*schief*

"Tantalizing reading…the honest, natural fun and the playful then consuming love that emerges are best of all. Great entertainment!"

—*Long and Short Reviews*

"Greenwood's talent is obvious…she is an author to keep an eye on!"

—*RT Book Reviews*

"Filled with humor, passion, and a lovely ending!"

—*Proserpine Craving Books*

"A delightfully charming read, sprinkled with mischief…refreshing, fun, and entertaining."

—*Lily Pond Reads*

"Emily Greenwood makes a strong debut with a playful series about young ladies who discover that a little mischief can be a good thing!"

—*Fresh Fiction*

"There's a certain whimsical nature to the plot, the hero is quite devastatingly gorgeous, and the writing is well-crafted."

—*All About Romance*

"Truly a pleasure to read… I look forward to seeing what comes next from this new author."

—*Debbie's Book Bag*

# MISCHIEF by MOONLIGHT

# EMILY GREENWOOD

sourcebooks
casablanca

Published by Sourcebooks Casablanca, an imprint of Sourcebooks,
Inc.
P.O. Box 4410, Naperville, Illinois 60567-4410
(630) 961-3900
Fax: (630) 961-2168
www.sourcebooks.com

Printed and bound in Canada.
WC 10 9 8 7 6 5 4 3 2 1

*For my parents*

# One

IN THE YEAR AND A HALF SINCE THAT FATEFUL NIGHT, Colin Pearce, the Earl of Ivorwood, had wondered many times what might have happened if he hadn't invited his best friend to his party. Whether, if Nick hadn't met Josephine Cardworthy that night, Colin might himself have had a chance with her.

Since Colin had been away from Greenbrier for years, he hadn't been around to see Josie's transformation from a scamp of a girl into an enchanting young woman. But he'd only been home a few weeks before he'd begun to think he and Josie would be very good together.

He'd been on the verge of declaring himself the night of the party, but Nick had arrived before he'd had a chance. Nick, at whose feet women had so often thrown themselves—why had it never occurred to Colin that Josie, too, would find him irresistible?

*Who is that?* she'd said at the party, grabbing Colin's forearm. Her sapphire eyes had been sparkling, her sable hair glossy, her creamy skin a persistent distraction, and he'd had to force himself to focus on her words and not the pleasure her touch was bringing him.

*Captain Nicholas Hargrave*, he'd said. *My closest friend*.

Her eyes hadn't left Nick in his dashing scarlet uniform. *Oh, good. You can introduce me*.

And Colin could only watch as his best friend twirled her about his ballroom and talked with her the whole night, and took the place by Josie's side that he'd wanted for himself.

Six weeks later Josie and Nick had become engaged.

Colin had made certain from that day that no one— least of all Josie—would notice he was badly smitten with her.

Left to his own devices, he would have abandoned Greenbrier and stayed far away from her. But Nick had been required to return to Spain before they could marry, and he'd asked a favor.

*You live so near*, Nick had said. *It will be the easiest thing in the world for you to look after her for me, to visit her regularly since I cannot*.

As if Josie Cardworthy needed looking after. She was the most self-sufficient woman Colin knew.

But he'd promised Nick, which was why he was currently walking along the path behind Greenbrier that led away from the splendor of his ancestral home and toward Jasmine House, the Cardworthys' manor.

Girding himself for an evening of conversation and the exquisite torment that Josie's presence brought, he passed through the doorway in the high stone wall at the eastern border of his property that led to the Cardworthys' garden. The late May dusk was just settling in, turning the soft yellow brick of their home a rich orange where it could be glimpsed through the thick cover of jasmine and ivy vines that threatened to smother it.

Jasmine House was lit up for the evening, its modest grandeur somewhat diminished by the rioting state of the garden and the clutter of an overturned wooden bench that had been serving as a fort for Josie's brothers earlier that week.

A grin teased his mouth as he remembered how she'd mounted a sneak attack on the two boys, dumping a bucket of water on them as revenge for some misbehavior, her shining brown hair tumbling loose as she laughingly escaped their clutches at a speed no lady for miles could likely have matched.

Josie had a way of stirring things up and making life seem to sparkle.

He let the grin fade with accustomed ease and reminded himself that it would be a mistake to stay very long tonight. At least there would be other guests to distract him from Josie.

He passed a battered doll hanging upside down by a long strand of yarn amid the canes of a raspberry bush and chuckled. The Cardworthys were nothing if not unusual.

❧

Josie Cardworthy knocked a second time on her sister's chamber door, but still there was no reply. She entered, and there was Edwina, sitting at her vanity with a book in her hand, but staring out the window. As Josie pulled the door closed behind her, her sister didn't turn. At least one worry could be put to rest: Edwina was dressed for the evening.

"It's almost time to go down," said Josie, who was wearing her one fancy gown, a shining silver-blue silk satin. "The Biddles will arrive soon."

"I'm sick," Edwina said, not sounding sick at all. As usual, her posture was so stiff a board might have been strapped to her back. She was wearing her lustrous moss-green gown, and her black-as-night hair was dressed in a high, pretty coiffure. From the back, she looked as beautiful and inflexible as a statue.

"You're not sick."

"It's consumption. I've been hiding it. Just tell Mrs. Biddle and they'll leave directly."

The corner of Josie's mouth inched up. Mrs. Biddle worried constantly about sickness.

"You're coming downstairs," Josie said firmly. "It's astonishing that we're even having a little party, let alone one to which an eligible gentleman has been invited."

The evening was a rare attempt by their mother to help Edwina find a husband, and Josie was determined her sister wouldn't squander it.

"I'm old," Edwina said. "That's as good as being sick. Tell them," she began as she finally turned around, but then she gasped.

"Your hair! What on earth have you done?"

Josie laughed. "As you see. Don't you like it?"

"But your hair was so beautiful. Why—" Edwina caught herself. "I mean, it does look nice now with the curls framing your face and that blue band around your head, but why on earth did you cut it all off?"

"I just had a sudden urge to change it." Josie ruffled her fingers through the shiny brown curls that now fell softly against her cheeks and nape. She was *mostly* glad she'd done it. At least the haircut was a harmless thing to do.

"It reminds me of the time you pierced your ears when you were fifteen and Papa bellowed for an hour." Edwina lifted an eyebrow. "What if Nicholas doesn't like it?"

Josie didn't suppose Nicholas would care—or did she? She considered for a moment that she'd cut her hair as some kind of test for him to pass when he returned, a sort of reaction to his recent letter saying he'd be back in two months.

But no, surely it was just that old recklessness. And thank goodness she was going to be married before long to a wonderful man: being married would stop her from doing impulsive things.

"Never mind my hair. Why are you in here, being a coward?"

Edwina's perfectly shaped lips pressed together glumly. "There's no point in this idiotic party. Men find me pretty but they don't *like* me. Papa always said I didn't have pleasing ways, and he was right."

Josie came closer and sat on the bed. "Papa liked to say outrageous things to stir people up, as you know very well."

Edwina frowned, as though remembering something unpleasant.

Having spent his life in India until he inherited his estate from a cousin, Mr. Cardworthy had never stopped missing the more exciting life he left behind. When he'd arrived at his new property—then called Hartwood—he'd promptly rechristened it Jasmine

House and made it apparent he had no interest in any of the neighbors, whom he called "the locals."

It was partly Papa's fault Edwina wasn't married. Their gruff Papa had never allowed the girls to receive any gentlemen, because he'd had plans for his daughters to marry wealthy nabobs, friends of his from India. But Papa had died four years ago, before that could happen. And Mama had promptly gone into her Decline.

"And you *do* look lovely," Josie said. "That's always a good start."

Josie knew she herself was pretty enough, with nice blue eyes and a pert nose. But her sister, with her shining black hair and blue velvet eyes and Cupid-blessed rose lips, was beautiful.

Edwina would have long ago been married—she was now twenty-seven—if it hadn't been for her hedgehog personality. Stiff, prickly, and often difficult, Edwina always said whatever she liked. Josie was used to her and knew she had a heart of gold under her peculiar ways. But they knew almost no men, and how could a stranger come to appreciate Edwina if she wouldn't even try? Sometimes Josie suspected her sister had given up on ever marrying.

"Anyway, what do we know of Mr. John Biddle?" Edwina said dismissively.

"He's a lawyer," Josie said.

Edwina rolled her eyes. But then a faraway light came into them. "We were meant to make brilliant matches."

"I know." Josie guessed Edwina was thinking of Mr. Perriwell, but she didn't dare speak his name. Their brother Lawrence had once mockingly called him "the manly suitor of long ago," and Edwina had looked ready to do him an injury.

The dreamy light disappeared from Edwina's eyes. "Well, *you've* made a brilliant match, and for that I'm glad. It would be piggish to suppose there'd be someone as wonderful as Nicholas for me."

"Maybe John Biddle *is* someone wonderful," Josie said. "But you'll never know unless you make an effort when he comes." She narrowed her eyes. "You know how it goes when you're *not* making an effort."

Edwina lifted her chin haughtily. "I simply can't make myself say the things men like to hear."

"Yes you *can*." Josie tugged the front of Edwina's bodice a half-inch lower to show a little more of her bosom. Though Edwina was the elder by five years, Josie sometimes felt like the leader. "And it shouldn't be hard. Mr. Biddle will surely be kind—he's Vicar's brother, so he's bound to be considerate and thoughtful, as Vicar is."

"Two people can be born into the same family and be entirely different," Edwina said, pulling her bodice back to where it had been. "Look at us. You're sweet and I'm sour. I'm good with numbers and you hate them."

"You're not sour," Josie said generously. "And I don't hate numbers, I just wouldn't get the satisfaction you do from doing the household accounts."

"It would be more satisfying if Mama would stop fretting about every penny when in fact we're practically wealthy. This is the only nice gown I've got, and I've had it five years."

It was true that their clothes were old—Mama

insisted that one fine dress each was adequate, and that had proved true since they were hardly ever invited anywhere.

"Here, let me help you with that ribbon," Josie said, reaching for the dark green band around her sister's neck from which was suspended a small cameo. "If it were a little higher, it would draw attention to your lovely neck."

Edwina batted Josie's hands away. "You go. No one will miss me, and anyway, I have things to do. Say I have the headache."

"You're not going to sit in here reading like you do all the time. Just make an effort with Mr. Biddle. You can talk about books—that's an easy topic for you. Ask what he's reading, that kind of thing."

"Men make me nervous," Edwina whispered plaintively, "and I'm too old for this."

Ignoring her, Josie tugged her to her feet. "Smile," she said, ushering her out the door.

"Oh, girls, there you are," their mother said as Josie and Edwina came into the sitting room. Mrs. Cardworthy was dressed for the evening in a gauzy cream gown and frilled cap, her person draped, as it was for all the waking hours of every day, on the aging blue divan she hadn't left since Mr. Cardworthy died.

The maids had made the fading divan look festive tonight, if a tad garish, by draping it with a pink and orange shawl Mr. Cardworthy had brought from India. Fortunately, the sitting room showed to advantage in the kinder light of dusk. The collection of carved sandalwood elephants and Indian brass dishes that had decorated the room for as long as Josie remembered had been neatly dusted and looked, if not charming atop Mrs. Cardworthy's good end tables, then at least interesting. Among the collection was a wooden tiger with fierce yellow and black stripes and red eyes, which had always seemed to Josie to embody the spirit of her father.

If only Rickett had been able to trim the bushes, the view of the garden would have been perfect, but their gardener was getting to be long in the tooth, and it took him a while to see to things.

"Edwina," Mama said, "go find my elixir to strengthen me for the evening. Josie, look down the garden path and see if Ivorwood is coming. Oh, if only your father hadn't left us."

"Mama, you *must* stop phrasing it that way," Josie said as she made for the door that gave onto the garden, "or people who don't know us will think he deserted us."

"It's the same effect," Mrs. Cardworthy said, though with less rancor. "Dead is just as gone as left."

Mrs. Cardworthy had been forty when she had her last child, and her husband had been a decade older. They'd never been the most lighthearted of people, and losing her strong-willed husband had only enhanced Mrs. Cardworthy's inherent gloominess. New experiences were to be avoided, and new people were suspect.

Though her mother had never admitted it, Josie knew she thought it would be no bad thing if her children never left Jasmine House; what better, safer place could there be for them? Doubtless she also thought it would be best if Nicholas Hargrave never returned from the war to marry Josie and carry her away.

Josie felt there were a number of subjects on which her mother was *quite* misguided.

"Oh, good," Josie said as she spied a familiar tall gentleman coming along the path, "here's dear old Ivorwood now."

"Really, Josie," Edwina scolded, "you must stop calling him 'old Ivorwood.' He's an earl, and he's not even old."

"But Colin's such a dear old friend, and I think of that first about him. And he was such a friend to Papa, when no one else was."

In truth, Josie had come to see Colin in recent months as a very close friend. The frequent walks they shared in the garden, often discussing various aspects of history—he was writing a book about the kings of England, and she loved the weird details he found through his research—were an escape from a house that often resounded with her mother's megrims.

Things were not exactly stagnant at Jasmine House; helping see to the household kept Josie engaged, and the daily pandemonium created by her younger brothers provided exasperation and amusement in equal measure. But a visit from Colin had become her favorite diversion.

Colin was different, with his reserved ways, and comfortable, like a favorite stuffed chair. He always had intelligent things to say, and he was as solidly reliable as a boulder. Also, because he was Nicholas's best friend, being with him was in a small way like being with her fiancé—and ever more, lately, she'd needed any reminder of Nicholas she could find.

She pushed away the anxiousness that thoughts of

her fiancé had brought and focused her mind on the evening before them and, most importantly, the good it might do her sister.

"But you're right," Josie said as she watched the earl skirt around the bench lying across the garden path, "he's not any older than Nicholas—it's just that he seems older. Perhaps it's because he's reserved."

"He's such a handsome man," Edwina said. "All that glossy black hair, and he's tall and always immaculately dressed. It's a shame he's so unforthcoming, though. I can't imagine him courting anyone. Although maybe he behaves differently with the ladies in London. Not that we would know since we are never to be there."

"Edwina," their mother said from the divan, taking a healthy swallow of her elixir, "you know that London is far away, and not a safe place to visit. Never mind the expense."

Josie watched Colin approach. True, he was handsome—she just never thought about it, perhaps because she'd always known him. From the time she was twelve or thirteen, she could remember him coming to call on their father; they'd held discussions about books and history that often lasted hours. But she'd been too young then to be noticing gentlemen as men.

And then he'd gone away for years, and when he'd returned she'd thought, *Well, look at that, Ivorwood is quite smart.* But she'd met Nicholas and thought no more about it.

She was planning to talk to Colin tonight about Edwina. Josie was worried about her sister's prospects, and she meant to ask him for help. Because if Edwina didn't find a husband soon, Josie didn't see how she could marry Nicholas without feeling she was abandoning her sister to a spinster's existence.

She and Edwina might joke about how Mama never left her divan, but spending a lifetime attending to a woman who refused to do for herself would be suffocating. Of course no one expected Will, Matthew, or Lawrence—twelve, fourteen, and fifteen—to dance attendance on their mother. They were sons, and it would never be their lot in life.

"Ivorwood, here you are," Josie said as he approached the door.

He looked quite fine, but then he was always well dressed, as if he'd turned his formidable intellect to the consideration of what he ought to wear. His coat was a sharp green satin that made his sage eyes look more vivid. He had no quizzing glass, no large family rings or gaudy buttons; the quality of his clothing was the only thing about his appearance that suggested he was a very wealthy man.

Which wasn't to say he didn't have quite a bit of presence; he was tall and rangy, and his black hair and general lack of lightheartedness gave him a dark, aloof quality that seemed pronounced tonight. Then there was his nose—hawkish, jutting, it gave a hint to ancestors who'd doubtless done all manner of rough things to secure power.

"You've changed your hair," he said, coming inside. "I quite liked it long. But this new style suits you."

"Thank you," she said. "Come take a turn around the room with me while we wait for the guests. You don't count as a guest, of course."

"Well, thank you very much."

She laughed and slipped her arm over the bend of his elbow and tugged him toward the edge of the room. She lived in a house full of boisterous and argumentative people, and space, things, and even sometimes the best bits of food were constantly in contention; Colin, in a way, was something that belonged especially to *her*.

"Of course you're not a guest—we know you too well. You're as good as part of the family."

He merely grunted in reply. His arm felt stiff against her, and she pressed him encouragingly, to draw him out of his shell.

❧

Colin had no idea what Josie was saying because he was so distracted by the feel of her arm against his. He alternately wished she would not touch him and lived for those moments when she did. They were always accompanied by bitter scolding from his conscience reminding him she was Nick's fiancée, as if he could forget.

She seemed to be waiting for a reply.

"I'm sorry, what did you say?" he said.

She laughed. "I said that you look especially brooding tonight. No doubt your thoughts are caught on some historical old man. King Canute? Edward the Confessor?"

He wished his thoughts were on old men, as idiotic as that sounded. Instead, he was trying not to notice the way her new short coiffure played up the light in her eyes, and directing his arm to stop sending him excited little missives about the delicate curves of her arm.

He made himself think of Nick, off fighting a war while Colin lived a soft earl's existence. How he wished he might change places with him. Nick should be here with Josie, and Colin ought to be out there being shot at. He deserved to be shot for wanting Josie. His fascination with her was wrong for so many reasons, and if there was a way to cut out the part of him that wouldn't stop thinking of her, he wished he might know it.

She squeezed his arm again as if to encourage him. She had no idea.

Lately he'd felt like a powder keg whenever he was around her, ready to explode with the slightest touch. He'd been thinking of a trip to conduct research for the history he was writing, and he knew he'd been putting it off, but he was weak, and he wanted to be with her. He told himself he was only doing as Nick had asked him to do, but that was a lie.

He shouldn't have come tonight.

The door to the salon opened just then, admitting Sally to announce the Biddles: Vicar, his wife, and his brother. Colin hoped they would distract him from Josie, though he had to acknowledge that was not likely to happen.

# Two

JOSIE KNEW SHE SHOULDN'T PIN TOO MUCH HOPE ON Mr. John Biddle, but he seemed quite likable. He was a pleasant-looking blond man with a serious expression, and he'd all but gasped when he'd taken in the beauteous sight of Edwina.

Within twenty minutes of his arrival, however, Josie's hopes for him as a suitor for her sister were already slipping. Edwina, with that tense look she tended to get around strangers, had begun by telling him about her latest sewing project. She was an accomplished seamstress, and the one who made over their dresses when Mama declined to buy new fabric. But details of fitting and hemming were hardly of general interest.

Seeming at last to remember that she must engage him, Edwina had asked to know his favorite book, then dismissed his response as "a trivial volume."

Edwina was usually serious on the subject of books, and Josie realized now that it had been a mistake to encourage her to discuss them. Edwina and Colin sometimes had spirited debates about a book they'd

both read, but Colin would have taken her sharp
dismissal of a favorite volume as an opening for conversation, while Mr. Biddle clearly would not.

Now Edwina was on to lists. "I don't like coffee,
mutton, apples, or toast," she said tartly. "No syllabub.
Also, I detest cheap cotton."

Josie all but groaned. John Biddle might be pleasant,
but he was certainly not a nabob, and she didn't think
Edwina was trying very hard.

Mr. Biddle's gaze moved toward Colin, and shortly
he excused himself to take up a point of history with
the earl.

Edwina turned toward Josie with a tight look on
her face. "See? I told you there was no point. I could
tell he didn't like me."

"And so you made no effort to change his mind."

Edwina waved her arm dismissively. "He'd rather
talk to Ivorwood, and I don't blame him. He's the
most interesting person in the room."

*Ivorwood...*

It was at that moment that Josie got an idea which,
strangely, she'd never considered before, probably
because *they'd* never considered it before.

Why shouldn't *Colin* be a suitor for Edwina?

He was the best man they knew, and even though
this wasn't saying much, considering how few gentlemen they knew, he really was a prince, and worth
a hundred of any old nabob. Smart, handsome,
considerate—why, just last week he'd helped her
family avert disaster when Matt had been caught trying
to steal a kiss from a farmer's daughter. Whatever
Colin had said to her brother after settling things with

the farmer must have been compelling, because Matt had been as meek as a lamb ever since.

Even better, Edwina and Colin had something important in common: they were each of an inward disposition and loved quiet pursuits like reading.

She entertained a vision of the two of them sitting cozily in the sunny morning room at Greenbrier, their noses buried in books from which they periodically stopped to read each other entertaining tidbits. They would doubtless both love it.

Actually, that sounded like bliss to Josie as well. It wasn't that she didn't like to read; she did. It was just that she also loved to go for punishing horseback rides, and run across a sunny meadow just because, and get Cook to teach her to make things. She loved to be *doing*, and she loved to try new things.

Her mother often said to her, *Can't you keep still, girl?* But Josie was not at all good at tatting or needlepoint, and she had no patience for the piano. She knew how to plant roses, though, and where the best walking paths were, and she could make a fabulous custard à la française. She hoped one day to learn how to do pottery.

One of the things Josie had liked best about Nicholas, and which she thought would suit her perfectly, was that he was always in motion.

But Colin courting Edwina: the only problem she saw with this was that the two of them had known each other for years and never shown a bit of interest in one another. Yet wasn't this likely because of their tendencies toward being self-contained? What if someone gave them a little push, opened their eyes to what was right in front of them?

What if she tried getting them together in a round-about way—say, if Colin thought he was helping Edwina? Josie had planned to ask him to do so that night anyway. What if, in ostensibly getting him to help Edwina, she could get them to spend extra time together, so that they might naturally come to focus on each other?

Surely then Colin would come to more deeply appreciate the quiet virtues buried under Edwina's prickly exterior, and Edwina would come to welcome Colin's subtle attentions.

෧෨

Colin had just extricated himself from a long discussion with Mr. Biddle and was wondering if it was too early to slip away politely when Josie came and linked her arm through his again.

"Not thinking of leaving yet, I hope?" she said. "I know how fond you are of your own company and how little you like chat. What were you and Biddle talking of, anyway?"

"He read my book on Henry VIII and wanted to probe the motives of Sir Thomas More."

Colin moved close to a small table and picked up a volume lying there, an excuse to withdraw his arm from hers. He really ought to leave, because he was only spending every moment trying to keep his eyes from the pretty curve of her lips.

"How is work going on your new book?" she said. "What's it called again—*Kings and Their Notions*?"

His lips twitched. "*The Decisions of a King*, as you know. It's coming along." He was writing as fast as he could, as often as he could—it was the only thing that took his mind off her a little.

"And when can I read it?"

"Ha," he said. "I think it will be some time before anyone will be allowed to see it. In fact, though," he said, "I think I shall be taking a trip shortly, to do some research."

Her face fell and she moved closer, so that her scent reached him, touching him deep, where lived the cherished memories of all the conversations and laughter and friendship they'd shared over the last year, memories that wanted him to believe they were meant to be together.

He turned away from them with long-established ease. Self-discipline had been something he'd demanded of himself since childhood, when he'd come to understand that his out-of-control parents had none.

"Listen, Colin, you won't go away just yet, will you? I'm worried about Edwina."

He glanced across the room at Edwina, who was standing stiffly with Mrs. Biddle. He could only just hear her sharp tone as she told Mrs. Biddle not to buy some new sort of fabric from the shop in town because it was of inferior quality.

"Is something amiss?" he said. "She seems quite as usual to me. And very lovely she is tonight, in her green gown. It sets off her black hair remarkably well."

His words seemed to cheer Josie in some way, because she smiled. Her smiles had such a ridiculous effect on him, and there it was, the little lift they always gave him.

"She *is* fine. But you know how our mother has not much helped her in finding a husband. I'm certain she wants Edwina to stay at Jasmine House forever and take care of her, even though Mama is perfectly able to get off the divan and start really living if she would only choose to."

"She does seem to spend a lot of time on the divan," Colin said.

Josie gave him an exasperated look. "You know that she only gets up to go to bed. She even has her meals on the divan! Aside from the fact that we have so few friends in the neighborhood, it's one of the reasons we never have anyone but you to dinner."

"Yes, a bit difficult to dine like that."

"And you know how Papa refused to have governesses for us because he didn't want us to become worldly. Never mind that he chased away every man who ever tried to court Edwina or me because he was going to marry us to nabobs."

His eyes lingered on hers, and he felt a smile tugging at his mouth. He really tried not to smile too much in her presence—it made him too happy, which resulted in a sort of hangover once he'd gone back to the enormous, quiet rooms of Greenbrier, where he would have been content in his solitude were it not for what Josie Cardworthy did to him.

"And yet you seem to have managed very well. And Edwina shall do, too, doubtless. Why should you be worried about her?"

"Really, Colin, I can only wonder if all that time alone thinking about the ancient kings of England hasn't entirely dulled your brain to the life around you.

But then, *you* don't see anything wrong about people not marrying—you like to be alone all the time."

"Not true," he said quietly. She had an idea of him that was not, in some respects, the way he really was. Oh, she knew him through the connection of the true friendship they shared. Their conversation was genuine and effortless, their shared silences companionable. They respected and sought each other's opinions and enjoyed disputing with each other.

But she was young and innocently unaware of the ways of men. She'd certainly be shocked to know how much he wanted to think about her body and the effort he spent making sure he never did.

She thought he spent his days sitting soberly writing at his desk for hours, and he could only imagine how startled she'd be to see him as he usually was at home: in bed shirtless and unshaven with his books splayed out around him, their pages both his main pleasure and his distraction from the woman of whom he must not think.

And she couldn't know that he'd given up on other women when he'd fallen under her spell. He'd never been fond of casual dalliances, nor much interested in widows and courtesans beyond the occasional liaison. But in the last year, he'd stopped finding other women appealing at all.

She had no idea that he planned his occasional short research trips to avoid spending too much time in her tempting company. In her mind, he was a sort of dear, sexless older brother, and he had to let her keep this skewed idea, because it put the distance between them that had to be there.

"Well, *I'm* worried about her being alone always," she said in a low, vehement voice. "Edwina is a wonderful person, but it would take someone special to appreciate her."

This was certainly true. Edwina Cardworthy was beautiful and difficult, and while he had a great deal of brotherly affection for her, he could easily see why she'd not yet made a match. He inclined his head noncommittally.

Josie was getting impassioned, and her blue eyes glimmered. They often did when she was caught up in some excitement, as she had been last month when she'd insisted Colin take her to an execrable traveling actors' production of *Romeo and Juliet* set up in the market square.

Though he never would have gone to such a thing of his own choice, he couldn't resist her enthusiasm, and he'd agreed. She'd made him wear a large, disguising hat and plain clothes, and they'd sat in the back murmuring wry comments to each other the whole time. He'd never enjoyed a play more.

Now she said, "You know how delightful Edwina is in her unique way. But with the lack of eligible bachelors and the general ill feeling toward my family in Upperton, she has no chance of making a match here."

Colin raised an eyebrow at her. "Come, Josie, you are exaggerating."

"You know I'm not. And even if the neighbors could forgive us for all those years of keeping to ourselves, Edwina always speaks her mind."

True, and she was also prone to complaint.

"And what do you wish me to do about this supposed problem?"

Josie bit her pretty pink lip, which he wished she wouldn't do; it made him imagine teasing and pleasurable torments.

"You could hold a dinner party and introduce her to some of your eligible friends," she said.

He lifted an eyebrow.

"Yes, I know you *avoid* holding dinner parties, but I know you are capable of it, and I think people like your parties better than anyone's."

"You've seen through me. I only hold a few gatherings so people will feel deprived, and thereby be more appreciative if I do ever invite them."

"Oh, be serious! We're talking about Edwina and how, earl that you are, you might make a difference for her. Like, by taking her on a stroll through town so everyone can see her with you."

"But if she appears with me, won't that discourage other gentlemen?"

She slid him a sidelong glance. "You might take her to London for the Season."

He gave a bark of laughter. "What, me? A single gentleman, escort a single lady to London?"

"I'm sure something could be arranged in the way of a chaperone."

He crossed his arms. "Your mother doesn't like London."

"Mama doesn't like any place that isn't our sitting room," she said. "But Edwina deserves a *chance*. She ought to have the opportunity to be seen and appreciated in a much wider circle than Upperton. Couldn't you get your aunt to sponsor her, the one who lives in London?"

Colin frowned slightly. This was getting complicated. He was a solitude-loving bachelor, and having been the only child of a bitterly unhappy marriage, he had nothing helpful to offer anyone wishing to marry. Much less did he see himself as the appropriate person to get embroiled in such complicated female affairs as the launching of young ladies into society.

On the other hand, he was an earl, and as such burdened with all manner of responsibilities. Though he did try to keep others' expectations to a minimum.

But this was Josie's sister and his old friend Cardworthy's daughter. Josie was right that the neighbors thought the family odd and unsociable, and he doubted any of the local mamas would consider the haughty Edwina Cardworthy for their sons. Perhaps he could set something helpful in motion and step away.

"I'll think about it. But simply taking a woman to London won't ensure her happiness, Josephine. Plenty of terrible marriages are made there."

"I know." Her blue eyes twinkled merrily. "It's incredibly lucky for me and Nicholas that you brought us together at Greenbrier."

"Indeed," he managed to say. He was beginning to wonder how much longer he could stand there talking to her, because once she began thanking him for bringing her and Nick together, the conversation always turned to Nick's fine qualities. And while his friend did have many, listening to Josie sing his praises made Colin wish he were deaf.

"Tell me again how you met him," she said.

Not that story again. He knew why she loved to hear it—Nick came off heroically, and hearing about him was the closest she could get right now to being with him. Buoyant, roguish Nick, who made Colin laugh better than anyone. Underneath Nick's golden-boy looks and charm lurked a sharp mind and a competitive streak that had lured Colin into all manner of contests, though never once over a woman.

*And they weren't in competition over a woman now.*

A surge of jealousy coursed through him, but he told himself this was the best possible thing, that recounting Nick's deeds to Josie would strike a blow against every wrong thing in him that was yearning for her. He forced himself.

"It was the heady days of university," he began in a long-winded tone, but she rolled her eyes, a long-suffering smile quivering at the edges of her lips.

"I know that. Get to the good part."

He sighed theatrically, which made her laugh, thus defeating the purpose of telling the story to make himself face how much she was not for him. He got on with it, this medicine he needed to spoon down.

"I was punting on the Cherwell River and facing backward because I'd caught a fascinating view of some of the university buildings. Unfortunately, I had neglected to notice the low bridge ahead, and was knocked on the head as I passed under it and fell unconscious into the river.

"But fortunately for me, someone was walking by at that moment. This was one Nicholas Hargrave, Cambridge student, and as I was at the superior institution of Oxford, as yet unknown to me. He was strolling purposelessly along the banks, doubtless thinking of mundane things. Unfinished work, dreamy calculations of his athletic prowess, what he wanted for dinner. Old Nicholas—"

"Colin," she interrupted with a satisfying note of exasperation, "you have to tell it the right way."

"You mean in which he is thoroughly painted as Sir Galahad? It is painful to gush so about a man. But I suppose to please a lady…Well, Nick saw me disappearing under the water and dove into the Cherwell and pulled me out. And very gloating about it he was, too, when I finally came round, going on about how much better Cambridge punters are than Oxford punters."

She was laughing heartily now, her eyes all lit up and crinkling at the edges, and even though she was laughing at him and enjoying the past triumph of her hero Nick, Colin was the one who'd made her laugh, and for just that moment, he allowed himself to be happy that he'd given her this pleasure.

"Ungracious of him," he continued, "with me lying there, an enormous lump forming on the back of my head."

"You never told me about the lump before. Poor you."

"You don't seem very sorry for me."

She put her hand on his forearm and squeezed gently. "Oh, Ivorwood, who could feel sorry for you? You're the perfect person to laugh at because you're the earl, and you already have everything."

Right.

Something flickered in her eyes. "Except a wife, of course," she said playfully.

Now here was a conversation he definitely didn't want to have with her.

He was saved by the sounds of someone beginning a lively tune on the pianoforte. It was young Matthew Cardworthy, who'd taken up the piano as a sort of challenge; he liked to play music at a vigorous pace with an ironic tilt of his head, though Colin perceived that the boy did in fact quite love playing, however much it was meant to be the province of ladies.

Mr. Biddle and his brother, with Mrs. Cardworthy calling out encouragement from her divan, were pushing aside the furniture in preparation for dancing, assisted by the boys' hunched, retiring tutor, Mr. Botsford. Colin almost groaned. It was his intention never to dance with Josie—to have her in his arms when she would never be his would be torture. Fortunately, he'd managed to avoid it so far on the few occasions when there'd been dancing.

She tipped her head up at him. A curly lock of her sable hair was bouncing comically against the blue bandeau she'd tied around her head, a small vulnerability that charmed him. The early summer evening was warm, and her cheeks glowed softly apricot. "Now you will finally have to dance with me, Colin."

"I must certainly dance with Edwina first, as you are wanting me to 'lend her consequence.' And then," he said lightly, "there is the matter of the cow."

This was a game they played, a necessary game for him, through which he'd managed to avoid ever dancing with her by coming up with nonsensical and fanciful excuses. It was part of the joke that each time he had to find a new, polite-seeming reason not to dance.

She inclined her head, joining in the game. "And which cow is this?"

"The one who even now is watching at the window—no, don't look, she's very testy. I shall have to go over and mutter Greek poetry at her. It's the only thing that stops her from charging about. Otherwise, she will certainly vault through the window and run about in here, ruining all your furnishings."

She laughed and he moved off to find her sister.

Josie watched Colin bow to Edwina and take her hand while Matthew began a new tune that was almost too fast for dancing. How was it that she'd never thought before tonight of Colin as a suitor for Edwina?

The more she considered it, the more she believed she could wish no better mate for her sister. The difficulty was going to be that he was such a contented, solitude-loving bachelor.

He had friends of course—Nick, and any number of other gentlemen. He was not some shy, fumbling rube unable to be in company. No, he was perfectly able to be warm and witty, but he simply didn't much *need* company. And he seemed entirely content that after him the title would go to his cousin. But wouldn't he—wouldn't Edwina, too—be happier with a companion, someone to share life's joys and sorrows?

He was going to be something of a tough nut to crack, marriage-wise. But worth it, if her matchmaking skills could bring it off.

❧

Later that night, unable to sleep, Josie took a candle and slipped down to her father's library. The neglected room had a quietude that seemed to welcome her wayward thoughts, and she went to the brandy decanter and poured a small measure and stood there drinking it.

It wasn't quite right, drinking alone, but she felt out of sorts and she didn't know what she wanted, and the brandy seemed to help.

Another sip, and with it a mutinous spurt of truth-telling. She *did* know what she wanted: to leave Jasmine House. She was twenty-two and engaged to the most wonderful man possible, and she wanted to get on with it. Get on with the leaving and the marrying and the life of which she dreamed.

But she was here, waiting. Existing.

She traced a heart in the light frosting of dust on the desk, putting in her initials and Nicholas's. She knew what she needed: patience. He'd been gone for so long, a year—and she was forgetting what he was like, and that scared her.

He sent letters from Spain, very properly addressed to her family. And she treasured them, but apparently they weren't enough. How greedy she was. Any other woman would have been satisfied even to have a fiancé, let alone one as wonderful as Nicholas Hargrave.

His latest letter had said he would be home in July, just over two months away. It had given her a feeling of panic. And maybe that panic *had* had something to do with the hair-cutting.

She took another sip of brandy, glad it burned on

the way down, as though it could burn away all the things that were wrong with her. The doubts she shouldn't have about those six blissful weeks she'd spent getting to know Nicholas. The worries that he would feel differently about her now, after a year. And worst of all, the fear that marriage would make her feel like a caged bird.

How could she entertain such thoughts when he'd told her he loved her?

It had seemed brave, his speaking so easily of love. No one talked of love at Jasmine House. Deep emotions were kept hidden in her family, as though they were an embarrassment. The stiff upper lip and deprecating humor prevailed.

Nicholas was offering her a marriage that surely would be entirely different from what her parents had shared, and that was what she dearly wanted. Her parents' marriage might have looked tolerable, but it had never looked like love.

And she loved Nick, of course she did.

She threw back the rest of the brandy and almost cast up her accounts when it hit her stomach. This wasn't helping. Nothing could help because *nothing was the problem*.

All she needed was to stop thinking so much. And not do rash things like cutting her hair off. Or far worse.

She forced herself to bring up the shameful memory, to acknowledge that she'd let a traveling horse trader take her for the ride of her life—and almost been discovered in his arms.

*What a beauty ye are*, the young man had said when

she'd happened upon him while out walking in a field. *As welcome a sight as the first daffodil of spring.*

He'd been walking his horse, and she shouldn't even have stopped to talk with him. But he'd had sparkling dark eyes and a lilting Irish accent, and she'd accepted his invitation for a gallop on his horse.

She was a pure young lady—so how could she have climbed up on a horse in front of a man she knew only as Sean and let him put his arms around her as they raced across fields yelling with joy?

And how could she have allowed him to press his lips against her neck while the horse walked? But she'd *liked* it—and been so caught up that she hadn't seen Mr. Whitaker coming around the bend in his cart.

Falling off Sean's horse as she flailed in surprise was the only thing that had saved her from being compromised in the arms of a stranger who wasn't even a gentleman.

No harm had come of her lapse in behavior. But she'd seen what she was capable of, how the thrill of abandoning rules and propriety might call to her like a siren song. When she met Nicholas a month later, she knew that, as wonderful as it was going to be to spend her future with him, marriage would also save her from her fatal impulsiveness.

She put the glass back with the decanter and resolved in that moment that there would be no more midnight brandy-drinking. She would focus on worthwhile things, the most important of which would be helping Edwina and Colin see how good they might be together.

# Three

THE NEXT DAY, JOSIE GOT STARTED ON HER PLAN. SHE began by mentioning to Edwina that Colin had said she was looking especially fine the night before. Her sister was not impressed; as she was accustomed to everyone saying she was beautiful, this was nothing.

Josie continued her campaign by trying to steer Edwina toward Colin during his visits in the following days, suggesting to Edwina that he would be especially interested in hearing about the book she was reading, or her thoughts on formal gardens. But Edwina merely looked at her blankly.

Finally exasperated, Josie discreetly suggested that Edwina consider Colin as a suitor. This, unaccountably, made Edwina laugh.

"Ivorwood, courting? I can't imagine it. Can you see him telling a woman she's the light of his life and he must have her?"

Edwina had a point: that fatal reserve of Colin's. Well, fatal if you wanted him to be effusive. Unfortunately, Edwina had the idea that a suitor must treat her like a princess.

"Well, perhaps not those words. But he might say something nice."

"If a man's not going to say those words or something like them to me, then he's not the man for me. But I think we all know marriage is not in my future anyway."

Josie frowned. "You can't just give up on marriage because Mr. Perriwell behaved badly."

Edwina's eyes darkened at the mention of the wealthy suitor their father had produced six years ago. Mr. Perriwell and Edwina had seemed to really like each other, and it had looked as though an engagement were imminent. But then their father had gotten sick with the illness that killed him, and Mr. Perriwell had stopped visiting. They heard later he'd married.

"I don't want to talk about this," Edwina said, a husky note in her voice.

"But—you have to. I mean"—Josie lowered her voice—"at Jasmine House means dancing attendance on Mama while she refuses to leave the divan. And I know there will be a nice portion for each of us, but everything else will belong to Lawrence. After Mama…do you really mean just to live here with him and be a spinster aunt?"

Edwina shrugged dispiritedly. "I don't like to think too far into the future."

Edwina was in other ways such a practical person—she kept all the household accounts, for goodness' sake—that her depressed view of her future made no sense.

"Anyway, life is unpredictable," she continued. "Who says I won't perish before Mama?"

Josie rolled her eyes. "Now you're just being dramatic. But you can't give up on finding a husband before you've even begun. And wanting a fantasy man to sweep you off your feet is just another way of ensuring you don't risk your heart with a real man."

"Josie," Edwina said fiercely, "there's no point. I am nice to look at, but that's it. Even Papa told me I'd have to rely on my beauty, that I didn't have anything else to recommend me."

Josie remembered how their father had sometimes said to Edwina, *You've got no spirit, gel, not like your sister.* Edwina had been prone to tears as a girl, and afraid of dogs and horses, which had annoyed their father—a man who'd valued boldness so much that he'd given his daughters mannish names. But he'd said so many ridiculous things, Josie had early on stopped paying attention—why hadn't Edwina?

"It was wrong of him to say that—surely you see that? Papa said all sorts of wrong things."

A shadow flitted across Edwina's face, making her look surprisingly vulnerable. "Well, I certainly didn't have enough charms to keep Mr. Perriwell's attention."

"That's ancient history. Forget about it." Josie grabbed her hand and squeezed it encouragingly. "You do like Colin, don't you?"

"Yes, of course I do," Edwina said with a sigh. "He's a lovely man. Smart and witty, and quite nice to look at."

So Edwina *could* see his virtues.

"But it's ridiculous, the idea of him courting me," she continued.

*Only because you're not ready to embrace something*

*good for yourself*, Josie thought. But if only Colin might court Edwina in the right way, who knew what might happen?

At least she'd already asked him to help with finding suitors for Edwina; surely this would force him to look up from his books and think about her, and then who knew but that they might really start to see each other?

True to his promise to help, Colin held a picnic on his estate the following week and invited every unmarried gentleman in the neighborhood—and, helpfully, a slightly smaller number of single ladies, making a group of about a dozen.

He was most hospitable at the gathering, deftly finding opportunities to present each gentleman to Edwina throughout the day. Though she was glad for the opportunities this afforded Edwina, Josie felt a little discouraged by the equanimity with which he offered other men to her sister, when he might be seeing Edwina as a prize he now wanted for himself.

But an incident near the end of the picnic luncheon gave her hope.

The guests were all sitting on blankets in the softly dappled shade of an old oak tree, and one of the ladies, Christabel Brown, had been holding court for some time. She was a pretty young woman with a tinkling laugh, and Josie had noticed that the men's eyes were drawn to her as often as they were to Edwina.

Miss Brown was delighting the group with tales of her young cousin. "An amazing, witty child! Only four, and he's already known for his advice. 'You mustn't arrange your hair like that, Uncle,' he says to my father, 'combing over the little bits of hair. It makes you look like a walrus.'"

There were shouts of laughter, and Mr. Trilby, a spry, witty young man sitting next to Edwina said, "Ho, the knave!"

"Yes," she went on, her eyes twinkling, "and he told me I mustn't wear my pink muslin, as it doesn't flatter my figure!" More laughter.

Josie, glancing at Colin, saw him staring off into space as though he weren't paying attention.

Edwina sniffed and said, "He sounds rude. He should be corrected, or he'll end up truly unpleasant."

A heavy silence greeted these words. Tact had never been Edwina's forte.

And then, murmured into the silence but easily intelligible by all, someone said, "*She* ought to know about being unpleasant. Got a talent for it, she has."

Josie's eyes flew to her sister's face as titters broke out. Edwina, looking very stiff, opened her mouth, doubtless to say something truly unrecoverable, but Colin spoke first.

"I must agree with Miss Cardworthy," he said, turning to bestow one of his rare smiles on Edwina. "Disrespectful children frequently grow into the most awful people. Now, who's for cake?"

And just like that, everyone was trotting out stories of people who'd grown up to be rude and selfish. Edwina had several examples to offer from literature, and they were met with amusement and acceptance that made Edwina blink with pleasure and smile her thanks at Colin.

Josie saw him smile back at Edwina, and strangely—it

was like being hit with something—she had a momentary, strong reaction to the sight, as though it were wrong. As though, for some unknown reason, she didn't like that Colin had just rescued her sister.

She looked away and gave herself a sort of internal shake. She was *happy* for what Colin and her sister had just shared. It was just the kind of progress she'd been hoping for.

And it was perfect, she told herself sternly, when Colin chose to walk next to Edwina as the party left the picnic grounds, the two of them chatting happily about Shakespeare. Certainly she knew Colin better than Edwina did, and had been particular friends with him these many months. But he didn't *belong* to her— why should she feel funny about seeing him looking at Edwina with such pleasure?

What was important was that now things were progressing.

But over the next days, Josie began to grow impatient again as no more progress seemed to occur.

True, on Colin's visits to the Cardworthys, he now paid Edwina more attention, but his manner was as reserved as usual—in no way the sort of courting Edwina had said she wanted—and Josie began to despair again of their coming together after all. And yet she still felt they each deserved the happiness the other might bring them. Their shared smiles the day of the picnic had been so warm.

By the end of the second week, Josie had grown so frustrated with Colin's reserve that, while sitting with him in the garden at Jasmine House, she spoke more directly.

"Ivorwood, don't you think Edwina looks especially lovely today?"

He glanced at her. "Yes, certainly. Yellow is a most becoming color for her."

"Why don't you go and talk to her?"

"About what?"

"Oh, anything," she said as nonchalantly as possible.

His eyes settled on her, and she was startled for a moment by something sharp in them. "Josie, I am not in need of a matchmaker."

*Caught.* Still, perhaps it was best now to be plain.

"But come, Colin, perhaps you are. After all, you are an only child and an earl. And, poor you, an orphan."

He gave her a dry look. "My parents were still alive and making each other miserable when I was twenty."

"Nevertheless, there is no one now to press you toward marriage. You ought to have a countess, and yet you behave as though marriage never occurs to you. How can you think of letting the title go to your cousin? Don't you ever mean to fill your nursery with little Pearces?"

He inhaled what sounded like a long-suffering breath, which was odd since it wasn't as though she'd tried to steer him toward marriage before.

"Josephine. Setting aside the fact that you are an unmarried lady of only twenty-two and thus can have little insight into matchmaking, I would point out that a thirty-year-old man need hardly rush into marriage."

"Rush! I can't imagine you've ever rushed into anything in your life. You're so deliberate."

"I am not ready to marry," he said firmly, "and would therefore make any woman a miserable husband."

He was resistant—what, really, should she have expected?—but Josie noticed that he hadn't said he *didn't* fancy Edwina. She would take that as a hopeful sign. And he had been so particularly thoughtful toward Edwina at the picnic. Sweet, really.

"But *why* don't you wish to marry? Why, when you are all alone at Greenbrier? It must be positively echoing there. And heaven only knows what you do in Town."

"I do have a *few* friends, Josie."

"Of course you do. You know very well that *I* think you're a lovely man. The nicest man imaginable."

There was that sharp flicker in his eyes again. "You don't know that I'm nice."

A raspy note in his voice made the little hairs on the back of her neck stand up in an exciting way that startled her. She blinked. Was he teasing her? Though he didn't look amused.

"But of course you are nice."

She thought she heard the sound of teeth grinding.

"You have no idea how many things about me are not *nice* at all."

"Nonsense," she said, though she felt another prickling along her neck and supposed she was fidgety from drinking too much tea after lunch. "And you can be completely charming when you wish, only you don't seem to wish to charm the young ladies very often. So I don't see how you shall ever get on with the right sort of women—the ones who will like you for yourself and not for your wealth and title."

"I assure you I'm content to wait until I'm able to discern who is merely after my money."

"You are being contrary. Doubtless you're used to doing exactly as you wish, being that you're an only son with no one about to gainsay you. You've likely become spoiled, indulged as you are by your servants."

"Very likely. And I should therefore be little more than a curse as a husband."

She groaned. "But you like Edwina."

"I do."

She wished he would elaborate, but he didn't.

"A wife would keep you civilized," she pointed out.

"My cousin Nathaniel may have the title with my blessing. He's a good fellow, and he already has children."

She tipped her head. "Is all this because your parents didn't have a happy marriage? I was so much younger when they died, and you never speak of them."

He gave a bark of laughter. "Who knows how many dishes they broke against the walls over the years?"

"Oh, Colin, I didn't know," she started to say in a soft voice, but he cut her off.

"I've no need of sympathy. A person can develop great self-reliance in such situations, so I would say that I thank them."

She slid a glance toward the house, where on the other side of the sitting room window her mother could be seen reclining on the divan with a plate of cake. The bright pink and orange shawl that had been draped over the back of the divan the night of the party was still there, giving Mrs. Cardworthy the look of some raja's indulged wife nibbling sweetmeats.

"My parents didn't have a wonderful marriage either, but I have hope for myself. I think we *must* have hope that we will do better."

He didn't say anything for a moment, and her fervent words hung in the air. Finally he said, "I'm sure you're right."

She narrowed her eyes. "No you're not. Why, Colin Pearce, I never realized what a pessimist you are."

"Yet another reason I'd make an unpleasant spouse. So," he said briskly, "I trust I'll hear no more of matchmaking."

"Oh, very well," she said with an ill grace that seemed to make his lips twitch, "I shall say no more about it."

෴

Josie was walking through the woods the next day with a basket of things she'd bought in town. Pretty blue wildflowers decorated the path generously to either side, and she was glad she'd taken the long way home, though now she was remembering that the gypsies who sometimes stopped in the woods had returned.

Her mother was afraid of them, but they seemed peaceful to Josie, and as she drew near their camp, she heard the cheerful sounds of laughter and music being played on a stringed instrument. It was a pretty tune, and as she walked, it made her smile. Nicholas had written that he and his men had been trading with gypsies, and perhaps he'd heard similar music.

Her wandering thoughts were doubtless why she didn't see the old woman sitting on a rock until she was practically in front of her. Obviously one of the gypsies, she wore a kerchief over her hair and a dusty man's waistcoat over her dress. As Josie drew near, she wished the woman good day.

"Mistress," the woman said, dipping her head. "Tell your fortune?"

"Oh—no, thank you," Josie said, meaning to keep walking.

The old woman chuckled, then started to cough and cough, and it seemed uncaring to simply continue on. Josie was on the verge of pounding her on the back when the woman sucked in a long breath and the coughing abated.

"Give me your hand, girl, and I'll look into your love-future."

"No, truly," Josie began, but then the gypsy's words caught her attention. "What do you mean, my love-future?"

"Your hand, my lady, and I'll tell you what is in the heart of your true love."

The idea that looking at Josie's hand could allow the woman to know anything about Nicholas's heart made her want to laugh.

But. There *were* those restless, doubting feelings about Nicholas that nagged her no matter how she tried to avoid them. Tentatively she held out her hand.

The crone stroked a fingertip across it. "All is not well," she said after a few moments.

"Pardon?"

"The man. He does not understand love."

This was hardly what she'd expected—she'd imagined some cheering story meant to inspire a tip—and she tried gently to pull her hand back. But the gypsy held on firmly.

"Oh, well," Josie said carelessly, "who does understand, really? Isn't love supposed to be a mystery?"

The gypsy flicked her a glance, as if irritated that she wasn't properly concerned. "There is trouble ahead. The course of love may not run smooth. It may not run at all."

These words sent a shiver down Josie's spine, as if this woman had looked into her heart and seen the hesitation there. Seen down to the untrustworthy part of her that had felt bottled up for so long and that yearned for something she couldn't name.

She told herself not to be stupid. The woman's words were meaningless, made up to create an illusion.

Yet she couldn't let go of the unsettled feeling that had come over her. What if, when she and Nicholas could finally be together, being together wasn't as wonderful as she'd remembered it? What if her dreams for their future were all wrong?

"Oh," she said quietly.

The gypsy's eyes narrowed. "You can help it along."

"How's that?"

"The course of love. I have a potion."

Oh, good heavens, a potion! But this silly suggestion had at least broken the spell. "Thank you, but no."

A piercing green gaze met hers. "You scorn what you do not understand. But the ways of your people are complicated, and often the wrong people marry each other."

Well, that was certainly true. But why was she standing here getting advice about life from someone who lived in the woods?

"I really must be going." Josie tried again to pull her hand back, but the older woman had a very firm grip.

"Don't be a fool!" the crone said vehemently. "He will never be able to love you if you don't act. And you will miss out on the love of your life."

The words poked deeper at that little seed of anxiety. *The love of her life.* That was what she so hoped for, what she dreamed about. Nicholas was the love of her life, of course he was.

He'd said he loved her.

She was foolish and weak to doubt their future, to be listening to this woman who knew neither of them.

Before Josie could speak, the woman reached into a pocket in her coat and pulled out several objects: a root and two small bottles. Finally releasing Josie's hand, she selected one of the bottles and pushed the other items back into the pocket.

"Take this," she said, grabbing Josie's hand again and pressing the bottle into it. "All that is needed is to put three drops—no more!—into the man's drink, then let him see the one he is meant to love."

Josie stared at the bottle with its tea-colored liquid. Even though she hardly believed in such things as love potions, an idea was forming in her mind about what this potion might do.

An idea that had nothing to do with the connection she and Nicholas had formed.

But no, it was beyond ridiculous.

"Thank you," she said, "but I don't believe in magic."

"Is something magic because we cannot explain it?" The gypsy shrugged. "The potion is made partly from the seeds of a beautiful vine from the hot climates across the southern ocean, given to me by a friend who journeyed there. There, people take the seeds to open their minds. Here, we have nothing similar." She tapped the bottle. "Except in your hand."

Perhaps she could tell that Josie was a little tempted, because she folded Josie's fingers over the bottle. "Where it is needed, it can help. Where it is not needed, it will do no harm."

*Where it is needed.* Josie did know somewhere a love potion might be needed. If such a thing might really work.

She felt a little charmed by the fairy-tale quality of the whole thing. What if she did try—with Edwina and Colin? What if this potion might be just the little push needed to get Colin to wake up to the idea of courting Edwina?

He seemed to have something against marriage, and with parents who'd apparently been very unhappy, that was somewhat understandable. But he was too good a man to be so grim on the subject of companionship, too good a man to be always alone. And he'd showed that he cared for Edwina.

Using the love potion was a wild idea. And yet, what did she—or any of them—have to lose?

Josie dug in her reticule for a coin for the gypsy, ignoring the voice of reason that pointed out she was spending her money on plant juice. If there were even the slightest chance it might help, it was worth it.

Now she just needed to find the right moment to give the potion to Colin in Edwina's company. Perhaps she could do it at tea the next time he stopped by Jasmine House.

"One more thing," the crone said. "Do it tonight—there will be a full moon." She winked.

"We gypsies respect the power of the moon. It will enhance the potion."

"Oh. Very well." Josie would send him a note then, and invite him to come for an evening visit that night. Perhaps the shadowy cover of night was better anyway for using potions—she didn't want to be caught looking as though she were trying to poison him.

# *Four*

COLIN HAD BEEN HAPPY TO RECEIVE JOSIE'S INVITATION to come for an evening visit, but now that he was sitting with the Cardworthys drinking a late-evening cup of tea, he knew himself to be a fool. Not because the conversation kept threatening to divert to a discussion of fichus, though it was a topic that would never fascinate him, but because Josie looked so beautiful tonight in her plain cream gown he'd seen a hundred times that it was making him contemplate writing to Nick to say that he'd better hurry up and return.

What the devil was taking Nick so long, anyway? He ought to have found some way to return months ago and made Josie his wife and taken her away. Nick was a fool.

Josie was talking about the merits of poetry now—he guessed she didn't want to discuss fichus either—and he felt tempted to start a debate with her, to rile her and make the color come into her cheeks and her blue eyes flash. To make her lose her composure and engage with him, if only in words, which was the only way he could connect with her. It was a wrong idea, but he still wanted it, the way a hungry person yearned for food.

He dragged his gaze away from the pink scarf she'd tied in her hair, which echoed the rosy color of her lips, and settled them on Edwina, who was sitting in the chair next to him. Mrs. Cardworthy was, as usual, draped on the divan.

"Have some more tea, Colin," Josie said.

He gave her his cup and forced himself to think of topics that would take his mind from her: Henry the Eighth, the Puritans, his tenants.

"Oh," she said, standing up with his cup, "I think there's a tiny crack in it. Let me just see."

She went over to the window, apparently to use the light of the full moon, which was spilling in through the glass and brightening the room considerably in addition to the candles. She stood there, facing away from them and examining the cup for what seemed like a long time, but then she turned around and said, "No, I was wrong. It's perfectly fine."

She came back to the table and poured him some tea. She knew just how he liked it, and he watched her stir in the milk. He'd once found a glove of hers that had been left behind one winter evening when her family had come to Greenbrier, and held it up against his own hand and marveled that anything so small and slim as her hand could accomplish tasks.

He accepted the tea but refused the plate of biscuits she held toward him because he knew he wanted to take one only because *she* was offering it. The biscuits were some Indian confection that Mr. Cardworthy had called sweet *kachoris*. They weren't bad, though they were extremely dense, and Colin wondered at the faithfulness of the recipe Cardworthy had provided his cook. The Cardworthy children, who'd grown up with them, ate them happily. He sipped his tea and looked at the carpet and thought about the Puritans some more.

In the middle of listening to Mrs. Cardworthy talk about the shocking cost of linen, he began to feel a little strange. A bit drowsy, though not exactly as if he were tired. More like dull-headed.

Josie's voice forced him to focus. "Ivorwood, have you seen the beautiful painting of violets that Edwina made yesterday?"

"I...no, I haven't had the pleasure." What was wrong with him? Blurriness teased the edges of his vision.

"Do go show it to him this instant, Edwina," Josie said with cheerful enthusiasm. "Then we can discuss it."

"Whatever would there be to discuss?" Edwina said. "It's a picture of flowers."

Josie cleared her throat. "Ivorwood is a connoisseur of art. Doubtless he'll have thoughts to offer. Just go look at it, you two."

Colin couldn't think why Josie kept going on about this painting, but he seemed to lack the focus to come up with any direction of his own. He stood up.

"Edwina?" he said, offering her his arm. She stood and walked with him over to the far corner of the room, where an easel held her painting.

"It is indeed very handsome," he said, feeling that his words were now blurry as well. Could words be blurry? Why was he thinking about this? He must be coming down with something. He forced himself to offer some compliments about the composition, though it smeared before his eyes into shifting purple blobs.

"Thank you, Ivorwood. But I don't know why Josie sent us over here. She's being strange."

"Actually," he said, "I'm beginning to feel strange myself."

He closed his eyes, focusing his thoughts. When he opened them, Josie was coming toward them.

"Are you all right, Ivorwood?" Mrs. Cardworthy called from her divan.

"Just finding myself quite tired all of a sudden. I'd best go. If you will excuse me please, ladies?"

"Colin?" Josie said in a voice that seemed oddly urgent. He couldn't think what was so urgent. He couldn't really think at all.

He said good night and made his way in a stupor to the back garden. As soon as he was outside, he felt, bizarrely, as though the enormous full moon were focused solely on him, as though it were somehow his special companion as he stumbled along the path to Greenbrier.

Somewhere along the way, though, the fatigue pulling at him shifted into a surging feeling of delight and a wonderful sort of freedom the likes of which he'd never known before. Suddenly he felt empowered and infinitely alive, and he began to run, on fire with urgent purpose, the pulsing energy of the big moon spurring him on.

When he reached Greenbrier, he tore through the front door and hardly took note of anything as he rushed euphorically upward, taking one staircase after another until he reached the top.

Colin rolled and tossed uncomfortably, not quite awake as the images of a dream tormented him. His bed was hideously uncomfortable, and he felt strangely damp, but it was the piercing brightness battering his eyes that finally dragged him from a heavy sleep.

A bright ray of sun burned into his face, and he shifted his head and blinked as his vision adjusted to a wide view of sky and a stone wall. No, it was *battlements*, which the sun's rays were just now cresting.

Good God. He was lying on the roof.

He'd apparently *slept* on the roof of Greenbrier.

He lay there, blinking up at the blue morning sky.

And that dream. He'd dreamt of Josie, and it had been more than a dream; it had been a vivid erotic fantasy. Josie, in a diaphanous blue gown, crawling toward him, her small, soft breasts catching fascinatingly on the fabric as she went.

He swallowed hard.

From his right came the sound of a throat clearing.

He sat bolt upright. His butler stood by the door to the roof.

"My lord," he said. "I trust you are well."

Colin paused. More memories of the night before were crashing over him, and they weren't good. No, surely he hadn't...

"Ames, yes, I am well."

Neither of them said anything as Colin stood up and brushed himself off.

"I'm afraid I had some bad tea," he said.

But no, that couldn't be it—the effect had been immediate, and the Cardworthys had seemed fine.

He could remember being at Jasmine House vividly now—the initial fatigue, leaving quickly (thank God he had), and the feeling of exultation that had come over him as he made his way home in the extra-bright light of that full moon. Maybe some kind of moon madness had come over him. Lunacy, certainly.

"Or something," he continued. "Perhaps some temporary fever I picked up in town. In any case, I wasn't feeling quite myself last night."

"No, my lord," Ames agreed equably.

"Did I…" Colin said, "that is, did you happen to hear anything last night?"

Another throat clearing. "I believe you shouted several times. You had already stopped by the time I arrived to make certain all was well."

"I see."

"You insisted you wished to 'sleep under the moon that shelters us all,' was how I believe you put it."

He'd spoken that drivel? What had *come over* him last night?

"Could you hear what I was yelling?"

"It was rather hard, but it sounded like 'Posy.' Or"—there was a pause—"might have been 'Josie.'"

"It must have been Posy," Colin said firmly, pushing down a bolt of horror. "I saw a very nice posy at the market yesterday. Must have taken my fancy."

"Very good, my lord."

Colin sent Ames away and leaned out over the battlements, needing to understand how he'd broken nearly every bond he'd placed on his behavior.

The roof offered him an expansive view of a large swath of countryside, but all too close was Jasmine

House, with its unruly garden and unusual jasmine-covered chimneys. So close they might have heard him yelling. Though probably not *what* he was yelling.

Josie was there, possibly still sleeping, innocently unaware that nearby was a man who wanted to do wicked things to her. She would be there at Jasmine House until Nick finally came back and took her away, a daily temptation.

Had he not left the Cardworthys abruptly last night, he might easily have revealed what must never be spoken. This was appalling.

All this time, he'd thought himself in control, believed he could take for granted that no matter the temptation, he would resist. He was used to self-discipline, and he expected nothing less of himself. But last night, he'd behaved like a fool. A fool at the mercy of his emotions.

Just what he'd learned from his very earliest memories was a mistake.

He thought of his tempestuous mother, how whenever she'd fallen into a fury with his father, she'd thrown the fact of Colin's existence against him. *The child*, she'd called him; she'd called him by name rarely enough as it was, but when she was angry, she stirred up her grievances, and at the top of the list was being forced to marry the wrong man and bear his child.

Inevitably such scenes would end with his mother doing something like spitting in his father's tea, and the earl throwing it at her. Even as a young boy, Colin had realized that some people never grew up, and he'd known he never wanted to be like that, which meant never letting himself be ruled by emotion.

Clearly, despite his years of self-control, he harbored an appalling potential for emotional indulgence that he'd never suspected. And now he knew that he could no longer trust himself.

He wanted Josie badly, she belonged to his friend, and last night, with the shouting and the dreaming, he'd been given a warning that his own code of behavior was not inviolable. How could he trust himself around Josie, knowing this? What might he say to her? How might he allow himself to be ruled by emotions that would push him to find out if it was really love that she shared with Nick?

He had to get away from her.

He got up and began preparations to remove himself to London.

❧

Josie was puzzled and a little hurt when she discovered that Colin had left Greenbrier suddenly, and without telling her. But mainly, she missed him. She missed their conversations about history, the simple walks they took together, and how easy it was to talk to him about Nicholas. His absence had shown her how much she'd come to rely on his presence, and now she was lonely when she hadn't been before she'd gotten to know him so well.

Of course she had her family, but that was not the same. Between her and Colin was something different and deep, as if, despite their differences, they were alike in the substance of which they were made. Which made sense, since they both cared for Nicholas—they would have to have quite a bit in common, wouldn't they?

But she was also disappointed he'd left because she'd had such hopes that he and Edwina might be growing closer.

Not surprisingly, the ridiculous love potion seemed to have been a failure. She'd actually been concerned that the doctored tea had made him ill, because she'd accidentally put in rather more than three drops. And then she'd felt quite guilty about having given herself permission to be putting things in people's drinks.

But she'd sent over to Greenbrier early the next day to ask after him, and apparently he was fine, because he'd already left for London.

He'd been gone almost a week, and each day seemed longer than the one before.

Nor were things around Jasmine House very cheerful. Will and Matt, while practicing fisticuffs, had gotten out of hand, with the result that Will had broken his arm. And Edwina seemed to have settled into a dispirited acceptance of her future that worried Josie.

"I heard from one of the maids that there's to be an assembly in town in two weeks," she said to Edwina as they sat in the garden sewing one afternoon. "Wouldn't it be lovely to go? Mr. Trilby and some of the other gentlemen we met at the picnic might be there."

Edwina shrugged, which made Josie press her lips together impatiently. "Edwina, you *must* make an effort."

Edwina gave a mirthless laugh. "Oh, Josie, you are such a dreamer. I shall finish out my days here at Jasmine House. And really," she said seriously, "I'm grateful to have a family and a roof over my head and steady meals."

Just then their brothers burst through the doors to the garden. Will was howling, with Matt following.

Their tutor had gone out for the afternoon, and they'd been running wilder than usual.

"Blast you!" Matt shouted at Will. "You've ruined my best horse figure."

Will only laughed as he vaulted over a line of bushes, ignoring Josie's warning that he stop before he hurt his broken arm.

The yelling continued until Will tripped over a broom that had been left lying in the grass and landed hard on the stone path. He gave a pained yelp that caused Josie to jump to her feet in concern. Edwina merely rolled her eyes.

"Serves him right," she said mildly, continuing to sew. "He was the one who left the broom out there to begin with."

"But his arm," Josie said. "We should see if he's hurt."

"I'm sure he's fine. He just wants attention. Will always has to be the center of attention."

That was possibly true, but it was also a shrewish comment.

Will picked himself up and walked off in a sulk. It would have done the boys good to gallop out across the fields and release some of their energy, but the Cardworthys only kept two horses, and Mama didn't like them to be ridden hard lest they go lame. Papa might have been a rough man, but since he'd died, Jasmine House had become too tame a place for high-spirited boys. Too tame a place for anyone with spirit.

Josie sat back down. She felt certain that there was some underlying fear or unhappiness that made Edwina sharp. If only it might be somehow resolved.

Josie said with soft urgency, "I want for you to find

a husband, more than anything." She paused. "Won't you please consider setting your sights on Ivorwood?"

Edwina just stared at her for long seconds. "Why? Has he expressed a fascination with me to you?"

"No," Josie said carefully. "But he might if you showed a particular interest in him when he comes back."

"I'll just snap my fingers, shall I, and get him to pay attention to me instead of you?"

Josie frowned. "But that's different. We're only good friends. But you might be so much more to each other."

"Is that so," Edwina said frostily. "Ivorwood's never shown half so much interest in me as he has in you. And I won't take any woman's leavings, especially not yours."

"But who will you marry if no one's good enough? You don't want to end up like Mama, do you?"

"Just because I don't want to entice a man who's clearly not smitten with me, it doesn't make me like Mama."

Josie knew she was walking on thin ice, but wasn't it time to speak honestly? So much was at stake. "Mama gave up on her future when Papa died. Didn't you give up on yours when Mr. Perriwell left?"

A dark flush spread over Edwina's face. "That was different. Papa kept us so sheltered we couldn't meet anyone."

"Papa's been gone for years," Josie said gently. "When are you going to let go of his hold over you?"

Edwina looked away. "Don't you see that I have?" she said in a rough voice. "I *learned* from him. And from Mr. Perriwell. That's why, if I were ever to marry, it would only be to a man who would treat me like I'm the sun in his sky. And since that's not going to happen, I shall be perfectly happy staying at Jasmine House."

She stood up. "Keep your pity, Josie. I don't need it." She tossed her sewing on the chair and left.

Josie swallowed uncomfortably. Clearly her match-making efforts had been an utter failure. And though Edwina might talk bravely, she seemed still troubled by their father's thoughtless comments and Mr. Perriwell's abandonment.

But what Edwina had said about Colin being particularly interested in Josie…someone listening might have gotten the impression that he was drawn to her in something more than friendship.

Of course it wasn't true. But she remembered the funny way she'd felt when Colin had smiled at Edwina, and it gave her the strangest shiver.

Later that afternoon, feeling peevish, Josie took out the small stack of letters from Nicholas and reread them. And suppressed, as she found herself doing more and more lately, the wish that he wouldn't address her as though she were some sort of goddess of perfection. He only wanted their future to be perfect, she told herself, just as she did.

*Dearest Josephine*, he'd written as a postscript to the family letter, *when we are finally together, all shall be as it should be. You are all that is good, and I cling to the memory of you as one clings to a light in the darkness.*

Muddled as she was, though, she didn't see how she could be anyone's guiding light.

She did not feel any better the next morning when, awakened by a shriek, she emerged from her chamber to find one of the maids in the corridor staring at her brothers' tutor, who was sitting dazedly on the floor by Edwina's door with a startled look on his gaunt face. Next to him lay a large bunch of weeds tied around with a cravat, like an enormous bouquet; the hallway smelled strongly of onion tops, which could be glimpsed among the clover and dockweed.

Edwina opened the door to her room and nearly fell over the pile of weeds. Mr. Botsford, who was rubbing his face vigorously and trying to stand up, looked as though he would shortly be ill.

"What on earth is going on?" Edwina demanded as their brothers arrived.

"I'm so slor…sorry!" Mr. Botsford said, finally managing to stand by dint of pushing himself up along the wall. "I cannot for the life of me tell you how I ended up here." He stood there quivering and blinking his large brown eyes rapidly, looking like a cornered field mouse.

"What about all these weeds?" Edwina said in a cold voice. "Is this some sort of joke, Mr. Botsford?"

He stood there in mute horror.

It eventually came to light that Will had found the potion bottle in Josie's room when she sent him to fetch something, and he and Matthew had thought putting some of her "elixir" in Mr. Botsford's tea would be hilarious.

She explained the potion away as something a gypsy had pressed on her, and was relieved that Mr. Botsford seemed to recover quickly. As he led her brothers sternly off to atone through some disagreeable tasks, Edwina prodded the weeds with her foot.

"Doubtless the only bouquet I shall receive this year."

Josie leaned down to pick up the weeds. "I suppose the poor man has a *tendre* for you."

Edwina merely put a hand over her face and retreated into her room.

As the maid bore the pungent bouquet away, Josie thought of how abruptly Colin had left Jasmine House the night she'd potioned him and worried guiltily that the potion had had some ill, if temporary, effect on him.

And what if he'd somehow seen her putting it in his tea? She shuddered at the thought.

She resolved to pour the potion out, but her brothers seemed to have lost it—though she turned their bedchambers upside down, she couldn't find the wretched thing.

# Five

COLIN NEVER LIKED BEING IN LONDON AS MUCH AS THE country, even though he had a beautiful home in Mayfair, as befitted the Earl of Ivorwood, and the city meant gatherings filled with plenty of lively conversation and music and art. He liked music and art, and he valued the project he'd recently undertaken with his friend Hal, Viscount Roxham, to build a hospital for wounded soldiers, which, along with meetings of Parliament, kept him busy.

But he didn't like to be with people around the clock, and in London, with all the people who knew him because he was the earl, they were hard to avoid. He missed the slower pace of life at Greenbrier, the endless hours he could spend on reading and writing. And of course, he missed Josie, the one person whose company he always wanted.

Lately he'd been trying to convince himself that her beauty had enchanted him to the point that he overlooked things about her that should have annoyed him. Like the way she sometimes told him what he ought to do. A flaw, surely.

She was also far too likely to do things without considering consequences, as when he'd come upon her standing on a branch in the old apple tree in front of Jasmine House last fall, insisting she could reach the apples the gardener had said couldn't be gotten. Colin had nearly expired at the sight of her feet on that narrow limb, and he insisted she get down immediately. But she'd only laughed and pelted him with apples.

He pushed away the thought that perhaps she'd gotten engaged to Nick on a whim, that the two of them had had only six weeks of courting and maybe they shouldn't have let their feelings run away with them. That she tended to look on the bright side of things and disregard consequences, and she thought marriage was a fairy tale.

People got married on the strength of much shorter acquaintance than six weeks, he reminded himself, and it didn't matter one whit what Josie and Nick did because it was entirely not his affair.

He had no business thinking of her at all, but even though he wasn't with her every day now, he couldn't seem to stop. That erotic dream had put the kind of images in his mind that he'd fought hard never to nourish, and now they were there, waiting to ambush him in weak moments as though they were actual experiences they'd shared.

And, raging desire aside, Josie had become such a close friend that he simply missed her.

He felt bad about leaving so abruptly, but he knew he must not invest any more in their friendship, that doing so would only draw him further into the temptation the dream had shown him: the temptation to think he had as much right as any man to want a woman who did not yet legally belong to another man.

He would not behave like a scoundrel to his two closest friends. He owed them far better.

Which was why, as a sort of apology to Josie, he was currently engaged in writing a note to his aunt, Mrs. Maria Westin, who was in Town for the Season, asking her to sponsor Edwina.

He was fairly certain Maria would do it, and he knew it would please Josie, who was so concerned about her sister's future. Not without good reason, he thought wryly as he signed the note and sprinkled sand over it. At least he'd disabused Josie of the idea of matching him with Edwina.

Josie would be invited, too, naturally, but he meant to keep enough distance between them that it would be as though she were hardly there.

❧

As the Earl of Ivorwood's coach drew Edwina and Josie through London on a soft June afternoon a week later, Josie stared avidly out the little window on her side.

"Aren't you going to look?" she said as a high-perch phaeton pulled past them, driven by a man with a fillip of blond hair pluming over his forehead and a garish yellow waistcoat. "Our first visit to London! I didn't think we'd ever be able to come."

"I know. I'm very excited," Edwina said in a flat voice. Edwina had closed the curtain to her window when the carriage had clattered by a marketplace where people were shouting and the smoke of a brazier had hung thickly in the air. The smells and sounds and sights of London were intense, but Josie liked how different they were from the quiet familiarity of Upperton.

"You don't sound excited," she said, and she thought she knew why: after so many years stuck at Jasmine House, maybe London looked daunting to someone of Edwina's temperament. Perhaps Edwina was afraid of not being a success, afraid she would be overlooked or rejected, and she didn't want to get her hopes up. Josie tried to cheer her. "It's amazing. The whole town is a wonder."

"The whole town smells awful," Edwina said from the far corner of the coach, where she had withdrawn. "Why don't you close your curtain?"

"Edwina," Josie said, turning to give her an encouraging look, "if you even just pretended to be a little enchanted, I think you'd soon come to feel that way, like the way humming a cheery tune can give you a little courage when you're feeling low. It really was so kind of Mrs. Westin to invite us, and of Colin to ask her to do it."

"I know," Edwina said and forced a small, tight smile. She tried gamely to expand it into what she must have thought looked like enchantment, but the expression was actually fairly ghastly.

"Never mind," Josie said kindly. "I'm sure all will go well if you just let London work its magic on you."

When Mrs. Westin's invitation had arrived several days earlier, they'd all been surprised. Maria Westin's letter had hinted that she'd had particular success in guiding young ladies in finding husbands, and though Josie caught her mother looking dismayed at the thought of Edwina finding a husband, it was hard for anyone to argue that Edwina didn't deserve this chance.

Josie had been so glad at this sign of friendship from Colin, since she knew he was helping Edwina because she, Josie, had asked him. She felt especially grateful that, despite the way she'd pressed him about courting Edwina himself, he still meant to help.

Even if Edwina was approaching London with trepidation, Josie held out hope that, perhaps with guidance from Maria Westin and enough of the right kind of exposure, Edwina might catch the interest of a London gentleman. Preferably one who knew how to be lavish when courting.

Whatever happened, though, one of the things Josie was most looking forward to in London was for Colin to show it to her. For surely once she and Edwina were installed at his aunt's house, they would see him regularly.

Mrs. Westin's town house, which was in the fashionable district of Mayfair, was tall and slim and elegant. A dapper, surprisingly handsome butler opened the front door for Edwina and Josie.

Inside, the foyer made Josie think of a beautifully wrapped present. Every surface gleamed, from the dark wood of the stairway banister to the brass sconces on the walls. A small marble statue of a Greek woman stood on a waist-high pedestal, accenting the salmon wallpaper behind it, while on the opposite wall, miniature gold-framed paintings marched up the stairs. Everything smelled cleanly of lemon.

Mrs. Westin was waiting to greet them. She was petite and slim, with the sharp, alert quality of a bird, and perhaps it was because her hair was such a striking auburn color that her skin looked just like porcelain. Her apple-green silk dress fell in perfect soft folds and kissed the tops of tiny dark yellow satin shoes. Josie could not have said how old Mrs. Westin was—she might have been forty, but a confident worldliness in her manner suggested she was quite a bit older.

"Well, my dears," she said, leading them into a handsome dark blue and gold drawing room and ringing for tea, "lovely as you are, you will certainly attract attention. Now tell me, have you ever been to London before?"

"No, Mrs. Westin," Edwina said. She was blinking a lot, which she did when she felt out of her element.

"Stop blinking, child," Mrs. Westin said in a kind voice. "Fix your eyes on something if you must, and focus there until you can gather yourself."

Edwina's eyes dropped to the floor.

"Never the floor, Miss Cardworthy! You are a regal young woman, not a schoolgirl being scolded. People will treat you as you present yourself to be treated. And the last thing you want is a husband who wishes you to be a little girl for him to scold."

That brought a smile to Edwina's face. She raised her head and lifted her chin. "I should hate such a man."

"So should I." Maria Westin spoke in such a decisive way that Josie wondered if the widow's husband had been such a man. Though Josie couldn't see her *allowing* him to be.

Maria Westin turned her sharp eyes on Josie. "And

what about you, Miss Josephine? My nephew tells me you are engaged to Captain Hargrave."

"Yes, ma'am."

"A handsome gentleman to be sure. And he's been off fighting Napoleon for some time, hasn't he?"

"I haven't seen him in over a year."

One of Mrs. Westin's slender eyebrows lifted. "So he engaged himself to you, and then went off to war? Isn't Captain Hargrave worried that you'll forget about him? And aren't you a bit worried that some lovely foreign lady might catch his eye?"

Her frankness was startling. And also refreshing. To say such things out loud, to voice the hidden, unwelcome thoughts that tormented Josie in the dark of night—well, it made her feel oddly comforted.

She hoped Nicholas had received her letter telling him that she and Edwina would be in London for the Season. His last letter had indicated that on his return to England in late July, he would stop at his London town house first. That was only next month, and if he didn't receive their letter, how surprised he would be to find Josie in Town.

Edwina waved her arm dismissively. "Nicholas wouldn't dare lose interest in Josie. She's too perfect."

"Edwina," Josie said, frowning at her sister's tone.

Their hostess laughed, an airy, elegant sound. "But it's a charming thing to say, as long as the tone is not sarcastic. Tone is everything, my dear Edwina, and you never want to look shrewish or envious. But we can discuss such things further before you two venture into society."

"Shall we see Ivorwood soon?" Josie asked.

"Not just yet. I believe he is quite busy at the moment."

Josie tried not to show her disappointment.

"Anyway," Maria Westin continued, "*we* shall be far too busy to see *him*. I'll send a note to let him know you've arrived."

There followed several intense days in which Colin's aunt tutored Edwina and Josie in London ways and fashions and took them to shops. She invited them to call her Maria, and seemed quite sweetly happy to spoil them.

"Since I am widowed with no children," she said as she led them into a linen drapers on Bond Street that was overflowing with rich satins and silks, "I want to play fairy godmother to you both." And she bought them each enough beautiful fabric, in pastel hues that looked straight from the garden, to make three gowns.

As they got to know their hostess better, Josie couldn't help noticing that while Maria Westin wasn't telling Edwina anything Josie hadn't already suggested herself, Edwina actually seemed to be listening to her.

❦

Maria took Josie and Edwina to a dinner party at the end of their first week, to begin introducing them to society. The ladies met a number of charming and flirtatious gentlemen, and by the next morning, Maria said that people had already begun talking about "the beauteous Cardworthy sisters."

As each day passed, Josie observed with amazement that her sister seemed to blossom more. Some of this blossoming was surely due to Maria and all she'd exposed them to, but Josie suspected some of it was due to the magic of London itself, with its crowds and grand buildings and city energy. It was as though some sort of scales had grown over Edwina during the years at Jasmine House, and they were falling away now amid the excitement of London.

Most afternoons the three ladies strolled about the city, wandering among ancient lanes and grand buildings and exploring Hyde Park, and Josie often wished the still-absent Colin were there to share it all with them. She'd missed him as the ladies had stood outside the Tower, where she recalled all the things he'd told her had happened there.

And how he would have teased her if he'd been present when she'd almost fallen into the Serpentine while chasing an adorable dog who'd snatched her reticule, which had been full of sweets.

But there was no sign of him; he was apparently very busy. She missed how easy it was to see him at home.

At a party near the end of their second week, Edwina caught the attention of one gentleman in particular, Lord Mappleton. Josie had never seen her sister smile so much as she did when he lingered talking with her, though Josie couldn't see that there was so much to smile about: Mappleton was wealthy and titled, but he didn't seem to have an original thought in his head, and there was something almost too agreeable about him.

There were, Josie was dismayed to acknowledge noticing, many finer men on whom to set one's sights. London gentlemen were…fascinating. She was beginning to see how being kept apart from society, even the small society of Upperton, had closed down her view of the world, so that coming to London made her feel like a child in a sweetshop.

She was enjoying herself far too much, and she was ashamed to realize that she'd gone whole days without thinking once about Nicholas. This was terrible, as was the sense she kept having that marrying would mean giving up so much *potential*, which was greedy and also ridiculous, because marrying Nicholas wouldn't mean giving up parties and balls—as his wife, she'd likely attend far more. He had a family house in London as well as one in the country, and marrying him would be the beginning of wonderful things.

So why had her impending marriage started to seem like an ending? She loved him, didn't she? He was handsome and charming and so much fun.

*He'd told her he loved her.*

So why was she so peevish and unsettled?

Oh *where* was Colin? They'd been in London for over two weeks, and still they hadn't seen him. It was almost as though he were avoiding them.

✦

When Colin finally appeared at Maria's house at the beginning of the following week to escort the ladies to their first ball, Josie was so happy to see his familiar face that she almost rushed forward to hug him, though she knew that would be excessive.

He wore a black tailcoat and a snowy white shirt, and though she'd certainly seen him in black before, tonight there was something about him that whispered midnight things to her. Black hair, black coat, yes, but it was more to do with something dark and remote in his manner and a shuttered quality in his silver-green eyes.

His greeting, while friendly, was detached—he merely nodded to her with a polite smile, then moved on to greet Edwina. He was preoccupied, or subdued, but whatever it was, he was far more reserved than usual. He might be that way with other people, but he'd never been like that with her. She tried to catch his eyes, but his gaze was always elsewhere.

As the other ladies were adjusting their wraps, she moved closer to him and said, "Colin, I haven't gotten a chance to thank you properly for asking Maria to sponsor Edwina and sending your coach for us. It was so very good of you."

"Think nothing of it."

"How can I, when I know it must have been some trouble to you?" She smiled, wanting to encourage him not to be so remote, but he only gave another of those detached smiles.

She reminded herself of how reserved he was and put extra warmth in her voice. "I know very well that the world of debutantes is not your realm. You did something extra for us, and especially for Edwina."

He inclined his head courteously in reply then looked away and told Maria they had best be on their way. As he escorted them out the door, never once did he show by any word or glance that it made any difference to him that she, Josie, was there.

She felt a little crushed.

On the way to his gleaming black carriage with its

golden family crest, he enthused politely over their gowns and said what a fine evening it was for a ball. Josie was wearing one of the new gowns Maria had bought for her, a white silk with a bluebell-colored sash tied under her bosom and a matching bandeau in her hair. Her new blue satin slippers made her feet want to skip across a dance floor. She felt pretty and gay, and she thought Colin might say something particular about how she looked tonight, but he didn't.

He handed them deftly into the carriage and sat next to Edwina and opposite Josie, wearing a pleasant smile that suddenly seemed out of place paired with the bold jutting of his large nose and the black slashes of his brows.

He asked after their family and the news from Upperton. The conversation was polite and general, and it could hardly be otherwise, as they were not alone. Nor would they be; this was London, not the back garden at Jasmine House, she told herself.

But where was the subtle warmth she usually felt from Colin?

She began to wonder if something had changed, if in coming to London they now might not be as they'd been in Upperton. Perhaps he'd left Greenbrier so abruptly because there were important things here she knew nothing about that required his attention.

But she acknowledged how much she was used to being one of the things on which he liked to spend his attention, and she didn't want it to be any other way. Where was the man who'd told her such diverting tales of his historical investigations in small villages? Who'd shown her his childhood journal wherein he'd carefully recorded all the minute doings in his house-hold over the course of an entire month?

This new Colin, with his eyes that sought other views and his air of command, was someone she didn't quite know. She needed his friendship...didn't he need hers?

They arrived at Lord Worthing's manor, where the ball was to be held, and he got out to hand them down. When it was Josie's turn, she gave his hand a friendly little squeeze, but he didn't squeeze hers back. When she realized that she felt a little rejected, she told herself she was being silly and too sensitive. Surely he was just preoccupied. Or was something perhaps amiss?

Or was it her—*was* he in fact being cool to her for some reason?

She examined her conduct on the last occasions they'd been together, but she couldn't see why he would be.

Unless—she thought guiltily of poor Mr. Botsford and his bouquet—he'd seen her put the love potion in his drink. But surely Colin would have said something at the time, demanded to know what she was doing? Unfortunately, she could hardly come right out and ask him.

"I wonder if Mappleton has arrived yet," Edwina said as they paused a moment before the grand, lit-up manor. Lively music could be heard, and even as they stood there groups of people were going inside. Maria looked on with the impassive air of a general approaching a good position on a battlefield.

Josie wanted a moment with Colin, to ask him if all was well, but when they entered the grand

foyer, a footman announced the arrival of the Earl of
Ivorwood, and their hostess, Lady Worthing, rushed
forward to welcome them.

Colin presented Josie and Edwina to her. "The
Cardworthy family are some of my oldest and dearest
friends," he said, sounding quite as usual.

Josie gave herself a sort of internal shake and told
herself she ought not to scrutinize him so. But thoughts
about Colin's mood were quickly replaced by wonder
as they moved into the enormous ballroom.

"Why, it's amazing," Josie said, gazing at the beautifully dressed people dancing beneath the chandelier
glow of hundreds of candles. Flowers decorated every
surface, and the introductory notes of a fiddle floated
through the room, filling her senses.

"Softly," Maria whispered wryly, "lest you seem too
pleased. The fashionable people will think you a rube."

"Then I shall be glad to be considered so, for to be
in such a glorious place and not be amazed would be
wrong. It's pure magic."

"Josie," Edwina said with a hint of exasperation,
"you are far too inclined to like things. Why, listen to
that woman's laugh—she sounds like a donkey. *That's*
not magical."

"Ladies," Maria said cheerfully, "let us remember
our *tone*."

Lord Mappleton appeared then and invited Edwina
to dance. Maria presented Josie to a very handsome
blond gentleman who turned out to be Viscount
Roxham, one of Colin's good friends. His wife, Lady
Roxham, was dancing with someone else, and he
smiled kindly at Josie and offered her his arm.

"Nick told me about you," Roxham said as they began the steps of a quadrille.

She blushed. "I seem always to be hearing of him from other people." And it struck her that, yet again, she'd forgotten about him. She hadn't thought about him once all that day.

The knowledge made her a little sick.

"It must be odd," Lord Roxham said with a rueful smile, "to find yourself discussed by people you've yet to meet."

"A little," she said weakly. What she *had* been paying attention to was Viscount Roxham's hand-someness. People called him Lord Perfect, and she saw why: he had golden hair and sparkling blue-green eyes and these very fascinating little slashes that formed in his cheeks when he smiled. Truth be told, his smile made her feel a little breathless, *and what on earth was wrong with her?* Roxham was a married man, and she was engaged!

She moved her eyes away from his male beauty, but they only settled on a man behind him who had curly brown hair and a wonderfully deep laugh that made Josie want to stand in front of him and see if she could make him laugh more. Dear God, maybe she even wanted to kiss him, this handsome stranger.

Almost frantically she swung her eyes about the room as she danced, but everywhere she looked were gentlemen who seemed fascinating. Handsome, dash-ing, playful—she wanted to know them all, know their stories, hear them laugh, feel what it would be like to be with them.

Heaven help her, she was an emotional hussy.

Somehow she finished the dance with Roxham, only to be invited to dance by the curly-haired gentleman, an Irishman named Mr. Kit Standish, it turned out. She said yes to him, and to all the other men who asked. She loved dancing with them, but all the time her conscience kept demanding to know what she thought she was doing. It accused her of liking their attention too much, and forced her to admit that she had a deep appetite for all of this—for the compliments men gave her, for their charm and their male beauty and the feel of their strong hands on her.

Anxiety mingled with the pleasure of the dancing, so that her head spun.

Colin, the only man with whom she felt she might safely dance and avoid this turmoil, had not come near her all night. She caught a glimpse of him dancing with a lovely woman wearing a feathered turban, and another time with an exquisitely dressed stout woman. But he didn't seem inclined to catch her eye or come to chat with her or ask her to dance. She began to wonder if he was avoiding her.

By the time the dinner break came, she felt quite disgusted with herself, and while the others were leaving to find the dining room, she lingered at the table where cups of ratafia were set out.

She took a glass and sipped it, feeling the now-familiar burn of brandy behind the sweet flavor of the cherries and spices. It went to her head almost immediately, and she began to think it might help take away the mixed-up feelings that had overtaken her as she realized how much she was dazzled by the men of London.

She finished one glass and took another. A few moments later, she saw Colin passing near her, unaware of her presence. She stepped forward and grabbed his arm.

# *Six*

COLIN TURNED IN SURPRISE.

"Didn't you see me?" Josie said, an unwanted husky note in her voice betraying that she was upset. But they'd been such good friends, and he was treating her like an acquaintance, and she hated it. She needed him now.

She took another sip of ratafia, willing it to relax the lump of feeling in her throat. She felt odd and out of sorts, as if she didn't know herself anymore, or what she might do.

For a moment his face wore the strangest expression. She might have said it was anguish, but it was gone in a moment.

"Josie," he said. "I trust you are enjoying yourself?"

"Yes. No. I don't know," she said, wanting to tell him everything but too ashamed.

His eyebrows went up. "Curious."

Colin was older and wiser—she could tell him about how muddled she felt. She so wanted someone's wisdom. And just as much, she wanted him to stop being remote.

She grabbed his hand and tugged him around behind an enormous column near the drinks table to give them a little privacy from the dwindling groups of people who were passing toward the door leading to the dining room. Away from the chandeliers and their glittering crystals, the little corner of the grand room was shadowy. Behind them, an ornate, gold-painted double door to a balcony was open to catch the breeze.

A heavy pause ensued. She had the sense he wanted to be away from her, and she couldn't understand it. The little fan of lines around his eyes seemed pronounced tonight, as though he were especially tired. He'd probably been up late with some old book.

She caught sight of Edwina across the room, passing through the doorway to go into dinner in company with Maria and Lord Mappleton.

"Ivorwood," she said quietly, "what is it? You don't seem happy to see me. And you left Jasmine House so abruptly the last time we were together, as though you were taken ill. Was something amiss?" This was as close as she could get to asking what had happened after she'd put the potion in his tea without admitting she'd done so.

She thought he stiffened, but perhaps she was imagining it, because he only said, "Just a temporary indisposition. It was nothing."

"Then have I somehow offended you?"

"No, of course you haven't offended me," he said kindly. "I was simply needed in London. And of course I'm glad you and Edwina are here."

"Then you'll dance with me after the dinner break? I know you're often so busy, but just this once?"

The dancing joke again, Colin thought grimly. Though this time she looked as if she really did wish him to dance with her. He laughed a little, though it sounded dull to his own ears. But what else was there to do when Josie was quizzing him about why he didn't want to dance with her?

*Because having you in my arms will only make me want to touch you more. Because I won't want to stop. Because holding you will make me sick with wanting and jealousy, and I can't bear to be a man who is lusting after his best friend's fiancée.*

All words he could never say.

He conjured an ironic smile and shook his head a bit.

"You know how it is for an earl. We have those special, secret duties, and tonight I'm sorry to say they involve a small, opinionated female monkey someone's brought. It's my duty to entertain her while her master is dancing so she doesn't become jealous, and I'm afraid that between her demands and the dances I'm required to share with every matron and debutante in London, the night is already taken up."

Usually she would be laughing by now, but he caught the shadow of hurt in her eyes and the conjured smile faded from his lips. It had been a mistake for both of them, becoming such close friends. He should never have agreed to watch over her for Nick—it had only given him an excuse to see far too much of her. Now they were so connected in friendship and he needed distance from her, and she wouldn't understand.

She was upset about something, though surely not

the dancing? It was practically expected at this point that he wouldn't dance with her.

She downed the rest of the ratafia in her glass. It was an especially potent batch, he'd noticed when he'd taken some earlier, and he was surprised she was drinking it.

One of the little curls that framed her face had gotten caught in the edge of her thick lashes and he longed to brush it away. She was so beautiful tonight that every time he'd looked at her his heart had skipped a beat, and standing there with her was making him feel as though he'd just run a race. Never mind that her pretty white gown exposed more of the gently curved rise of her petite, perfect breasts than he'd ever seen before. All night, he'd forced himself not to look, though it hardly helped.

Ever since he'd come near her in Maria's foyer, he'd been in a constant state of arousal. The proximity of the carriage ride had been hell, and as he'd sat with his knees only a few inches from hers in their insubstantial white fabric, he'd forced himself to list every king of England in order in a futile attempt to take the edge off his lust.

In the ballroom only a few courting couples lingered across the parquet floor, along with the musicians, who'd put their instruments aside while they mopped their brows and drank lemonade. He and Josie were as good as alone behind the wide column with the draping plant fronds to either side of them, which suddenly seemed like a good thing when he saw, to his astonishment, tears brimming in the corners of her eyes.

"Josie?" he said, unable now to maintain the coolness. "What is it? You don't truly wish to dance, surely?"

She drew in a heavy breath and pressed the backs of her hands to the edges of her eyes. "I hate tears," she said angrily and turned away from him and moved out to the balcony.

He followed her. "Josie?" he said again. She'd stopped in a circle of light from one of the pair of torches lighting the balcony. Her hands were resting on the stone balustrade, and she seemed to be staring at the tops of the trees, whose lower portions glowed in the light of the torches on the ground.

"It's not the dancing with you," she said, her voice still husky. "It's the dancing with all the gentlemen. I am a terrible person."

"You are a terrible person because you've been dancing?" He laughed, relieved. "Josie, it's London. Everyone—married or engaged or single, ancient or young—dances and flirts. It's the done thing. You must know that."

She finally turned around, and he was cravenly relieved to see that the tears were gone. "I do know that," she said. "But I didn't expect to like it so much."

"There's nothing wrong with having a good time. It's why you came."

"No, I came to be a support to Edwina. I'm engaged to Nicholas—I don't need to be dancing with other men. I don't need to be—I don't need to be—admiring them!"

He wished his first gut response weren't jealousy. But he knew it was only a reflex, and he forced himself to assume the measured air of the friend she so clearly needed. Though what she actually seemed to want was a confessor, he thought with a repressed groan. Of course it would have to be him.

"So you find yourself admiring the London gentlemen."

"Yes," she said miserably, her gaze dropping to the stone floor. "I am ashamed. An engaged woman. I don't deserve Nicholas."

In the garden below them, an unseen woman's voice rang out in a flirtatious trill, followed by the sound of masculine laughter.

Colin suddenly wished he hadn't made it possible for Josie to come to London, with its shallowness and fast living, as if the city and its people would crush all that was fine in her. But it was wrong of him; Josie didn't need sheltering from life, and London had charms she deserved to experience. He was only envious that he couldn't share all her pleasure in discovering them.

"That's not true," he said. No woman could have deserved Nick more. "Come, Josie. There's nothing wrong with appreciating the beauty of creation, a great deal of which is found in other people."

Her eyes darkened with anguish, and he yearned to sweep her into his arms and comfort her.

"Colin, it's not just tonight, though now, tonight, it's suddenly been made more apparent to me. It's as though some part of me that was always asleep, some animal part, has been awakened, and it wants…everything, everyone. It wants pleasures. It's impatient, and it feels terribly forceful."

"It's an appetite," he said with an inward slide

into despair. God, that they should be discussing this. "Desire…it's an appetite like the craving for food or sleep. Though it is doubtless not an appetite of which young ladies are made aware, or expected to have, except in a very limited way. I suppose the way young ladies are raised, some of them might even avoid having this appetite awakened forever."

She seemed to mull his words. "So you're saying that desire"—she said the word in a hushed, husky voice that he knew came from embarrassment but which *did* things to him—"is awake in me now like some kind of monster, and I must manage it?"

"It's not a monster," he made himself say. For all that he wanted her and suffered because of it, he did not condemn what was natural. "It's part of the whole person. Perhaps it's that you are now just more aware of it since you have passed fully through childhood."

"Childhood! I'm twenty-two."

He thought of Jasmine House and how old Cardworthy had, in his benevolently dictatorial way, isolated his family and pushed others away. Of how Mrs. Cardworthy had kept to her divan for the last four years, and the way the children had been so little guided. The lack of a governess and Mrs. Cardworthy's anxious self-absorption and the likelihood that whole realms of human experience had never been addressed.

"I mean the way a child looks on things as being the way they always have been. The body's familiar needs of hunger and thirst and sleep are there from birth. Sexual desire is a new appetite when it develops."

She was blushing furiously—probably helped along by the ratafia—but she wasn't looking away. Josie's courage was one of the things he admired most about her. But this conversation was killing him.

⤸

Josie's head was whirling a bit, though not in a bad way. It felt daring and extremely interesting to talk about the things they were discussing. And talking about them with Colin was safe.

She realized now when it was that desire had been awakened in her: when she'd gotten on the back of that horse trader's horse and let him touch her. Before then, while she'd enjoyed the admiration she'd received from the few gentlemen she'd encountered in Upperton, it had all been chaste on her part. Admiration was rather distancing if it wasn't returned, and she'd never admired any man in Upperton except Colin, but that was different. She admired him as a person and a friend, not a man.

"It's different for men, isn't it?" she said. "The awareness of desire."

"Right," he said in a voice that sounded oddly hoarse.

"You know, Ivorwood," she said slowly as a thought unfolded, "I think it might be a problem that Nick is the only man I've ever kissed."

Colin looked as though he were about to choke. "It's not a problem," he said stiffly. "It's admirable to be chaste."

She frowned. She'd been chaste all her life, but lately she'd felt such a sense of wanting to throw that off. To rebel against all the rules and customs that bound her life and everyone else's. Her father had been excessive in guarding his daughters, but that had only been an exaggeration of the custom that kept young women apart from the company of gentlemen almost until they were ready to marry them.

She knew it was a stupid wish, this rebellious urge to experiment, but it was pressing on her. She felt unsettled, and she burned to do something about it.

"Just now it doesn't feel admirable to be chaste," she said, swaying closer to him. She was getting an idea that was giving her that old familiar thrill. "It feels unwise."

"Now that is certainly the only time I've ever heard chastity called unwise."

"Hear me out." Perhaps it was the ratafia, or the dancing, or the truth-telling with Colin, but she felt extra warm, and sort of fuller, larger, smarter. She leaned closer to him and caught the familiar scent of his soap, but she was close enough now to also detect the scent of his warm skin, and it was fascinating.

She looked into his gray-green eyes, which were watching her almost warily under those serious black eyebrows. His large beak of a nose made his face seem arrogant, which made her smile. Colin was too nice to be arrogant.

"I'm beginning to think it might be better," she continued, "for young ladies to have some experience of gentlemen before they marry."

He lifted an eyebrow. "That's one of the reasons people go to balls and parties."

"But there's no chance, really, for young ladies to get to know desire, so that it isn't so mysterious. Hidden things feel shameful. And scary. But also, too enticing."

He frowned. "We should be going into dinner now, Josie. I think you could benefit from something to eat."

"I'm not hungry, thank you." She moved a little closer, and his eyebrows lowered sternly. "I have an idea. Something I want you to help me with."

"Whatever it is, I have the feeling it's not a good idea. Listen, Josie, I think you've had too much ratafia. It's gone to your head, and you need to eat something."

"Nonsense. Actually, I haven't felt this good for ages. And it's not as though I'm swaying and swaggering about. I'm not drunk, Ivor W."

He squinted at her. "*Ivor W?* What is that?"

She grinned. "A nickname. We're close enough, surely, for nicknames."

He gave her his haughtiest look. "I'm an earl, Josephine."

"I know!" She felt quite giddy now. "But you're also my friend. Of course there's Nicholas, but he's been gone so long, and I've had all these wonderful months with you. And, well, we do make excellent friends, don't we?"

"Yes," he said with a wariness that only made her smile to herself. Colin was so reserved.

"So I want you to do something for me. Or maybe, I should say, let me do something."

His eyes opened wider, as if he had an idea that what she was going to propose was improper. He was always so trustworthy and considerate—she knew he'd be shocked by what she wanted to do.

But suddenly it felt like the best idea possible for gaining a broader experience of men, the experience which thoughts of marrying had suddenly made her want. Surely she might have a little bit of experience with her friend Colin, and then that would banish those unsettled, doubting feelings she'd been having and resolve all the yearning with no harm done, really, to anyone.

She moved forward, to where he stood in the shadowy corner of the balcony where the balustrade met the wall of the manor.

"Josie," he began in a warning tone, but she lifted up on her tiptoes at the same time as she curled a hand around his neck and tugged him lower, and she quickly pressed her lips to his.

❧

Colin froze. He was instantly in heaven and hell at once. Heaven, dear God, to have Josie's lips pressed to his. *She was kissing him.*

And hell. *Nick.* She belonged to Nick.

No matter how much he wanted this, it was wrong.

He tried gently to lean away from her, but she had hold of his neck, and she kept him there.

As if he truly wanted to move.

Her lips were so soft against his. And not shy. Pliable, friendly, they urged him to join in, to do what he so badly wanted to do. The tip of her tongue brushed unskillfully along his mouth, leaving a trail of brandy and innocent sin. Even as he steeled himself not to respond, a bolt of lust shot straight to his already painfully aroused groin.

His first kiss from a woman in over a year, and it was from Josie. He stifled a groan.

He should already have stepped away from her, but he could not. She swayed and the tips of her breasts brushed the front of his coat, and he might as well not have been wearing a shirt and waistcoat and tailcoat, because they burned right through all the layers of fabric. He forgot everything else but her, and he kissed her back.

Heat raced through him as his tongue touched the gently questing tip of hers and he felt her respond to him. *To him.* Josie was responding, wanting him. She whimpered, and the sound drove him further. He brought his shaking hand to the graceful curve of her shoulder and slid it slowly across the cool satin skin exposed by her low bodice, every inch of her a revelation.

She still clutched his neck, and now her other hand came around his waist to hold on to him as though he were there to rescue her from something. Their kiss grew wilder, nothing but naked hunger, and Colin knew he was barely holding on to his control, because he wanted everything from her.

She leaned into him fully, so that her breasts crushed themselves against his chest and his erection jutted into the soft fabric of her gown. His eyes rolled back with lust.

"Colin," she whispered against his lips, her voice holding a note of pleading mingled with something else, as though she'd been surprised by him, as though she hadn't been the one to start the kiss. She was sweet and soft, and she smelled amazing. Every breath he took was filled with the intoxicating scent of her.

But now a new note reached him—the pungent

odor of pipe smoke. Someone in the garden below was smoking a pipe, and whether that person might even be able to see Colin and Josie in their dark corner mattered not: his stomach dropped as he remembered who he was and who she was. What they were doing was wrong.

What he so violently wanted could not be.

With every part of his being screaming in revolt, he broke their kiss and gently tugged her hands away. He stepped back, forcing his breathing to calm.

Her eyes flew open, dark blue pools that held desire and confusion. And dawning guilt.

Of course. They were both guilty. But while Josie the innocent had taken too much ratafia and run away with a silly idea, he was entirely sober, and as the man who'd been lusting after her for months, the only one truly at fault here.

He'd forgotten the lesson of that night he'd shouted her name to the rooftops.

She gasped, her hand flying to her mouth. "I'm— I'm so sorry, Colin. I don't know what came over me." She dropped her hand. "Can you ever forgive me?" she said in a voice of awful anguish.

But she wasn't the one who needed forgiveness. He'd been tempted, and he'd faltered.

"Nothing to forgive, dear girl," he said. "You've had too much to drink. And I—"

"It wasn't the ratafia," she broke in. "It—was an impulse. A wild idea that should never have gotten ahold of me. I didn't mean anything by it," she said, devastating him without the least idea she was doing so. Her eyes drifted to the floor. "I'm so ashamed."

Her remorse was killing him. "Don't feel ashamed. You got caught up in a whim, and I should have been able to resist the temptation of kissing a woman, no matter how beautiful she is." Kissing *you*, he wanted to admit, but that would make this more personal, which would only be worse.

"You think I'm beautiful?" she said quietly, and he thought her lower lip quivered. But then she drew her brows together with sober discipline. "No," she said. "This was my fault."

This was in fact the second time he'd been kissed as a sort of ambush by a beautiful girl—the first time had been with his friend Hal's too-young sister, Eloise, who'd had a *tendre* for him. With sweet young Eloise it hadn't taken much resolve to resist. With Josie it couldn't have been more different.

"Don't," he said. "We'll simply put this moment behind us. Forget about it." Though a rotten part of him wanted to take what had happened and build on it. Cozen her, entice her into doing more—into seeing him as more than a friend.

*The heat in that kiss hadn't been all him.*

What if she *was* attracted to him?

*She was not married yet.* The final choice was not yet made. Wouldn't he and she be throwing away something potentially amazing if they didn't pursue what had happened tonight? What if he kissed her again?

*No! Absolutely not.* That was exactly the wrong kind of thinking. Scoundrel thinking.

Josie, who had always seemed to him so in command of herself, had shown him her dawning curiosity and her vulnerability, and he must help her guard it, not exploit it further. He owed that to her and to Nick.

"I wish Nicholas were here," she said in a small voice. "Then none of this would have happened. I wouldn't be tempted to be so impulsive."

"Yes."

"I, um, I don't think we should tell him about this. It was sort of an accident."

Colin didn't say anything at first. He so didn't want to talk about Nicholas right now. But after all that brave talk about mastering desires, he could hardly shy away from what he owed his friends, both of them.

"Right."

"I miss him," she said.

"I know," he said quietly, her words tearing at him. "Of course you do."

"He'll be home soon, but..." Her sapphire eyes were dark with trouble. "What if he doesn't care for me anymore? It's been so long."

Ah. He began to see even more what was behind the kiss, no matter that he wanted to believe he alone had inspired it. Of course she would have doubts—it had been a year since she'd seen Nick.

"Josie, he engaged himself to you. I'm certain it's thoughts of you that cheer him each day."

"But what if something's changed?" she whispered, as though she could barely stand to entertain the thought. "A year is a long time. What if he's thought better of his choice? Or if I..." Her voice trailed off.

*Don't do this to me, Josie*, he thought. *Don't make it sound possible that there could be any other future for you than with Nick.*

Something in him rebelled at the emotions she had stirred in him, at this power she had over him. He'd given in to temptation tonight, surrendered reason to the surge of passion, and now he allowed a silent fury at himself to take over and put the tumult to rights. This was what came of allowing emotions to rule. Emotional excess was how he'd ended up on the roof of Greenbrier, shouting out her name.

He despised emotional volatility.

He moved farther away from her. "I'm sure nothing's changed," he said, knowing they would both be best served by the coolness he allowed into his voice. It should have been there all along. "You'll see when he comes back."

He turned away and went through the balcony doors.

⚜

Dinner cleared Josie's head of some of the ratafia, and a long conversation with a Mrs. Turner on the subject of holidays by the shore allowed her to avoid thinking about her behavior with Colin. He kept to the other side of the room, and she made herself not look at him. She didn't feel his eyes on her once, either.

After dinner, the guests wandered back to the ballroom, taking the noise and distraction with them, and Josie followed them, wanting desperately not to be alone with her thoughts, because she'd done it again—given in to the urge to be reckless—and this time was worse than anything she'd ever done before.

Oh, God, why, why, *why* had she kissed him?

The kiss she'd pressed on him had been startling, jerking at the foundation of so much she'd thought she'd known. The jolt of pleasure and happiness that had rushed through her when their lips touched had been as unexpected as a firework going off in a dark, blank sky. And for a few moments, her world had turned on its axis toward something entirely new, a rich, bursting feeling for Colin that she hadn't expected. *Passion* for Colin.

He'd responded, hadn't he? Hadn't that been desire in his kiss, and in the touch of his hand on her décolletage? Why had he been so cool afterward?

Was it because she was engaged to Nicholas? Or because he didn't want her?

And what was the matter with her that she was even thinking these things?

Colin was her friend, and what was just as bad, he was Nicholas's friend. And she'd had the urge to kiss him and told herself it would just be a lark, when it was so wrong.

She entered the ballroom, where Colin was just leading Edwina out for a dance. It felt queer watching them. She didn't like it, and she didn't like herself for disliking it.

He'd kissed her back, and there'd been desire in his kiss, but she forced herself to face what had to be true: she was a woman, and men desired women. He'd told her himself: *I should have been able to resist the temptation of kissing a woman, no matter how beautiful she is.*

He found her beautiful, and that made him want to return her kiss, but he probably wanted to kiss every other pretty woman in the room as well. Men were attracted to women, and she was a woman. She'd opened the Pandora's box of desire when she'd kissed him.

She saw now that the idea of being such good friends with a man had been fatally flawed. The pull that existed between the sexes must touch the friendship at some point. But clearly, from the way he'd retreated, only his desire had been touched, the desire he'd feel for any attractive woman.

While she…Josie swallowed a lump of emotion that was pressing against her throat. She could not separate the desire she'd felt in his arms from the deep, deep fondness she had for him. It was beyond fondness, she forced herself to admit. She couldn't bear how easily he'd been able to walk away from her, because she needed him.

She watched him twirl by with her sister, both of them smiling as though they hadn't a care in the world.

*I'm a terribly shabby person*, she thought as she fought to conquer the emotion rioting in her chest, *but let me not have ruined everything*.

&

Colin bowed to Edwina at the end of their dance and forced himself not to cast his eyes about the room for Josie.

*That's it!* He was going to have to start pursuing other women.

Pursuing any women at all, he reminded himself harshly, because he certainly wasn't pursuing Josie.

He was master of himself. And he wasn't going to think about her anymore. At all.

Obviously, lust was pressing on him. He was going to have to make an effort with women (though not Edwina, who was, anyway, being courted by

Mappleton). Very likely what all this was telling him was that he needed a wife.

*Fine!* He hadn't in the least been wanting to marry—with the example of his parents' marriage it was hardly appealing—but apparently he must do so or risk becoming a devil.

He forced himself to dance every dance for the rest of the night, even staying late to partner the bold, cynical widows who remained when the sweet young things had all gone home to bed. He stayed past the point when he himself wanted his bed.

It was necessary, he told himself as he led the lovely Lady Denborough out in what was likely to be the last waltz of the night—even the musicians were yawning. It was necessary because he knew that every part of him was yearning for Josie. Because now that he'd tasted her lips, she'd unleashed something in him.

Touched something in him.

Pulled him deeper into a realm he must have nothing to do with.

There must be nothing further between them, even though very likely he wouldn't even be able to smile at her now without wanting to follow it up with an embrace. He'd have to stay away from her.

His pretty dancing partner made some comment about the music, and he forced himself to reply. He was in command of himself, and he simply would not be in thrall to Josie Cardworthy. Clearly, extreme measures were called for.

When he arrived home as the sun was rising and far after his customary retiring time, he didn't allow himself to seek his bed right away, but instead took up the pile of invitations on the silver salver in the foyer that he normally would have ignored, and he made himself accept every one.

# *Seven*

EDWINA LOVED LONDON. INITIALLY, SHE HADN'T thought such a thing could be possible, but she felt suddenly so new and different, and hopeful, as she hadn't in perhaps forever. Hopeful in general, but more specifically as regarded gentlemen and the possibility of marriage with a really fine man.

Quite simply, for the first time in her life, she'd been having success, and she knew there were two main reasons for this: Maria Westin's guidance, and her friend Lady Hermione Stellan's decision that Edwina was A Find.

Lady Stellan loved nothing so much as what she called A Find, whether the new thing in question was a beautiful fabric that everyone else had overlooked or a musician who'd gone previously unappreciated. And now she insisted no woman currently in London was lovelier than Edwina, and behaved as though Edwina's age were a distinctive seasoning that added a certain indefinable quality to her beauty.

At gatherings and events, Lady Stellan introduced her to everyone and in general treated her like a prize horse. Edwina was under no illusion that her race would last forever, but it now seemed possible, as it hadn't since she'd met Mr. Perriwell, that she might secure the affections of the right sort of man. A man like Lord Mappleton, she thought with a smile as she floated out the front door of Lady Stellan's on his arm after a particularly lovely luncheon.

A most presentable gentleman in possession of a large estate in the Cotswolds, he'd treated her as though she was special from their first meeting. During luncheon today he'd seemed fascinated by the (much-edited) things she told him about her life in Upperton. She'd made certain to listen to him carefully, as Maria had advised, and to repeat back to him—rephrased—some of what he said to her. He seemed to delight in this.

He *was* a good twenty-five years older than she was, but she mustn't ask the moon.

As he escorted her now to Maria's barouche, which awaited her, he assured her he was looking forward to seeing her at a party the following day. She smiled at him in that slightly excessive way Maria had insisted looked genuine, and thought that this time she actually meant it.

She stepped into Maria's waiting barouche as though she were alighting a cloud. The summer day was very pretty, and as the open carriage rolled away from the town house under the gentle late afternoon sun, a breeze whispered against her face while a lark swooped ahead in gracious arcs. All was bliss.

Even the smells of London were growing on her, or at least, the smell of dirty cobblestones was becoming familiar. She smiled as she thought of how the foreign scents and sounds of the city had assaulted her at first. She felt like a part of London now.

They had just reached Regent Street, with its fine shops and crowds of strolling, fashionable people, when the coachman, astonishingly, began to whistle.

Since it was the middle of the afternoon and the top of the barouche was down, anyone could see her riding with this driver who was making a spectacle of himself, and she called up to him to cease at once. He seemed not to hear her and carried on whistling. A lady passing in a high perch phaeton frowned at them.

Edwina's furled parasol lay on the seat beside her, and she took it and rapped the driver on the shoulder.

He glanced back at her, and she realized he was unfamiliar. She hadn't noticed earlier, but then, why would she?

"You're not one of Mrs. Westin's coachmen," she said. "Who are you?"

"Jack Whitby, miss. I'm doing some work on Mrs. Westin's furniture. But the coachmen have all taken sick, so I was asked to help."

"You're a *carpenter*? Couldn't someone else have filled in for the coachman?"

"Cabinetmaker," he corrected her, incredibly, "and no. It seems a number of the servants ate some bad custard, and they're—"

"Never mind," she said sharply, "I get the idea."

He turned back around and started whistling again. She rapped him on the shoulder again, and he glanced back.

"You don't need to keep hitting me, miss. You can use my name."

Of all the cheek! As if she would be dictated to by someone like him.

"What do you mean by whistling?" she demanded.

"I don't suppose I *mean* anything by it," he said. "I am simply enjoying this fine day."

"Well, you may enjoy it silently. The whistling is inappropriate."

His only reply was an eyebrow that lifted and quivered, as though in mirth. His eyes were a startling light, icy blue, his hair a deep, shiny chestnut. His boxy cheekbones held her attention longer than they should have, and she couldn't help noticing that his coat hung across his shoulders in a way that suggested a very hard frame was underneath.

It was because she was old that she was noticing what she should not, she told herself disgustedly, as though her body sensed that her fading beauty would soon make it impossible to find a husband and so was calling her attention to any virile man she encountered. She looked away.

Shortly they drew near a shop selling ladies' accoutrements, and remembering that she'd wanted to purchase a little rouge for her cheeks—she meant to use only the smallest amount, but she needed something, as there were so many dewy young debutantes about—she told the Whitby fellow to stop. He pulled to a stop near the shop and handed her down.

&

Jack watched Edwina Cardworthy make her way to the ladies' shop with a smile curling the edge of his mouth. She'd looked like an angel coming down from heaven as she'd stepped out of Lady Stellan's town house, but by the time she was beating him on the shoulder with her umbrella, the customary sharp, calculating look had come back over her beautiful face. He'd seen her about the Westin household several times in the last few days, unobserved by her, of course, since he would be invisible to a lady. But those odd glimpses had been enough to show him a complicated woman.

She had the kind of beauty that would have made his father itch to capture her as a Helen of Troy or Diana, but it would have taken all his artist's skill to penetrate behind her layers to the real woman underneath. Though if any of the Whitbys were going to inspire Edwina Cardworthy to surrender her secrets, he didn't want it to be his father.

As she approached the shop, she drew near an elderly woman who was standing there while the other pedestrians moved around her. The woman was raw-boned and sturdy, and she wore the kind of plain frock that might have suited a governess.

Miss Cardworthy, however, stopped to speak with her. Jack's eyebrows rose as, a few moments later, she escorted the older woman down the street.

By the time five minutes had elapsed, he was growing concerned that Edwina Cardworthy still hadn't returned, and he was just about to go look for her when she reappeared and went into the shop. Some minutes later she emerged with a wrapped package, and he got down and handed her up into the barouche. Her hand, slim and protected within the fine fabric of her glove, tugged at his attention.

"Any trouble with the old woman?" he asked as he flicked the reins lightly and the horses took off.

"She was only lost."

Out of the corner of his eye, he could see her stiffening—well, stiffening even more—as if scolding herself for having spoken with him beyond what was necessary.

"Look here," she said, "have you no deference?"

He laughed, not turning around.

"Really!" she said. "Anyone would think you fancied yourself a gentleman."

"That I do not," he said seriously, "though I've known my share of them. My father is a portrait painter, and many's the aristocrat who's come to his studio. I can't say I've admired any of them for their arrogance, or their talent at inheriting money."

He smiled as an irritated silence reigned behind him for a minute while she absorbed his words.

"Is your father William Whitby, then?"

"Yes."

"I've seen his work. It's quite good."

"It is."

"And you didn't wish to follow in his footsteps?"

"Cabinetmaking's an art as well."

"I suppose," she said. But her thoughts had clearly moved on to other things, because she said no more.

She was twice as beautiful as any woman in Town that Season, and well aware of it, but there was far more to her than the selfishness of a woman who was used to being admired. He thought of the way she'd helped the old lady, and of a conversation he'd overheard while working on a wardrobe in one of the unused guest rooms at Mrs. Westin's.

Edwina had been in the corridor with one of the maids, and as he listened it became clear she'd discovered that young Leah didn't understand the value of money and had no sense of how to make a pound. Edwina was trying to explain it in a way the girl could grasp, but poor Leah wasn't bright. Edwina persisted, though, explaining as thoroughly as a governess intent on the best effort of her pupil, and some glimmer of understanding had dawned in the girl as he listened. He'd been charmed.

He knew very well that men such as he weren't meant to converse with women such as Edwina Cardworthy. But he'd never seen why his gifts of intelligence, skill, and art shouldn't be of as much significance as the value society put on things that hadn't even been earned. He believed in who he was, and he prized directness.

He glanced over his shoulder. "You have a kind heart."

Edwina was startled by the carpenter's compliment. Ridiculously, it made her feel warm all over, as though his words were a balm for something that had been ailing her. But this was wrong. She couldn't be having a *conversation* with this man.

"What do you mean by speaking to me so personally? You have no sense of your place," she said, and that stopped him, as she'd meant it to, from saying anything else.

When they arrived in front of Maria's town house, he handed her down. She made certain not to look at him, but she couldn't ignore the sensation of his hand on hers. Even through the fabric of her glove she could feel the strength of his fingers and how much larger his hand was than hers. Before today, she'd never held the hand of a man who labored with his hands.

And she had no need to do so now. She pulled her hand away.

Josie had come out to meet her, and Edwina pushed away thoughts of the carpenter and leaned close to her sister to enthuse about what a successful gathering it had been and how much she'd enjoyed Mappleton's company.

Josie had seemed subdued over the last week, and Edwina wondered if it was because they hadn't seen anything of Ivorwood since the ball held by Lord and Lady Worthing. Or perhaps she was only anxious for the return of Nicholas. Edwina made a note to invite Josie for a cheering stroll in the park.

After a minute, Josie's eyes flicked over Edwina's shoulder, and Edwina turned to see that the carpenter-driver was lingering behind her for some reason.

"Excuse me, Miss Cardworthy," he said, not sounding particularly unhappy to bother her, "you left your parasol behind."

Her delicate cream parasol looked odd in his hands, which were tanned and nicked with little cuts. She took it quickly, glancing to see if he'd smudged it; she didn't have so very many parasols. But he'd done nothing to it, and she made herself acknowledge that though his hands obviously did much work, they were also quite clean.

She felt his eyes on her and looked up to see them

laughing, as though he knew she'd expected his touch to dirty her things. She turned away from him without a word.

But she saw Josie's eyes follow him as he led the barouche away.

"An interesting man," Josie said, "though he makes a different sort of driver."

"Apparently he's filling in for the coachmen, who've all taken ill. But he'd better stay a carpenter, out of sight of polite people."

"Oh, Edwina," Josie said.

"Don't 'Oh, Edwina' me. There are times when a lady is perfectly in her rights to judge and dislike a person, and this is one of those times. Anyway, who cares about him when we can talk about Mappleton?"

"Oh. Yes, let's do," Josie said with a gameness Edwina knew very well was put on. Edwina was under no illusion that Josie was enchanted by Mappleton, but she didn't need her to be.

❧

Josie had begun to wish she and Edwina might return to Upperton, though she wouldn't have dreamed of saying so. She knew that Edwina was having the time of her life, and she couldn't have been happier for her sister, who was currently twirling about yet another ballroom on the arms of a handsome gentleman.

But coming to the ball meant Josie would be invited to dance as well, and after what had happened with Colin four days ago, she'd decided she mustn't dance a single other dance while in London. Nor had she allowed herself to probe what had happened with him or consider what *he* might think about it—thinking too much was clearly her downfall—and she'd been nothing but glad that she hadn't seen him since then.

Avoiding dancing at a ball was proving difficult, however, since the gentlemen continued to ask, and she'd just declined another invitation when Maria appeared at her side.

"Josephine my dear, you really must give up this bizarre refusal to dance. It does you great credit that you are so fond of your fiancé no other man will do, but it is only making the gentlemen more desperate to dance with you."

"They only look on me as a challenge, and they'll soon tire of the game."

"Nonsense. You're a lovely unmarried young woman at a ball. It's in the natural order that you should be dancing with a gentleman."

"Truly, I'm content to watch the dancers."

A shrewd light came into Maria's eyes. "Have you seen Ivorwood, then, dancing with Lady Denborough? I just heard from a friend that my usually reserved nephew has been seen about town with a succession of fashionable widows, Lady Denborough among them. The word is that he's looking for a wife."

Josie's stomach lurched at these astonishing words.

"Oh, look," Maria said, "the dance is over. Let's go over and greet him."

"Let's wait," Josie said. If she saw him, she'd likely say more than she should, because the thought that he was suddenly interested in beautiful widows was making her alternately sick with inappropriate jealousy and furious because he'd rejected her plan for him to court Edwina. Which was a little insane.

But Maria ignored her and linked their arms and began leading her toward where Colin was standing with a beautiful blond woman in a dazzling red gown. And then they were all standing together and Maria was presenting Josie to his beautiful blond companion.

Colin looked every inch the earl in his snug black breeches and midnight-blue satin tailcoat, with a gold brocade waistcoat underneath.

"Ah, Josie," he said mildly, and she was annoyed to find that his calm demeanor made her feel as though he'd forgotten about her, as though she were some barely remembered little neighbor-girl. She was a little disgusted with herself.

She ground her teeth and reminded herself that she was the one who'd opened Pandora's box when she kissed him. Perhaps he'd already forgotten all about it. Apparently he'd been busy with numbers of very pretty ladies. Perhaps he'd kissed all of them too.

She was horribly jealous, and she knew this was wrong, but she couldn't seem to be reasonable.

"Colin," she said, "it seems you are all the rage."

Lady Denborough smirked, while Colin frowned.

"Lady Denborough," Maria said cheerfully. "I had thought you were in Cornwall."

The widow gave one of those fashionable smiles that did duty for a laugh. "I am unfortunately required to go to my estate there now and again. When his lordship was alive, of course I couldn't acknowledge its flaws, out of respect for his childhood home. Now that he is, sadly, gone, I mean to renovate the entire place. But I can only spend so much time there before I risk dying of boredom."

This woman was Colin's idea of a future wife? Josie arched an eyebrow at him.

His frown deepened, but he turned toward his companion and said encouragingly, "No doubt you shall have it in fine shape in no time, Lady Denborough, and then you'll be besieged by guests."

She gave a tinkling laugh and put her hand on Colin's forearm. "And *you* shall come to my very first party. I can hardly wait."

Colin smiled at the lovely widow—Colin, who'd always behaved as though he preferred books to people. Josie felt a little furious.

A tall gentleman appeared then and reminded Lady Denborough that he'd reserved the next dance. With a longing look in Ivorwood's direction, she allowed herself to be led away.

Maria watched her go. "Shall we be hearing wedding bells soon, nephew?"

A dark look passed over his face. "Really, Maria," he said. "Can a gentleman not escort a lady to an event or two without causing idle speculation?"

Maria laughed. "Of course he can. But when that gentleman is a sought-after bachelor earl who's never pursued *any* available lady, you may be certain it will be perceived as an indication of interest. Wouldn't you agree, Josie?"

She reminded herself that she'd been his friend, that he was a good man, and that she had absolutely no business being jealous if he chose to pursue women, because *of course* he couldn't pursue her. In no way should she wish him to.

"I suppose Ivorwood does not care to be the subject of gossip," she said.

"Exactly so, Josie," he said, and she felt him looking at her as though he sought understanding in her eyes, but she refused to meet his gaze. It was his business if he wished to spend time with lovely, eligible women, and it was *better* for her if he did, no matter how much she hated watching it. But on Edwina's behalf, she felt angry with him because he'd insisted he didn't want to court her, insisted that he was uninterested in marriage. She knew she was being childish—he'd likely only been trying to be politic—but his lack of candor still stung.

"Don't be coy, Ivorwood, it doesn't suit you," Maria said. "I'm your only female relative of consequence, and I think I can be said to have an interest in the matter if you are thinking of marrying. I might even wish to propose some candidates. Like a debutante. Why start with the widows?"

Colin seemed to be gnashing his teeth. *Good.* He deserved torment.

"I do not wish for interference in my private affairs," he said.

"Private? Ha," Maria said. "What could be of more public interest than an eligible earl's marriage prospects? Frankly, I'm surprised you haven't been overrun already by mamas trying to get your attention now that you finally seem to have taken note of the fairer sex."

A flush spread up Colin's cheeks, and Josie guessed

that the matchmaking mamas were already importuning him. Once, she might have felt bad for a poor, quiet man who just wanted to be left alone, but not now.

"It's funny," she said, turning to Maria, "because I've heard him more than once insist he didn't wish to marry."

"Perhaps he's changed his mind," Maria said.

❧

Colin had known that sooner or later Josie would discover that he was squiring ladies about. But after their kiss and the regret they'd admitted, how could she blame him?

She was angry with him. She wouldn't understand that their kiss had shown him he couldn't trust himself where she was concerned, that he had to make a future for himself, even if the thought of sharing it with any of the lovely widows he'd met inspired nothing beyond a sense of reasonable acceptance.

"Perhaps I've decided to marry sooner than I had previously thought," he said. He flicked a glance at Josie, who was now examining a fingernail as though she couldn't have cared at all what words came out of his mouth. He clenched his teeth.

She looked so pretty and soft tonight in her pink silk ball gown, with its little embroidered roses that spoke of sweetness and innocence, and a darker rose bandeau tied around her tumble of sable curls. She looked like home, but she wasn't. She was going to be Nick's wife, and he, Colin, needed to make a home with someone else.

"I knew you'd come to your senses, Ivorwood," Maria said. "For a handsome earl to scorn marriage is simply wasteful." Her eyes shifted for the barest moment toward Josie, and he wondered if Maria had an inkling he was attracted to her. But she merely said, "You must allow me to hold a party for you. I'll invite all the most eligible young ladies."

"That won't be necessary," he said tightly. He'd focused his attentions on the widows because, unlike the debutantes, they had an experience of men and thus were not dreaming of a knight in shining armor to adore them. He was very leery of his capacity to adore any woman who wasn't Josie, and he didn't want to set up expectations.

Josie looked up then, and he was startled by the hard glint in her eyes. "Oh, but really, you ought to be thorough when looking for a wife. You won't want to settle for just anyone."

She meant Edwina. She thought he'd told her he didn't want to marry because he was trying to fob her off about her sister. She thought he'd lied to her.

"I'm not in a rush to marry," he said. "It was only after coming to London that I began to think it a good idea. Before then, I really hadn't thought to marry soon."

Did she understand?

She gave him a smile that was formal and lacking all the liveliness and impishness that was Josie, and it made him furious that things had come to this.

"So London has changed your mind, then. And why not, when it is so full of beautiful, accomplished women? I wish you the best of luck finding the perfect wife."

# Eight

As the round of dinner parties and soirees continued, Josie tried to stay in the background while also helping Edwina shine as best she could. If she had to look away whenever Colin was present, dancing and talking with the beautiful women who now seemed always to surround him, that was just as well.

She still didn't understand why he'd altered course so abruptly since coming to London, but the truth was it didn't matter that he wasn't including Edwina among the women he was courting, because her sister had so many suitors of her own.

Increasingly, though, Josie was becoming concerned that, in her eagerness to find a wealthy, doting husband, Edwina was ready to make a bad match. One evening as they were preparing for another of Lady Stellan's parties, she decided to broach the subject.

"Do you really like Lady Stellan?" she asked as she watched Edwina pluck at a stray eyebrow hair.

Edwina, who'd just sent the maid away, looked ravishing in a ruffled ashes-of-roses gown that deepened the color of her lips and gave her a sensual look that played marvelously against the raven black of her hair. She tried out a pouting expression in the looking glass before pinching each cheek soundly.

"Lady Stellan plans the best parties."

"But she's always saying cruel things about people."

Edwina shrugged and pulled experimentally at one of the curls that framed her face. "It's what people do here. You have to go along with it or you can't be successful."

"Successful at what?"

"At being sought after. What else is there for a woman?"

Edwina's words pushed against Josie's idea of marriage as the way for love to bloom. Despite the example of their parents' marriage, she'd always hoped there could so much more to it than two people who got along tolerably well. But what if her sister was right after all?

"Your perspective has shifted quite a bit since we left Jasmine House," Josie said, "and of course I'm so happy you feel ready to consider new possibilities for your future. But the idea that your only option is being sought after...it sounds a little desperate."

Edwina gave her a hard glance in the looking glass. "I'm being practical. I have a plan for my future—I have to, if I want to catch a suitable husband. You know that. And why do you look so leery? I thought I could speak plainly with you of all people."

"Of course you can," Josie said carefully, "but don't you think it's important to speak plainly with everyone?"

Edwina turned to face Josie and crossed her arms. "No. Anyway, you've been encouraging me all along to hide my sharp ways."

Josie pressed her lips unhappily. "Surely it's one thing to choose your words carefully, but another to make yourself into an entirely different person to catch a husband?"

"I don't care about such distinctions when there's so much at stake."

"But do you want to end up in the kind of marriage our parents had?"

"Our parents had a poor marriage because Papa was a bully. I'm going to marry an easy man, someone who has *my* best interests at heart."

"Like Mappleton. Do you really enjoy his company so much that you wish to see him morning, noon, and night?"

Josie ignored the little voice prodding her to consider whether she could say the same about Nicholas. Marriage *was* a gamble. But surely if the couple started out at least truly caring for each other, that would be the best chance for happiness. Surely six weeks of bliss in a man's company were enough to know that you'd suit. Weren't they?

Edwina cocked her head. "I like Mappleton well enough. And when did you turn so grim? You used to be so optimistic."

"I just want the best for you."

"That's exactly what I want," Edwina said, making for the door. "The best possible match."

As Josie followed Edwina downstairs, she thought glumly that Edwina hadn't heard her at all. The way Edwina had changed since they'd come to London worried her.

So did the way she couldn't stop thinking about Colin.

❧

*What a successful evening*, Edwina thought as she stepped into Mappleton's luxurious barouche, to which were harnessed four of the most beautiful white horses she'd ever seen. Lady Stellan's dinner party had been sparkling, and Mappleton's attentiveness the whole night had made her feel as bubbly as the champagne that had been served with dessert. Life in London was amazing.

Of course she was sorry that Maria had developed a headache by dessert and had to leave. But Maria and Josie departing early had opened the way for Mappleton to take Edwina home in his carriage, with the top down for propriety. The moon was little but a murky yellowness hiding in the clouds, the only light it offered being a faint glow that picked out the gold paint trimming the carriage.

As they passed under the glow of a street lamp, its light caught a roll of flesh pushed up under Mappleton's chest, the unfortunate sign of a corset. But she reminded herself that he was a good listener, and *biddable*, and that those virtues were more important than physical perfection. Besides, his milieu was conversation and dining, not the kind of activities that produced taut muscles.

Her mind veered toward the memory of Whitby's hand, how it had given her such a sense of strength. There had been other details that were beneath her to notice: the way his sleeve caught on the well-defined muscles of his upper arm as he held her parasol out to her; the taut contours of his neck, visible since he wore no cravat.

*Enough*, she told herself sternly. The carpenter was

just a man, and an unimportant one, who was far too pleased with himself. She had no reason to be thinking of him while she sat across from Mappleton.

Her companion smiled. Surely she was imagining that his eyes lingered on her mouth? Was he thinking of stealing a kiss when no one was near? Should she allow him if he tried?

She had little notion. Mama, who was mortified by anything to do with bodies, had never offered any guidance about being with suitors.

He didn't lean closer. "It must be very different in London, compared to Upperton."

She laughed. "Yes. The society here is more refined. No talk of cows."

Mappleton laughed. "Cows, eh? Let's talk about you. *You*, my dear girl, are utterly delightful. And may I confess, Miss Cardworthy, that your loveliness makes me forget myself a bit? You really are the most exquisite creature."

What wonderful words, just the sort she'd been hoping her whole life to hear. He was looking at her intently, and a frisson of something that, strangely, felt like revulsion ran through her.

*Idiot*, she scolded herself. She was exactly where she'd wanted to be: in the company of a wealthy, important gentleman. Why should she feel anything but delight when he was complimenting her?

"You are too kind, my lord."

The carriage was slowing down—they must be near Maria's—and he hesitantly reached for her hand. She accepted his overture, though she wished that he would be more sure of himself.

He gave her a regretful smile. "I must journey to one of my estates on a matter of business, and shall unfortunately be gone for a few weeks. But when I return, I hope, Miss Cardworthy, that you will be at home when I visit. There is something I should very much like to ask you."

He meant to propose!

"I'm certain I would always be at home for you, my lord."

He smiled wider at her words, and she thought they might have encouraged him to do something besides just grinning at her. But he merely waited until they stopped moving and got out to hand her down. He bent low to kiss the back of her hand and wished her good evening.

Perfect enough. Yes, he would do nicely.

He climbed back into the carriage, and one of Maria's footmen stepped forward and closed the door after him. It wasn't until the carriage took off and Edwina noticed that the footman was still standing there with her, watching it go, that she realized the footman was Jack Whitby.

In the glow of the lanterns hanging outside the house, she caught an insolent glint of amusement in his eyes.

"Just what is it that so amuses you?" she asked sharply.

He raised his eyebrows, as if to suggest that he wasn't amused at anything, and tipped his head in a sketch of servility that sat ill with the proud cast of his features, but he made no reply.

She lifted her chin. "So now you are filling in for the footmen," she said.

"It seems the custard was very powerful."

She let her eyes rest on him, a sort of weighing meant to remind him that she, as a guest of his mistress, was in a position of power over him. A hard look, she made no doubt, of the sort that she could never show to Mappleton lest he crumble. Whitby seemed not at all affected.

But the pause to look at him only gave her a better chance to notice the masculine lines of his face and the intelligence in his icy blue eyes. He was *handsome*, and something about him—a capable energy—held her interest when it should not.

She forced herself to ignore all that. The enormous gulf of social class stood between them, though he had an apparently unconquerable dignity that seemed to suggest such gulfs were irrelevant. He was wrong, and she would put him in his place.

"You are a carpenter," she said in a bored tone, as if this information were so inconsequential she could hardly remember it.

He dipped his head, but predictably, the motion seemed more ironic than deferential. "A cabinet-maker, as I believe I mentioned before."

He knew very well that he had, along with the fact that his father was a celebrated painter. She found herself wondering what it might have been like to grow up in such a family. Jack Whitby was certainly not lacking in pride, and something about the way he valued himself so highly tugged at her.

She gave him her haughtiest look, aware she was reaching for a mask but knowing she could not do otherwise. "So you are accustomed to working on fine

pieces. Good. My jewel box broke during our travels.
It will require very delicate work."

His eyelids lowered, though she was certain it was
in sly amusement and not meekness. His eyelashes
were thick and dark, and they lent a note of beauty
to the hard maleness of his face. If this man had been
a lord like Mappleton, every woman in the *ton* would
have been seeking his attention.

"I have built many such boxes," he said. "I can
easily repair yours."

"I'll send it down to you," she said and turned to go.

"I don't know that Mrs. Westin would like that,"
he said, arresting her motion. "I'm here temporarily
to do repairs on her furniture. And I've been happy to
help during the servant crisis. But I'm not certain she'd
care for me to use my time otherwise."

Edwina stiffened. He knew she was asking a small
thing that Maria wouldn't mind at all, but he wanted
to push back.

"Of course I shall check with her before I send it
to you."

He inclined his head.

Edwina swept up the stairs, telling herself she'd
already forgotten him.

❦

Jack whistled as he walked through the kitchen, where
Cook was tidying away the last of the day's things and
making arrangements for the morning. He grabbed a
biscuit from the tin kept for the servants, and Cook
scowled at him, but she couldn't keep her features
stern as a smile broke through.

"Ta, what a knave you are, Jack Whitby. That's at least the third biscuit you've taken today."

He grinned, turning to walk backward as he made for the door that gave onto the mews. "Only because they're so good, ma'am. Sure, even a saint couldn't resist your biscuits."

Cook was blushing as Jack passed through the doorway and made for the carriage house behind the town house, where he had set up his tools. He had his own shop in Cheapside where he did much of his work, but for jobs like Mrs. Westin's involving large, heavy pieces of furniture that would be difficult to move, he often came to work on-site.

So far he'd lost a little time filling in for the sick servants as Mrs. Westin had asked him to do, but he'd been offered a generous amount to help, and he'd agreed, planning to work later into the night. Things at home were sorted out, and he could afford to spend extra time here. And truthfully, Edwina Cardworthy was making him want to linger.

As he gathered a few things to bring up to the library, where he was repairing the damaged surface of a large mahogany desk, a smile tugged the corners of his mouth. With her stiff spine and intelligent, hard gaze, Edwina reminded him of a beautiful owl, one who would fiercely object to having her feathers ruffled.

He shook his head, chuckling a bit as he folded a work cloth and piled on the tools he'd collected. Edwina Cardworthy had doubtless never been properly ruffled in her life. But his next thought pushed the grin from his face, because he knew he wanted to be the man who ruffled her.

# Nine

As much as Edwina loved London, she was beginning to wonder if it wasn't working some unpleasant spell on everyone.

Her normally buoyant sister, for instance, seemed more subdued every day, which was strange, considering that Josie's long wait for Nick was almost over. But when she'd asked Josie if she wasn't delirious with happiness that her fiancé would likely return in a week or two and carry her off to the altar, she'd said "of course" in a snappish voice.

Perhaps Josie's peevishness had something to do with her friendship with Colin, who, now that he'd astonishingly become the gentleman about whom all the Town ladies were talking, seemed not to have much time for her anymore.

As Edwina wandered distractedly from the sitting room to the garden one afternoon, then plopped down to take tea with Josie and Maria, she knew that she herself didn't feel quite as she should either. In fact, she was becoming the tiniest bit tired of London.

This made no sense, especially now that Mappleton

seemed likely to propose when he returned to Town. But there was getting to be a dull predictability to the social whirl, and she didn't want to think that dullness had anything to do with the way a certain arrogant, blue-eyed man made her feel lit up inside.

She'd wasted all those years at Jasmine House feeling sorry for herself, but that was behind her now. No longer content just to accept what fell to her, she meant to seize her future with both hands, and it looked to be a brilliant future: a family of her own with the best possible husband.

She would be eternally grateful to Ivorwood and Maria for making her London visit possible, because it would not be an exaggeration, she was fairly certain, to say that it was going to change her life.

The ladies were to go to the theater that night, and before Edwina left she sent her broken jewel box down to Whitby with a peremptory note. She told herself that reminding him how far beneath her he was would stop him from being impudent. And stop her from thinking about him.

But after the ladies returned from the play, she'd had an almost overwhelming urge to talk to Josie about Whitby and the way he made her feel. She could only be glad that her sister had gone straight to bed, which had saved her from putting into words what she shouldn't even be thinking.

She tossed in her bed all night. When the first streaks of dawn began creeping across the carpet, she rose and dressed and rang for a maid to bring a tray to her room.

The bread and chocolate were some time in coming,

as it was so early and the servants were just stirring, and after she ate, she wandered the house aimlessly. Maria and Josie would likely not be awake for an hour at least.

Deciding to get a book, she went into the library and didn't at first realize that anyone else was in there. But shortly she became aware of a soft sound coming from the room's large, exquisite desk, and noticed a distinctive, not unpleasant smell, and she went over to look.

Jack Whitby was crouched behind the desk, rubbing a cloth over the dark wood of the desk.

He flicked a glance at her but said nothing and kept working.

"I should think the maids would be responsible for the polishing," she said.

"I'm not polishing, I'm repairing the finish."

She ought to leave right then; to be alone in a room with a man and the door closed was highly improper. And Jack Whitby, with his persistent lack of deference and his air of mockery mingled with vigor, made it seem all the more improper. But she couldn't make herself go. She told herself it was only her usual contrariness keeping her there and moved away from him, making for the bookshelves.

They existed quietly in the room together for several minutes, the only noise being the sound of his cloth and the rustling she made as she pulled books off the shelves. She poked through a collection of novels, but the silly heroines in their pages irritated her and she moved on to a group of scientific books.

She couldn't have said how long she stood lost in

a book that finally engaged her when she noticed that the polishing sounds had stopped. She looked up from the book, and there he was at the end of the shelf.

"Oh—you scared me." The stupid words spilled out without her volition. She wasn't *scared* of him, though he did unsettle her. But she certainly didn't want him to know that.

The corner of his mouth inched back. "I find it hard to believe you are so easily scared, Miss Cardworthy. Though I'm certain there are any number of men who might be afraid of *you*."

She expelled a little breath of outrage. "How dare you make such personal comments to me!"

He shrugged. "You only dislike them because they're not flattering. But that doesn't mean they aren't also true."

She blinked at him, her lips pursing. She could feel herself growing tighter, as if a rope were being wound around her, drawing her further into herself, to a lonely place. She didn't like herself like this—tight, closed-off—but it always seemed to happen when she felt threatened. She wasn't afraid of Whitby though, she reminded herself. She didn't have anything to lose here. She straightened her spine.

"And who are you to tell people who they are?"

"A man who earns his own way. Perhaps you'd like me to be faceless and voiceless and without opinions because I work with my hands. But I can read and write, same as you, and I've got a brain in my head, and skills most of the men you know do not."

A shiver ran down her spine at his prideful words. At the suggestion that he might have all sorts of talents she couldn't imagine but that a woman might appreciate.

*Stop this.* She was not some ninny, to be beguiled by a handsome face and a forceful demeanor.

His gaze drifted down to the cover of the book she held below her chin. "*The Mathematical Repository,*" he read. His eyes flicked to hers. "I like mathematics. Are you partial to them?"

"Why, yes," she said, her irritation momentarily forgotten. She did love mathematics, with their clear answers and the order they brought to her sewing and knitting, but it wasn't often she met someone else who liked them. People always thought mathematics were dull. "They're the best sort of puzzle."

"I, too, prefer things that need measuring and pondering to solve," he said. But then she realized he was trying to get a rise out of her.

She gave him a bored look and opened the book and stared down at a page full of calculations. "Don't you have somewhere else to be, Mr. Whitby?"

Out of the corner of her eye she could see that he was smiling—why did she so want to wipe that smile off his face?

"I should have that box of yours repaired by tomorrow."

"Well, good." She closed the book and turned purposefully away to put it back on the shelf, a dismissal. She needed him to go, because she was strangely afraid she might say or do something she didn't mean to. He ought not even to register in her awareness beyond the useful help he could provide. But he did, and she didn't trust herself.

"You're welcome," he said to her back.

"Really!" she said tartly. She looked over her shoulder, thinking to cow him with her hardest look.

He only laughed. "You might be used to saying whatever you like, Edwina Cardworthy, but don't think I'll let you walk all over me."

Something softened in those icy eyes, making her skin prickle. "Sweet Edwina. There's a velvety soft woman underneath that sharp exterior, but you're afraid to let her out, aren't you?"

His words threw her off balance. It was as though he'd seen through the beauty and the demeanor that distracted everyone else, seen the person she was underneath.

But she shouldn't be listening to such appallingly familiar talk. She reached for maidenly outrage, but something else came with it, something exciting and unfamiliar. "How dare you."

"Easily," he said with a grin and turned to go. But she hadn't had the last word, and she grabbed his arm and tugged. And knew immediately that she'd just asked for more than she could handle. He easily broke her hold on his arm and moved toward her, backing her into the bookshelf.

"What is it, Edwina Cardworthy?" he asked in a soft voice. "What is it you want?"

She couldn't think with him so close. He smelled of wood shavings and the varnish he'd been rubbing on the desk, and the warmth of his body brushed against her skin, making her want to lean into it. The squareness of his jaw was fascinating her almost irresistibly. Everything about him was as chiseled and hard as the wood on which he worked. He didn't

have the refined elegance of a gentleman, and yet he
was not coarse. But he was too direct, and blunt, and
everything she did not look for in a man. He *worked*
for a living.

"I—nothing." She was stumbling over words, but
she felt stupid and overwhelmed. Jack Whitby standing so close to her was incredibly exciting, in a way
she'd never been excited in her life. "Excuse me,"
she said in a husky voice she hardly recognized. "I
shouldn't have grabbed you. It was only a reflex."

A glimmer of amusement twinkled in his eyes and
broke the spell.

"Move back, Whitby," she said, annoyed with the
quaver in her voice. "You are crowding me."

But instead he leaned closer. "Giving orders again?
I don't think what you need from me is obedience."

Her mind might be struggling to assert that she
needed to get away from him, but his nearness was
doing something else to her. Turning her brains to
porridge, apparently. Definitely making her heart race.

"You are impertinent," she said, but it wasn't
the scold it should have been and instead came out
breathy. Flirtatious. "Unbelievably arrogant."

"Agreed." He moved closer, though so slowly that
she could easily have protested. But she didn't, and
then there was nothing between them but a wisp of
air. The sound of his breathing sent a thrill through her.

Along with the scent of wood shavings and varnish
now came a more personal scent that she knew was
his skin, a warm, salty, human scent. There was some
force in him, a unique and fascinating force, and she
wanted to touch him, to accept it.

He leaned still closer and his lips touched hers, nudging her, coaxing with a deft and tender arrogance that undid her. She parted her lips.

His mouth surprised her, so supple as it was on hers. But firm at the same time, and purposeful. The intention and force behind his kiss intoxicated her. His tongue stroked along the soft skin inside her lips and encouraged her to stroke him back, and she did, leaning in to him and stealing a shaking hand up to touch the front of his coat. The fabric was rough, the sort of cloth she would have passed over as utterly unacceptable for anyone she knew.

He was the first man she'd encountered who hadn't focused on her beauty, and she couldn't resist that about him.

He slid his hand along her neck, the rough drag of his calloused palm telling a history of strength and effort. It made her skin spark.

He kissed along her jaw and down her neck.

"You smell amazing," he said in a voice that sounded like a groan. "Like clean linen baking in the sun, and lavender flowers."

He was talking to her, seeking more of her just because he liked who she was, and she loved that.

*No*, an ugly voice whispered, *it's a mistake. He's only kissing you because of your beauty, the beauty that draws all men.*

"I'll be twenty-eight in August," she gasped out as his hot mouth moved lower. Deep in the secret heart of her, desire gushed like a spring river escaping its banks to flood parched plants.

"I'll be twenty-seven," he said with a dark chuckle

that turned into a groan as his lips reached the plump, upward swell of her breast. "Are you thinking of a party to celebrate?"

"Oh God, you're younger," she moaned. Her knees wobbled and her back slid a little way down the bookshelves. He caught her around the waist.

"What, do you think you're on the shelf? You couldn't be more wrong." He pressed slow kisses on her cheek in a line heading toward her mouth. "Any man would be a king if you chose him."

Her heart skipped a beat at his words.

And then the click of the library door opening made them spring apart.

❧

"Edwina?" Josie said in astonishment. It was hard to believe her own eyes, but as she'd moved into the library, what she'd seen was her sister with her arms around Whitby, the carpenter. And she'd been kissing him.

They stood apart now—Edwina had moved quickly away from him, and she looked pink and flustered.

"Josie," she said in a hoarse voice but then seemed at a loss for words.

Whitby was apparently the only one who didn't feel overwhelmed with awkwardness. "Miss Cardworthy," he said to Edwina, inclining his head to her as politely as any gentleman might have. "Come by my workshop anytime to collect your box."

He took up his bag of tools with a sweep of his arm and moved toward the door, tipping his head to a speechless Josie as he passed her on his way out of the room.

She quickly shut the door behind him and rushed over to Edwina, who had slumped back against one of the bookcases.

"Edwina? What on earth is going on?"

"I...don't know," her sister said. But then she seemed to gather herself and stood up straighter. "I made a mistake, that's all. That man." She gestured toward the door. "Whitby—"

"Did he force himself on you?" Josie asked, even though the way Edwina had been pressed against him had looked very much like permission.

"No," Edwina said firmly, though the blush of pink in her cheeks suggested she didn't feel as in control as she wanted to be. "He didn't force anything on me. I think he simply benefitted from a sort of...curiosity I hadn't realized I had."

"You mean you were curious about passion?" Was Edwina, too, feeling topsy-turvy?

"Apparently! But that's all—it was a sort of exploration on my part."

Edwina gave her a hard look. "And don't be judging me, when you've doubtless been kissed soundly by Nicholas."

Josie looked away, feeling like a sneak and a terrible fiancée and sister. She hadn't been thinking of the single, chaste kiss she'd shared with Nicholas, but the too-memorable one she'd placed on Colin.

"Yes, Nicholas kissed me. Only once, behind the oak tree at Jasmine House. It was lovely."

There were about a hundred other things she could have said about kisses after what had happened with Colin, but listening to Edwina dismiss what she'd been doing with Whitby didn't encourage confidences about her own weakness.

Edwina snorted. "Lovely? I'm certain I shall never feel that way about kissing Whitby, of all people. He's the most arrogant man I've ever met."

"But..." Josie said, peering at the fading blush on Edwina's face, "you liked it, didn't you? Maybe you like *him*."

"Like Jack Whitby? A cabinetmaker? Are you out of your mind? In no way is he a gentleman. Never mind that I don't even like him."

"I suppose," Josie said. "Though I've often thought you don't like anybody." She immediately felt terrible for being so blunt.

Edwina laughed, but it was a bitter sound.

"I'm sorry," Josie said. "That was unkind. And not true, I know. Ever since we've come to London, you've seemed to take more pleasure in company."

"No, there is truth in what you say." Edwina dropped her eyes and began to pick at a thread on her cuff.

She knew Edwina would retreat behind her prickliness and reserve, and she felt such a sense that she mustn't. Though she was closer to Edwina than anyone but Colin (and now she didn't even know if she could count him), they never shared their deepest feelings. Josie had never spoken of her fears about choosing Nicholas, and if Edwina had second thoughts about what she wanted for her future, she'd kept them to herself. Mightn't it help if they could really talk?

"No, really, you mustn't think that. I expressed myself badly," Josie said. "I think it's more that if you think people might not like you, you decide not to like them first."

A vulnerable look came over Edwina's face. "I know I'm impossibly particular. I sometimes wish I weren't, but I can't seem not to be. Even Mappleton—I like him well enough, but he doesn't *dazzle* me the way ladies in novels are always being dazzled."

But then she crossed her arms, as though regretting saying too much. As though the two of them couldn't really trust each other.

"What about Nicholas?" Edwina said.

"Yes, I did feel dazzled when I met him."

"And now? After a year apart?"

Josie was about to admit that perhaps things had changed when Edwina said, "But how could you possibly not? He'll make the perfect husband."

She didn't want a perfect husband—such a man didn't sound real at all. But she realized that Edwina, with her hopes for a wealthy, important husband, might not understand.

And yet, Josie suddenly felt certain that her sister had been stirred deeply by Whitby.

Was it like the way she herself had been stirred by Colin?

With a feeling of panic, she tried to conjure an image of Nicholas, even something so minor as the shape of his hands. Surely they were long-fingered, like Colin's, if perhaps not quite so long? But she couldn't remember.

"Josie?" Edwina said. "Why are you frowning?"

Josie lifted a trembling hand to push a lock of hair away from her eye. "It's London, isn't it? Ever since we came here, it's been doing strange things to us. You with Whitby. And I...I don't feel quite myself."

"I am not 'with' Whitby," Edwina said tartly. "And I believe Mappleton is going to propose. He told me there's something he wants to discuss when he returns."

Josie sucked in a breath. "Oh. So soon."

"But you encouraged me to marry! And now you act as though my getting engaged wouldn't be good news."

"It's just that Mappleton's so soft," Josie said urgently. "You'll lose respect for him."

"You're wrong," Edwina said in a hard voice. "He's of good family, he's got money, he thinks I'm wonderful, and he can give me children. I don't want anything else from marriage."

She swept out of the library, and Josie knew that, if anything, she'd only made Edwina want to marry Mappleton more. Why could they never *talk* to each other?

She was worried. Edwina saying she wanted to marry Mappleton when she'd just been kissing Whitby seemed an awful lot like desperation. She did realize that, considering what had happened between herself and Colin, this was the pot calling the kettle black, but that was different. She cared about Colin, however wrong that was. What a tangle everything had become.

She needed a walk to clear her head, so she summoned a maid and set out for the modest pleasure garden a few streets away, which was located behind a teahouse. She liked the garden because it had a pond with a graveled path around it, which was overhung prettily in several spots with arbors dripping with grapes and climbing roses. She told the maid she might sit on one of the benches while she, Josie, walked round the pond.

It was mid-morning, and the only people about were those interested in the teahouse. She had the path to herself for several laps, but as she emerged from a thickly vined arbor, she was startled to see a gentleman approaching.

His dark head was down, as if he were concentrating on something, but there was no mistaking who he was. He must have sensed her presence because he looked up and was clearly startled to see her there.

"Josie."

"Colin."

They hadn't spoken in days, not since she'd seen him with Lady Denborough, and the memory gave her an unpleasant twinge to go along with the awkwardness of standing there so stiffly with him.

After a moment, he said, "I hope you are well. And your sister."

"Yes, thank you, we are. And you?"

"Quite."

He pressed his lips together. She stood there frozen. Silence.

So it had come to this: all they had to say to each other were mundane courtesies. The knowledge stung, but considering what had happened at the ball, she supposed this must be for the best. Their gazes drifted apart, and the only thing left to say was "Good day."

As they moved past each other, she wished so much that she'd never come to London.

She'd gone perhaps five steps when she couldn't stand it anymore, and she turned and called his name. He turned around, waiting, and she moved closer.

"I hate this awkwardness," she said. There was so much else, none of which she could say, but this was the essential truth. She couldn't bear the distance that had grown between them.

She thought he wouldn't respond—he didn't move closer—but then he said, "Yes." His voice sounded a little hoarse.

He was wearing her favorite of his waistcoats, which had a pattern of light and dark blue stripes, and it made her feel even more keenly how she'd missed him. "And I'm sorry that I was unpleasant when I met you at the ball with Lady Denborough."

"I understood," he said. "But my change in plans really was genuine. I didn't lie to you about not wanting to court women when you encouraged me to consider Edwina."

"I know that now," she said seriously. He looked fairly serious too, and she wished he'd smile, but Colin had never been one to be grinning all the time.

"Will you walk with me?" she asked.

"Very well."

They set off on the path around the pond. Ahead of them, an elderly man was now strolling as well. The maid who'd accompanied Josie was still on the bench; she appeared to have fallen asleep.

Colin was struggling to listen to what Josie was saying. He'd been working hard in recent days not to think of her, and to put his feet on the sensible path of marriage to an appropriate woman. He'd moved on from Lady Denborough and the other fashionable widows, whom he'd found to be far too fashionable for him, and had since met a quiet lady named Miss Susanna Alcott, with whom he'd had a surprisingly enjoyable conversation at the opera. He meant to see her that night, at a dinner being held by his friend Hal.

So when he'd come upon Josie so suddenly, he'd been caught off guard. Her olive branch had touched the weak part of him that still wanted her desperately.

"I must tell you though," Josie was saying, "that I worry about Edwina. It's wonderful that she's had such success here in Town, but I'm worried she's going to make a bad choice for her future." She lowered her voice. "Lord Mappleton seems likely to propose."

"Ah. Well, he's all right. She could do worse."

"But surely she could do better. He's like a piece of dough. There's no force in him."

"Perhaps it's a compromise she's willing to make."

"But I don't think she should compromise on her future."

Since Colin was heading in the direction of compromise himself, he had nothing to offer to this. They walked in silence for a few minutes, overtaking the old gentleman and passing under a long arbor that was heady with the scent of grapes.

He realized she'd been very quiet for a while, and when he glanced at her, she had an unhappy look.

"Colin," she said softly, "I can't forget what I did at the ball. It was such a bad mistake."

They couldn't talk about this. He couldn't. But he hated that she was suffering over it.

"We both made a mistake," he said. "I know it can be hard letting go of mistakes, as if thinking about them over and over would allow us to go back and undo them. But we can't, and sometimes you just have to refuse to think about them anymore."

She sighed heavily. "I think perhaps men are better at forgetting things than women. And I feel I've made quite a few mistakes of late. I feel quite flawed."

"You just have to shrug and move on. For instance, last week I stopped to visit a friend and left with someone else's horse."

"What, really?"

She laughed a little, and the sound made him realize how much he'd missed her liveliness. His life seemed so dull without it.

"That's so unlike you. Still, it wasn't intentional." She paused. "I feel I ought to confess another stupid mistake, because it involved you."

He glanced at her. "I can't think what you mean."

"It really was a very silly thing, and I hope you'll see the humor in it." She cleared her throat. "It happened at Upperton, back when I was thinking you and Edwina would make such a fine match." She paused.

"Yes?"

"I'm actually fairly embarrassed to tell you this."

"I'm sure it will be fine. Clearly it can't have been such a terrible mistake if I didn't even know about it."

"Well…I happened upon a gypsy one day, and she

told me this ridiculous but amusing business about a love potion, and how it was the very thing to help people find true love, and I thought of you and Edwina and decided to try it."

He didn't like the sound of this. "You didn't."

"I did. The gypsy assured me it was only some plant juice, completely harmless, and it sounded like a lark. So I put it in your tea one night when you came to Jasmine House."

"You gave me a *love potion*?"

"It was an idiotic thing to do, but I thought that, as you two had some very good things in common, it might work. And I didn't like the idea of either one of you being lonely in life, without a spouse."

He was actually quite furious. He'd been nothing more than a pawn to her, to be moved around as she thought fit. Or kissed when the mood struck her, as it had at the ball. While to him she'd been the star shining in his sky, however much she shouldn't have been, she'd been making a fool of him.

"I'm so terribly sorry," she continued. "It was incredibly high-handed of me, and I hope you didn't experience any ill effects of the potion."

When he didn't respond, she said in a small voice, "Colin? Can you forgive me?"

He must be grateful she'd confessed about the potion. It was what he needed to hear—it would make him remember what he'd done after she'd given it to him, how it had released the bonds he kept on himself. He needed to remember himself yelling like a fool from the roof of Greenbrier, how his need for her had made him give in to emotion and indulge himself.

He needed to be reminded of how he might stumble, because knowing the way she'd responded to his kiss, he couldn't trust himself never to try for more.

"It was a mistake," he said.

She nodded eagerly, a look of relief coming over her face. "I'm so glad you see that. I've worried about what that potion might have done to you," she said ruefully. "My brothers gave it to Mr. Botsford—"

He stopped. They were just about to enter the grape arbor again. "I don't mean the potion," he said, "though it certainly was a ridiculous thing to do. I mean that it was a mistake, our talking like this. The distance that had grown between us—it was for the best."

The smile fell away and her eyes darkened unhappily. "How can you say that? I thought we were going to forget past mistakes. And…I hated how it felt, the distance between us. I missed you. I miss you still—I miss the way things used to be."

He closed his eyes, needing to shut out her face, because he so wanted to touch her cheek and smooth all this away. "Don't. Don't miss me."

"But—"

"Josie." He must trust her with the truth. It would at least be an explanation for all those times when he would have to turn away from her. "I'm attracted to you. I'm *hideously* attracted to you. You have no idea how much I want to touch you."

Color flooded her cheeks. "Oh," she whispered.

The old man was approaching them at a remarkably improved pace, and he gave Colin a hard look as he passed them, as though calling him a blackguard. Colin could only agree.

She moved closer to him, and something in her eyes seemed to reach for him, as if she were yearning toward him. As if she wanted him.

Desire surged in him, tempting, urging him to sweep her into his arms and kiss her until she melted for him. Told him they might have a future.

God, this was so wrong!

He wrenched his eyes away from her.

"Maybe I shouldn't have admitted this," he said, disgusted by the hoarseness in his voice. "But I need you to understand now why I can't be around you anymore. Why we mustn't spend any more time together."

"But," she said, "I couldn't bear it if you simply disappeared from my life. Something could change. This can be mastered—"

"No, Josie, it can't."

He left her there. He would always remember the hurt astonishment in her eyes, and how achingly beautiful she looked with her hair falling in soft curls and the green of the arbor behind her creating a dream image of a beautiful future that would never be.

# Ten

JOSIE WAS STILL SHAKING HALF AN HOUR LATER WHEN she returned to the town house. Maria was in the foyer, speaking with the housekeeper when she came in.

She peered at Josie. "Are you quite all right, my dear? You look flushed."

She repressed a hysterical sob. "I've been walking, and I think I took too much sun. I shall go lie down."

Once in her bedchamber, she sat down at the small desk and let her head fall into her hands.

She'd been so happy to reconcile with Colin. Those few minutes they'd spent walking around the pond before he'd spoken so seriously had made her feel better than she had in so long. Perhaps it was his collectedness that always made her feel grounded, or maybe she'd never know what it was, but something about him answered something in her, so that she felt more like herself with him than with anyone else.

*You have no idea how much I want to touch you.* The memory of his words stirred the same hot flush in her now as they had at the garden. Wrong though it was, she'd loved hearing them. She'd wanted to touch him too.

*I'm hideously attracted to you.* Hideous. He knew what honor required, and he was right, no matter that she hated the idea of their friendship being truly broken.

She was going to have to forget about him. All she could do was move forward in the right direction, the direction she'd chosen a year before.

She reached into the desk and pulled out the packet of letters Nicholas had sent over the long months, and she made herself read through every one.

And then she began a reply.

> *Dear Nicholas,*
>
> *I miss you and thank God each time we have a letter from you, a sign you are still alive. But I don't know how much longer I can wait for you to come back. It is so hard, in so many ways I never expected. I suddenly feel I don't know myself at all, or of what I'm capable. I need grounding, and you would do that for me.*
>
> *Please, please come back to England as soon as you can. Come back and marry me, and we'll live on your beautiful estate and all will be perfect. Keep yourself safe.*
>
> > *Your affectionate,*
> > *Josie*

Upon completion, she read the letter over once and stuck it in the fire. Then she dropped her head into her hands and acknowledged that she was in trouble.

༄

Colin needed to punch something. He'd never felt more uncivilized in his life.

He settled for several rounds with the fencing master at the school where he sometimes practiced, and when Hal showed up, he went at it hammer and tongs with him as well, until the sweat streamed down their faces and their chests heaved.

"I get the sense there's something you're trying to work out," Hal said, running the back of his hand over his forehead as they stood by an open window trying to catch a breeze. "You are relentless today."

Colin leaned an arm against the windowsill and shut his eyes, but that only made Josie's face appear. How was he ever going to forget how it had felt to stand so close to her, to breathe in her rose scent, to feel the hint of her bodily warmth? A life of desperation stretched before him.

He wondered bleakly if he would ever be able to be intimate with another woman when he wanted Josie so much. He couldn't see how. There was far more to what he felt for her than just wanting.

"Just feeling a bit pent up," he said.

Hal laughed. "Too many parties and balls for your taste, if I know you. Can't avoid them here, can you?"

Colin grunted. Hal knew him well. Though he knew nothing of Colin's fixation on Josie. "No."

Hal nodded thoughtfully. "And you've been playing the good host to your old friend Cardworthy's daughters. They're very pretty and interesting young ladies. I can easily see what Nick finds to admire in Josephine. And Edwina is one of the most beautiful unmarried women currently in London."

"The most beautiful *married* one being Lily, of course," Colin said, referring to Hal's wife.

"There can be no question." A secret smile teased the corners of Hal's mouth, the smile of a blissfully married man. As much as Colin wished his friend happy, the sight of it gave him a bitter stab of envy.

"But as for her sister," Hal said, "I wonder what Nick could have been thinking, not marrying Josie before he left. A year is a long time, and engaged isn't married."

*Don't tempt me to think I can change things*, Colin thought fiercely. Because for one moment by the pond, when she'd drawn closer to him, he'd thought he'd read in her eyes that she needed him, and he'd wavered. A wicked voice had encouraged him to press his suit and let her choose between them. It had taken everything he had to force himself to say the right thing.

"There wasn't time for them to marry before he had to return to Spain."

"And so she waits for him when, charming and pretty as she is, she might throw off the engagement and choose from any number of men."

"She wouldn't do that."

Hal arched an eyebrow. "Dunleavy is smitten, and that rogue Kit Standish told me he wants to change her mind."

Colin's jaw tightened. "Why?"

Hal shot him a look. "Sometimes I wonder about you, Colin. Why indeed would a man wish to spend his days with a pretty, charming, witty wife? Gad, man, you've been keeping to yourself too long, and you're turning into a hermit."

It would be better if he actually had, Colin thought. Then he wouldn't be doing battle with the dawning awareness that he *needed* Josie Cardworthy. He needed her like he needed water when he was thirsty. Already, knowing he must nevermore be close to her, his body craved just to be in the same space as her. Simply telling her their friendship was over hadn't made him stop wanting to know everything about her.

He'd been so, so close to losing control and pulling her into his arms.

There was nothing he hated more than people who were out of control. He'd had a daily example of this in his parents, a daily view of the stupid and selfish things people did under the influence of emotions.

*Go on,* his mother would taunt his father, *hit me. You know you want to do it.*

He supposed the saving grace of his father was that he never had. But he'd used words like fists, and there'd never been peace between the two of them.

*You're not worth the trouble,* his father would say to her in that cold way of his. Which only enraged Colin's mother, who then threw things. Usually, Colin would have slipped out of the room by the time the throwing commenced, and found his way to one of his many hiding places. One of the benefits of a large home. He'd kept his hidey-holes stocked with books and would disappear there for hours at a time.

He'd had enough of strong emotions to last his whole life. They were like an intoxicant to be avoided, and he knew better than to let them lead him.

"I can hardly be a hermit in London," he said.

Hal laughed. "Well, if anyone could, it would be you.

Though you did develop that out-of-character interest in lonely widows a few weeks ago. Lily didn't approve."

Oh wonderful, his friends were gossiping about him. "She doesn't approve of lonely widows?"

"She says you are too nice a man for 'hard, calculating women.'" He grinned. "But she does approve of Kate Alcott."

"Hal. You know I think Lily is all that is gracious and good…"

"But you don't want any help finding a countess." Hal laughed heartily, and Colin considered wielding his foil anew. "I shall try to discourage Lily, but it will be difficult because she adores you so. She thinks you are 'the loveliest, most noble man.' She's always admired you for the way you handled Eloise's infatuation."

He'd never felt less noble in his life than he had today. "It was nothing."

Hal made a face. "I'm certain I don't want to hear any more details about that kiss my sister foisted on you than I already know," he said, clapping Colin on the shoulder.

Later, when Colin, his self-disgust not at all mitigated by the hours spent fencing, reached his town house, a letter from Nick was waiting for him. The sight of his friend's handwriting pierced him and accused him of being treacherous, selfish, a bastard. He snatched the letter and took it to his bedchamber. It was dated May, and from the stained condition of the envelope, it had obviously had a circuitous journey.

Nick wrote:

*Colin Old Fellow,*

*I hope this finds you well. I am for the most part still in one piece, despite Boney's efforts here in Spain. I miss England's cool weather, and so many things about home. Last week I wrote to Josie, letting her know I should return in late July. I so look forward to seeing her—it's been thoughts of her and home that have sustained me at trying times.*

*But…ah, but. All seems to grow murkier, and I feel the need to confess.*

*It's to do with a woman I've met, someone who's come to fascinate me though she should not, and not only because of Josie. She is not English, and truly the most ill-mannered woman I've ever known. Yet she delights me. This is wrong, I know. But though I would choose to avoid her, I am required to spend time with her constantly. It is a sort of torture.*

*There's really nothing to be done about this, is there? I only needed to say this aloud, in a manner of speaking, to someone who would listen. I know which is the right direction—the only direction. Only now I'm not certain I'm worthy of it.*

                              *Nicholas*

Colin's first reaction was anger. He had no trouble reading between the lines of what Nick couldn't write—he knew his friend had sometimes been called on to conduct dealings with French spies, and that the spies were both men and women. That had to be what he meant about someone he was required to spend time with: a French lady-spy. And now he was apparently tempted by her.

While also wanting Josie. Josie, who looked on Nick with such stars in her eyes, this man who'd dabbled and played with women from the moment he was able. Nick was a good-hearted man, yes, but he was also something of a rogue used to having whatever woman he wanted, and happily accustomed to enjoying the adoring attentions of beautiful females. Colin had thought Nick had stopped all that when he met Josie.

*Hell.* He scrubbed his eyes. How could Nick have sent such a letter? How could he be wavering when he was engaged to Josie of all women? Colin felt tortured by the Fates, mocked, tormented. Bitterness clawed at him.

Nick was wavering. He was tempted, just as Colin was tempted by Josie.

But Nick was in a difficult situation nothing like the peaceable existence Colin knew. Nick was being shot at, living often miserably among the elements, forced into extra danger in his work with spies. Some days he surely wouldn't know whether he would live or die. He had likely already lost many friends to battle and disease, and seen men wounded and suffering. It wasn't surprising that he might yearn for comfort.

But if Nick truly loved Josie, how could he yearn to find comfort with another woman?

Along with his anger on Josie's behalf was the unwelcome knowledge that part of him was rejoicing in Nick's weakness. That he secretly wanted Nick to stumble and fall off the pedestal on which Josie had placed him and open a way for Colin himself.

It was weakness that he allowed such thoughts for even a second, and he despised this in himself. He'd closed the door on his friendship with Josie, but he would always care about his friends' happiness.

He wished Nicholas were there so he could shake some sense into him. Nor would a letter likely reach him before he might leave for London.

"Come back to her," he murmured fiercely. "Come back to her as soon as ever you can."

# *Eleven*

THE DAYS PASSED SOMEHOW FOR JOSIE, DAYS OF WAIT-
ing for Mappleton to return and propose to Edwina
and for Nicholas to come back and their marriage to
take place. A thousand times a day, she replayed her
conversation with Colin, and each time she came to
the conclusion that, however much she missed him,
he was right that they mustn't be together.

She saw him across ballrooms and made no attempt
to greet him. At a dinner party, he sat across from her,
and they managed not to speak a single word to each
other while also appearing congenial. She and Edwina
encountered him walking in Hyde Park, and they
greeted one another with casual cordiality and nothing more. If Edwina raised an eyebrow at their bland
conversation, at least she said nothing.

Colin didn't know that Josie was powerfully
attracted to him as well, and that was the one thing for
which she was grateful. He wanted her sexually, and,
oh yes, she wanted him that way too. But there was
lust, and there was love, and nothing about the way
he'd behaved had spoken of love.

He'd said he was "hideously attracted" to her. But of tenderness, affection, openness—all the things she knew she wanted from a man, he had expressed none.

Nicholas was open. He'd talked freely of love and emotion with her. She'd chosen him with all the wisdom she'd gained growing up with a view to a marriage devoid of tenderness and openness.

Colin was hidden. He'd always kept a portion of himself to himself, with his books and his research and his solitude. Since coming to London, he'd been withdrawn and dark and inscrutable. And while a reckless part of her was thrilled by the excitement of the challenge and puzzle that he was, the reasonable part of her knew what happened when she reached for thrills.

She did, though, find it bitterly ironic that Colin, whom she'd once considered as predictable and comfortable as an old chair, had turned into an enigma—and one who was dangerous to her heart.

In her more generous moments, she forced herself to hope that he would soon meet a woman who might be his wife, or at least that he was enjoying the company of his fashionable widows, but it was a very unenthusiastic hope.

Nicholas hadn't sent any more letters, but the last one she'd gotten months before had said he'd be back in England in late July, which it now was. Edwina would likely become engaged any day, and when that happened, the sisters would return to Jasmine House with the good news and begin preparing for the wedding. In which case, if Nicholas still hadn't come, she would await him at home. When he finally returned, she meant to welcome him with nothing less than enthusiasm, and she'd make sure she deserved him.

⁓

The ladies were together in Maria's pretty drawing room one hot and sunny morning, trying to keep cool with lemonade and debating which to accept of the invitations that had arrived. Josie's contributions to the conversation were few. She was standing by one of windows that had been opened to catch a breeze, watching a robin peck at a spot of bare earth near a shady patch of lilies of the valley and wishing life were as simple as the birds must find it to be.

A maid appeared in the doorway to announce a visitor.

"So early for a caller," Maria said with a hint of disdain.

"It's Lord Ivorwood," the maid said.

"Why didn't you say so? My nephew is always welcome."

Something stirred in Josie at the news he'd come, but she forced herself not to acknowledge it. They weren't friends anymore, and she must treat him as an old acquaintance whose presence provoked only mild interest, however much she yearned for just the sight of him.

He appeared in the doorway, tall and dark and so handsome she could hardly bear it. But his expression looked oddly grim, and the knot of his cravat was askew, as though it had been hastily tied. He lingered in the doorway, and a tingle of alarm coursed through her.

"Colin?" Maria said, standing. "Is something amiss?"

He pressed his lips together. "I'm afraid so." He moved into the room but didn't meet Josie's eyes. "Perhaps it would be best if we all sat down."

The alarm tingle grew to a clang. The ladies sat on a divan, and the earl took a chair across from them. He ran a hand through his black hair, disheveling it, and Josie saw that his eyes looked haunted. Something was very wrong. Her stomach dipped and she gripped the arm of her chair.

"There's no easy way to say this, so I will just say it: I had a letter this morning from Nick's commander. Nick is missing and believed dead. He was mortally wounded with his troops as they were trying to take a farmhouse held by the enemy. The house caught fire, and there were no survivors."

Silence met his speech. Josie blinked, his words repeating in her mind until she felt as though they were being muttered at her from the far end of a long tunnel. She forced herself to speak.

"I don't accept this," she said. "He could still be alive. People survive all sorts of injuries."

She was vaguely aware that on either side of her, Edwina and Maria seemed both to have frozen, because neither of them was saying anything, neither was contradicting these awful, unwanted words.

Colin reached out and took one of Josie's hands. His grip was cold, and when their gaze finally met, she almost crumpled at the anguish that passed wordlessly between them.

"The battle occurred almost three weeks ago," he said in a hoarse voice. "He was seen lying in the doorway of the house with a crippling injury to the gut, the kind of injury that would never have allowed him to escape the fire. I'm so very sorry."

Unable to bear the compassion in his eyes, she looked away and let her hand fall from his. Edwina slipped an arm around her and hugged her hard.

"Oh, Josie," she said in a raw voice, "I'm so sorry."

"He was a fine man," Maria said. "What a loss for us all. Words are inadequate."

"Yes," Colin said.

They all sat there silently with the news. At some point Josie realized Colin had left, though she found she didn't care who was present or where she was.

Maria brought her a glass of brandy, which she drank with shaking hands. Then Edwina guided her up to her room and loosened her gown and helped her lie back on the bed.

Josie looked up at her sister's dark head hovering over her. The emotions roiling within her felt like poison. Sorrow, guilt, anger, remorse, and confusion crashed through her like waves, threatening to drown her.

"I wanted to know him so much more," she said through the tightness in her throat. "I wanted there to be time."

"I know, dearest." The tender compassion in Edwina's voice tugged at the last bonds Josie had on her emotions. "Life is cruel."

"I'd like to be alone now," Josie whispered. Edwina nodded and slipped quietly out of the room.

Josie lay on the bed on that bright, sunny English afternoon with robins chirping outside her window, while miles away Nick was gone from where he'd been and the battles raged on without him. Just as she would now have to carry on without him and the future of which they had dreamed.

Colin stepped out of his carriage in front of his town house and walked up the steps as though in a dream. He was dimly aware of the sounds of someone knocking at a door down the street, a carriage rolling by, the angry barking of a dog in the mews. Life carrying on as usual.

As if anything could be usual again.

He'd known Nick for ten years, during which time they'd grown into men. Buoyant, playful, roguish Nick, who'd been part of so many of the best moments of Colin's life.

And now he was gone.

Colin hadn't realized how much his idea of the world had depended on his friend being in it.

He trudged up the stairs, his whole being heavy and stupid with grief. It had taken all he had to pay the visit to Maria's, to speak the words that Josie had never wanted to hear. To break her heart.

And he had, he'd seen that. The devastation in her eyes had nearly killed him.

As he passed through the foyer and up the grand marble stairs, ignoring the carefully quiet movements of his staff, he suffered the bitter realization that now he and Josie were finally sharing a truly deep connection, though one he'd never have wanted: grief.

He entered his bedchamber, threw off his coat, and reached for the brandy bottle. He didn't even like brandy in quantity, but now he welcomed its harsh intensity.

He thought of Nick's letter, and, guiltily, how furious it had made him. But the letter had also stirred a craven spark of hope, because part of him had—even if only for a second—rejoiced in Nick's attraction to that lady-spy.

He'd *doubted* Nick, however momentarily.

And now Nick was gone, just as if he'd wished him away.

*Had* he? Dear God, he didn't know himself anymore. Maybe he had. And now Nick was gone and he was left with nothing but bitterness and sorrow.

He had no sense of time, no awareness of it passing. All was gloom and shadow.

Alone in his grief as he deserved to be, he kept to his house, for once glad to be so important that his order not to be disturbed was obeyed scrupulously.

❧

Mornings, afternoons, and evenings slipped by, but Josie, lying on the bed in her chamber at Maria's, had little awareness of them beyond the waxing and waning light. Occasionally sounds penetrated, or someone would come to see if she wanted something, but it was all muffled and distant.

She'd come to understand what it meant to hate yourself.

With a part of herself that had seemed to detach when she heard the news of Nicholas's death, she acknowledged that she'd always thought this phrase overly dramatic: How could a person truly hate herself when our instincts drew us toward survival and pleasure? Of course she'd been angry with herself before, and disgusted with mistakes she'd made. But nothing had ever been like this.

There she'd been, frolicking around London, delighting in discovering new joys, questioning her engagement, finding other men fascinating. Kissing Colin.

How stupid and silly and useless it all had been. Childishly, selfishly, she'd been indulging herself while Nick was off fighting, his days and nights fraught with suffering and tragedy. And now he'd given his life for his country. For all of them.

She was unworthy of him. Unworthy of his memory.

And she couldn't even cry.

She understood why this was. It was because she was a terrible person, a reckless, selfish person, driven by greedy desires.

Cold fury bubbled inside her, mingling bitterly with sorrow for Nicholas, and she forced herself to lie still, to not give in to the need to distract herself from what she was feeling by seeking the company and solace of her sister. It was just as well that Colin had broken off their friendship. She deserved to suffer.

⁂

By the end of the week, Edwina and Maria had become very concerned. They stood in the corridor outside Josie's chamber after lunch, talking in whispers.

"I've never seen her like this," Edwina said.

"She's had a terrible shock." Maria's sharp, petite features were drawn with worry.

"It's a tragedy," Edwina said, not for the first time

since they'd heard the news. The grimness of it all just kept washing over her. But while her heart was wrung with sorrow for her sister, Josie was beginning to scare her.

"She still won't leave her room under any circumstances, and she's taken nothing in days but water and a bite of toast I made her swallow. She just turns away when I come in to see her."

Maria nodded grimly. "She looks awful. Haunted. The frozen way she lies there, with that empty look in her eyes." She shook her head. "She's going to waste away or fall ill if she keeps this up."

Edwina wished for the hundredth time that none of this were happening. Josie had always been such a resilient person. She was the optimistic one of the two of them. For Edwina, filling the role of someone who might give another hope was as foreign as it would once have been for Josie to lie in bed all day with a dull look in her eyes. She knew her sister was terribly sad, but this seemed like something more, as though there were some particular force behind her grief.

"Maybe we should send for Colin," she said. "Perhaps they have grown a bit apart in London, but they were always so close before, and he shared her deep affection for Nicholas."

Maria agreed, and they dispatched a note to the earl.

# Twelve

IT HAD BEEN ONLY A WEEK SINCE THE NEWS OF Nick's death, and already Colin had been drawn back into the rhythm of life. The needs of his estates and his staff couldn't be neglected. There'd been a fire that had spread to several of the buildings at his estate in Yorkshire, and he'd needed to consider the best way to rebuild. And then the board of governors for the soldiers' hospital he and Hal were establishing had had to meet to make necessary decisions.

Too, his body had recovered its drives for food and activity, though he cared nothing for what he put in it to make it function. Even though he'd known Nick was in constant danger as a soldier at war, somehow he hadn't expected anything to happen to him. Nick had been canny and agile and strong, a golden boy who always came out on top with a grin. It hadn't seemed possible all that might be extinguished.

He thought of his friend all the time. The way they'd always teased each other, their middle of the night philosophical debates at university, the months

MISCHIEF BY MOONLIGHT 161

of travel together in their early twenties. Nick had been the brother Colin never had, though he'd never told his friend as much.

As he sat at his library desk in the early evening, forcing his mind to focus on St. Bede's *Ecclesiastical History of the English People*, a knock sounded at the door. His butler entered with a note from Maria.

It said that she and Edwina were worried about Josie. Her spirits were very low, she wasn't eating, and she was refusing to leave her bedchamber. They thought a visit from him might help her.

He put the note down, the news of her anguish twisting his gut. She was obviously terribly depressed about Nick's death, and no one could understand that better than he could.

He didn't want to go. He'd broken with her. And he didn't think he could bear to see her now, with both of them so raw with pain. He needed to stay in his house, detached and apart. Solitude had always been his answer to the storms of life. He craved nothingness and detachment.

But for once it was eluding him, and what he had was sorrow and bitter regret. They would be his companions whether he was in his study alone or out in the world. Seeing Josie would only turn the knife of remorse and pain in him, but he couldn't refuse to help her if she needed him.

He pulled on the coat hanging on the back of his chair, uncaring that it was a shabby old brown one he kept for poking through dusty volumes, and left.

Edwina met him at the door to Maria's town house with an anxious expression. Her eyebrows drew together slightly at the sight of his dusty coat and early evening stubble, but she made no comment.

"Ivorwood, I'm so glad you've come. We just now managed to get Josie to leave her chamber, and I think it was only because she knew you might be coming. Perhaps if you could convince her to take a walk, it would bring her back to herself a little."

Edwina took him to Maria's small but elegant sitting room, where Josie sat in a gilt chair by the marble fireplace. She was wearing black, which only emphasized the unhealthy paleness of her face. Her playful, short coiffure had grown out, and the curls sagged loosely against cheekbones grown too prominent. Deep smudges under her eyes contributed to her hollowed-out look.

"Josie," he said softly as he came into the room, not wanting to startle her. She was staring at the empty hearth and didn't look at him as he moved closer. He'd spoken so bluntly to her weeks ago, when he'd insisted they could no longer be friends. But the reason for that—her engagement to Nick—had been removed, and now he didn't know what they had.

The sight of her struck at the rawness in him and prodded that barely quieted need for her life. He wished violently that he could do something for her, anything to relieve the pain that must be crushing her.

"I've come to see if you'd like to take a walk. It's quite nice out just now, with the early evening cool settling in, and we ought not to forget how we need a little fresh air every day."

He sounded like an idiot. But seeing her like this, he knew Edwina and Maria were right to be worried.

She didn't respond to his words or even seem to care that he was there. As awkward moments passed, he thought he must go and leave her in peace, no matter how it pained him that he could be no comfort to her. But then, without looking at him, she spoke.

"Will you please take me for a carriage ride, Colin? Just the two of us?"

He glanced at Maria. It would be improper, but he was a very respectable earl, and Josie was struggling with a terrible blow. No one could think anything untoward would occur at such a moment.

"Yes, why don't you?" Maria said. "Some fresh air would be just the thing."

Colin handed Josie into his carriage and sat across from her. The heat of the summer day had broken and the orange sun was already sinking below the housetops of Mayfair. He told the driver to take them toward the outskirts of town, thinking the peace of a quieter setting might cheer her after the weeks in London.

They sat in silence for some time while the carriage bore them along. A lovely three-quarter moon was rising, and he tracked its progress through the window on his side. He lifted a hand and gestured at it, hoping the heavenly sight would comfort her somehow. But she only turned her face to the view for a moment and let her eyes slide away.

He had a sudden memory of walking through the Cardworthys' back garden that night he'd done his unexpected howling at the moon. What a long time ago that now seemed, before Nick had been lost and so much had passed between Colin and Josie.

He thought perhaps the two of them wouldn't speak at all now, and that was probably for the best. Her wordless presence comforted him, though, as nothing had in the last week.

But then she surprised him by speaking. "Thank you for coming." Her voice was hoarse, as if from disuse. "Though perhaps you did not want to."

He knew his need to end their friendship, however necessary, had hurt her. "I wanted to come. I...have never stopped caring."

She closed her eyes, as though absorbing his words. "You're the only one who understands."

"Anyone would understand. The man who was to be your husband is gone."

When she opened her eyes, he was struck with the flatness in them, which matched the dullness in her voice. He felt a spurt of anger that death had done this to her.

"But you *knew* him," she said.

"Yes." He looked away. She was twisting him up inside, making him feel awful. Nick had been a fine man, but he'd been no saint. In some ways, Josie hadn't really known him very well—how could she have, after only six weeks?

Certainly, as a woman she'd known him in ways Colin never could have. But she didn't know about that French spy, for one thing, and how he'd been tempted by her. Josie loved Nick, loved his memory, and she could never know that, under the terrible pressure of war, Nick might have strayed.

He was startled when she reached across the carriage and took his hand. He felt he would do anything to relieve the bleakness in her eyes.

The carriage hit a rut and jerked them, but her urgent grip didn't slacken.

"I am so angry," she said in a ragged voice and squeezed his hand hard. "What is wrong with me that I have lost my fiancé and I feel so angry? I can't even feel sadness."

"You are overwhelmed. It's too much that you are feeling, not a lack of feeling. Really, anger ought to be the most natural reaction to death, our deep cry to the universe that demands to know why the hell this has to happen at all."

He'd meant to shock her a bit with the rough language, because for all she said she was angry, the frozen way she looked was scaring him, and he'd thought to startle her out of it. But she seemed not to have noticed.

"There is no excusing it." She hung her head. "I'm a terrible person."

"Stop this!" he said forcefully, giving her arm a shake. Their hands fell apart. "Stop being so hard on yourself. You are grieving, and grief is wild, it is its own beast. When you care about someone who dies, that love pulls you a little way across the divide between life and death. Grief turns everything you know upside down."

She absorbed his words but then closed her eyes and pushed a hand roughly through her hair, unconsciously giving herself a wild look as the curls stuck out here and there. Even in her sorrow, she was beautiful.

"But that's just it," she said in a bitter voice. "I had serious doubts. I don't even know if I really loved him! I don't *know*!"

Colin stared as her words penetrated his mind. Had she not been in love with Nick after all? Could it be?

*No.* This was not the time for such thoughts. Surely, with the memory of Nick between them, it never would be.

But he couldn't bear to see her in despair. Before he realized what he was doing, he'd reached across the carriage and taken her hand back, and he held it lightly. It was fairly dark in the carriage now, with only the moon to light them, and perhaps that made it easier to touch her, as though right now they weren't part of the everyday world. He wanted her not to feel she was alone.

"Josie, you two were apart for more than a year. Anyone would have had doubts." He forced himself to say what was right. "It's a shame you didn't have more time together before he had to leave."

"But he deserved better from me."

He'd deserved better from Colin, too, than a best friend who'd wanted to take his fiancée into his arms. But things were more complicated than Josie knew.

"Who's to say he didn't have doubts as well?" he said. "We are all only human."

His words seemed to have some profound effect on her. She gazed at him and slowly lifted her hand, taking his with it, and pressed the back of his hand to her cheek. She inhaled a shuddering breath. A tear seeped onto his forefinger.

Her anguish pierced him, and he turned his hand and cupped her cheek, wiping her tears with the pad of his thumb.

"Oh, Colin," she said in a ragged voice. "I need you so."

With those four little words, a barrier within him suffered a crack.

*She needed him.*

He allowed himself to consider—to truly entertain for the first time—that she might have come to care for him. That the kiss at the ball and what he'd read in her eyes at the garden meant something after all. Did he dare hope?

*Stop this!* How could he even be thinking such thoughts, and at such a time? What she needed from him right now was comfort, and that was all. He could offer her the comfort that a brother would share. Human comfort.

He moved across the space between the facing seats and sat next to her, and it felt like the most natural thing in the world to pull her into his arms in an embrace meant to share her burden of grief.

She wrapped her arms around his torso and squeezed him tightly, burying her face against his neck. His heart pounding, he kissed her forehead lightly in what he told himself was brotherly affection, though he knew he was treading on shaky ground.

She tipped her head back and sought his lips.

The crack in the wall of his restraint split into a deep fissure. Her soft lips rubbed against his as they had once before, at the ball. But now everything was different.

He gave in to his need for her and took over the kiss, licking along the seam of her mouth. She let him in.

And then things went a little wild. They fell on one another as though each was the only rock for miles in a savage sea. He pulled her so she sat sideways across his thighs. Devouring mouths, pulling at necklines, grabbing the tops of shoulders, their hands scrabbled over each other, shaping arms, shooting up along backs.

But this was the wrong moment for what was between them, and their touching was too fast, too wild. The tenderness and awe he felt for her were being pushed aside by desperate urges. And she was like a wild thing, undone by grief, surely, even if it was mingled with desire.

She ripped at his cravat, her hands tugging it and working inefficiently until she finally loosened it and pushed it aside and buried her face in the crook of his neck. A sob broke from her and forced him to full acknowledgment of what they were doing in a carriage rolling through London.

"Josie," he said hoarsely, trying gently to pull away.

"No!" she said in an urgent, hoarse whisper, and her hands clenched his lapels. "Don't you dare stop."

He should put a stop to what they were doing, of course he should. She was clearly in a desperate state, and he was not much better. Right, yes, he would stop—in a minute. It was just that she seemed to so want what they were doing, and wanting didn't even begin to explain his need to touch her more.

But after all the months of yearning just to be able to touch her sleeve, never mind her actual skin, he wanted to savor what they were doing, while she seemed to be in a tremendous rush.

She shifted so the side of her sweet rump came against his nearly painful erection, and he groaned. "Josie, slow down."

"I know," she said, her words like wisps. Arresting

the urgency of her motion, she lifted a trembling hand and slowly feathered her fingertips across his jaw and trailed them over his lips.

This would be enough, he told himself. Just having her touch him like this, with affection and desire, was more than he ever thought he'd have.

She lingered on his mouth, tracing over the shape of his lips, and his heart whispered a wordless prayer of gratitude. He kissed her fingertips, and she leaned forward and replaced them with her mouth. Curious, daring, sweet Josie—she could have no idea how violently she was fanning the lust that had been boiling in him for so long.

*This* would be enough, this kiss—in a minute he would gently break their embrace and they would go back to sitting appropriately and return to Maria's as soon as possible.

But she swirled her tongue against his with a quiver of eager experimentation, and rockets of desire shot through him, pushing aside his good intentions. They could kiss more…what harm would it be?

They kissed and kissed, their breathing growing loud in the small space, though not loud enough to rise above the thump of the carriage wheels rolling over a rough road. They would be near the outskirts of London.

Colin reached out and jerked the curtain across the little window, shutting out the moonlight. It was instantly black in the carriage, though an insistent sliver of light still found its way past the edge of the curtain, as though intent on accompanying them. John Coachman would keep driving until Colin said stop, which he wanted to be never.

She worked at the collar of his shirt. "I need to feel more of your skin," she whispered.

Need...she was killing him.

"Could you...take off your shirt please?"

He made a choking sound. "My shirt?"

"I've never seen a man's bare chest."

"You won't see it now. It's too dark." He lifted a shaking hand to shape the curve of her waist, and she leaned into his hand. He explored upward until he met the soft give of her breast. His blood thundered, the lust roiling in him yelling *This! This! This!* while his better nature shouted *Stop!*

"I have to feel you," she insisted, working at his shirt until it was spread wide and her hands were on the bare skin of his chest.

Her desire and her touch unleashed him, and he began undoing the buttons on the back of her frock, barely registering when his clumsy fingers sent a button flying loose to hit his boot. The small, useful muscles of her bare back fascinated him, and he stroked them over and over, unable to get enough of her.

Oh yes, he wanted what they were doing. And *she* wanted it. In the back of his mind the specter of marriage loomed like permission, and he pushed her chemise wide over her shoulders and freed her breasts. His trembling hands moved deliriously over the silky skin. He rubbed the tips with his thumbs, wonder and lust filling him equally, and she arched into his hands.

With a sigh that came from the depths of his being, he buried his face against her breasts as she clutched him to her. A whimper of pleasure escaped her.

*She wanted him.* Something in him sang out even as

the animal force of what they were doing pushed him to nudge her legs apart and lift her skirts and pull her to straddle his legs.

Her small hand moved to the fall of his trousers and began to trace the shape of his erection with gentle curiosity, and he fought not to explode from the yearned-for pleasure of her touch, the most exquisite torture of his life.

Josie was vaguely aware of the carriage rolling on, its motion adding to the urgency and propulsion of what they were doing, and the darkness made it something outside of everyday life, and grief, and everything she couldn't bear to think about. What they were doing was taking her out of herself, now when she so desperately needed it to.

But there was so much more to what she and Colin were doing. He was here, right here with her in this moment, and it felt like they were both discovering something new, something almost healing. Though she knew he was a man of thirty who'd been about in the world and must have experienced such things before, she didn't want to think about him being with other women. His kisses and his touch felt special, and only for her, and that was all she cared about.

How like a prayer answered it was to be in his arms, to know he needed her as she needed him. And pleasure, too, of a kind she'd never truly known, the warm, urgent uprising of desire.

He took her nipple in his mouth and teased her with his tongue and dragged his teeth lightly over the swollen skin. She clutched the sturdy width of his back, holding on to him hard as a thrilling heat raced through her. While he turned his attention to her other breast, she ran her hands over him, making herself slow down so she could trace the flatness of the muscles that lined his ribs. He made a sound like all the air had been sucked out of him as she skimmed lower, across the jutting bones of his hips.

He worked his hands up under the fabric pile of her skirts, which had mounded up between them. His fingers stroked slowly up her calves as though he didn't want to miss an inch of her skin, making her feel worshipped. When he reached her inner thighs, he stopped to linger. Did he know that she desperately wanted him to touch where she was aching for him?

"You are so soft," he said in a hushed voice.

He seemed amazed by her, as though her womanly curves and hollows were a revelation.

His fingers moved slowly along her flesh in that maddening, worshipping way, and—*there*. Slowly now, he stroked her. Everything in her shivered, attuned completely to the almost unbearably rich pleasure of his touch, and to the oneness she felt with him in that moment. Any boundaries that had ever been between them seemed to have fallen away.

"Does this please you?" he asked in a husky voice as his fingers circled and rubbed, making her limp with desire.

"Yes," she whispered, glad now it was dark because this was so intimate, and she was so open to him and vulnerable. And yet, she'd never felt more protected.

"A wonder," he murmured in a thick voice, his lips against her neck.

"Mmm?" Her voice had gone blurry.

"You. A wonder," he murmured.

Her heart seemed to tip forward then, as if straining to meet his, and she knew that what she'd shared with Nicholas had been only the barest beginning, and nothing like what she felt for Colin. Every moment in his arms only pulled her deeper.

He tugged at the ties of his breeches and the thick weight of him fell toward her. It was shocking, this strange, hidden part of him, but also fascinating. She leaned back a little and lightly touched the smooth hardness with her fingertips. He bucked, and combined with the jerky motion of the carriage, nearly pitched them off the seat.

His hand came over hers and helped her squeeze him harder than she would have guessed he'd want, but he groaned in a way that could only be pleasure. She heard the sound of teeth grinding, then he swept her hand away and pulled her closer.

"We'll get married," he murmured urgently against her ear.

Marriage…she didn't want to think about anything practical now. Hazy with passion, needing to be as close to him as she could, she wanted only what they were doing. The trust and the bond that had always been between them seemed to deepen every moment as their passion burned brighter, consoling her and making her feel more cherished than she'd ever felt in her life.

He tilted his hips, and a shudder wracked his body as they slid together.

"Oh God," he groaned. He drove into her, past the momentary resistance of her maidenhood, past propriety and restraint. With a sudden plunge, he sheathed himself fully inside her.

"I'm sorry," he gasped. "Too rough."

"I don't care," she whispered, struggling to adjust to the feel of him inside her.

She had only moments to absorb the stretching and welcome the increasingly pleasurable sensation of their joining when, with a shudder that seemed dragged out of him, he abruptly found his release.

# Thirteen

JOSIE LAY ACROSS COLIN'S CHEST, HER FACE PRESSED into the seat upholstery behind him. He was very still, as if gathering himself. Or maybe he'd even fallen asleep.

Now that the force of what they were doing had collapsed and their breathing was quieting, she was aware of the jumbling of the coach wheels turning, of the thump of the horses' hooves. It was entirely dark in the carriage; she supposed it must be getting on for ten o'clock. Edwina and Maria would be wondering where they were.

She hadn't felt the release toward which their joining had been drawing her and which had clearly had such an effect on him. But what they'd shared had been something important and deep. He'd touched her heart, and she knew she'd never be the same.

She knew now that she loved him.

Of course she did—she'd only been hiding it from herself all this time. What else could she have done, being engaged to another man, an equally worthy man?

But what she felt for Colin ran much, much deeper than what she and Nicholas had shared. She and Colin were connected at the deepest possible place. They understood each other. Wordlessly, they knew each other. *This* was what she had been reaching for. This was the reason behind her unsettled feelings.

These last months, some part of her had known that the man she'd thought of as her friend first and a man second was really her key to the mysteries of the heart.

They shouldn't have done what they'd just done—it was the wrong time and ignored the gravity and respect that grieving Nick called for, like shouting out a birthday greeting in a quiet church. It had been an impulsive thing to do, but it had still somehow been the right thing to do. This was love, finally; how could it be wrong?

He shifted beneath her cheek and she slid onto the seat with her heart melting in her chest as softly and gratefully as a pat of butter on a piece of warm toast. The ache over Nick was still there, as sad as the loss of any friend would have been, but it was bearable now because she was not alone. And because now she truly knew love.

She began to put her gown to rights, grateful for their shared silence. She could hear Colin doing up his breeches.

"I'm sorry," he said quietly. "I would have wished things had not gone as they just did."

A stiffness in his tone arrested her hands as they probed an unfastened buttonhole on the back of her gown, feeling for a button that seemed to be missing. "What do you mean?"

Yes, she was a little ashamed that she'd so easily stepped away from her grief and into his arms. But she didn't care about that right now—what she cared about was that profound connection she'd just shared with him.

Was he disappointed with what they'd done? It had ended so abruptly. Why would he not reply?

"Colin?" she said, letting all the softness she was feeling into her voice. Surely this man who knew her so well would sense what she needed to hear.

❧

Colin was struggling to gather his wits. He knew he was in danger of pulling her into his arms so they might ride in his carriage endlessly through the night, with no destination. Just the two of them, outside of time and space.

Touching Josie, making love to her, had exploded over him like an unexpected storm, though if he'd ever allowed himself to imagine a first time making love with her—and he hadn't—it wouldn't have ended with his release occurring abruptly, and before hers. He'd wanted her so badly, though, and for so long.

But now the bliss was fading, and he could no longer avoid the voice of his conscience. He scrubbed a hand roughly over his face.

"Colin?" she said softly. He could hear the yearning in her voice, and it tore at him. He'd let his emotions and his passions run away with him, when he should have held them in check. She'd been vulnerable, and he should have been strong.

He'd behaved so weakly.

He also, already, wanted another chance to make love to her, to make it far better for her than his falling-off-a-cliff climax had allowed. A million more chances, actually.

He could feel Josie's eyes on him in the darkness that had made what they'd just done more acceptable at the time. The silence was stretching out, and he knew she'd want a response. Remorse and shame washed over him more urgently each moment.

"We shouldn't have done what we just did," he said.

"I know," she said, her voice full of feeling that seemed to yearn toward him, and for a moment he entertained flinging open the carriage door and pitching himself out into the night to escape all this emotion.

"I know," she said again. "I don't quite understand how it happened. But…I'm not exactly sorry that it did."

She was going to frame this as something good, he saw, and he must not allow that.

He couldn't be at the mercy of desires. That wasn't who he was.

Maybe all this time when he'd been wanting Josie, he'd yearned for her precisely because he couldn't have her. She'd been safely engaged to Nick, and now she wasn't.

He'd thoroughly compromised her. She might even be with child already. How could he have so abandoned reason and honor?

He must atone. However much he didn't want to, he must retake the hard line he should have maintained where Josie was concerned.

"What we did was an insult to Nick's memory. We acted reprehensibly."

She drew in a breath sharply. His words had been hard, but they were true, and every moment he saw more clearly how badly he'd transgressed what he owed his friend. He stirred up anger with himself over this so he wouldn't have to think about the part of him he needed to close off to Josie.

That too-soft part told him they'd done what they had because there was a very real connection between them, which went far deeper than what had existed between Josie and Nick. That soft part of him wanted him to acknowledge that the attraction he and Josie had been hiding had pulled them together because of something incredibly important.

But he couldn't listen, because what he needed now was to take the right actions that would put things between him and Josie back on an even keel, even if they were changed.

A heavy silence had taken over the carriage, and he opened the curtain to the moonlight and pulled out a small tinderbox to light the lantern on the wall, needing it to dispel the last traces of what they'd done.

"Reprehensibly," Josie repeated in a flat voice.

"Yes." She paused, then said, "Would you ask the coachman to take us back to Maria's?"

He knocked on the roof and stuck his head out the window and gave the order.

His words had been blunt, but they had to be. Josie made him feel like someone else, a person he didn't recognize who careered around doing crazy things, and he had to be clear.

Of course, they would have to marry. He *wanted* to marry her. To be with her, to make love to her over and over. But he refused to be overwhelmed by her. He would always need to keep the deepest part of himself back.

She had withdrawn into the corner, her head turned away from him, chin up and eyes fixed on the upper corner of the carriage wall.

"Josie," he began, "you know we will have to marry now after a respectable delay."

"I know nothing of the kind."

He blinked. This was nonsensical. "Of course we have to marry. I've compromised you—" He thought she flinched at his words, but they must speak plainly. "And beyond that, you might well be increasing."

"I doubt it."

"You can't know that. It can't be determined for weeks, surely." He raked his hand through his hair, incredibly uncomfortable with this conversation. Did she have to be difficult? "Josie, you must see reason. The very fact that we've been in this carriage alone together for so long is damning."

"No one will think anything of it," she said in that new, flat voice he was starting to hate. "You're the irreproachable Earl of Ivorwood and I'm a grieving fiancée. And make no mistake, I do grieve for the loss of Nick. I couldn't be more sorry he is gone. And I agree with you that what we just did should never have happened. Starting from now, I'm going to pretend that it didn't. Barring a pregnancy, there need be no consequences from this for either of us."

The starkness of her words surprised him, but he

knew some of her sudden remove came out of hurt at how abruptly he'd spoken, how he'd focused on the mistake they'd made.

He softened his tone. "Josie, would you look at me so we can talk about this like reasonable adults? We have to get married." He paused a moment. "And the sexual encounter…it can be so much better."

She made an outraged sound. "I'm sorry if it wasn't up to your standards!"

"That's not what I meant at all. I meant better for you."

"Stop. I don't want to marry you, and I *don't* want to talk about this any more. If there are any consequences from tonight, we can talk about them when it becomes necessary. And now," she said, letting her head drop back against the squabs, "I should like to rest. I suppose you will understand that I'm quite exhausted."

And just like that, though the small space of the carriage meant they were close enough to watch each other breathe, she dismissed him.

❧

The ride back to Maria's was the longest of Josie's life. As the wheels rolled onward, their regular rumble echoed the rhythm in her head: *He didn't love her, he didn't love her.*

Thank God he'd revealed himself before she had.

She kept her head back and her eyes closed as though she were resting. She didn't much care if he thought she was asleep, or guessed she was only pretending so she didn't have to talk to him.

He was disgusted with what they'd done, evidently.

She hated that stiffness which had come into his voice, a note she'd never heard from him before.

Of course she agreed with him that they shouldn't have done what they had. She'd felt so full and changed, though, afterward, and willing to forgive them, in consideration of love. But he didn't love her, so why would he forgive?

His offer of marriage made her angry. She supposed she should be grateful that, instead of still being paralyzed with fury at herself over having been a bad fiancée, she now realized she'd had doubts about marrying Nicholas because her friendship with Colin had turned into something so unexpected and important. She could forgive herself now, a little, for the mistakes she'd made while waiting endless months for a man she'd known for six weeks to return to her.

And yes, she could forgive herself for what had just happened with Colin. It had opened her eyes, and she couldn't be sorry for the fuller knowledge of herself and life and love that it had given her.

But she was angry with him for rejecting it. For withdrawing, as he so often did. Maybe he'd felt nothing beyond the pleasures of the moment, or maybe she just wasn't enough for him, or maybe he couldn't risk his precious solitude to find out if she might be. It didn't matter why he didn't love her, but she saw how it would be between them if she did marry this man who so clearly hated unruly emotions of the kind that ran through her. She could never marry him.

"Josie?" he said quietly and touched her arm. "We're close to Maria's now. Come, we must talk."

She kept her eyes closed and didn't respond. After

a few moments, he removed his hand. She could feel his eyes on her, and childishly, that made her even angrier.

That she might become pregnant had seemed insignificant to her when she'd been caught up in the need to join herself to him. This was without doubt the most foolishly, dangerously impulsive thing she'd ever done in her life.

Perhaps if she were pregnant, she'd go away, maybe even have the baby in India. Everything was different in India, Papa had always said. Life there was rougher and wilder, and no one would know her there—she could pretend to be a widow. She could teach the children of the nabobs, and she and a baby might have the adventure of a lifetime.

But such plans were for later. For now, she just wanted to get away from him.

He didn't say anything else until the familiar sounds of other carriages and the sophisticated chatter of people strolling the streets indicated they were in Mayfair.

As the carriage slowed on its approach to Maria's house, he said, "We'll talk about this when you're feeling more the thing."

The carriage stopped, and they heard the sounds of the driver getting down. The door would open in a moment, and Colin leaned forward to get out and hand her down.

"Please don't," she said without looking at him. "And—I don't wish to see you anymore."

She felt him flinch at her words, and he reached forward as if to grab her before she got out, but the door was open and she stepped out and escaped, glad for the lights and glow of Maria's house before her. She rushed up the stairs and felt grateful for the front door closing decisively behind her.

Neither Maria nor Edwina said anything about her long absence, though she could see from the concern on their faces that they hoped she'd been helped by her outing. She managed a small smile, and when she asked if she might have a tray with a sandwich in her room, they lit up as though they'd just heard good news.

Tucked into her bed a short time later after eating a little of the sandwich and drinking some water, she lay very still, her arms at her sides as she stared up at the pretty white canopy over her. The tightness in her neck and shoulders that had been there for days had eased somewhat.

Now that her guard had relaxed, her throat swelled and she had to work a little to breathe. Fat tears pooled in her eyes and dripped down her temple, and she let them. Tears for poor Nicholas, and for her own sins, and for all the things in life that never quite worked out enough to let people be happy.

When they had dried, she slept deeply.

The next day, she returned to Jasmine House, leaving Edwina to stay with Maria.

# Fourteen

EDWINA MISSED JOSIE. LONDON WASN'T THE SAME without her, and though Josie had seemed a little improved at her departure, Edwina was still worried about her, and sad for her sister's heavy loss. She hoped Jasmine House would offer the solace that Josie so clearly needed.

And it was strange, but without Josie around to needle her about Lord Mappleton being a bad choice for a husband, Edwina was finding herself thinking about her sister's concerns, when previously she'd been so able to ignore them and focus on her goal. Well, perhaps it had been the case that because it was *Josie* who was speaking about Mappleton's appeal as a suitor, she hadn't paid attention.

*"Do you really enjoy his company so much that you wish to see him morning, noon, and night?"* Josie had probed.

Edwina really couldn't afford such thoughts. Mappleton was all she'd ever hoped for in a man, and very likely he was going to propose. He would be back in Town any day.

Then she would be free—free of the stifling

world of Jasmine House and its pinchpenny living
and, most of all, though she could never have
admitted it so baldly, free of a future as Mama's
companion. She loved her mother, but now that
she wasn't dragged down by gloom, she could admit
that she didn't want to live out a spinster's existence
caring for her.

So it would be Mappleton, if he proposed, and
no looking back. She might not think his company
scintillating, but she was confident she could control
things between them, and to ask for more than that
from marriage would be greedy. She certainly didn't
expect it would be anything as exciting as what she'd
felt with Whitby, and that was as it should be.

What had happened with him in the library had
shown her she was vulnerable to fairy-tale wishes,
to the dream of a man who would love her just for
herself, one she could love in return. But she was
a practical woman, and she knew that marriage,
as much as she'd ever seen of it, had little to do
with love. And she'd been burned enough by Mr.
Perriwell to know that she didn't dare risk her heart
with any man. A smart marriage was about power
and playing your cards right. Mappleton was going
to offer the family and future she'd been hoping for,
and he would *do*.

A knock on her bedchamber door arrested her
hands in the process of tidying a few stray hairs as she
examined her coiffure in the looking glass. She had
on one of the pretty dresses Maria had bought her, a
gown the color of bluebells that fell in long, soft lines
to swirl in a cloud around her feet.

"If you please, miss," said Letty, one of the maids, "Mr. Whitby says he's misplaced the jewel box."

Edwina ground her teeth. She'd sent Letty down to collect the box.

"Go back and tell him that I expect he'll be able to find it within an hour."

An hour later, Letty returned to tell her that the box was still missing.

"Is it, by God," Edwina muttered.

"Miss?" Letty said.

"Nothing. That will be all, thank you."

She knew what he was doing: he'd told her to come down for the box herself, and he wanted her to know she wasn't going to get it until she did.

She told herself that not doing as he'd directed was the appropriate response to a man who seemed to think he could order her around, but she knew there was more to it, that she was also having to resist the urge to see him again. She'd found herself unable to stop thinking about him, and about what would have happened if Josie hadn't come into the library.

*Something inappropriate and wrong, that's what.*

She made herself wait until the late afternoon before she went out through the garden to the carriage house, where he'd been given space to do his work. She would collect her box and make certain Jack Whitby understood that she was *not* his for the ordering about. That in fact, this was the end of any interaction between them.

The door to the carriage house was half-open, and a rasping sound was issuing from within. She paused in the doorway and poked her head a little way in.

Maria kept just the brougham; it was parked near the wooden door to the alley, which left space for Whitby and a number of pieces of furniture.

He was a few feet inside the house but facing away from her and crouching down below a high window, by whose light he was rubbing glasspaper along the leg of a chair.

The rough, light cloth of his shirt seemed just the right complement to the hard shape of his muscula- ture, which was being intermittently described by the motions of his arm. His sleeves were rolled up to the elbow, revealing a tanned forearm and a neat wrist. His hands were surprisingly elegant in a sturdy way, his fingers long and their motions deft and economical. None of which should matter to her.

"Are you coming in or not, Edwina Cardworthy?" he asked without turning around, giving her a start. She'd been so quiet—how had he known she was there? She drew herself up and spoke to his back.

"I've come for the box. If you've managed to find it, that is."

He put the glasspaper down and stood to face her, and something unruly in her rose up.

"It happens I have." His light blue eyes held a glint of mischief that, idiotically, made her want to smile. She disciplined her lips into a line and lifted her chin.

"Why, what a surprise." She remained in the doorway and held out her hand to indicate she would collect the box and be done with him.

He refused to look at her hand. "Come in. I'll get it."

"I'll wait here."

The corner of his mouth inched up, provoking her. She let her hand drop exasperatedly. "Do finally tell me what it is, Whitby, that you find so perpetually amusing about me."

"Well, you *are* funny. It's the way you seem so stiff."

He moved closer, and a whiff of his scent came to her; the clean scent of wood shavings, for goodness' sake, was giving her a thrill. But it was familiar now, and it whispered of closeness and excitement. "You're wound up tight as a spring, when if you'd only smile, the world would fall at your feet. But you won't smile. You can't let your guard down."

What did he mean, *the world would fall at her feet*? Did *he* want to fall at her feet?

No, she didn't care what he wanted. Nor would she think about how he might *unwind* her.

He was closer now—she didn't know when that had happened—and she had to tip her head back a bit to see him.

"I have no idea what you are talking about," she said, horrified by the wayward huskiness that had crept into her voice. And the awareness that she desperately wanted him to kiss her again. Hadn't she been wanting his kiss all the time she'd been waiting to come down here? Hadn't the awareness of how much she'd been thinking of Whitby been the main reason she'd sent Letty first?

He crossed his arms and leaned his shoulder against the brick wall near the door, and a mocking glint came into his eyes. He had such an assured quality about him, as though nothing would ever set him off balance.

She told herself it was only to move away from him—she certainly wasn't going to *run* away—that she pushed the door wider and entered the carriage house, mustering her most queenly demeanor. A bee came in with her and buzzed lazily about the sunlit and shadowy spaces in the quiet room.

With the brougham to one side, he'd set up a number of pieces of furniture. There were two more chairs like the one he'd just been working on, plus a small round table upended onto its top. Beyond these, against the wall and near the brougham, was a singular piece that caught her attention.

She moved closer, drawn by its exquisite lines. "Oh. It's beautiful."

It was a trim, delicate desk, just the size that a woman might like for writing letters. The modest top was large enough for someone to spread her things out a bit, and she envisioned an inkwell and a few sheets of paper and perhaps a bud vase neatly arranged. The wood was a rich, many-hued honey color, simple but not plain, and on each side a single, sturdy leg decorated with carved leaves descended toward a footed bar that elegantly held the desk's weight.

"Mrs. Westin commissioned it," he said from behind her, "and I'm just putting on the finishing touches."

"The wood is so rich-looking. Is it something unusual?"

"Oak. Strong and solid."

But it looked elegant, artful. "I didn't know oak could look so rich."

"If it's in the right hands…"

"Did you design this?"

"I do all my own designs."

She acknowledged then what she hadn't wanted to consider: how much of an artist he was, an artist in wood. He made beautiful things—items of lasting worth—for clients like Maria Westin who could appreciate his work. Very likely one would have to be as wealthy as Maria to afford it.

He was socially beneath her, but he deserved to be proud of what he contributed to the world: beautiful, useful objects. And he was. She envied Jack Whitby his pride. He knew his own worth, and he would never let anyone convince him it was less than excellent. What would her life have been like if she'd believed in herself as deeply?

She saw now that all her life she'd engaged in a sort of reverse pride, believing that the only appealing thing about her was her looks. What if she could allow that there was much more to her of value, aspects that might even deserve respect and approval?

Those aspects might not be her recently acquired talents for charming the fashionable people of London; she wasn't *really* carefree and lighthearted. But maybe that didn't mean she was lacking—just different.

What if she, like Whitby, looked for and honored what was good in herself instead of always focusing on things not to like? She could celebrate the good qualities she had. Like loyalty; her family might aggravate her interminably, but she would always love them. Also, intelligence; she could solve complicated mathematical problems and appreciated books of all kinds, and she was capable enough to oversee the Cardworthys' finances. And she was very, very good with a needle and thread.

Accepting herself, she suddenly saw, could be a choice. So simple, and yet a revelation.

If only it hadn't been the wrong man who'd helped her see it. They couldn't be anything to each other, yet he did something to her. And she needed to know, truly, how much she affected him.

She turned to face him. "Why do you tease me? Why did you kiss me in the library?"

"Can you not guess?" He laughed softly, but there was something deep in his eyes. "You captivate me. Like a fine piece of oak, I suspect you've so many layers to you that a man could never uncover them all. You're like infinity."

A burst of happiness sped through her. She wanted to rush into his arms.

But this man was not from her world. She *must* not allow herself to trust him.

"You compare a woman to a piece of wood," she said, forcing disdain into her voice, needing to remind them both of the distance that must exist between them. "A gentleman would never do such a thing."

He crossed his arms. "And there are many other things gentlemen do that I would not. I'd never beget a bastard, for one thing."

She blinked at the bluntness of his words.

"There, see? My frankness didn't send you into a swoon. Do you know, Edwina, I once cared for a young woman who was fragile. I had to watch what I said all the time or she'd collapse in tears, and I eventually became glad I'd never been tempted by marriage. Many women are so sensitive that a man could never disagree with them properly. They sulk and fuss, or crumble to pieces. But you're not fragile, and you don't mind offending people if you disagree with them. I like that about you."

"You like me because I'm difficult?"

"I like your spirit."

She blinked. "You think I have spirit?"

"Of course you do. You speak your mind, and you care about what's right. You could have married years ago, but you never met the right man, did you?"

It scared her that he seemed to know so much about her. She straightened her spine, needing to arm herself so he didn't cozen her. "You're wrong. Any number of men in London understand my value and wish to treat me accordingly."

"You may think you want to be put on a pedestal and admired. But I'd never do that to you. You're a woman to hold and touch and kiss. A woman to talk with and fight with and make love with."

She sucked in a breath. His words showed her something completely new. They moved her. Her lips burned, yearning desperately for him to move closer and complete that in her which needed him so much. She struggled against it.

"I don't know what made me stand here listening to the words of a carpenter," she said in a voice that should have been sharp, but it came out husky.

He looked at her steadily for long moments, so that she wanted to squirm under his gaze, but she held firm. Finally, as if coming to some decision, he said, "You're right. Forget what I said. No one would ever say we might be together."

"It would be wrong," she said.

But suddenly she hated him a little for starting all this, for teasing her and kissing her and ignoring the prickly shield she kept raised, for speaking words that made her believe she was special. In his arrogance, he'd stepped across the societal divide between them and done things that had made her want him more, and now, suddenly, *she* wanted that power.

The power to initiate and to stop. The power to leave him helpless with yearning, the way he'd left her.

Her eyes fixed on his, she took a step closer to him, and he backed up a little between the brougham and the wall.

She only had time to see his brow furrow before she crushed her lips against his. With a gasp of surprise, he opened to her, and his tongue met hers.

Heaven.

She lifted shaking hands to touch the sides of his chest, the taut muscles telling of heavy lifting and hard pushing of tools against wood, of work. He growled as her hands moved up over the wideness of his rib cage, and it struck her as an animal sound. That was what he made her feel: animal urges, the wants of a creature for touching and rubbing.

But he was leaning away from her. "We can't. It's too risky, and you don't want this."

"Don't tell me what I want," she said and kissed him again.

He inhaled sharply, as if he were caught in some way, but he seemed to accept what she was doing, because he pushed his hands up along the curves of her waist and groaned in pleasure.

She shouldn't be in here with him, shouldn't be doing this, but she wanted him almost desperately. She'd forgotten the anger that had pushed her to pursue this, because beneath it was something in her that had lifted up so gratefully when he'd said all those things to her. He understood her. And she needed him in some fierce way she didn't comprehend.

Surely she could allow herself a moment of indulgence in this incredible pleasure?

He kissed her back with gentle thoroughness and slid his hands over her shoulders and up the bare skin of her neck with a slowness that told her she had all his attention. His touch made her shiver, and she wrapped her arms snugly around his back, knowing she was letting him see too much about her, but helpless to stop.

He leaned into her, and she reveled in the press of his hard body against hers. The unwelcome thought flitted through her mind that he might be a skilled seducer, that he might know just what to say to bring women like her into his arms. Aging women like her who, after years of neglect, were vulnerable to male attention. Maybe what he was doing with her was something in which he indulged all the time. He was handsome and irresistibly virile.

She concentrated on the feeling of his mouth as he dragged it along her jaw.

"You surprise me," he murmured hoarsely.

She was surprising herself. She slid her hands up his back and along his shoulders and over the outsides of his arms and squeezed his bulky muscles.

"Hush and kiss me."

He moved his mouth lower to press moistly against

her clavicle, and she gave a little hum. Then he was inching the scooped neckline of her gown lower. "It's not good for you to always get what you want."

As if *that* was what happened all the time.

But she did want something now, and badly. She wanted more of him, a deeper experience of his body. She grasped his shirt and tugged it upward, her movements clumsy, unaccustomed.

Not all her sense had fled, and it shouted in outrage at her. *Stop this!* But she didn't want to. It felt too good, and who was to know? He wasn't from her social circle—it was like something with no cost or consequences.

*No it's not!*

But she gave sense and decorum the cut direct and shoved her hands up under his now-loose shirt and shocked herself when she moaned at the feel of his hot skin over the work-hardened muscles of his back.

He groaned, his mouth still pressed against the upper curve of her breast. She slid her hands to his front to explore the hard, curving architecture of his chest.

"We have to stop," he ground out, though she could feel his torso shivering under her touch. He moved his mouth up to rest against the place where her shoulder met her neck. "Are you mad?" he asked more softly.

Yes, she was mad, clearly out of her mind. "I don't care."

"You will." He took hold of her arms and gently but firmly pulled them out of his shirt and quickly pushed the loose fabric back into his trousers.

"Your bodice," he said, gesturing with his chin

to the place where he'd tugged it lower to expose the outer edge of the puckered, rosy skin around her nipple. When she didn't move, he pulled it into place. His eyes, normally the color of an icy mountain stream, had turned a dark, stormy blue, and the grim set of his mouth told her it was costing him something to stop what they were doing.

Still, how could he stop so suddenly, how could he sweep her up beyond the bounds of sense and propriety and then simply stop? She stepped closer and pressed her chest against his, as though she could push him to say how much she affected him.

"I thought you found me so…captivating, wasn't it?"

He looked down at her. "I do. But you don't want a future with a cabinetmaker, and I won't be your plaything."

His words were like fuel to the fire burning in her, and she pushed more fully against him and lifted up on her toes, dragging her body along his, and brushed her lips against his.

But he'd frozen, and he was trying hard to push her away even as she became aware of the rustle of footsteps on the stones outside the house. She was just moving away as someone stepped into the room.

Cook was standing there in her apron with a plate of biscuits in her hand and her mouth hanging open. The space behind the brougham might have felt like shelter, but clearly she had seen enough.

Oh, dear God, Edwina thought as the full horror of what she'd just done came crashing over her. Caught *twice*, kissing Whitby, but this mattered in a way that Josie coming upon them hadn't.

*What had she done?*

"What in heaven's name," Cook said in a voice like thunder, "do you think you are doing, Jack Whitby? Get away from Miss Cardworthy, you filthy ox."

He had already moved away from her, toward the chairs by the window, but Edwina didn't look to see his face. She couldn't.

Cook came forward and put an arm around her. "Are you all right, miss? Are you hurt? What ever were you doing out here?"

"No, of course I'm not hurt," Edwina said, ignoring Cook's last question. She felt as though she were far away from the room, as if this moment turned suddenly disastrous were happening to someone else.

Kissing a man in public—and a man who worked with his hands. What on earth had she been doing? Did she want to ruin her life? She'd never find a suitable husband if this became known. Mappleton would certainly be done with her.

Cook was still talking, though Edwina could hardly focus on the words.

"It'll be the sack for you, Jack Whitby, and no mistake," Cook said in a hard voice. "You'll never work among the quality again, I can tell you that. Mauling a lady! You deceived me well—I thought you were a decent man."

Edwina wanted to shout that Cook was wrong, that Jack Whitby *was* a decent man. A very good man. But she couldn't say the words.

Jack had said nothing as yet, and now, finally, Edwina looked at him. He was watching her. Waiting, she imagined, for her to say something to mitigate the damage that would accrue to him and his livelihood. Perhaps to admit she'd been the one to initiate the embrace.

Cook talked on, promising doom for Jack, and still he said nothing.

"Cook," Edwina interrupted, forcing herself to speak, "it would be best if this were simply forgotten. It wasn't what you think…just an accident of proximity."

The older woman's eyes widened as this suggestion. "Don't you be thinking you have to defend this scoundrel, Miss Cardworthy. I know what I saw! He was being familiar with you, forgetting his place," she said, pointing at Jack as though he were some kind of rat. His mouth was set, and he didn't so much as blink as he stood there.

Edwina wanted him to speak, to come up with something, anything to deflect blame from both of them, something that would lift this burden of disaster. For she could see that Cook was going to make as much outraged noise as possible, and the more Edwina spoke against what she said, the more she would draw questions about her own behavior.

He was being unbearably noble, this man who wasn't even a gentleman.

"Please lower your voice," Edwina said as she heard muffled sounds on the bricks outside, as though someone were out there listening. "No one will benefit from this incident being made public. If you will refrain from speaking of it, no one need know."

Cook fixed a piercing eye on Edwina and drew herself up. "And leave him to tamper with the maids and anyone else? Certainly not. The housekeeper will hear about this outrage directly. And the mistress, too, I'm sure."

Before Edwina could utter one word more, Cook turned away and marched out of the carriage house like a woman on a mission. Edwina considered running after her—but what could she say in the face of so much determination?

She could feel Jack's eyes on her and she turned to face him. "I'm sorry," she said, inadequately.

"There's no need. She's right. I had no business kissing you."

He was being generous. If she hadn't insisted on kissing him that last time, they wouldn't be in this mess. But she couldn't admit this to him. "Um…"

He turned away from her and began to gather his tools. "You'd best leave if you don't want to be part of another scene," he said in a remarkably even voice considering the way he'd been insulted by Cook and the likelihood that he was about to be thrown out on his ear. "My guess is the housekeeper will be here in a matter of moments."

"I…" she said feebly, watching him put a hammer and a couple of files into a box, but he didn't stop or turn, and she had the sense that he was already done with her.

She turned away and went back through the sunny garden. She stopped in the upstairs corridor to look out the window that gave onto the mews, waiting for the reaction to what she'd so stupidly helped set in motion.

Sure enough, fifteen minutes later, Jack Whitby emerged from the carriage house, a hat on his head, shoulders straight as the square lines of the toolbox in his hand. He set off down the street. She wondered how fast the gossip about her would fly.

# *Fifteen*

JOSIE WAS GLAD TO BE BACK AT JASMINE HOUSE. SHE was still sad that Nicholas was gone, and wrung out from what had happened with Colin, but she wasn't numb anymore. She could eat and talk to people and just keep going, even if she did so with a heavy heart.

Her courses had arrived three days after she returned home, releasing her at least from that worry. But the fantasy of going to India had taken hold, and she held on to it as a possible future for herself. It would be an adventure, an idea to entertain her when she felt like herself again, however fanciful it seemed that she would be able to do it.

As the days passed, she had to acknowledge that, though she was still angry with Colin, she also yearned to hear something from him. She wanted him to send her a letter, to come back to Greenbrier and rush over to Jasmine House and say he'd been wrong and he loved her. She so hoped for even the tiniest of signs he was thinking of her.

But there was nothing.

Clearly he wanted to put all that had happened

between them behind him. He would go back to his books and be grateful for the detachment from life they offered.

She reminded herself that she'd bluntly rejected his offer of marriage, which would hardly encourage him to woo her. But she'd rejected it because it had been made out of duty and perhaps affection, but not love.

She had far more than affection for him. She needed Colin because she loved him. But sufficient unto himself as he'd always been, he didn't *need* her, and he certainly didn't love her.

She wished his home weren't so near; she could see part of it from her bedchamber window. Nestled prettily on a slight incline amid its handsome grounds, the hall was cozily if grandly framed by towers at each of its four corners. With its pale stone and its air of timeless quietude, Greenbrier, despite its magnificence, had always seemed friendly. Now it felt foreign, as though it had secrets she knew nothing about.

Days at Jasmine House fell into their customary routine. Josie's brothers still ran about shouting and wrestling with each other, trailed by their long-suffering tutor. Though Lawrence did seem to be cultivating finer manners and was suddenly interested in spending time in the village on market days.

Mrs. Cardworthy still lay draped across the divan all day with her pile of novels.

Having been away from Jasmine House for so long, Josie had a new perspective, and it struck her that the sitting room, with the Indian touches she'd always liked, now seemed to bear her father's stamp. Every time she thought of the hurtful things he'd said to

Edwina, it made her angry, and she thought that, four years after his death, it was time to put the past behind them and start a new era. But her mother wouldn't hear of changing anything.

"I like these things," she'd said when Josie suggested new furnishings. "They remind me of happier times."

"Truly?" Josie had said, trying not to sound incredulous. She would never have described her parents' marriage so enthusiastically. "Or perhaps you like them simply because they are familiar," she'd said gently, but her mother had looked away, signaling that the discussion was over.

Mrs. Cardworthy had been kind since Josie's return, but her compassion also came with a restrained, rueful smile that said, *Isn't this the way life always works out, anyway? And isn't it better not to put oneself out there in the world?*

At the end of Josie's first week back, Mama began to make requests. Could Josie read to her, as her eyes were tired? Though not too tired, Josie noticed, to do tatting while Josie was reading to her.

Would Josie go tell Cook that she'd changed her mind about the dinner menu?

Would Josie fetch her a shawl?

It was the old familiar pattern: Mama wanted someone nearby to dance attendance on her, and as the boys would never be expected to be that someone and Jasmine House was perpetually short of the amount of servants really needed, that left her daughters. Now *daughter*, since Edwina was still in London.

Josie began to wish quite violently that her mother would stop behaving like an invalid, but all gentle suggestions toward that end were dismissed. She tried the inducement of nature: There was the most beautiful patch of lilies of the valley at the far end of the garden, and didn't Mama want to see them? Her mother had Josie cut the flowers and bring them inside. The suggestion of a brief walk to see a family of ducklings that had taken up residence by the front gate brought only chuckles, followed by the request that Josie pay the chandler's bill and go through the accounts for the last month.

This last activity set Josie's teeth on edge, revealing as it did that there was a veritable mountain of money available to the Cardworthys, certainly enough to pay for more servants so the ones they had needn't work quite so hard. But when Josie brought the books to the divan to point this out to her mother, Mrs. Cardworthy had said, "That's money put by, in case anything happens. We dare not spend it."

"But it's an enormous sum! We'd barely touch it if we added another maid and another gardener. Rickett is getting quite old and really can't manage everything."

"Absolutely not. It isn't wise not to plan for the future."

"But what about now?"

Mrs. Cardworthy gave her a dismissive look. "You only say that because you're young and you think everything will work out well."

"No I don't! I lost my fiancé three weeks ago."

"I know, dear," her mother said, patting her arm. "There, you see how it is? So many things don't work out after all. Most, really. It's best in life to be content with what one has. Hand me the biscuits, dear."

Josie had finally, with quiet fury, spoken her mind.

"Mama, you have to get off the sofa and see to things for yourself. Get up and live! I'm not deliriously happy either, but I'm not just sitting in my room."

Mrs. Cardworthy's lips drew together and she blinked several times, as though tears were threatening. "You are so hard," she'd said stiffly. "You have no idea what it's like to be a fifty-two-year-old widow."

"No, I haven't, but I don't see why it means you have to stay on this divan. Be practical, Mama. If you don't get up soon, your body is going to turn to soup and you won't be able to use it at all for things like climbing stairs."

Mrs. Cardworthy's face had crumpled. As this happened any time someone tried to urge her off the sofa, Josie didn't even scold herself for the hardness she felt.

"I *can't* leave the divan. You of all people, after losing Nicholas—you of all people should understand that I need to rest. You know Dr. Denton said I was to rest."

"Papa died four years ago!"

But Mrs. Cardworthy had just turned away, lower lip quivering, and faced the back of the divan. She then spent the whole afternoon and evening ringing for the servants to bring her tea, and her elixir, and more tea, and toast, and generally kept them dancing such attendance on her that dinner was late. Though not her own, which she took on a tray on the divan as usual. Afterward she announced she would retire for the night.

When Josie offered her assistance with going up the stairs, Mama said in an injured tone, "No, thank you. I will not trouble you. Sally shall help me."

Josie had sighed. "Mama, I only spoke for your own good. Surely you see that you can't spend your life on a divan like some character in an old fairy tale?"

Mrs. Cardworthy had tipped her chin up. "It's all right for you, Josephine. You've got all that youthful energy, but soon you'll see that life closes doors on you and narrows your prospects, and you'll understand that one must cope in whatever way one can."

And she'd trudged upstairs, leaning heavily on poor Sally.

The next day, as if bestowing favors, Mrs. Cardworthy had demanded more than ever from Josie, who complied and kept her mouth shut.

The only spot of hope Josie felt at all was for Edwina, and she watched each day for the post, hoping to hear news of her sister's engagement. She began to appreciate better Edwina's wish to marry Mappleton.

A letter finally arrived one afternoon, but the astonishing news it brought was decidedly not happy.

*Dearest Josie,*

*I write to tell you about my troubles before you hear of them from anyone else.*

*The plain fact of it is that I was caught kissing Jack Whitby by Maria's cook. Of course it's a scandal. It was blamed on him not knowing his place, but I'm considered damaged goods now and no one wants to know me.*

*I'm so ashamed. That I should so far forget myself twice…that I should be so strangely drawn to him. I cannot explain it. I know it is wrong, and that there is—there can be—nothing between us. He is not a gentleman. And yet, I will tell you that he is an honorable man, and so different from anything I have expected.*

*This disastrous kiss has provided the worst sort of fascinating gossip because it happened below-stairs, and without the direct witness from someone in accepted social circles, it is considered believable but unproven. But it's enough to make invitations dry up. And though I know Mappleton is back in Town, he has not come over to ask me that question he wanted to ask.*

*I've ruined so many things, not least our family's good name, and I'm so very sorry. Can you forgive me?*

Here the ink was blotched, as though a drop of something had fallen on it, like a tear.

Her sister sounded so different. Humble and unsure of herself, but also more open.

Josie's heart twisted for her. She was astonished that Edwina had kissed Whitby again, but now there could be no denying that he'd made a significant impression on her. Edwina sounded as though she admired the cabinetmaker, which astonished Josie, especially considering the qualities Edwina had sought in a husband. Did she love Whitby? Josie could hardly judge her if she did.

She took up the letter again.

*Maria insists I must stay here though it is painful, because if I return home now it will look like running away and make me appear guilty. So I go about with my head held high, walking with*

*Maria in Hyde Park, though no one will talk to
us. Maria is very brave, though I don't think she
really cares what other people think, which I have
come to admire.*

*I have made such a mess of things.*

Josie felt immediately that she ought to go to
Edwina. But Mama, when Josie discreetly divulged
the news, disagreed.

"She was so eager to get away from home," Mrs.
Cardworthy said with a whiff of triumph. "Let her see
what it is like now."

"Mama! That is so hard. You must let me go to
her."

"Josie, you know I cannot spare you. And how
would it look, anyway, with you having just lost
Nicholas, rushing all about? No, you had better stay
here, and write to Edwina that she must come home
as soon as possible."

"But Mama, if she cannot repair her reputation,
what will our neighbors think?"

Her mother waved a careless hand. "Oh, the locals.
Who needs them?"

Josie bit back anything else she might have said.
What was the use? She sent the most encouraging
letter she could draft to Edwina, and said a fervent
if unrealistic prayer that this disaster might somehow
be undone.

❧

The church of St. Stephen near Winnetfield was
ancient and crumbling. Set away from the town and

neglected, the only signs of activity Colin noted as he wandered its grounds were the chirping of a robin and the skittering of small creatures among the dry leaves. Built in the fifteenth century, it had been constructed on the site of a bitter struggle between two brothers vying for the ducal lands of the family estate, a battle that had engendered the raising of armies and consumed many members of both families, including, brutally, the brothers' wives.

Colin had come to Winnetfield several days ago to research details related to the ducal estate, whose once-stout castle was now only broken walls of stone, but he'd been unable to focus clearly on historical matters and, frustrated, had found himself wandering the grounds of the estate aimlessly.

The cemetery to the side of the ancient church held the tomb of the victorious brother, whose line prevailed for two hundred years, though the faint indentations of his name barely remained on the weathered headstone. Next to this stone was another that had always, as far as records indicated, been mysteriously unmarked.

The two stones were set apart from the other graves, as if linked. Was the unmarked grave that of the brother? Were the two finally reconciled in death? He supposed the brothers' story would be fascinating to explore, though he felt none of the usual energy that thoughts of a potential book generally gave him.

Still, he was glad to be away from London and people he knew and obligations, and it did feel grimly appropriate to be in this cemetery. Nick was somewhere in Spain, his grave unmarked and lost now, too. And Colin could never ask for the forgiveness he needed.

He sat down in the grass, his back against the cold, blank stone, and a predictable line of poetry came to him.

*The grave's a fine and private place / but none, I think, do there embrace.*

Nick would never embrace Josie. He'd never share the ultimate physical connection with her that they'd been meant to share.

And in their grief, Josie and Colin had done just that.

What the hell would Nick have thought?

Colin could easily imagine Nick planting him a facer. He wished, actually, that Nick were alive to do it.

But Nick had also experienced for himself the press of life, how it pulled a man to entertain thoughts and actions he'd never expected to consider. And this was weighing on Colin: Would Nick have forgiven him for what had happened in the carriage?

He supposed what he wanted was some sort of blessing from Nick's spirit. Forgiveness. And permission.

"Of the two of us, I knew her better," he said aloud to the deserted graveyard. "I understand instant connections. I felt them with her, too. But I know her more deeply than you ever had a chance to do. And I can care for her now when you cannot."

It was an appalling thing to say to the memory of a dead man he'd loved like a brother. But it was the truth.

No thunderbolt hit him, no tree fell on him. Nothing greeted his words but birdsong and leaf-rustling. The sounds of life going on.

Was that in itself an answer?

Nick had died because of all the things humanity could not get right. Death and war and heartbreak dogged life, but life was also goodness and joy and peace. Nick had cared for Josie and Colin both. How could he not have wanted that to carry on?

A fat, warm raindrop hit his nose, followed by more as a late summer shower started.

He got up, more at peace than he'd been since he'd heard of Nick's passing, and headed back along the road to the inn where he was staying. As the rain drenched his hair and ran off his face, he allowed himself to think of Josie.

The carriage ride had been the wrong moment to do what they'd done, and he knew it hadn't been exactly wonderful for her, but touching her had been amazing for him. Considering the heat that had burned between them, he knew he could do far better with her. He wanted them to do it again and again, to get it right.

He'd not heard any news of consequences from their encounter. He was grateful—he didn't want her to feel forced into marrying him. But they had a solid foundation of friendship and a passionate attraction. What more could they need?

She was still grieving Nick, of course. Her last words had been said in anger and pain, but he would never allow those emotions to define what was between them. Time did heal.

The future suddenly felt so *possible*.

He'd go to her right away—today—and find a way to be a solace to her until she was ready to hear what he had to say.

But upon reaching the inn, he saw that his return to Greenbrier would not be immediate. A letter from Maria was waiting for him, telling of scandal for Edwina.

&

*Dearest Josie,*

*I can hardly believe it, but I am not ruined after all! And it is dear Ivorwood who has rescued me.*

*He had been away, but he came back when Maria wrote to him. He drove me in his curricle on Rotten Row at the fashionable hour and greeted quite an amazing number of people, considering he is not what one would call gregarious. But he seems to know ever so many people, or at least, there are many who would like to know him.*

*Then he held a large dinner party and invited all sorts of important people. Viscount Roxham and his wife were there, along with a marquess, a bishop, and a number of people who'd been avoiding me.*

*Mappleton was there too, though he kept apart from me at first. But when we sat down to dinner and everyone saw the kindness Ivorwood and Roxham showed me, my scandal was forgotten. Mappleton sought me out after the meal, and I even heard one of the matrons saying that rumors from below-stairs can never quite be believed. Though I know it is wicked to be glad that Cook, who was not lying, is now considered a liar, I am glad.*

*Love,*
*Edwina*

Josie couldn't have been happier for Edwina, and indeed all of them, as the scandal would eventually have reached Upperton, and no matter what her mother said, Josie for one hoped to get to know their neighbors. The Cardworthys might even become a real part of the Upperton neighborhood. Who knew but that they might even make some friends?

She wasn't surprised that Colin had come to Edwina's rescue. Just thinking of his many virtues brought a huge, unwanted lump to her throat, but she reminded herself of how painful it had been when he'd cut things off between them, how easy it had seemed for him to be so blunt, and that helped.

Still, they *were* deeply indebted to him, and she urged her mother to write to him. Mrs. Cardworthy, though, said surely it would be enough to thank him when he returned to Greenbrier. When Josie insisted they must write, her mother finally said, "Oh, very well, you write it and I'll sign it."

Josie began and discarded five different letters and finally wrote a very simple note of thanks, which was duly signed by her mother and dispatched to London. Afterward, she took an extremely vigorous walk in an effort to settle herself, refusing the whole time to look in the direction of Greenbrier, though its dominating bulk required some effort to avoid.

&

Since her scandal had been brushed away, Edwina had been to several balls, and the day after each one the reception room at Maria's had been filled with flowers for her. Mappleton had renewed his attentions, and at a concert gathering the night before, he'd followed her onto the terrace and kissed her.

"I think you are a very, very interesting lady," he'd said to her afterward. And kissed her again. Not only was this not as exciting as Jack Whitby's kissing, but she had the impression Mappleton thought she was in some way accomplished at kissing, that he expected her to take charge, and this thought didn't please her.

"Why?" she'd asked in a voice that was far more tart than it ought to have been. She'd found herself slipping at times into her former less-pleasing ways. "Why should I be any more interesting than the other ladies you know?"

A light came into his eyes. "You are bold." Apparently he thought she was an adventuress, and that excited him in some way.

After the disaster caused by the kiss with Jack, she knew she ought to be glad for Mappleton's devoted attention. Nothing had been said by either of them about his absence during her scandal, nor was the scandal itself even mentioned. Edwina was happy to put it behind her.

Only…she felt different now. When the scandal had broken, she'd instantly gone from being the fascinating newcomer to being ignored, and it was hard now to be delighted by the attention of people who'd avoided her. She was utterly glad to be a pariah no longer, but now the idea of marrying into the fashionable world, with its glossy exteriors and hard hearts, didn't hold the same allure.

For the first time in her life, she craved the welcoming messiness of Jasmine House. But she told herself this was pure idiocy, and that she only missed Josie.

Over the next week, Mappleton lavished gifts on her. He took her to Gunter's for ices and invited her and Maria to join him in his box at the opera. He lingered in the dark outside the carriage when he was meant to be handing her in, blinking expectantly at her as though he was waiting for her to steal a kiss from him.

He began to truly annoy her.

She hadn't thought it possible that a gentleman could be *too* nice to her. But he was, and the more his niceness began to annoy her, the more difficulty she had being pleasant to him herself. And the more peevish she was with him, the more he seemed to be kind to her. It was almost as if he wanted her to dominate him in some way.

Then he proposed. Having begged a private word with her in the drawing room at Maria's, he briefly touched her lips with his cool, dry ones and begged her to do him the honor of being his wife. He told her he would make her his goddess.

Her stomach plunged at the thought.

The next day, as she took tea with Maria in her garden, she told her about Mappleton's proposal.

Maria raised her eyebrows at the resigned manner in which Edwina spoke. "And?"

"And I'm to think about it."

"He is titled, well-to-do, handsome enough. He seems a very pleasant man."

"He is. I suppose. Pleasant, that is."

Maria waited while a footman settled a plate of cakes

on a small stone table between them and then left. She gestured for Edwina to take a cake, a small crease deepening between her brows. Finally she spoke.

"And you don't want a pleasant man who is going to shower you with compliments and gifts."

Edwina, who'd lost her appetite for cakes, sighed. "I don't understand it. He's just the kind of man I've always dreamed about. He says he wants to make me his goddess. And what woman wouldn't want to be treated that way?"

"Oh, I don't know," Maria said. "There's appreciation, and then there's adulation. Adulation goes in one direction, generally, doesn't it? It's not really a basis for conversation."

"He listens to everything I say as though each word is a pearl of wisdom. I even tried saying stupid things to him, as a test, and he loved those too."

"Oh, well, a man in love…" Maria said.

"Is this love? Or is it only admiration? I didn't used to think there was a difference."

Maria looked away, across the garden. "Admiration won't chew you up inside."

Love. That was just it. Edwina hadn't expected love or sought it. She'd always wanted admiration, always felt that no one at home really appreciated *her*. Papa, especially, never had. And now here was a man who behaved as though she made the sun rise, and being with him was starting to make her feel she might cast up her accounts.

Edwina felt disgusted, with herself and with Mappleton. And what was most troublesome, she'd begun worrying about Whitby.

Almost from the moment she'd been discovered

kissing him, she'd been able to push away thoughts of him. Nor had she allowed herself to worry about what had happened after he'd been sent away from Maria's. Being in the grips of scandal had easily filled her mind with panic and despair, so that she'd had no space for him.

But Mappleton's kisses—what they made her think of was not Mappleton, but Jack and the way his touch affected her so deeply. She asked Maria now, as nonchalantly as she could, what had happened to him. Maria gave her a penetrating look.

"After I sent him packing? He went back to his shop. I wonder how it will have affected his custom, though. His pieces were quite sought after, but the most respectable families won't want anything to do with him now."

"I see. Of course that would happen," Edwina said with a dry throat.

Maria nodded. "On the other hand, there are less respectable families with plenty of money. I don't think he'll starve, but as for the kind of patrons who commissioned him to make art, well, those may be gone for good."

Edwina felt awful and guilty. All day, thoughts of Jack occupied her so much that she began to think she wouldn't be able to accept Mappleton until she saw Jack again and apologized. Surely it was only the wrongness of what had happened that was bothering her, and it was certainly no small thing.

Besides, he still had her jewel box. Unless he'd burned it out of vengeance.

And so she found herself the next day in a carriage en route to his shop. She'd gotten the address by snooping through the accounts on Maria's desk; she wasn't proud of having done so, but she could hardly admit she was going to see him. She'd been ashamed to find herself surprised that the address was quite respectable.

She brought no one with her but a coachman, and she had him stop two blocks from Whitby's shop and wait there so he wouldn't see where she was going.

The shop was at the western edge of Cheapside, next to a silversmith on one side and a furrier on the other. In the large front window was displayed a handsome chest of drawers and a small, round table. A neatly lettered sign hanging above the window read "Whitby, Cabinetmaker."

A bell jingled as she opened the door, and though no one else seemed to be in the shop, an open doorway at the back and a tapping sound indicated someone was there. Inside, it smelled of the pleasant sawdust scent she associated with Whitby.

"I'll be with you in a moment," came a voice from the back room. *His* voice, and it made her feel like a firecracker had just gone off inside her.

She forced herself to relax and wandered through the shop, where several handsome pieces of furniture were displayed. A pretty rocking chair with a slim spindle back and a satin-smooth seat made her want to test its motion. An exquisitely fashioned grand mahogany table conjured an image of a father and mother and several children happily gathering for dinner. Would Whitby create such beautiful pieces for his own family some day? Undoubtedly. Longing pierced her, and she knew she couldn't bear to think of such things.

She trailed her fingers over the pretty inlaid mosaic top of a desk, amazed by the smoothness of the joining, and acknowledged how much he'd achieved through his labor and artistry. Were these pieces here because he'd been abandoned by customers who'd once commissioned his work?

As she moved through the room, she saw two coffins, plain but sturdy, and she was afraid she had her answer.

The sound of footsteps drew her attention to the doorway, and there he was, wearing a dark apron across his front. He stopped when he saw her. He didn't smile.

"Miss Cardworthy."

He'd called her Edwina once before, but there could be no more of that.

She cleared her throat. She'd forgotten how icy blue his eyes were, and though before they'd been so often lit with amusement, now they gave her a chill.

The sleeves of his coarse white shirt were rolled up to the elbow, and the sight of his bare forearms gave her a pang as she remembered how they'd touched each other. His brown hair was tousled and a strand hanging across his brow was dusted with a scattering of the wood shavings that also decorated his forearm. It wasn't hard to imagine him rubbing his arm across a forehead grown warm from work.

She swallowed. He looked very capable, very male, and not at all happy to see her. Now that she was here, she suddenly felt unsure of what she wanted to say to him.

"Mr. Whitby," she began, and just speaking those proper words twisted her inside. "What happened at Mrs. Westin's house...we both know it wasn't your fault."

He crossed his arms and leaned back against the door frame. Aside from the light coating of sawdust, his dark apron was tidy.

"Is that right," he drawled. His eyes gave nothing away.

She'd never been much for apologizing, but she knew she owed him honesty. "I was as much a participant in what happened as you."

The corner of his mouth tilted arrogantly. "A participant. I like that. Sounds official."

A growl of frustration pressed at the back of her throat, seeking escape. "You shouldn't have lost your work at Mrs. Westin's over what happened. It was wrong."

He shrugged, his hard expression giving nothing away. "It's the way of things. I knew that when I kissed you. Both times."

She had to know the full impact of her willful behavior on him. "Have you," she began, but her voice had gone dry and raspy, and she cleared her throat and pressed onward. "Have you lost other work because of what happened?"

His eyebrow crept up—for sheer arrogance, a duke would have had nothing on him. "You can put your conscience to rest, if that's what this visit is about."

Not an answer to her question; apparently he didn't wish her to know what he had suffered. She shouldn't be surprised. He was the proudest person she'd ever known.

"Well—I'm sorry. About what happened." She'd forced the words out, though they made her feel terribly vulnerable.

"You don't need to take any blame."

"Yes, I do," she said, growing impatient with his calmness. "You tried to warn me off, but I wouldn't listen."

His eyes were hooded, so she couldn't see their expression as he spoke. "Perhaps I didn't want you to listen."

*He's saying he only wanted your body*, she told herself harshly. *He's attracted to you, and you're attracted to him, and that's all there was to it.*

She ignored the inner voice trying to remind her how tender and sincere he'd been with her, how he'd told her she had a good heart. They were words she'd never have used to describe herself. She was judgmental and difficult and pessimistic, and he couldn't possibly know her at all.

Before she could succumb to the urge to beg him to hold her, she thrust her hand into her reticule. "I should like to collect my jewel box if you still have it."

"If I haven't destroyed it, you mean?" he said with a mocking twist of his mouth. He called over his shoulder for someone to bring the jewel box.

"I would have left it at Mrs. Westin's," he said to her, "but I supposed leaving just that one thing would only bring more attention to you."

She gave a curt nod in acknowledgment.

Something caught her eye in the doorway behind him—movement. A child of perhaps seven was standing there.

"Here it is, sir," the boy said, and Jack turned and took the small box as Edwina looked on, speechless.

"Thank you, Robbie," Whitby said.

Edwina had frozen at the boy's appearance. He looked exactly like a small version of Whitby.

"I've finished the table leg," the boy said.

"Very good," Whitby said. "You can do the chair, then."

The boy let his glance fall on Edwina for a moment, then he nodded and disappeared.

Whitby had a son? But he'd said he'd never been married. A bastard, then? But how could he be so duplicitous, when he'd mocked gentlemen for that sort of behavior, sworn he'd never do such a thing? She'd believed him.

She didn't know what to think, but a reflex asserted itself and told her she'd been fooled again by a man, made to believe she'd meant something to him when she didn't. Even knowing a future with Whitby was impossible, she'd still felt they'd shared a true connection. She'd been wrong again.

"You have a son," she said in a voice that suggested everything she didn't say.

His expression turned hard, any hint of angry flirtation now gone from eyes that might as well have been made of sea ice.

"You're asking if I have a bastard," he said in the coldest voice she'd ever heard.

Though she was trembling, she forced out the hard words that would defend her against the softness she felt for him. "Some people will allow themselves anything. They have no standards."

"I couldn't agree more," he said. "Now, if you will excuse me, my nephew requires my help."

A gasp escaped her. "The boy is your nephew?"

"I don't need to explain myself to you." He turned to go.

"Wait—I'm sorry! I misunderstood."

He glanced back, his expression so remote she wanted to cry. "No, you *misjudged*. It's what you do. You judge yourself and everyone else so harshly that you'll never trust anyone."

"But...but I don't know how," she whispered in anguish.

Her words had no effect on him as he moved through the doorway to the back room and left her standing in the shop.

She was shaking. The boy was his nephew, but she'd assumed the worst, just as she'd been doing for so long about so many things. Because assuming the worst protected her from being disappointed: she was always already unhappy.

And now she'd just insulted Whitby terribly and shown her own profound snobbery, a disdain she now realized had little to do with how unsuitable other people might be, and everything to do with her fear that others would find *her* unsuitable.

She could hear the boy's high voice in the back room, and the deeper timbre of Whitby's reply, something about a tool.

Unhappiness rolled over her like a carriage wheel and came to rest on her heart.

She left the shop and walked the two blocks back to where the coach awaited her. She was grateful for the privacy it offered, which allowed her to sob unobserved the whole way back to Maria's.

# Sixteen

In Upperton a hot, rough September wind had been raging all morning, and Josie, catching sight of the elderly Rickett trying to stake the rosebushes in the back garden, had gone out to help. The red and pink flowers were in full glory, and ever since coming home a month before, she'd found herself gazing at them with an almost physical need for their beauty. But they would be battered and broken by the wind's rough treatment if they weren't protected.

As she worked, she pondered the letter she'd received that morning from Edwina. Instead of the news of an engagement that Josie had been every day expecting, it had held a brief description of the soirees Edwina had attended and an account of what her sister had worn. The letter held no enthusiasm or excitement, almost as though Edwina were simply going through the motions.

Perhaps, Edwina's earlier letter notwithstanding, being in London was proving awkward even though the scandal was over, and perhaps Mappleton hadn't proposed after all. She would write her that night and gently ask.

Josie and the gardener worked for some time together, tying the roses around stakes, until a particularly violent gust uprooted the ancient, half-dead apple tree near the front drive, and Rickett went around to see to the damage. So she was alone, on her knees among the roses she was trying to gather, when she glanced up to see Colin walking through the tall, mis-shapen boxwood bushes at the back of their garden.

As he passed the weather-beaten carved wooden elephant statue by the iris bed that had often served as a perch for the Cardworthy children, he gave it a cheerful pat. His long-legged stride, so familiar to her, now looked cocksure whereas before she'd hardly noticed it. He wore a dark blue tailcoat and fawn breeches with shining tall black boots, and he seemed jauntily unbothered by the wind whipping him, only lifting a hand to brush away a leaf that had landed on his black hair.

He looked commanding and handsome, an earl who made whatever place he occupied into his realm. Why had she never seen before that the arrogant jut of his substantial nose, while certainly inherited from bold ancestors, was also just as much a mark of his own power?

Her stomach took a large dip.

She immediately looked back down at the tall white roses, which were being bent nearly in half by the wind, and focused on gathering them with her gloved hands. So Colin had come back to Greenbrier. Why shouldn't he—it was his house. It had to happen at some point, so why not now? He would be stopping by for a neighborly visit. She would be polite. Of course she would—she owed him that, considering what he'd done for Edwina.

Surely he was as eager as she to forget what had happened. She took a deep, slow breath and straightened her shoulders, and decided she would not feel anything beyond politeness for him. But then she had to stifle a bitter laugh as she recalled how well trying to be indifferent to him had worked in London. So she told herself the feelings she had for him were her own business, and with time she would simply root them out.

She made herself look up again with a mild expression. He was close enough now to greet, though the sound of the wind made it necessary to shout.

"You've come back," she said unnecessarily, but she had to say something. "I hope you are well."

He crouched down next to her. "As you see," he said reasonably. "Here, let me help."

"Oh, no, you needn't. Go inside and they'll give you tea. Mama will be happy to see you."

But he ignored her and wrapped his arms around the thorny bundle of roses she had gathered, so she could only let go and take the twine and tie it around the stems while he held them.

"Are you doing the rest of them?" he half shouted over the wind, jerking his head toward the patch of red roses she hadn't yet staked.

"Yes, but really, you needn't help. I've got a method. Do go in and make yourself comfortable."

He gave her a look. "It will take twice as long if

you do it alone. And I don't want to go in. I came to see you."

A hot blush swept up her neck, along with annoyance that he was ruining her equilibrium. She wanted to tell him he couldn't say things like that to her anymore, but she swallowed the urge. She'd known she'd have to talk to him someday, so she must simply be…mature? Was that the word for braving conversation with the man with whom you'd impulsively had intimate relations in a carriage?

She gathered her composure as he pulled together an armful of the red rose stems. He held them, waiting for her to put the string around them, and she wished doing so would not involve leaning close to him and passing the twine within inches of his chest. She forced herself to do it and kept her hands pressed so close to the roses that the thorns scratched her.

While he moved to gather the next bunch, tying them himself, she sat back on her heels and surveyed the rest of the garden as though he was only there to help with this task and didn't require her attention for any other purpose. She could feel his eyes on her.

"You'll have to look at me sometime, Josie."

"I know," she said dully. She let her eyes roam over the groups of tied of flowers and was dismayed to see that the work was all done, because now she supposed she'd have to go inside and have tea with him. Could she plead a headache? That wouldn't look believable, but she didn't think she cared. Why couldn't he have waited longer to have this first awkward visit? A year would not have been too soon.

She finally looked at him, then wished she hadn't.

The strong set of his chin, the hard angle of his cheek, the jut of his prominent nose, the silver-green of his eyes…his male beauty made her heart thump. Why hadn't his appearance had an effect on her over all those months of togetherness before they went to London?

His masculinity now felt like a dark and secret force against which she was vulnerable. When she'd touched all those parts of him kept hidden by his clothes, she'd stirred up mystery about a man she'd thought she'd understood.

She wondered if he was still courting the fashionable widows. Perhaps he'd already proposed to one of them. Surely those women had been able to see what she, in her blindness, had missed for so long: that he was an extremely desirable man. Perhaps all those times she'd thought he was off doing research for his books, he was really with fashionable widows. Very possibly what they'd done in the carriage had been just one more pleasurable experience for him.

Except, that wonderful newness she'd known in his arms and the way he'd responded to her had made her believe it had all been new for him as well. But her mind skittered away from the memory of that London night, and she was glad for the brightness and mundane familiarity of her own garden.

"It's been several weeks since you left London," he started to say, but she cut him off, the blush heating her neck again.

She leaned close so she wouldn't have to shout into the wind. "I am not increasing," she said. "There's no cause for concern."

She didn't know what reaction she'd expected, but it wasn't the flicker of disappointment in his eyes. Surely he wanted to celebrate that their ill-advised coupling would have no results?

"Josie, how can you think I wouldn't be very concerned about you regardless?"

She *really* didn't want his concern. "Colin," she said briskly, "it can't, of course, be the way it used to be between us. I do realize our friendship is ruined. But it's done, and it can't be helped, and we'll both be best served if we simply try to be polite to each other and keep our distance."

"Our friendship isn't ruined. It's simply been broken open."

She frowned. She had no idea what he meant, but he was looking at her intently and she didn't like it. Why was he making this so hard? It would have been easier if he were being cold, but instead his eyes glimmered with a hot light that was making her want to squirm. She was annoyed with him for making her feel this way, and at herself for feeling it.

"But it's good you're here," she continued in a businesslike manner. "I want to say again how grateful we all are for what you did for Edwina. You saved her—us—from disaster."

"It was nothing."

The wind threw a scattering of dry leaf bits against them and pulled strands of her now shoulder-length hair out of its knot and whipped them against her face in messy snarls. "No it wasn't. I know you weren't even in London at the time, but you chose to return. You held a party for all the significant people and lent my sister every bit of consequence you could."

She wanted to look away from his steady gaze, but she would force herself to thank him properly. "And you didn't have to. After what happened between you and me, I'm sure we both felt we'd had enough of each other for a very long time."

"I spoke harshly then," he said. "I felt keenly that we'd offended Nick's memory. But on reflection, I've come to believe we ought to be forgiven."

Her eyebrows shot upward. "Well. This is quite a different tone. We 'acted reprehensibly' I believe were your words."

"I spoke too harshly then. Come, Josie, it wasn't such a bad thing we did. And I believe Nick would have understood our need to…connect as we did."

When he said "connect," the corner of his mouth tucked back a bit, as though there was something about the memory of that night that made him feel smug.

But of course: men wanted sexual relations. It was just that she'd never thought of Colin wanting them, and certainly not with her.

She had, before London, so handily dismissed any thought of him wanting such things. He'd been available for conversation and friendship with her, but she'd never imagined him having unknown or mysterious desires of his own. Because he was reserved and kept to himself and spent so much time alone reading and writing, she'd assumed he wasn't much caught up in the bodily urges that consumed other men. She'd actually thought herself more worldly than he was.

How casually arrogant she'd been. But she'd thrown

herself at him in the carriage, practically forced herself on him. Shame burned in her chest as she remembered how she'd told him so fiercely not to stop when he'd tried. How she'd torn at his clothes.

"I suppose," she said, "what I so freely offered was irresistible."

He flinched. "That is needlessly harsh toward both of us. It's true that I never had intended to do such a thing with you. And I never would have dreamed, with the news of Nick so raw…" He looked as though he were blushing, though surely it was just the wind reddening his skin.

"But I told you the truth in the garden that day: I wanted you. I'd wanted you from the day I first came back to Greenbrier and saw you all grown up. And I still want you."

At these words, something decidedly wicked glittered in his eyes. In *Colin's* eyes. Wickedness. The world had gone upside down.

A lock of Josie's hair blew across her eyes and she pushed it away impatiently. "You were confused by grief, as I was," she said. "That's all it was."

"I wasn't confused. I want to marry you."

*No.* She couldn't take this. She wanted to shout for him to stop being so considerate and forgiving and persevering. It was just a pose he'd adopted, as though he believed it was the considerate way to behave— because she didn't believe what they'd done had really touched the heart he kept so guarded.

"Look, Colin, I've…I have a tendency to do dramatic things on a whim. That's what happened in London. I was overwhelmed with emotions I didn't want, and it suddenly seemed that what accidentally started up between us would take them away. We've agreed it was a mistake. And now I don't want to talk about it anymore."

His jaw hardened. "You're being absurd. There was more to what happened between us than happenstance. We get along famously, and as someone who's seen firsthand the disaster caused by two incompatible people marrying, I can tell you that friendship is the best possible foundation for marriage."

So he wanted her body *and* her friendship.

"Stop talking about marriage!" she said. "I don't want to marry you. Just forget what happened. You don't need to feel guilty or as though you owe me anything."

His brows slammed together. "Why are you being so unreasonable?"

"Unreasonable?" she said, wishing her voice hadn't gone a little shrill. "Does a woman want to be reasoned into marriage? I don't. You just think reason and compatibility are the most important foundation for marriage because your parents didn't behave well toward each other."

"That's right, they didn't, and it was a mess. They couldn't agree on anything or forgive each other a single mistake. My mother could never forgive my father for being the man she was forced to marry, and he could never respect her. It was the perfect example of how people at the mercy of emotion behave like idiots. Why would you want to take a chance on marriage being like that, when you could have companionship and peace?"

She just looked at him. Finally she said, "I

understand perfectly, Colin. The last thing you want in a marriage is emotion, because unruly feelings, to you, are inherently something to be avoided. In which case, and considering how emotion clearly carried at least me away in London, I can't see why you would want to marry me."

He frowned. "I didn't mean it that way."

"What did you mean, then?"

His jaw clenched.

"Never mind," she said when he didn't immediately reply. "We're going to simply forget about all of this."

"No, we won't," he began with an ominous note in his voice. But at that moment the door to the sitting room opened and Matthew called across the garden to them.

"Mama asks if you won't come in for tea, Ivorwood. She says she's longing to see you after so long." Matthew grinned. "Do come and have tea. We can always use another fellow."

≈≈

Colin was clenching his teeth so hard he was probably in danger of cracking them. Josie had accused him of scorning unruly emotion, but *unruly* pretty much described how he was feeling right now.

She held his eyes with hers, willing him, he knew, to decline.

"Thank you, Matthew. Tell your mother I would love a cup of tea."

He stood and held out a hand to help Josie up from her kneeling position. She ignored it and got up on her own. She insisted on walking a few steps behind him as they made for the manor and tea.

The whole time he sat across from her, he wanted to leap across the table and sweep her off somewhere so he could explain things better. And then ravish her thoroughly. Instead he watched as she volunteered to get extra cream for the table, fetch more biscuits, and adjust the drapes, and in general eagerly did everything she could to spend as little time in his company as possible.

By the time he returned home to Greenbrier an hour later, he was extremely grouchy and frustrated. He buried himself in his books, but they provided no solace from thoughts of Josie.

How could she be so contrary? She wasn't even going to consider his offer of marriage?

Eventually he threw down his quill and went out to the stables. He took his horse out for a punishing ride meant to disperse all the bloody *feelings* that had overtaken him. Two hours later, he was physically spent, but he'd accomplished nothing toward mastering his emotions, which only made him furious. Was he to be like his parents after all?

He made for his library and buried himself in his books.

At dinnertime, deeply annoyed with his lack of focus, he had a plate of sandwiches sent in and disciplined himself into concentrating on the words. But no subject shared the pages of history with honor and death so frequently as love, and when he found himself starting to have some sympathy for the intemperate Henry the Eighth, he slammed the volume before him shut with disgust.

It was no good. His lifetime of reading had given him a thorough exposure to the human animal in all its glory and heartbreak, and he could no longer avoid the diagnosis of his own state: he was in love with Josie Cardworthy.

And she showed no signs of loving him back.

If anything, she'd been nothing but irritated with him the entire time he'd seen her today, and she'd clearly wished him gone. She definitely wasn't treasuring any blissful memories of their time in the carriage.

He wasn't happy with the vulnerable way love was making him feel. But at least there was a saving grace in all this: she didn't know how he felt. And she wouldn't—not yet, anyway.

He'd convince her to marry him *somehow*. She'd had friendship for him, and desire. He could easily remember the passion they'd shared in the carriage, and he refused to believe that had been based on nothing or that it had all simply gone away. She wouldn't acknowledge her affection for him, but now that he'd admitted to himself that he loved her, he felt very inspired to court her.

She had to care for him at least a little, and as soon as he could get her to care for him as much as he cared for her, he'd let her know how he felt.

# *Seventeen*

HARDLY HAD JOSIE DISPATCHED A CHEERING LETTER TO Edwina when, a few days later, instead of a reply, her sister herself arrived at Jasmine House, conveyed there in Maria's carriage and accompanied by one of Maria's maids.

Josie thought Edwina looked thinner, and her sister's greeting was strangely meek. But of course, travel was wearing, and after the family welcomed her home, no one thought anything was amiss when she promptly took to her bedchamber.

Since Josie hadn't told her brothers about Mappleton, none of them were curious on that score. And with Mrs. Cardworthy on her divan as usual with her novels, and the boys occupied with some scheme in the back garden, the family didn't pay much notice to Edwina's withdrawal. But by the afternoon of the second day, Josie was beginning to worry.

"Edwina?" she called from the hallway after knocking on her bedchamber door. She chose to take the muffled sound from within as permission to enter.

Edwina was sitting on her bed with an open book of theorems in her lap. Josie knew her sister found the way complicated mathematical problems could be neatly solved satisfying, but it didn't seem as though the book was holding her attention.

"Are you unwell?" Josie asked, coming to sit at the foot of the bed. "You've not left your chamber since you arrived."

"Oh," Edwina said quietly. "No, I am quite well."

Her normally lustrous black hair lay loose and lank over her shoulders, and there were shadows under her midnight-blue eyes. She was wearing a very old, quite ugly brown gown, the sort of thing she might normally have worn only to help in the garden or sort items in the dusty attic.

Had something happened in London? Had there been any more contact with Whitby? Josie meant to tread carefully.

"I was hoping to hear more about London."

"There's not much to tell." Edwina looked down at her book and turned a page.

Silence. Obviously something was wrong, and Josie felt the gulf of distance between them. They were such different people. She thought of how everything about a sister could be as familiar to you as yourself, and yet the two of you might not really know each other at all.

"You seem rather low," she said carefully. "Did something happen in London? What about Mappleton?"

"He proposed."

*What?*

"Then why aren't we celebrating?"

"Because I turned him down."

"Turned him down? But it was such a triumph for you to catch him!"

"I didn't love him. I don't think I even liked him in the end. He only wanted to admire me." Edwina looked up. "And I know what you're thinking. He sounds like just the man I wanted, doesn't he? But I began to feel I couldn't respect someone who was so entirely enraptured by me."

She seemed so different now.

"Then it sounds as though you've made a good decision." Josie moved her hand to rest on top of her sister's and gave a gentle squeeze. "This doesn't have something to do with Jack Whitby by chance?"

A stain of pink crept over Edwina's cheeks. "How could it?" she said, though her voice no longer sounded defensive when speaking of him, but resigned. "He's a cabinetmaker, in trade."

"But you have feelings for him, don't you?"

"Yes," Edwina whispered miserably. "I do. He is a remarkable, honorable man, an artist and educated, and he's worth ten of most gentlemen."

"And does he truly care for you?"

"I think he did at one time, only I've been so awful to him. It was my fault he was sent away from Maria's in disgrace. I was the one who kissed *him*, even though he tried to discourage me. But I was afraid to care for him, so I behaved as though he wasn't good enough for me, and I've been so wrong. He's far better than I am in every way that matters."

"That's not true. Maybe it was only a matter of him seeing your worth before you saw his."

Edwina shook her head. "It doesn't matter. It was always impossible."

"I suppose so, if you care very much what other

people think. Though I'm not sure our family ever has, and maybe now, for once, that could be an advantage."

Edwina managed a pathetic laugh. "You're right. We don't really have much to lose in the way of neighborhood standing."

She looked down again. "But I've burnt my bridges with him. And"—she took a deep breath—"you were right about Mappleton as a husband for me, but I couldn't listen because it was you. I was envying you so awfully for being engaged to Nicholas. I've always envied you."

"You had no need to," Josie said gently. "You've always been a wonderful person—you just couldn't trust that people would like you for yourself. I think Papa helped you to believe that, and it was very wrong of him. I'm sorry."

"It wasn't your fault."

"But I feel awfully as though I benefitted from you having to go first and take the brunt of Papa's bullying ways. You made it easier for me not to care if he blustered at me."

Edwina's eyes looked misty at the corners. "Then I suppose a little something good came out of Papa being disappointed in me."

"Oh Edwina, dearest," Josie said, "you are the best of sisters."

"Sisters *are* a wonderful thing," Edwina sniffed. "I feel a little better already."

They embraced and had a good cry together on Edwina's bed. Then Josie took a deep breath and told her about Colin.

"When I went for the carriage ride with him in London after we had the news about Nicholas…

well, we rather sought comfort from each other in a physical way."

"Josie Cardworthy!" Edwina said, but there was no hint of judgment in her voice, only a sort of indulgent surprise that made Josie feel a little better about what had happened.

Edwina lowered her voice. "Was it *a lot* of comfort?"

"Yes. But fortunately, there will be no consequences."

Edwina absorbed the full implication of Josie's words. "Well. I'm sure it was only natural to seek comfort at such a time, the two of you being such good friends. Are you in love?"

"No!" Josie said with a vehemence that made Edwina's eyebrows rise. "What happened was a mistake, but he felt that he'd compromised me, and he insisted we must marry."

"Ah. Insisting. Still," Edwina said, giving Josie an intent look, "you two might come to love each other."

"No," Josie said firmly, "it's not going to happen." She could see a look of lingering suspicion in her sister's eyes, and she said in the most cheerful tone she could manage, "Truly, it's all resolved and done with. And at least you and I will always have each other."

"Yes. And what a consolation," Edwina said drily, "that neither of us will be left as Mama's spinster caretaker. We can share the job."

"True," said Josie with a grim laugh.

Edwina smiled, and it made such a difference to the pale, drained look of her.

"We'll be the tragic lost beauties of Jasmine House," Josie said.

"Why are we lost?"

"Lost to gentlemen because we never found our true loves. And now we sail into the future undaunted."

Edwina flopped backward on the bed and threw an arm across her face. "You always were good at dressing mutton up as lamb."

"Listen, though," Josie said, flopping down beside her. "Since we are both going to be here, I think we ought to do something about Mama."

"What do you mean?" Edwina said from under her arm.

"Get her up off the divan, of course. And outside."

"Outside!" Edwina let her arm fall away from her face and turned her head to give Josie a deeply skeptical look. "Don't you think she'll go up in smoke or something if direct sunlight hits her?"

Josie laughed. "You know it's the very thing she needs. And it would make a huge difference for us as well."

Edwina seemed to entertain the idea for several moments. Then she shook her head. "I agree that she needs to get up, but it will never happen. Mama's been on that divan for four years. Four years! That argues to an incredibly stout mulishness. I don't even think she can walk much farther than the distance to and from her bed anymore."

"All the more reason to get her up and out," Josie said seriously. "It's the only thing, really. It will be our project."

Edwina put her arm comfortably back across her eyes. "It will be a failure. But clearly we lost Cardworthy beauties haven't got anything else to aim for."

∽

Mrs. Cardworthy, predictably, refused her daughters'
invitation the next day to drive out to a nearby town
for a glass of lemonade.

"Lemonade!" she cried, a novel dangling from
her fingers and a sweet *kachori* biscuit halfway to her
mouth. "What can you be thinking, to go all that way
for a glass of lemonade? Have Cook make you some if
you are in such need."

"It's not out of need, Mama," Josie said reasonably.
She and Edwina had prepared themselves for resistance
and were determined to be patient and persistent. "It's a
pretty little inn and there's a beautiful view of a garden."

"We have our own lovely garden," Mrs.
Cardworthy replied, "and one we've spent quite a bit
of money having Rickett maintain. I see no need to
go gallivanting about to look at anyone else's garden:
flowers are flowers."

Edwina shot Josie a look over their mother's head
that said *I told you so*, but she nonetheless put on a
cheery expression and said, "Do let's go, Mama. You
know how beneficial fresh air is."

"The windows are open, I can see our garden, and I
have all the fresh air I need." Mrs. Cardworthy patted
her daughters' hands amicably. "Really, my dears, I
have everything I need right here. My children are all
present in our happy home. We're all healthy. I have
my books. What else is there?"

"Rather a lot else, Mama. The world outside
our house, for one thing," Josie said, forcing herself not to sound exasperated. But her mother was
already frowning.

"I see what this is now. You want to push me out of the house. I'm a burden to you, an embarrassment, and you want to force me to do what I cannot."

Her voice swelled with hurt. "You don't care that I'm not fit for such undertakings. I've had a terrible shock, and *patience* is needed for a full recovery."

"Mama," Edwina said in a wonderfully kind voice, "aren't there things you're secretly yearning to do?"

Mrs. Cardworthy recoiled as though she'd been slapped instead of encouraged to seize the reins of her life. Her chin began to quiver.

"Sal-ly!" Mrs. Cardworthy called out before dropping her head back against the blue divan pillows, which were threadbare with overuse. Josie and Edwina exchanged glances.

Sally appeared and their mother directed her to bring her elixir. "I am quite ill," she said in a quavering voice.

Edwina and Josie moved to the doorway while the maid brought the elixir.

Edwina raised her eyebrows meaningfully.

"This just means we have to be creative," Josie whispered.

Over the next days, Edwina and Josie proposed a special luncheon in the garden (too many bugs, Mama countered), a carriage ride to see the church being built in the next village (it hadn't rained for a while, Mama pointed out, and the roads would be dusty), and a visit to the traveling pantomime show (a coarse diversion far inferior to books, their mother parried triumphantly).

Josie and Edwina explained their plan to their

brothers, who were in favor of it, and enlisted the boys' help in trying to entice their mother to get up. Thus another round of encouraging suggestions was begun, with the hope of eventually wearing Mrs. Cardworthy down. Their mother, for her part, seemed to enjoy the attention.

But their efforts had no effect, and even Josie began to feel a little discouraged. As she and Edwina stood aside for Sally to plump their mother's pillows two days later, Josie took up the bottle of Dr. Framer's Strengthening Elixir Sally had left on the table. The elixir had become such a part of their mother's routine that nobody thought anything of it anymore, and now she took a hearty sniff. It fairly made her eyes water.

Josie held the bottle out to Edwina with a grim look.

Edwina blinked at the fumes. "Heavens," she whispered, "this must be almost nothing but brandy."

Sally approached the door to leave, and the sisters stepped out into the corridor with her.

"Sally, how much of this elixir is Mama drinking?"

"Well, miss, she has a tot or two first thing in the morning, then after lunch, just before dinner, and before bed."

Edwina and Josie exchanged a look.

"Perhaps we should encourage her to cut back," Josie said.

Sally looked horrified. "Oh no, miss, she wouldn't like that. It relaxes her, like. And she'd never sleep without it."

They dismissed the maid and moved along the

corridor. "Our mother is a drunkard!" Edwina said in a scandalized whisper. "How could we never have noticed?"

"Because she never has too much at one time, I suppose. But I can only think it's helping keep her on the divan."

Edwina nodded. "Existing in a sort of mellow stupor. Sally's right, though. She won't want to give it up."

"Agreed. So we'll have to get rid of it for her. Let's go find all the bottles. And we'll tell the servants not to buy any more."

Edwina looked uneasy. "But she'll be furious. There'll be no living with her."

"Well," Josie said, "if she's angry enough, she'll have to get up and go look for the elixir herself, won't she?"

"You really are diabolical."

# Eighteen

WHEN COLIN STOPPED BY TO VISIT JASMINE HOUSE the next day, intending to invite Josie to stroll with him in the garden as part of his plan to besiege her defenses, she refused to leave the house. She told him she and her siblings had undertaken a plan to get Mrs. Cardworthy off her divan, and that it was her turn today to be a companion to their mother.

When he pointed out that her mother had always liked him and that perhaps he could be helpful, she deflected his offer of help and urged her brothers, who were just on their way to the lake down the road to test a skiff they were building, to take him with them.

So Colin went to the lake. The skiff turned out not to be lake-worthy, and Will was thoroughly dunked. Colin rolled up his sleeves and helped the boys refasten its muddied bindings. When he returned to Jasmine House with the boys afterward, Josie was suspiciously absent, and he had to go home without having a real chance to see her.

The next day when he came again to visit, she just smiled with a pleasant but impersonal cheerfulness and said her brothers were already down at the lake with the skiff and ardently hoping he would join them and offer more assistance. Then she muttered something about her mother and disappeared inside, closing the door in his face before he could reply.

He was glad if she was engaged on a worthwhile occupation, however much it did not look likely to succeed, and it had brought a spring to her step that had been missing the last times he'd seen her. If there remained a reserve and a tentative quality to her smiles, that was not surprising. But he could also see she was using this undertaking to keep him at arms' length. Clearly, he was going to have to make a grander effort.

The following day, he sent out invitations for a neighborhood ball.

It had been more than six weeks since they'd received the news about Nick, and though his loss must always leave a lingering sadness for all who'd loved him, it was time for both of them to rejoin society, and the smaller scale of a neighborhood ball should be the right amount of gentle festivity.

He worried that Josie wouldn't accept the invitation and that he'd have to find a way to force her to come, but on the night of the ball, both she and Edwina, along with their brother Lawrence, appeared, the other Cardworthys being too young, and their mother still declining to leave her divan.

From a vantage point at the corner of his grand ballroom, Colin stood watching Josie, Edwina, and Lawrence enter. The three siblings stood hesitantly to the side, aware that many in the village might still resent the way the family had kept to themselves, even if their presence tonight was a mark of the Earl of Ivorwood's favor.

But it would have been a hard-hearted person indeed who would have continued to hold on to the local grudge now that Josie had lost her valiant fiancé to the war, and the gentle efforts that Josie and Edwina and Lawrence made toward friendliness were quickly welcomed.

Before long the kindly old mayor of Upperton was leading Josie onto the dance floor. The mayor was, thank God, ancient, because she looked incredibly beautiful, a temptation to any man in her pretty hyacinth-blue silk gown with its violet satin ribbon tied under her bosom. Her glossy brown hair had been caught in a soft knot at her nape and wound around with a violet ribbon, but a few sections of her hair had escaped and were flirting with the tops of her shoulders. One strand lay invitingly against her neck, drawing his eyes repeatedly.

Already he'd noticed Freddy Lightfield staring at her with the look of a man who couldn't wait to dance with her. Young Freddy would have to get in line.

Colin made sure he was nearby when her dance with the mayor came to an end. As the opening notes of a waltz began, he was at her side. "Josephine, will you dance with me?"

She blinked, and a mocking smile teased her lips. "Surely you're not asking me to dance?"

"But I am."

Her smile slipped away. "But aren't there any animals requiring your attention? Sheep? A spotted dog? A lonely snake?"

"Nothing. I'm completely free tonight. Shall we?" He held out his hand and she stared as though she didn't know what to do with it.

Josie was dismayed at the apparent demise of their never-dancing joke, and she couldn't think of any polite way to decline. She hadn't thought she'd ever be dancing with Colin, or that she'd ever need to touch him again, though that hadn't stopped her eyes from following him since the moment she'd arrived. He looked incredibly handsome in his black coat and breeches and snowy cravat. A hank of his black hair fell across his forehead, giving him a careless, wicked air that made her a little unsteady.

There was nothing for it but to put her hand in his. They made their way among the other couples as the music swelled, and he set his hand on her waist and took her other hand in his. She conjured the mildest expression possible as they began to dance, though they were so close she thought he must surely notice the heavy thudding of her heart.

His hands felt warm and large on her and so welcome, but she forced herself not to think about the last time they'd touched each other, in London, when her bare hands had run over the hot skin and taut muscles of his abdomen and explored the width of his chest...

*Stop thinking about it!*

He danced remarkably well, and she told herself to enjoy this, that it was enough to be twirled around the room by him on a cloud of beautiful music. She would make herself be carefree with him, just as she'd been with him before the summer, before she'd fallen in love with a man who scorned the messy emotions that were so much a part of who she was.

"Sometimes I forget you're an earl and that you've been trained to do all sorts of useful things like dancing," she said. Conversation was good; it would crowd out other things.

"Don't you want to know why I finally asked you to dance?"

Did he have to tease her? True, they used to tease each other all the time, but now this special attention from him felt like too much. Maybe she wasn't going to be able to be with him after all. She repressed a heavy sigh.

"Very well, why did you ask me to dance?"

He leaned closer so his mouth was next to her ear and said in a low, husky voice, "Because everything's different now. And I wanted an excuse to touch you."

A tingle ran through her, as quickly as a ball of paper catching fire. She blinked and shifted her head so she caught his eye as he lingered close to her face. His gaze held a smoky look that startled her.

What was he doing?

"Colin?" she said. Surely that look in his eyes was just a trick of the light, because she thought she saw a flash of vulnerability.

*Did* Colin care about her more deeply than he'd said? Good God, she'd hadn't dared believe... No, it couldn't be.

And yet, he was looking at her with such a hot and tender gaze. Her foot stepped awry, and he caught her and kept her on her feet. Under his silvery green eyes, her lips grew warm, and she knew with sudden, surprising awareness that she wanted to kiss him.

His eyes held hers longer than they ever had before as he danced her around the room so gracefully that she might have been floating.

*Our friendship isn't ruined, it's simply been broken open.* He'd said that to her the first day he was back, but she hadn't allowed herself to probe his meaning.

"It's heaven to have you in my arms, Josie," he said quietly.

"What…what are you saying?" she murmured. The music was coming to an end, and around them the other dancers were slowing down.

"I think you know."

The dancers applauded the musicians, and Josie clapped as well, hardly knowing what she was doing.

"Come out to the terrace with me," he said. "I want to talk to you."

A warm blush spread up her neck. That smoky look in his eyes, the strong hints he was giving…she couldn't mistake his sensual intention. And it excited her. Her heart gave a little skip, that old impulsive skip, the one that wanted her to ignore consequences.

But his cool reserve would hurt her if she trusted him. And why was she even thinking about intimacy with him when only weeks before she'd been engaged to his closest friend?

Yet she wanted to hear what he had to say almost as much as she didn't.

*Just think of all the foolish things you've already done,* her conscience scolded. *There must be no more impulsive behavior.* She must learn from her past mistakes and focus on making careful, considered choices from now on.

"It's not a good idea," she said.

"It's a good idea," he said firmly, taking hold of her elbow before she could protest and steering her out the open doors that led to the terrace.

Torches had been set up, and the light from the ballroom spilled out into the night. The moon was bright, and the garden and grass were visible as silvery versions of themselves. He led her over to a stone bench at the edge of the terrace and pulled her down on the bench next to him.

"We shouldn't be out here," she said.

But she so wanted to kiss him.

He took her hand. "I know you've had a terrible time of it. But, Josie, one day soon you're going to wake up and want to make another future for yourself, and when you do, I want to be the man in it."

She drew in a sharp breath. "If this is to do with what happened in the carriage—"

"It isn't. What I want is the chance to erase all that." He leaned a little closer. "To give you something new to think about."

"Something new?" she breathed. The night air was cool, but the warmth of Colin as he moved closer stirred her.

*Move away, move away.*

But she didn't.

"Yes," he said. "Like this." He bent his head and touched his lips to hers. Softly, but not tentatively. He lingered there, teasing, coaxing her to open to him.

As she sat there, wanting suddenly to melt against him while knowing guilt would assail her the minute she did, his hands came up on either side of her neck, as if holding her so that he could beguile her better. He seemed suddenly masterful at this. She'd never thought...

But she was having trouble thinking, because he was distracting her with slow, importunate kisses at one corner of her mouth, then along her bottom lip, then the top, just as though he knew she couldn't resist him forever.

And what was Colin up to, anyway? He was Nicholas's friend, too. How could he allow himself to do this?

His mouth traveled along her jaw, and he stopped to linger just under her ear.

"Let me in, Josie," he murmured.

How she wanted to. But how could she trust him with her heart? He was being tender and warm now, but what about the cold way he'd proposed the first time, and the pushy, angry way he'd behaved the second time? She wanted closeness and love, not just desire.

She lifted a hand and placed it on his chest, half to push him away, half, she knew, to touch him more, a sort of exquisite agony. She was so vulnerable to him. The hard curve of muscle suggested itself to her through the exquisite fabric of his coat and shirt.

"We can't. Nicholas..." Her voice wasn't firm as it should be, but Colin wasn't paying attention anyway. He rubbed the delicate rasp of his incipient whiskers under her ear, releasing a shower of shivers.

"Nick cared about us," he murmured, pressing kisses along her jawline as he moved away from her neck. "He would have wanted us to seize what happiness we could, and not do penance our whole lives."

*Would* Nicholas have wanted that? And what kind

of happiness did he mean? If only he would speak of what was in the heart he kept so guarded.

She closed her eyes, thinking to treasure the feel of him for just this stolen moment. Her mind was so fuzzy with desire that she hardly remembered why she was protesting. His strength, mingled with that intoxicating tenderness, made her want to believe she could trust him with her heart.

"I," she whispered, not even knowing what she wanted to say. His lips hovered at the corner of her mouth, and she shifted so her mouth met his and opened to him.

He groaned and gathered her in his arms and their tongues met in a sensuous swirl. She lost track of everything as they kissed.

When he finally broke away, he buried his face in the crook of her neck. "Josie," he said in a voice that was almost a groan, "you'll make me wild."

*Wild.* She felt half-wild herself, and the realization brought her back to herself. She moved a little away from him.

"Josie?"

"I don't know what came over me," she said. In the ballroom yards away, a piece of music was just coming to an end amid enthusiastic clapping. Where they sat on the terrace was shadowy and well away from the louder noise and glow spilling out by the open doors to the ballroom. In the bushes behind them, she could hear the rustling of a small creature.

"I think you do," he said. "The same thing that came over me. If you only knew how much I want to be with you."

Did he truly? Now that she wasn't in his arms, she could focus her thoughts, and she was remembering all the reasons this was a terrible idea. But there was a look in his eyes of sincerity. What if there *could* be a chance for them?

Could she trust him with her heart? What if he turned cold again or pushed her away? She was horribly confused by her internal back and forth, and she needed to think, but she couldn't do it with him looking at her.

"I'm a bit hot," she said.

He chuckled, a sound of masculine gloating. She crossed her arms, forcing herself to be immune to this new, arrogant Colin so she could think clearly.

"Would you mind fetching me a lemonade?"

She watched him go back in through the doors of his grand manor. Tall, with that rangy frame, his clothes hung on him beautifully, the costly, impeccable attire of an earl who could have bought up her family's estate and thrown it away without feeling the least pinch.

Could he possibly feel as unsure and reckless as she did right now?

Could he ever open himself to her the way she dreamed of her husband opening to her? She wanted a union of souls, and she and he had had that in many ways as friends. But the unruly, emotional way she was feeling right now—could feel that way? Could he love her, and could love grow between them when he seemed to want to avoid undisciplined feelings? She was afraid of getting her heart broken trying to find out.

She gazed out over the garden and wished she were wiser.

As her eyes adjusted to the darker area beyond the light thrown out by the ballroom, she thought she detected some movement at the back of the garden, near the path that led toward Jasmine House. Was someone coming?

The feeble light played tricks on her, so that in one moment she thought she saw movement, and the next she was certain it was only those harmless little floating spots that sometimes appeared in her vision.

"Is someone there?" she called out, though the music had started up again in the ballroom, and it wouldn't have been easy to hear her. Was someone coming along the path from Jasmine House? "Is that you, Matthew? Will?"

No one replied, but out of the deep shadow of the big lilac bushes she was certain now that she saw a figure emerging. Someone tall, she made out as the shadowy figure moved closer, and wearing high, well-shined boots that caught the moonlight. Her brothers didn't have boots like those.

A shiver ran down her spine. Why hadn't the man responded? Was he a party guest just arriving? But why was he arriving at the back of the house, and from the direction of Jasmine House? The Cardworthys weren't expecting any visitors.

And then, as the man drew close, something tugged at her, something familiar about the way he moved. The moonlight caught the outline of curly hair and touched on the military erectness of the man's posture. She understood who it was just as he spoke to her from perhaps fifteen feet away.

"It's you, isn't it, Josie."

*That voice.* His voice. Yes. It was. It was Nicholas.

But she couldn't reply because it was as though all the air had been sucked out of her lungs. She could only stare as he drew nearer, and take in the now dimly visible details of his face and the forgotten way he swung his arms.

And then he was standing before her at the edge of the terrace. "Josie?"

She stood and found her voice. "Nicholas. You're here," she said stupidly, her voice hoarse.

His lips slanted ruefully. "The rumors of my death were somewhat exaggerated. I'm sorry to appear like this—it must be rather a shock."

He paused, and neither of them said anything, but just looked at each other. "I've just come from your mother," he said finally. "She sent me on here."

"Yes, of course," Josie said, drawing in a steadying breath to calm herself from the shock of seeing him. In the greater light afforded by the ballroom candles, his brown eyes shone with something that looked like eagerness. "And it is simply amazing to see you. Astonishing." Her voice was dry, and she was grateful for the darkness, because she thought guilt must be written all over her features.

She had, only moments before, been kissing Colin.

Never mind what had happened in London.

And here was her fiancé, back from the dead. If ever there were a time to faint, this would be it. She rather wished she could, or that a hole would open up and drop her away to some place where she could sort out everything that had happened in the last few months.

"Josie, Josie," he said warmly, shaking his head, "I can't begin to tell you how good it is to see you. If you only knew how thoughts of you have sustained me all this time." He laughed softly. "And how I wish," he said in a low, private voice, "that we had married long ago."

She could only stare, unable to speak.

"Nicholas?" said a deep voice behind her.

# Nineteen

OH GOD. COLIN.

Josie's thoughts, barely recovered from the shock of Nicholas's appearance, began to race. Colin was standing there holding the lemonade she'd asked for, an astonished expression on his face.

How much had he heard?

"Is it really you, Nick?" he said.

"Colin, old boy," Nick said with a smile, "you look like you've seen a ghost, and I can't blame you."

"My God," Colin breathed.

Josie could only watch as the men stepped forward to embrace, Colin handing her the lemonade as he did so. The heartiness of their embrace could leave no doubt as to how happy each was to see the other.

When they stepped apart, Colin said, "What happened? We were told you were mortally wounded in battle near a burning building, that you were missing but couldn't have survived."

Nicholas shook his head even as Josie still struggled to take in his presence. He was real, he was here. He was alive and safe, thank heaven.

"I nearly didn't survive. I was wounded in the gut, the kind of injury that's generally fatal, but it seems someone dragged me to safety, and I was still alive when the French came through the field after the battle. Being that I was an officer and thus possibly of use, they carted me off along with their wounded."

"And for your family and friends to be told you were dead," Josie said, thinking of all the suffering and trouble that had ensued. "What a thing."

Colin's attention was all on Nicholas. He seemed calm and clearly so happy to see his friend. As happy as she was. But oh, what a coil.

"Have you been to see your sister and brother yet?" Colin asked. Nicholas's parents were dead.

Nicholas shook his head. "I wrote them, but after stopping to see my commander, I wanted to come here first," he said, looking at Josie.

To see her.

Guilt stabbed her. She could feel Colin's eyes on her, but she absolutely couldn't look at him. If she'd thought she wanted the ground to open before, that was nothing to now.

Nicholas was here, and he'd had an awful, awful time of it, and right now could only be about him and the welcome he deserved. She took his hand. "I'm so grateful to those who took care of you."

⤛⤜

Colin watched Josie take Nick's hand. Relief and happiness ran through him in equal measures, along with the awareness that Nick's arrival also meant complications.

But Nick was back, and thank God for that.

He'd escaped certain doom at the hands of the French if discovered as a spy, which meant possibly that he'd had help from his French lady-spy, Colin thought, then pushed the idea away. He didn't care how Nick had been saved, only that he was alive.

Josie smiled at Nick, and a hideous, profoundly unwanted bolt of jealousy shot through Colin.

"I'm sure you will be giving people apoplexies right and left, Nicholas," she said.

Nick laughed, and the warm look that passed between him and Josie made Colin wish he were anywhere else. At the bottom of a swamp, alone in a desert—anywhere but here, where he could see the affection between Josie and Nick.

He felt wretched, as though he'd always had designs on Josie and acted on them the minute he was able. It wasn't true—he'd struggled hard against it becoming true, and only succumbed in a moment of weakness—but it felt true, and it would look terrible should Nick discover what he'd been up to with Josie.

He didn't know how he was going to do this—be with the two of them—especially now that he'd touched and known her. Holding himself back with her since he'd returned from London had been excruciating, but he'd done it, knowing he must win her over to the idea of them.

And now all that was smashed. Nick was here. If only he'd come home two months ago, before Colin had touched her, he would have been able to cope, to remain detached.

Damn, damn, damn!

He forced a genial smile. "You two must have quite a bit to say to each other after all these months apart. Why don't I give you some time to catch up while I go play host to all these guests? And then I can make an announcement, and Nick can come in and have a hero's welcome."

Nick made a wry face. "The public welcome. Not as wonderful as the private one. And I want to hear about everything I missed while I was dead, Colin. Have you solved all of history's riddles? How's the soldiers' hospital doing? And," he said with a mischievous look, "have you found a woman yet to be your countess?"

Colin could feel Josie's eyes on him, doubtless desperately wondering what he would say, whether he would reveal anything of what had gone between them.

"All in good time, Nicholas," he said. "You'll stay at Greenbrier of course."

Nick grinned. "I'd hoped you wouldn't mind. My carriage is waiting at Jasmine House."

"I'll have someone sent over to bring your things." Colin took out his watch. "Why don't I give you twenty minutes, and then I'll make the announcement."

"By Jove," Nick said exuberantly, "but I can't tell you both how good it is to be here!"

❧

"Well," Nicholas said to Josie with a laugh as Colin disappeared through the doors to the ballroom, "where to begin?"

Josie was glad for his laughter to ease some of the tension she was feeling, though she was afraid that if she started laughing herself, she'd surrender to hysteria.

"Begin by telling me everything," she said. "Tell me how you got here."

So he told her about his wounds, and how his recovery had taken weeks and weeks.

"I could barely even speak my name for the longest time, I was so weak. Then it took time to get strong again. But once I was well, a French doctor smuggled me out on a boat to England. The chap didn't care a fig for Napoleon, from what I gathered, and he couldn't stand the idea that he'd saved me only to have me be hanged for a spy."

"A spy!" Josie said. "And were you?"

"Let's just say," he replied in a low voice, "that it wouldn't have been good for any of us soldiers if I'd been forced to talk. So I'm doubly lucky to have gotten away."

A soft look came over his face. "But I've been thinking, ever since I realized I might truly see you again. You've believed these last few months that I was dead, believed that our engagement had been ended by death. I don't think it's fair to you to simply pick up where we left off a year ago, and I have a plan to which I hope you'll agree."

❧

At the end of a set of dances, Colin moved to the center of his ballroom and called for the attention of his guests. Then he introduced Nick as the hero he was, and stepped to the side and watched as his friend received richly deserved, thunderous applause.

With a gracious and humble smile, Nick thanked the guests for their good wishes.

"And I must extend my gratitude publicly to the French doctor who couldn't stand the idea that, I, his patient, would be tortured for information as soon as I was well. He helped me escape, so you see, not all Frenchmen are devils."

Laughter and a few ironic cheers for "the frogs" amid cries of "*one* good man among 'em."

Through it all, Josie looked on saucer-eyed. Colin would have given anything to know what she was thinking, but he had to suppose he wouldn't like what he discovered.

Finally, Nick summoned Josie to his side.

"More than a year ago I met dear, beautiful Josephine Cardworthy for the first time. We only had a short time together before I had to return to Spain, and then, after what was a very long year for both of us, she received the news of my death. I'm certain you'll all agree that our path has not been smooth."

Cheers and shouts of "hear, hear!"

"Which is why"—Nick turned to Josie, who was smiling stiffly—"I have asked her to set aside our engagement so that I can have the pleasure, and the delightful challenge, of courting and winning her all over again."

The room erupted into cheers.

And indeed, Colin himself was far from unaffected by this news.

৵৹

Much later, after Josie had danced twice with Nicholas and had a few minutes to talk and laugh with him in between all the people who wished to congratulate him and hear about his experiences in Spain, she saw him speaking with their voluble vicar and knew this was her chance to talk to Colin.

Ever since Nicholas had appeared, she'd been in agony—of happiness at his return, and guilt over all that happened while he was gone, all of which must now be put aside. It was for the best anyway.

The hope dawning tonight that there might really be something between her and Colin had been wishful and foolish, she saw that now. Nicholas had a right to her affections. And she knew that the kind of man she needed for her husband must be open, like him. She'd only been deluding herself over Colin.

Little waves of panic kept washing over her. Colin *must* know that Nick could never learn what had passed between them.

Surely he knew it?

She found him near the door to the entrance hall, having a word with his butler. She waited until they were finished, then grabbed Colin's hand and tugged him through the foyer. He didn't say anything as she led him into the library and shut the door behind them. She flopped back against it.

"What are we doing?" he said.

"We have to talk. Nick can't know anything of what happened between us. No one can know. Everything will have to go back to the way it was before he left for Spain."

Saying these words felt horrible. What had passed between her and Colin over the last months had been mysterious and sometimes thrilling, but it had also felt as if her heart had been tossed in a cart pulled by a spooked horse. It didn't matter, though, what had happened between them, because Nick was back and she owed him her devotion.

"But Nick's just said that you won't go back to the way things were," Colin said. "That you are not now engaged."

She pressed her lips together. "He still wants to marry me. You heard him: he wants to court me all over again."

He didn't reply but looked at her steadily, those familiar, intelligent, gray-green eyes weighing her. She knew the sudden, insane desire to rush into his arms and weep with emotional fatigue and confusion, but he wasn't her confidant and older-brother figure anymore.

His silence was starting to feel like an accusation. Finally she said, "You know that Nicholas and I were meant to be married—it was only circumstance keeping us apart."

"Was it."

He was being so cool, so controlled, and what else should she expect, or even want from him? It was the way he was. And cool control was what they needed. But there was something *leashed* about him now, too, that made her uneasy.

"So you'll promise never to speak of what happened between us." She tried to read his eyes as she'd once felt able to do, but they were shadowy now, when she so needed to know what he was thinking.

"No. I can't promise that."

"What?" She blinked. "You have to. It will be a disaster if he finds out."

"I don't agree with you. In fact, I wonder if we shouldn't tell him right now."

"Are you out of your mind? He would hate us both."

Anguish darkened his eyes. "Maybe. Probably at first."

The muscles of his jaw worked, as though he were clenching his teeth. "He is like a brother to me, and I rejoice that he is here and well. I so want for him to be happy. But things have shifted since we thought he was gone, and it would be false to simply paper over that fact. It would be unnatural."

"I made a promise to him," Josie said. "He's told me how that promise was a beacon for him. He's a good man, about whom I care very much. *There's nothing else to say.*"

"Josie," he said in a hard voice, "you two were engaged for a year, during which time neither of you saw each other. You don't even know him very well, do you? Do you know all that he's capable of?"

"I don't know what you're trying to get at."

He frowned but didn't say more, and looked away over her shoulder. If anything, his jaw looked harder.

"Obviously," she said, "I don't know him as well as I might, but we connected deeply enough a year ago to pledge ourselves to each other."

"Marriage is for life, Josie. It would be wrong to marry a man for whom you didn't care deeply, simply because you once said you would."

Impatient anger rushed over her, that he, who'd never spoken to her of devotion, should talk about caring deeply. "How dare you think to say whom I hold in my affection?"

Before she could even react, he'd moved closer

and grabbed her by the shoulders and leaned in, his eyes penetrating deep into hers. "How dare I? I'm the man with whom you shared the deepest embrace of your life. The man who knows you far better than Nicholas—knows your faults as well as your virtues—and wants you, all of you."

His eyes blazed into hers, and his words lit something inside her. She wanted to listen to him, but she didn't trust herself. So he wanted her. Wanting wasn't loving.

She tipped her chin up. This was how it had to be.

"I'm not changing my mind, and I shall certainly accept Nicholas if—when he asks again. He's the man I want as my husband."

She thought his breath gave a hitch at her words. Even now, when she knew absolutely that she shouldn't, she wanted to sway into him and feel the comfort of his embrace.

His eyebrows drew into two black slashes. "I don't believe that."

His forceful tone startled her, but she crossed her arms and faced him down. "You'll have to."

He stepped closer. "And you think that just turning away from what we have together is going to work. That you can simply forget it."

"We don't have anything together but friendship," she said firmly.

"Now you're just lying," he said.

Colin was struggling not to pull Josie into his arms and either shake some sense into her, or kiss her violently, neither of which was appropriate. Before Nick's return, Colin had been planning tonight as a significant step in his campaign to win Josie, but that was all changed.

She and Nick were no longer engaged, though there was an understanding between them. And yet, it was not that simple, because Colin and she had something too, something important and real. How could she simply put that aside to be with Nick—wouldn't that create a lie?

And Nicholas—what was he up to, breaking the engagement? Did he really mean to court her again, or was this a chance for them both to cool off and discover if they were really meant to be together? He couldn't forget that letter Nick had sent, telling of his deep attraction to the French spy. How did she figure into what Nick wanted?

"I have to go." She fumbled behind her for the door handle, but he put out a hand next to her head and held the door closed.

She closed her eyes as if to gather her forces, and the fringe of her lashes against the top of her cheek gave her a young, vulnerable look that tore at him, but he knew he couldn't afford to be merciful.

"Don't think that turning away from what's between us will make it disappear. That running into Nick's arms will wipe away doubt and erase your need for the connection we share."

She tipped her chin up and her spine seemed to stiffen. "Stop trying to tell me what to do."

"You have feelings for me. Remember that *you* kissed *me* first in London. Never mind what happened in the carriage."

Fury brought red to her cheeks, and he was glad for the reaction. However much he'd always despised strong emotion, he saw now that the last thing he wanted was for her to be unmoved by him.

"How can you bring that up? We agreed to forget about it."

"I said we would move forward. I could never forget it."

She turned her face away. "Stop talking about this."

"Not until you admit what you were feeling on the terrace, just before Nick came back."

Her closed-off expression said, *Never.*

After a moment she said, "I want you to promise you won't say anything about what's passed between us to Nick."

He took his time answering. "Very well, I promise not to say anything—*yet.* But I think you're just making it worse by waiting."

"What is *wrong* with you, Colin Pearce? If you were a gentleman, you wouldn't want to torment me with my mistakes and threaten the happiness of your best friend."

"It's a complicated scenario, isn't it? And it calls for a nuanced response. I'll do what I have to do, if it comes to it."

She clenched her teeth and looked pointedly at his arm holding the door closed next to her head. "If you will excuse me?"

"Certainly," he said, "as long as you understand that I have in no way surrendered." He lifted his arm and she yanked the door open and left.

# Twenty

It was late when Josie reentered the ballroom in a daze, and the guests had begun to leave. The musicians were playing a soft tune but nobody was dancing anymore. Most people were sitting in small groups talking, or making their way toward the cloakroom.

The vicar was still talking to Nicholas at one of the small tables near the edge of the dancing area. Edwina was talking with Lawrence and a young lady Josie didn't know.

Hardly able to think what she was doing, Josie moved away from the doorway, wanting to put as much distance between herself and the inevitable entrance of Colin as she could. She found a spot across the room near one of the large columns where she could prop herself up and gather her tattered spirits.

Nicholas was turned slightly away from her, so she could just see his profile, and she absorbed the details of his person that had faded from her memory over the last year. His light brown curls were touched with gold, doubtless from the Spanish sun, and the scarlet of his military coat announced his significance among men, along with the appealing erectness of his military-straight posture. His face in profile had clean, strong lines that any woman would find handsome. No wonder she'd been so smitten with him.

He must have sensed her gaze, because he turned and smiled. She smiled back, forcing herself not to think about how traitorous she was because everything else aside, she was so glad he was safe. He'd fought for his country and been wounded, and the whole time, apparently, she'd given him hope. She was glad.

But she was still shaken from what had happened with Colin, and the idea of being courted by Nicholas was too much to think about, so she didn't.

He parted from the vicar and made his way over to her.

"Josie, darling girl, I wondered where you'd gone to. Not that I wasn't well occupied during your absence," he said with a little grin. "I'd forgotten how Vicar can *talk*."

"I was only taking the air. It's warm tonight."

"You do look a bit flushed," he said with concern in his voice, unaware how guilty his observation made her feel.

*Of course she was flushed—she'd just come from Colin.*

She resolved at that moment to avoid Colin like the plague, because the only thing she knew anymore was that she did reckless things when he was around.

"I hope you're not unwell?" Nicholas said.

She forced cheeriness into her smile. "Not at all. But it's late, and I'd like to go home. I was just about to collect Edwina and Lawrence so we could walk back."

"I'll escort you. We haven't had much time together tonight, and there's so much to say. I've told you all about what's happened to me over the last year, but I've hardly heard anything about you."

"There's not much to report."

Behind Nicholas she saw Colin enter the room. He remained near the door, his host's duties keeping him there as he bid good-bye to parting guests. She collected Edwina and Lawrence and they made their way toward the door with Nicholas. Awkwardness pulled at her steps, making her legs feel like lead.

Edwina and Lawrence, the first to approach Colin, thanked him for a fine evening.

"I'm just going to see the Cardworthys home," Nicholas said, "and then I'll return."

Josie willed Colin not to look at her, and perhaps he felt her intention—though he'd hardly been acquiescent earlier—because he merely thanked them for coming and wished them a good evening.

They made their way back along the path to Jasmine House, though the familiar way felt changed and a little unfriendly in the darkness. Or perhaps it was that she felt guilty, and as though even the trees and birds must be judging her.

Lawrence, in between enormous yawns he tried to conceal, began to ask Nicholas all kinds of questions about his war experiences.

Edwina scolded him. "Lawrence, for goodness' sake, the man just survived a nearly fatal injury and spent months in the care of the enemy. Perhaps he doesn't wish to speak of it."

"No, no, it's quite all right," Nicholas said. The warmth in his voice reminded Josie of the open way he was, which had been so appealing from the first. It still was appealing, even if a little voice kept whispering that a man with mysterious hidden depths would fascinate her for a lifetime.

"I should have been extremely interested myself, in your place, Lawrence," Nick continued. "Though I'm here to tell you war is often far more adventurous-sounding in reports as opposed to the actual experience. We spent hours and hours doing hardly anything at all, sitting about in the hot sun waiting to engage with the enemy. It was, when we were not at risk of losing life or limb, often fairly dull."

"Dull!" Lawrence said incredulously.

They reached Jasmine House, and Edwina and Lawrence said good night. Josie, too, yearned for her bed and the peace of her bedchamber. She was exhausted, wrung out, and overwhelmed.

But Nicholas seemed unwilling to part just yet, and so she lingered in the garden with him. Inside the house behind them, Edwina lit a few candles in the now-deserted sitting room and moved about as if straightening up, giving them a chaperone but also privacy.

"Was it truly boring at war?" she asked. "Your letters spoke of the many delights you discovered. The beauties of Spain, the interesting people."

"Yes, that was part of it, too. I exaggerated a bit for Lawrence, not wanting him to dream of war as a valorous adventure when it is far more compromised than that. I make no doubt that illnesses alone are killing more men than cannonballs, and what a misery to die alone and suffering, far from home."

"And the French? How did it feel to have a whole country for your enemy?"

He was silent for a minute, and she thought he wouldn't answer. But finally he said, "The French are much like us."

He reached for her hands and held them lightly. Through the fabric of her evening gloves, she felt only a little warmth from his hands, as though she were detached from him. She knew this was wrong, that she'd been his fiancée and was on the way to being that again, but she couldn't see how to fix the trouble she was in, caught between her need for Colin and the devotion she owed Nicholas.

"Josie, dearest. In the whole last year, you were never far from my mind. When I wrote that you were the light that carried me through the darkest of days, I meant it. Thank you for being that light."

She swallowed, grateful for the darkness as guilt gripped her. This good man believed she was a paragon, and that was in no way true. But if the thought of her had brought him any relief from the hardships of war, she was grateful, and she couldn't bring herself to taint that by letting him know he'd put his faith in a deeply flawed woman. She could only resolve to be deserving of such esteem.

"I'm glad if in any way I cheered your spirits."

"You did, a hundred, hundred times. And I meant what I said about courting you anew. You deserve flowers and poems and every good thing, and I mean to provide them."

"Oh, no, that's not necessary!" For a moment, she desperately wanted to confess all, but she resisted that weakness.

He squeezed her hands lightly then let them go.

"Indeed it is. And now, as we are not engaged, I mustn't linger. But I hope I may call on you tomorrow and invite you and your sister for a walk?"

How was she ever going to stand the wrongness of this fine man believing he was courting a virtuous woman? But she didn't see a choice, because how could she ever admit what would hurt and disappoint him so?

"Oh, er..." she began, remembering the campaign to get her mother off the divan, which had not yet met with any success.

He looked puzzled at her hesitation, and she smiled. "Of course I will look forward to your visit, but I'm not certain Edwina and I will be free when you call." She explained about their plan for her mother, which he found amusing, and he assured her he wouldn't be offended if she was busy when he visited.

They said good night, and she watched him go along the garden path that led to Greenbrier, over whose roofline the moon was setting. She sent up a silent prayer that Colin wouldn't decide to tell Nicholas everything they'd been up to. She didn't at all know what the Earl of Ivorwood would do anymore.

❧

Colin was in the library late the next morning, reviewing accounts, when Nick came in. Colin smiled and put down his quill.

"In your favorite place I see," Nick said, dropping into the chair across from Colin's desk.

Colin gave him a dry look. "I do frequent other places, you know. And our very first meeting aside,

I think it's been well established that I'm a far better punter than you, never mind my fencing skills."

Nick gave a bark of laughter. "I don't at all agree any of that's been established, and I will concede nothing in the realm of fencing. Now that I'm back, we'll have to see about a round or two to measure our skills."

Colin smiled. "It really is quite amazing to have you here, when we all thought we'd said farewell to you for good. I'm having a bit of trouble getting used to it."

Nick leaned forward and plucked a slim volume off the desk and began flipping through the pages. "We had some jolly good times at university," he said. "Life was so uncomplicated then."

"Yes."

"Can't begin to tell you how sentimental a man gets when he doesn't think he'll see his friends and family ever again."

"It's understandable."

Nick was quiet for a minute as he flipped through the book some more. Not looking up, he said, "I want you to know that nothing happened in France, between me and the lady I wrote you about. Giselle."

Colin wondered specifically what he meant—that he'd never touched her? Because he'd evidently wanted her. And yet, nothing could be more understandable than temptation; Colin would be a hypocrite to suggest otherwise.

"But something might have," Colin said. "You might have wanted something to happen."

"Whether I did or not, the important thing is that nothing did."

"*Is* that the important thing?"

"Of course it is," Nick said impatiently, tossing the book back on the desk. "Nothing happened because the thought of Josie kept me chaste. How she is so lovely and lively. How she was waiting for me here, in England, where life is so much less complicated than it was in Spain. And far more perfect."

"I wouldn't say life here is perfect. Or uncomplicated."

"Oh, you know what I mean. Anyway, it's Josie who's perfect. She's the kind of woman any man would want for a wife. The kind of woman I've always wanted for a wife."

"A kind of woman? You make her sound like something you've chosen from a shop."

Nick's brows lowered. "What a thing to say."

"Well, Josie's not some sort of ideal of a woman. You knew her for less than two months before you got engaged—perhaps not enough time to see some of her less perfect qualities."

"Really, Colin," Nick said, the hint of tension on his face melting into laughter, "anyone would think you were warning me off her."

*Was* he doing that? Why the hell had he even said anything, when he couldn't trust himself to be impartial about anything related to Josie being with Nick? When he was still accustoming himself to the shock of having fallen in love with her? He didn't know how she felt about him—he might never—and it was making him crazy.

Nick deserved his chance with her—there was no question of that.

If his two friends truly loved each other, then so

be it. He would bow out. But until such time as he was certain that was the case, and that he'd gotten Josie to see she was making a choice—likely the most important one of her life—he wouldn't give up the hope of her.

"But of course," Nick continued in a reasonable tone that made Colin feel perfidious, "you know her better than I do. I rather envy you that—the chance you've had, living so close, to see her all the time, to know her family better." He chuckled. "I'm rather surprised you didn't fall in love with her yourself."

Oh, this was rich. Someday, perhaps when he was eighty and all his hopes for love and family happiness had thoroughly expired, he would have a belly laugh over it.

"Josie and I are extremely good friends," he said, but was that even true anymore? No. They'd gone far beyond friendship, and they couldn't go back.

He had no idea what that said about his future, or how he would cope with the hole that would be in his life if she chose Nick, because he knew for certain that if she did, he wouldn't be able to see either of them for at least a decade or two, until he could manage not to care.

Nick nodded. "You can't know how glad I am the two of you became such friends. I can't thank you enough for keeping an eye out for her while I was gone. It allowed me not to worry about her, knowing she was taken care of. And it was incredibly good of you, really beyond the call of duty, taking her and Edwina to London."

Colin swallowed hard, so tempted to just get it out in the open, to let Nick know he had competition for

Josie's hand. But he'd promised Josie he wouldn't say anything yet. He didn't like this, though—he didn't like it at all.

"I'm a friend of the family, Nick. With or without you in the picture, I would have been a friend to the Cardworthys."

"Of course. I know that, and I didn't mean to suggest anything—well, hang it all, I'm just so pleased to be here I'm not even certain what I'm saying."

He stood up. "I'm off to visit Josie, if you don't think it's too early for the Cardworthys."

"No," Colin said, realizing that if he wanted to see Josie today, he'd have to go now with Nick or find a pretext for being there on his own later. He decided to stay home. "It's not too early." He picked up a book he'd put aside on his desk. "And you can give this to Mrs. Cardworthy. It's part of the campaign to get her off the divan."

Nick read the spine of the book. "*Journeys in Italy* by Mrs. Renfrew." He glanced up.

Colin shrugged. "Inspiration to travel."

Nick laughed. "Much good it may do, after four years of chaining herself to a divan."

Colin watched Nick leave with a sense of relief. It sickened him that he might feel relief at having time away from his friend, but with all that could not be said, and the raging jealousy he must each moment force aside, he did.

Blast, what a muddle. What a secret, disordered, damned muddle.

Yet here was the thing he couldn't stop thinking about: Did Josie and Nick really love each other?

Or might she have been coming to love *him*, Colin?

How could she marry Nick, if that was the case, wounded war hero or not?

But could Colin really allow himself to be the cause of depriving his best friend of the woman who'd been his lodestar over the last year, when he'd been living through the hell of war?

❧

Mrs. Cardworthy, not having gone to the ball, was on the divan at her usual time the morning afterward and calling out to the servants for all manner of things.

Josie listened to their voices as she lay in bed. She didn't want to get up for the day. However, it wasn't long before Sally knocked on her door with the message that her mother was looking forward to seeing her as soon as possible.

Bleary with sleep, Josie dragged a brush through her hair and put on her yellow and white striped muslin gown, knowing that her mother would want to hear all about the ball, and not at all wanting to think about it herself. Especially her conversation with Colin.

As she descended the stairs, it occurred to her that it had now been two days since she and Edwina had discarded Mama's elixir, and yet their mother seemed so far unchanged by its absence. Josie had expected any day—any hour—that Mrs. Cardworthy would experience an unhappy withdrawal from the crutch that the elixir had become, but so far there'd been no signs, and now as Josie went into the sitting room, Mrs. Cardworthy seemed just as usual.

Did they really dare hope she would surrender the

elixir so quietly? And yet she'd been so needful of it. Josie felt rather too tired to think about it just then.

"Well, my dear, finally. Edwina is still sleeping," Mama said once Josie had sat down in the chair near the divan, where her mother was already surrounded by a pot of chocolate and a plate of toast. "So Nicholas Hargrave has come back, safe and sound."

"Yes." Josie really didn't want to talk about this, but such reluctance would make no sense to her mother. Anyway, Nicholas was back, and she must accustom herself to the way everything had shifted again. "It was astonishing to see him, of course. But how happy I am—everyone is—that he is alive and recovered from his ordeal."

"It's a great mercy. A blessing for us all." Did her mother pause then, as though collecting herself after saying words spoken reluctantly? Of course Mama was not unkind, but she *had* been rather accepting of the loss of Nicholas when they'd thought him dead.

Eagerness lit her mother's eyes. "Tell me all about the ball. What was Mrs. Townsend wearing? She's known to be fashionable. And the vicar's wife? How many young ladies did Lawrence dance with?"

But Josie was determined not to take the easy path of avoidance that had abetted her mother these last four years. "If only you could have been there, you would have been able to see for yourself." She let the silence stretch out as her mother waited for her to supply answers to her questions.

When it became apparent she would say no more, her mother said tartly, "You might have a little compassion for an invalid, Josephine. I must depend on others to bring the world to me, as I cannot go out to meet it."

"Mama," Josie said in the kindest possible tone she could summon amid the frustration she felt with her mother, "you can go out to meet the world anytime you like. If you would but agree to try to get up and go out, we would all of us help you."

But her mother made no reply, save for a hardening of her jaw. She took up the pot of chocolate and began pouring herself a cup. "And I suppose," she began in a hurt tone, "that now you and Nicholas will pick up where you left off and begin making plans for the wedding."

Josie pressed her lips together. She didn't want to think about the wedding. "In fact, Nicholas has asked me to break our engagement—"

"What? The scoundrel!" her mother said, but there was a note of glee underlying her outrage.

"So he can court me anew," Josie finished. "Because we had so much time apart, and because I believed for nearly two months that he was dead, he thought we needed a fresh start. And I agree with him."

Her mother's eyes lit up. "What a fine idea! Why rush into matrimony?"

Josie just sighed.

Nicholas appeared in the late morning, and Josie and Edwina went for a walk with him. She was grateful that he didn't press her for time alone yet, or even maneuver her aside for a private word. Of course they would have some chances for private words together in the coming days, and she would be glad for it, of course she would. But not just yet.

After Nicholas bid them good-bye to go into town to attend to some affairs, Josie and Edwina paused in the dining room to assess the state of the divan campaign.

"So," Josie said, "do you think Mama could somehow be getting elixir after all? She seems so agreeable today, just as though nothing's changed."

"Maybe she's going to accept things and go along with our plan for her improvement."

"And maybe our hens will fly into town."

Edwina cocked her head. "What's got you so gloomy? I should think you'd be on top of the world, what with Nicholas returned and wanting to court you all over again. I'm sure you were the envy of every woman at the ball last night: to be courted *twice* by a brave and handsome man."

"Of course I'm over the moon that he's come back. And I know how fortunate I am."

"Unless," Edwina said with studied unconcern, "you're having second thoughts about Colin."

"Of course not."

"Really?" Edwina said. "Because I've seen the way he looks at you when he thinks no one's watching, and it's hot enough to set the drapes on fire. And the more I've thought about it, the more I see that you must have been the reason he raced to London to help me."

"He came to help you because he's a friend of the family. Truly, what happened between us will stay in the past."

Edwina gave her a measured, rather skeptical look. "Well then, you won't have any regrets about choosing Nicholas a second time. I suppose you've had an entire year to think about being married to him, even if you didn't get to spend any of that time getting to know him."

She could hear Edwina's suggestion that she might be making a wrong choice, but she didn't dare entertain it.

"Listen, Edwina, if—when Nicholas and I get engaged again, I want you to know I won't fix a wedding date until we've gotten Mama off the divan. I am determined, and I won't leave you here to be responsible for everything."

Edwina waved a hand dismissively and glanced casually out the window, though not before Josie saw the corner of her mouth tremble. "Don't worry about me. I'll have everything I need here, and I always was going to be the spinster aunt. I really am quite satisfied with my lot."

"You're *not* going to be a spinster. If we can get Mama out in the world, and get her to spend some of this fortune that's just sitting around, only think of the gentlemen you might meet in Italy, or Ireland, or any old wonderful place. Or maybe," Josie said with a meaningful look, "you might go back to London and see if you don't run into Whitby again."

Bright color bloomed in Edwina's cheeks. "I could never," she began, then abandoned whatever she was going to say and cleared her throat. "Anyway, Mama looks no more likely to get off that divan than she did before we started our campaign. It's not going to happen."

Josie crossed her arms. "I *vow* that if and when Nicholas proposes, I won't accept him unless Mama gets up and starts really living."

"That's ridiculous and unnecessary. And Nicholas

will think you've lost your mind if you tell him you can't marry him because of this."

"Nevertheless, I won't leave with things as they are."

"We'll see," Edwina said in her best older-sister voice.

At lunchtime, a messenger arrived with an invitation for the Cardworthys to dine at Greenbrier that evening.

"I suppose you girls and Lawrence must go," Mrs. Cardworthy said dispiritedly.

"Mama, you are invited as well," Josie pointed out.

Her mother didn't dignify that with a response beyond saying, "Will and Matthew will keep me company. You may give my regards to Nicholas and Ivorwood."

Josie didn't really want to go—the idea of being in the same room with both Nicholas and Colin now made her feel ill—but it was going to happen at some point, so she knew it was best to get it over with.

"Honestly," Edwina said cheerfully that evening as the three of them walked up the path to Greenbrier, "you're moving so slowly, Josie, one would think you weren't eager to arrive."

"Maybe she's changed her mind and doesn't like Nicholas after all!" Lawrence said with gleeful, brotherly wickedness. "Wouldn't that be hilarious, and so like a woman."

"It would not," Josie said, "and if anyone is inconstant, it is young men. I heard you telling Matthew last week that Mary Warren is the prettiest girl in the world, and yesterday it was Lucinda Smith."

"Do stop bickering, the two of you," Edwina said, "or you'll make us unpleasant guests."

"Who are you," Lawrence said, "and what have you done with Edwina? She loves to bicker."

"Hush," Edwina said softly, and Josie felt a surge of affection for her, and sadness for the troubles that had changed her.

Dinner felt like a performance to Josie. Nicholas kept up a steady, respectful attendance that painted her as the golden girl of England, unknowingly miring her deeper in guilt. Colin said little, though she felt him smoldering at her from the far end of the table.

The only thing that made the evening bearable was her brother, who kept dragging the conversation back to the army, the navy, and the war. Josie had never thought she would feel grateful to Napoleon, but the topic kept the conversation neutral.

The men declined to retire from the ladies, and the party lingered at the table, talking of Spain, until Edwina stood and said they must go. Josie wanted to leave the room quickly, but Edwina had stopped Nicholas to ask him about the colors of fabric he'd observed in Spain, and Lawrence was asking about cavalry horses.

Colin was behind her at the far end of the table, but she didn't look at him as she made for the door. She wasn't quite there when he took hold of her arm.

She turned around. "Let me go," she whispered intently, not wanting to draw attention to them.

He smiled. "Never."

She blinked. "This is some sort of competition to you, isn't it? And to think I used to consider you sweet."

"Never consider a man sweet, my dear. You will be overlooking intentions of which you can have no understanding."

His voice softened in a way that reminded her of all

the friendship that had existed between them. "I miss being with you, dearest Josephine."

With a glance that told him the others had just moved through the doorway, he leaned forward and brushed his cheek against hers as though he were going to tell her something more, but he didn't. Instead, the light scratch of his whiskers gave her shivers.

And then he was standing next to her, gesturing for her to leave the room ahead of him in the most gentlemanly manner possible. She wanted to yell at him to leave her be, but of course she could not.

# Twenty-one

THE CACOPHONY THAT AWOKE JOSIE THE NEXT DAY was not unexpected. It was her mother, yelling angrily downstairs in the sitting room. Josie had a fairly good idea what it was about, since after Mrs. Cardworthy had gone upstairs to bed, Josie had gone into the deserted sitting room to search for hidden elixir.

She found it in the most safe, convenient place of all for her mother: under the divan seat cushions.

Now she scrambled out of bed and started pulling on clothes as the raging went on below.

"You will tell me where it is, Sally, or you can find yourself another position," Mrs. Cardworthy thundered as Josie hastily did up the ties on the first gown her hand touched, a white lawn gown with tiny pink roses embroidered on the bodice that she'd gotten in London.

"It wasn't me, ma'am," came the pitiable reply.

As Josie rushed down the stairs, she heard a cry and the sounds of the sobbing maid running out into the garden.

In the drawing room, Mrs. Cardworthy sat stiffly

upright on the divan, every line of her body emanating fury.

"Josephine Cardworthy," she said in a dark voice Josie hardly recognized that made her think of witches, "is this your doing?"

"Yes. I found your hidden elixir, and it's all gone now."

Her mother's face grew livid. "How dare you!"

Edwina appeared at Josie's side just as the wooden India tiger hit the wall by the doorway and landed with a clatter on the floor, minus its yellow-and-black tail.

"Gad, what do we do now?" she said under her breath.

"We can't give in," Josie whispered. Neither of them advanced into the room, preferring to stay out of range. Josie found herself wishing for Colin, for his steadiness and wisdom. He always seemed to know what to do in difficult situations. But these were the thoughts of a madwoman, because Colin wasn't simply Colin anymore: he was diabolical and beguiling, and she didn't know what crazy thing he would do next.

To her mother, Josie said, "Mama, the elixir was doing you more harm than good."

"Unfeeling child! All of you—you're the devil's children!" Mrs. Cardworthy said in that witchy, awful voice. "As hard as your father."

"She's terrifying," Edwina murmured. "I fear if we don't let her have the elixir, the servants will all desert us."

"We'll just have to distract her while she gets used to not having it. If we can get her past the craving for it, maybe she won't need it at all."

"I'm afraid of what would happen if she got off the divan in this state."

Mrs. Cardworthy threw several of the brass Indian bowls at her daughters. "Get out! If you're not going to bring the elixir, get out!"

They both retreated into the corridor, out of range.

"We can't allow anyone to see her like this," Edwina said.

"No, only family," Josie agreed.

Edwina gave Josie a serious look. "Not even Colin, or Nicholas, and he's meant to be courting you."

Josie, who'd begun to think she'd had enough time with gentlemen of late, didn't think a holiday from their company was a bad idea. In fact, when she thought about how she was meant to be laying the foundation for her future with Nicholas, she felt so confused and unhappy that she quite wanted at least a month's holiday from both of them, perhaps two.

She realized that where once she had rushed impetuously into decisions, she now felt inclined to postpone making them interminably.

"If Nicholas doesn't want to court me because I can't invite him inside, then he's made of less stern stuff than I thought."

They sent Lawrence in with a tea tray.

"You're her favorite," they said, putting a few biscuits on the tray as a treat, along with the toast their mother always had with her pot of chocolate. "She won't hurt you."

Lawrence returned their encouraging smiles with a grim look, but he took in the tray.

❧

Mrs. Cardworthy had worn herself out with fury by early that afternoon and fallen asleep on the divan. When Nicholas appeared for a visit, Josie invited him to stroll in the garden, where they would be unlikely to disturb her mother—or be disturbed by her, should she awaken and start shouting. Josie decided they would take it as progress that her mother had now gone for half a day without the elixir, however reluctantly.

The early October day was cool and dry with crisp notes of autumn, and the sun shone brightly in a vivid blue sky. A perfectly dreamy day, and here she was with perfectly dreamy Nicholas. This was exactly the sort of scene she'd conjured for herself in the first months after they'd gotten engaged.

He was telling her about everything he wanted to do, now that he was back in England.

"I want to tour the Lake District and travel all through Scotland. I've never made a proper visit there, and they say the fishing can't be topped."

"That sounds lovely," Josie said, even though she couldn't quite imagine it, couldn't imagine what it would be like traveling with a husband. With Nicholas for a husband. She didn't even particularly care for fish.

Self-disgust prodded her. It had been easy enough to dream of a future with Nicholas until she'd crossed over the line of friendship with Colin.

This thought in particular was plaguing her: How long had Colin wanted to touch her? And what was it that he did to her when he touched her? Because she seemed to lose all sense.

It didn't matter. She was going to be with Nicholas. That was the right thing to do.

He looked down at her and smiled. "But of course I hope you shall come with me on my travels, as my wife."

Something caught at her, as if she couldn't tolerate plans for the future, the idea that all those dreams they'd shared when they were courting would soon come to pass. *It's so final*, something in her whispered. *Of course*, she told herself sternly. *What else would it be?*

She put aside her vague reservations. "Aren't you getting a little presumptuous, Mr. Hargrave?" she scolded lightly, glad that the charade of courting again allowed her to keep more formality between them. She needed it just now, but surely with time, she told herself, the idea of marrying him wouldn't feel odd. She was so grateful to him for this chance to get to know each other again.

He grinned, enjoying the game. Fortunately, he seemed content to keep things light between them, for which she was grateful.

"What do you think of a jaunt into Upperton today, Miss Cardworthy? I've a longing for a pot of tea at the Hare and Hound, at one of those funny, half-broken little tables under the birch tree. We could bring your sister and brothers and make an afternoon of it."

"Perfect."

"Shall we send over to see if Ivorwood wants to join us?" Nicholas asked.

"If you like," she said, careful to keep her tone neutral.

A servant was dispatched with a message, but the reply came back that the earl was already engaged.

"Ah, well," Nicholas said, "if I know him, he's

too deeply entombed among his books to want to leave. Probably pondering some crusty old monarch this very moment."

But Edwina was happy to come, as were Lawrence, Will, and Matthew, who were excused from their studies. The group set out cheerfully on foot for the mile walk into town.

*See*, Josie told herself as she listened to Nicholas talk to her brothers, *he is an utterly perfect man. Polished, savvy, charming, and very, very handsome.*

She did wonder about his war experiences, which surely must have had some significant effect on him, but he didn't speak of them much, and when he did it was only in passing. She could easily understand his not wishing to speak of them at all.

They had their tea, and then Nicholas suggested a visit to the vicar, and so they walked to the vicarage and had more tea with Mr. and Mrs. Biddle. Josie was beginning to feel full of drink and a bit tired, but Nicholas seemed to have an inexhaustible supply of energy, and he proposed they make their way back over the hills to the east of the village.

When they got to the hills, he challenged her brothers to sprint down. The boys were quite game. Edwina and Josie stood at the top, watching them.

"Nicholas has a sort of constant motion about him, doesn't he?" Edwina said. "You must find it so diverting."

"Diverting. Yes," Josie said. Though traitorously, while once she'd loved his spirit of constant action, she now felt a little irritated by his need to keep doing things. Being with him was making her feel worn out, and she almost felt that he was *itchy* in her presence.

She couldn't put her finger on it, though, as he'd been nothing but gracious and enthusiastic, and she scolded herself for being silly.

"I'm going to run down as well," she said. "Join me?"

But Edwina only laughed.

So Josie pitched herself down the hill, yelling as her forward momentum almost sent her face-first into the grass, and it really was quite fun. She reached the bottom laughing, and for a moment wondered what Colin would have thought.

But it was good he hadn't come, because she was supposed to be forgetting him. She hoped he was forgetting her, and that he had no plans to reveal any of their secrets to Nicholas. How she wished there weren't any secrets to reveal.

Afterward, they all walked back to Jasmine House. When they arrived, Josie's siblings discreetly disappeared inside, and she walked around to the back garden with Nicholas. They stopped by the path that led to Greenbrier.

"It's been so good to spend time with you today," he said. "It's good to get back to normal. To the way things were supposed to be."

"Yes," she said.

"And I hope it won't be too long before…" He smiled sheepishly. "But of course, we've only just started courting. It's too early to speak of plans."

She didn't want to make plans yet either. Suddenly, she felt grateful for that vow she'd made to Edwina. She cleared her throat. "I should tell you that my mother is not doing very well. She's not exactly ill," she hurried to say as a look of concern came over his face, "it's only that, well, you know how we are trying to urge her to get off the divan?"

"Yes."

"It's not going well at the moment. That is, we've just realized she's been a little...adversely affected by the elixir she's been taking for quite some time, and she's just now given it up. So we're focusing on helping her weather the change."

"I see."

"So you understand, I hope, that I won't feel able to make any plans for the future just yet, until Mama has been helped to find a healthier way of living? That I won't feel I can in good conscience engage myself?"

He absorbed her words. "You wish to say that this undertaking may require some time?"

"Very possibly. I can't say how long. And of course I understand if you feel you cannot wait."

He moved his hand as though he were going to take hers but stopped himself and smiled instead. "Of course I don't mind waiting," he said with surprising cheerfulness. "You waited more than a year for me."

"Oh," she said, "how can you speak of the little I endured while you were away risking your life?"

"Waiting is always hard, isn't it?" A faraway look came into his eyes. "Anyway," he said, refocusing on her, "at least this time we won't be apart. It will be almost easy."

He smiled kindly, and she was relieved to see that he seemed to have taken the news well. She ignored the little stab of disappointment that her words hadn't discouraged him.

He set off down the path and Josie went inside

Jasmine House, where she was greeted with the news that her mother had insisted the doctor be called.

"And when he arrived," Edwina said, having gotten the report from Sally, "she told him she was in desperate need of Framer's Elixir. But it wasn't old Dr. Denton who came—it was his nephew, young Dr. Denton. And young Dr. Denton doesn't believe in elixirs. He examined Mama and told her that she needs exercise and that she must avoid spirits at all cost for at least six months."

"Well, now we have it officially."

"And she liked to hear it just as well." Edwina frowned. "Apparently, he also suggested she take up a hobby or go visiting. He recommended a visit with Mrs. Phillips, since she is also a widow, and won't they have so many things in common."

"How did she take that suggestion?"

"She told him she didn't need anything from 'the locals.' And he said, 'What about our Lord's command to love your neighbor as yourself?' There wasn't really anything she could say in reply to that. But it didn't make her get up, either."

⁂

Late that night, a clattering sounded at Josie's window, waking her up. She jumped out of bed and went over to peer out—and there was Nicholas, standing below.

"Come down," he called up in a stage whisper.

Her eyes widened. What a terrible idea.

"Come down," he whispered again. Worried that someone would hear, she decided to go down and send him on his way. She closed the window, pulled on a wrapper, and crept downstairs. Once in the garden, she didn't at first see anyone. And then he stepped out from behind a tree.

Moonlight glinted on something he was holding. A bottle.

She moved closer so he could hear her whisper. "You shouldn't be here. Go back to Greenbrier and we'll talk tomorrow."

"Josie, dear girl," he said fulsomely. "Come and have a tot of brandy."

"Brandy?" He seemed to have had quite a lot already.

He laughed. "I know it's not the kind of thing young ladies drink."

If only he knew.

"*Je plaisante.*"

*I'm joking*...French? Why was he speaking French?

She grabbed his hand and tugged him to the stone bench that stood at the backside of the great elm at the edge of the garden, so they wouldn't be seen from the house. They sat down, but he perched on the edge of the bench, fidgeting, as though he would jump up at any moment.

"You must go," she said again.

"Can't," he said.

Was he perhaps too bosky to think straight? "What are you doing here, Nicholas?"

He took a drink from the bottle. "Came to see my angel." He grinned at her and tipped the bottle toward her ironically, as though he expected her to be scandalized.

She'd never liked the idea of ladies being angels, all perfect and sweet and docile. But considering everything she'd done with Colin, she felt so far from angelic she might as well have been a fallen woman. If it ever got out, all that she'd said and done in the last few months, that's what she'd be known as. Though surely Colin would never expose her in this way.

"Do you know," he continued, "in Spain, I thought of you whenever I was certain that everything was going to *enfer*. Pardon my language."

He grinned roguishly, and she raised an eyebrow. She'd never seen Nicholas like this. He was drunk, for one thing, which he never had been before in her presence. But more than that, the things he was saying…it was like being privy to his secret thoughts.

"I missed you, too," she said.

He took another swallow of brandy and let his arm with the bottle rest on his knee. He shook his head. "It was more than missing for me," he said. "You were my guiding light. Like…like the essence of perfection. Pure and good and sweet. Clever, too." His words slurred. "Essence of all a woman should be. Fighting for you gave me hope, made the struggle worthwhile."

His words were making her uncomfortable. She thought of Colin, who seemed to like to tell her all the things he didn't like about her, even while he insisted he liked her. Well, he obviously lusted after her.

"I'm not perfect, Nicholas. I'm just a woman like any other."

He laughed and took another drink. She felt a surge of contrariness, and perhaps to annoy him since he'd insisted she wouldn't like it, she took the brandy bottle from him and swallowed a generous amount.

It burned awfully and made her cough because she'd drunk it too fast.

"See?" he said. "So innocent. That was your first drink of brandy, wasn't it? And it's really not the thing for you," he said, making a swipe to grab the bottle.

But she suddenly felt she had something to prove, to herself or to him, or perhaps she needed to thumb her nose at something about life that was making her very cross, and she took another large swallow. It burned a little less, doubtless because she'd already done so much damage to her throat with the first guzzle.

"Josie?" he said in a puzzled voice. "You don't like brandy, do you?"

"What if I do?" she said.

But he only laughed, which made her annoyed with him.

*How could she be annoyed with him?* He was Nicholas Hargrave, the man to whom she'd been engaged. A war hero. Clearly she was a desperate case. Very likely a lost cause.

Fatigue and a sort of emotional hangover dragged her shoulders downward. Already she could feel the brandy going to her head, and she put the bottle down. She needed to go back to bed.

She started to stand up, but he had other ideas. He grabbed her hand and pulled her back onto the bench. "Need to tell you something." His words seemed to come out more thickly with each passing minute.

"Very well," she said.

He cleared his throat and looked at her hand, which he was still holding, then dropped it and fell to his knees before her, startling her.

"Nicholas?" He wasn't going to propose, was he? Hadn't he understood what she'd told him about Mama needing her? Though she hadn't actually mentioned the vow she'd made to Edwina not to get engaged. But that aside, she didn't feel ready to even talk about marriage. She needed more time!

"I need to tell you about Spain. The work—some of my work was with a French spy. A lady."

Oh, what a relief—not talk of marriage. But spying? A French woman? She felt a little fuzzy in the head.

"I see," she said, though she didn't really see anything. She wished he would stop kneeling, but she wasn't certain he was even listening to her. From the earnest look on his face, she understood that he needed to tell her something at least as much as she needed for her to hear it.

"We were alone together often. And she's *très belle*. Not like you, but lovely in her way."

She absorbed his odd, French-sprinkled words with surprise. Had he had some sort of affair while he was in Spain? Something skipped within her; if he'd been involved with another woman, didn't that make her feel a little better about what she'd done?

What if he didn't even want to marry her anymore? The thought brought a wicked rush of relief. But he was squeezing her hand now so affectionately, and she didn't think that was what he was getting at.

Besides, their situations hadn't been at all similar. He'd been fighting for his life.

"Nicholas, you don't have to speak of this. I can understand if unexpected things happened during the war."

He waved his hand, as if dismissing whatever permission she'd been trying to give him. "I was attracted to her. She was exciting. A little hard. Mean, even. But interesting."

Would he never stop listing this woman's attributes? And why should he like a mean woman?

He gave her hand an urgent, rather hard squeeze. "But nothing happened! Nothing happened with her because of you. Because you were my guiding light, my dream of all that is *bon et parfait*."

Why did he keep lapsing into French? And why did he have to keep saying these things, about her being so good and perfect? It was as though she were some sort of statue that he admired for the grace of its construction.

"Nicholas, you have to stop thinking I'm perfect."

*I'm in love with your best friend, for the love of God, even if I'm struggling every day not to be. I want to deserve you—don't make it harder by thinking I'm so good.*

He laughed. "Of course you have your quirks. But the fact that you acknowledge this only makes you more wonderful."

She wanted to scream. What she was really itching to do suddenly, idiotic though it would be, was to tell him what she'd done with Colin. *That* hadn't been a perfect thing to do.

She stood and grabbed his hand and gave a hard pull to urge him upward. He was immensely heavy and unsteady, but he rose.

"I think you should go now. We'll talk tomorrow."

He lurched toward her, caught himself, and swayed backward before standing mostly upright. "Then you forgive me?"

"It doesn't sound as though there is anything to forgive," she said, feeling like the worst sort of hypocrite.

"Nothing happened. *Rien*," he said quietly. "Nothing."

❧

Nick knew he was terribly drunk, and that he shouldn't be at Josie's house. It was incredibly improper, and she was a gentlewoman. She wasn't from the mixed-up world of war, where people did all kinds of things simply because they needed to or wanted to, and why shouldn't they, with the chance that the morrow might bring death?

But after doing his best to fill their time together that afternoon with other people and activities because being alone with her made him restless, he told himself to stop avoiding what he must do. He'd needed to confess about Giselle, and the brandy had given him courage.

He'd been clinging to the idea of Josie for so long—this had been especially hard once he'd come to know Giselle—and the idea that he might lose Josie now that he'd finally gotten back to her was too much. Yet he knew he couldn't come to her without admitting he'd been tempted.

And now that he had, he felt a little more worthy of her. He would never be as good as she was, but she was a woman and thus more virtuous, so that could never be expected.

She turned him in the direction of the path to Greenbrier, whispered a quiet "good night," and gave him a gentle push. His bosky mind floated the idea of trying to kiss her, but his long experience of discipline pushed his feet to walk away. Besides, he still couldn't tell himself he truly deserved her, because even if he'd never touched Giselle, he still hadn't told Josie the truth.

❧

Colin, up late in his library poring over an early manuscript he'd recently acquired, was finding it impossible to concentrate. He knew Nick had left, having watched his departure through the moonlit back garden. The only question was whether Nick had been able to see Josie. It had, after all, been one thirty in the morning. But Josie was not a conventional miss, and it was easy to imagine her slipping down to meet Nicholas.

He pushed aside the tide of jealousy that had been lapping at him since Nick's departure and forced himself to concentrate on the page before him, only to look up several minutes later as he heard the faint sounds, discernible in the late night quiet, of someone at the back entrance to Greenbrier. It was the very same entrance Colin used himself when he visited the Cardworthys.

He pressed his lips together hard and returned to the words scrawled on the paper in front of him.

Before long the door to the library opened, admitting Nick. He was carrying a brandy bottle, and he moved with a wobble toward the chair across from Colin's desk. Colin raised his eyebrows.

Nick chuckled. "Been visiting Josie, but it's a secret, 'course. All *très* chaste, never mind th' impropriety of a midnight *rencontre*." His words were thick, his movements sloppy. And apparently being foxed now caused him to speak French.

"I see."

Nick tipped the bottle up to his mouth, though it didn't look as though much was left.

"Seems as though you've had a lot of brandy."

"Learned to hold quantities of drink in *Espagne*," he said. "Sometimes I thought all the troubles behind the war could have been resolved if we could have just sat down to a few bottles with the Frenchies."

Colin watched him through narrowed eyes. Something was amiss, and it wasn't just that Nick was extremely drunk. "I thought you hated Boney."

"Do. 'Course I do, hate him with a passion. No fire in hell hot enough for the man. He's caused so much misery."

"Then?"

Nick shrugged. "Not every French person's like him. Not even close. Some of those men who pulled me off the battlefield—they were kind to me. And the doctor. It's a shame we're fighting against them."

What exactly was Nick saying? Was there more to it? "And Giselle?"

Nick took a drink from the bottle of brandy he was holding. "We ought to be grateful to her, brother. She hates Napoleon so much that she risked her life to help us. To help England."

"Yes. And she betrayed her own country."

Nick turned and threw his bottle—apparently now empty—at the hearth, where it shattered, making a startlingly loud sound in the quiet house. Colin lifted an eyebrow at him, and Nick looked away with a tight expression.

"What would *you* do," Nick said, "if your country were in the hands of a man like Boney?"

"I don't know," Colin said quietly. "Certainly, some of the choices we make in life don't look good from all angles. But if a person is comfortable with his choices, if that person feels he did the right thing though others may disagree…" He was wandering into hazy territory here, considering his own doings with Josie and what he wanted from her.

"Exactly!" Nick said, flopping back against the divan and sliding a bit toward the floor.

"Anyway," Colin said, "I thought you said that nothing happened between you and Giselle."

"Right," Nick muttered. "Nothing happened."

But something about the way Nick said the words made Colin believe there was more to it.

"Nothing?"

"Don't want to *discuter* it," he said and slid all the way off the divan, his head thunking softly against the carpet. With a sigh, Colin got up, dragged him to his feet, and steered him upstairs to his room.

# Twenty-two

WHILE NICK SLEPT OFF THE BRANDY THE NEXT MORN-ing, Colin paid a visit to Jasmine House.

When he appeared at the garden door to the sitting room, he could see Mrs. Cardworthy on the divan, but things did not look quite as usual. Her white cap was askew, and there were several trays of dirty dishes in the room. Josie was in there with her, but she returned his jaunty wave with a grim look that said she hadn't forgiven him for the bossy way he'd been behaving. She took her time in coming to the door.

"You can't come in," she said in a peremptory whisper, opening the door only a few inches. "Mama is in a state."

"I hope she's not unwell," he whispered back, feeling a little silly.

"Not exactly. We found her hidden stash of elixir and threw it out, and she's furious. It's only quiet now because she wore herself out yelling." She started to close the door, but he wedged the tip of his shoe in the opening before she could.

She frowned. "I've told you we're not accepting visitors."

"I'm not a visitor, I'm practically family, as you've told me on many occasions. And you are being appallingly rude."

"Nothing else seems to have any effect on you of late." He smiled.

"Is that Ivorwood?" Mrs. Cardworthy said in a remarkably growly voice, having apparently recovered. "Let him inside! I must have my share in the visit."

"There, you see?" he said cheerfully. "She wants me to come in."

"You're not coming in. She just wants to complain to you about how we're abusing her."

He gave her a knowing look. "And this is not the sort of conversation you want to offer your suitors."

"You're not a suitor." A hard light came into her eyes, something he was unused to seeing in those normally lighthearted blue sapphires. "Anyway, suitors are the last thing on my mind now. I've vowed not to leave home until Mama abandons the divan. If you want to court a woman, I suggest you go back to your London widows."

He laughed. "A vow not to marry? Come, admit that's only a way of avoiding making the choice between me and Nicholas."

Her shoulders slumped a little. "Hush. Why are you making things so hard?"

"Because you're pushing me away. I want you, you want me, and you won't even listen. You're being obtuse and incredibly stubborn. Nick has released you from the engagement, and as far as I can tell, you two haven't rushed to get engaged again. There's nothing but guilt and societal convention stopping you from choosing the future that will make you the happiest, and you're refusing to do it."

Josie looked pained. "You wouldn't understand," she said.

"What? What don't I understand?"

"I—nothing."

"Jo-sie! Edwina!" Mrs. Cardworthy's shrill voice made his ears ring.

"I have to go," Josie said. "Please move your foot."

"You do realize, don't you, that you've only substituted yourself and your siblings for her elixir? If you want to stop her from being on the divan all the time, why don't you just get rid of the divan?"

"*Do* go away," she said. With a quick movement he didn't see coming, she kicked the tip of his shoe so it jerked backward, and before he could react she'd shut the door.

❦

That afternoon, Josie, exhausted from the night before, left her mother alone for a few minutes while she went to the kitchen to ask Cook to make something especially restorative for dinner. While Josie was there, Cook urged a cup of chocolate on her, which Josie gratefully drank at the kitchen table, feeling ten years old again and temporarily unburdened by cares.

She was surprised to see Sally in the kitchen doorway; the maid had been cleaning upstairs. She looked agitated.

"If you please, Miss Josie, I'm afraid I've done something bad."

Josie lifted her eyebrows. "Surely nothing so very bad."

Sally bit her lip. "It's the mistress. She's been pressing me something awful to find her another bottle of elixir, and I knew she wasn't to have any. But when I was dusting the hall table upstairs a little while ago, I found a bottle of liquid in the little drawer and put it in my apron pocket. And just now when I went into the sitting room, she saw the shape of it and demanded to have it—and I didn't know how to say no!"

Sally burst into tears.

Oh dear. Josie knew what that little bottle had to be—the love potion! One of her wicked brothers had surely hidden it there.

She started upstairs but hadn't quite reached the sitting room when she heard her mother burst into song.

"And manly parts to guard the fair!"

The tune was "Rule Britannia," the verse an unfortunate corruption. Mrs. Cardworthy, though, seemed pleased with it, because she was singing it again as Josie rushed into the room.

Still on the divan but far more upright and vigorous-looking than she'd been in ages, Mrs. Cardworthy held her arms outstretched as she began the verse a third time. The expression on her face was that of a person announcing something deeply meaningful.

Sally rushed into the room, followed by Josie's siblings.

"What on earth is she doing?" Lawrence said loudly, wincing as his mother repeated "manly parts" yet again.

Josie fixed her brothers with a hard look. "She managed to get her hands on that gypsy's elixir, which was supposed to be missing."

The boys had the grace to look abashed. Mrs. Cardworthy showed no signs of stopping.

"What must we do for her, miss?" Sally said, clearly horrified by the undignified state of her mistress.

Josie sighed, going over to pick up the bottle, which lay on the table near her mother. It was empty. "I think it will just wear off if we let her be. Who knows—it might even inspire her to get off the divan."

❧

"Josie wouldn't let me into Jasmine House at all," Nick said bemusedly to Colin later that afternoon, having just returned to Greenbrier. "I thought she might make an exception for me, but she came to the door and said her mother was too ill to be seen, nor could she herself come out. Though really, Mrs. Cardworthy didn't sound weak at all—I think I even heard her singing."

"She is in her way a vigorous woman," Colin said.

He was hardly disappointed that Nick hadn't been able to visit Josie either, even if he knew it would be for the best if Nick and Josie had a chance to spend time together. He wanted to be fair, but in truth he felt greedy. And there was the matter of Giselle, whose significance Nick had not fully explained.

"Josie seems to think this business with her mother could take quite some time," Nick said. "And she doesn't want to make any decisions about her own future until it's resolved."

Colin tried not to feel gleeful. "Let's go for a walk. We can climb Crumb's Peak."

"Oh, very well," Nick said morosely.

They set out from the manor at a brisk pace. Autumn had settled in, with its bright red and yellow leaves and cool dampness, and Colin welcomed the vigorous exercise. It wasn't long before they reached the base of Crumb's Peak.

"This won't be too much for you, with the injury, I hope?" he asked as they started upward.

"No," Nick said. "I'm quite recovered. Though perhaps I'm not in the same condition I was in before I sat about recuperating for several weeks. Still, we spent a fair amount of time when we weren't fighting doing contests of brawn with the Scots, and it made me rather fit."

And in fact, he had no difficulty in matching Colin stride for stride. They climbed in silence for a while, the countryside offering stunning views of the changing trees, though neither man paused to enjoy them.

Their pace grew steadily brisker. As they scrambled quickly over the loose rocks lining the long, craggy trail to the peak, Nick said, "I have the sense I'm competing with you here, old boy."

"Not at all," Colin said, pushing on a bit faster, "or rather, no more than usual."

Nick laughed and surged ahead, but he was not in the lead for long, as Colin sprang past him. They battled each other to the top, clambering and grunting and occasionally even putting out a hand to keep the other one behind (which was avoided with wrestling moves familiar to each from their younger days).

Finally they reached the summit, heaving and hot.

"I doubt anyone's ever climbed Crumb's that fast. You were running at the end," Nick said as they stood next to each other gasping and gazing out over a beautiful view of trees turning red and gold, which Colin knew was wasted on him that day. He grunted in acknowledgment of Nick's words.

Silence, until Nick said, "Is there some reason you're angry with me?"

"Angry?" Colin said.

"You're terse—well, more terse than usual. And you didn't come to the village with us the other day—"

"I was busy with accounts."

"So you said. But it hasn't escaped my notice that you're not much seeking my company."

Colin passed a hand over his head. Could any of this be more awkward? Part of him—wrongly, he knew—*was* annoyed with Nick, just for being there, because they were rivals, and Nick had no idea. Mostly he was deeply thankful his friend was alive.

"I simply meant to leave room for you to court Josie, as you said you wanted to do."

He'd promised not to reveal what had been going on between him and Josie, but his conversation with the brandy-soaked Nick the night before had convinced him that Nick had secrets of his own.

"But I am also…concerned," Colin said. "As Josie's friend, as well as yours. About Giselle."

"I told you nothing happened."

"And yet I get the sense there's more to it."

Nick kept his gaze on the countryside spread out below them. "I never touched Giselle once. Not once in all the time we were together. *Thrust* together, I might add."

"But you wanted to touch her."

"She's French! And as rough as a peasant." He ran a hand through his hair. "And unutterably noble," he said miserably.

"You're in love with her."

Nick turned, his face tight, the line of his jaw hard. "I never said that." But he hadn't denied it either.

Colin could feel his own jaw tightening. If he hadn't seen the anguish on Nick's face, he would have been tempted to send his fist into his friend's chin. Damn it all. "And so you plan to marry Josie because she's appropriate."

Nick crossed his arms. "What's with you? This is between Josie and me. Is there something I'm missing? Do you have an understanding of some kind with her? I suppose you got to know her much better while I was away."

"I already knew her very well," Colin said through clenched teeth. "And I don't have an understanding with her." *Not yet*, he didn't.

"Fine. Then know this: once we've had the chance to remind ourselves of all the things about each other that brought us together in the first place and she accepts my proposal, I intend to be the best husband I can to her. She'll never want for anything, and she'll always have my affection."

"But apparently not your love. You have to tell her about Giselle."

Nick turned to look out across the valley again. "I already did."

That stopped Colin short. "You told her every-thing? How you feel about Giselle?"

"Colin!" Nick said sharply. "Stop harping on this. Giselle is in the past and I mean to keep her there, so there's nothing more to be said."

"On the contrary. There's everything to be said if you're courting Josie while you're in love with another woman."

"You're not to say anything to her about any of this."

"It's wrong."

"I disagree. And I must have your word as a friend not to speak of it."

Colin looked away. This was Nick's affair, and he'd vowed not to interfere. But now, knowing how Nick felt about Giselle, things were different. Clearly Nick meant to do his best to court Josie in spite of caring deeply about a woman he couldn't have.

At that moment, Colin felt himself absolved of any worry that in courting Josie, he'd be acting dishonor-ably toward Nick. Nick didn't love her, no matter that he meant to care for her.

Which meant that Colin would have to win her first.

"Very well, I will say nothing." But as soon as he could, he'd tell Josie he meant to court her publicly. She was *not* currently engaged, and he'd had more than enough of secrecy and prevarication.

❦

The love potion did not in the end cause Mrs. Cardworthy to get up, though she did exert herself so thoroughly when singing and waving her arms that she fell asleep in the early evening and didn't wake once in the night to ask for anything. Lawrence remarked that the singing episode was likely the most exercise she'd had in ages.

In the morning, she seemed reinvigorated with energy for making demands of her children.

Josie didn't want to admit it, but Colin was right: she and Edwina and her brothers, with all the extra attention they were giving their mother, had filled the hole the brandy elixir had left. They couldn't live this way. Drastic action was called for, and late that afternoon she gathered her siblings and explained her plan.

"But that's cruel!" Lawrence said. He was the eldest son, the child on whom their mother doted, and Josie'd known he'd be the hardest to convince.

"None of us has anything to lose," she said. "At worst, Mama will be furious. And since she's already furious, she will only be *more* furious. At best—well, shouldn't we have hope?"

With grim faces, the five Cardworthy children came as a group into the sitting room.

"Have you come to your senses then, and brought my elixir?" their mother said.

They made no reply, but the three boys assembled around the divan as planned and, together, lifted it to the sounds of their mother's outraged shouts. With Edwina holding the door to the garden open, they carried her out and gently deposited her, facing away from the house and out over the back of the garden she hadn't entered for four years.

She was so angry she was spluttering. "This—outrage! Your father—never—wouldn't— Treachery!"

"Papa would never have stood by while you sat on the divan for four years either," Josie said gently. "We're sorry, but it's for your own good."

And they left her there and went back inside and assembled at the table in the sitting room. After a few moments, Matthew reached for a deck of cards.

"Cards?" Lawrence said. "At a time like this?"

Matthew shrugged. "We'll need distracting."

Mrs. Cardworthy began to moan pitiably, which could be heard fairly well through the open windows.

"Deal the cards," Josie said firmly. "Surely she can't last long out there."

But Mrs. Cardworthy had staying power.

"We should have known she'd resist. It's what she's good at," Edwina said two hours later as the early evening shadows lengthened. It was getting rather cool and would soon be dark, but fortunately the orange and pink India shawl draped over the back of the divan had made the trip outside as well, so their mother wouldn't be uncomfortable. Or at least, not very.

They kept doggedly at whist, and had sandwiches brought to them. The servants had been told to wait to serve the mistress her tea. Already accustomed to strange goings-on in the household, they didn't even blink at the sight of the sitting room divan in the garden, with Mrs. Cardworthy still lying on it and complaining pathetically in occasional sobs and moans.

Lawrence threw down his cards. "We have to go get her. It's clouding over."

"No," Josie said firmly.

Will was beginning to look grim about the mouth

as well. "It does seem a bit cruel to leave her out there. Maybe she just can't do it."

"It's more cruel to help her abuse her body by lying there all the time," Edwina said. "Deal the cards."

They played on, lighting candles as the light faded. A misty rain began to fall, though the garden was too dark now to watch what they all knew must be a pathetic scene. As the minutes dragged by, nobody could pretend anymore that the cards offered even a modicum of distraction.

The distant boom of thunder finally sent Lawrence to his feet. "That's it. This endeavor is a failure. We're bringing her inside."

Josie and Edwina said nothing as their brothers rushed toward the door to the garden. But before the boys reached the door, it was flung inward.

Their mother stood in the doorway. She was leaning on the door frame, damp and looking as though she might fall over at any moment. An intense glint lit her eyes.

"Mother!" Lawrence cried, rushing forward and trying to put a steadying arm around her. She avoided his efforts and pushed away from the door frame and slowly, haltingly, moved into the room on her own. Edwina called for Sally to bring towels and blankets.

Watching her mother advance unsteadily by slow inches was making Josie feel ready to have an apoplexy with worry that she'd fall over. But she also rejoiced in the determination that was pushing her mother's progress.

"Mama," she said softly as Mrs. Cardworthy passed over the vacant, dusty area of the floor where the divan had stood, "you're wet. Let me call for a hot bath for you."

"Later," Mrs. Cardworthy said in a hoarse voice. She reached the doorway to the corridor and slumped against the frame. "I shall have a meal in the dining room first. I am famished."

When her children just stood there staring in astonishment, she said, "Well, are you going to join me?"

They rushed forward, everyone talking excitedly at once. Sally arrived with towels and a blanket, and Mrs. Cardworthy was soon dried off and warmly wrapped.

It was the first time they'd all sat down to a meal together in four years. Looking around the table at her family laughing and talking, Josie realized this was the most lively they'd been together since their father died. It was as though a weight had been lifted from the household.

Their mother surprised them further by expressing a wish to pay a call on Mrs. Phillips.

"She's only recently lost her husband, apparently, and that's a turning point in a woman's life. She needs a new vision for herself. I could be of some help to her."

Her children were almost unable to believe the change in their mother.

"Well," Matthew whispered to his siblings after the meal as they all watched Mrs. Cardworthy make her way in infinitesimal steps out of the dining room, "she did have plenty of time to *think* on the divan."

The family stopped in the sitting room to gaze into the dark garden, unable to see the divan that was still out there, but aware it had long since been ruined by the rain. Edwina grabbed Josie's hand and gave it a celebratory squeeze.

"We'll buy a new one," Mrs. Cardworthy said as she stood by the window, leaning against Lawrence. "In fact," she said, turning to look at the sitting room, "I think we should redecorate this room entirely."

"It was a sort of desperate hope, putting her out there," Josie said quietly to Edwina once their mother, with the boys offering support, had started up the stairs. "I still don't quite understand how it worked."

Edwina didn't reply at first, and Josie saw that some deep emotion had stirred her.

"She did it one step at a time," Edwina said. "We forced the first step on her, but it had to be her choice to leave the divan. It's the only way anything ever gets accomplished, isn't it—one step at a time?"

"Yes. She was so attached to that divan, to that just-existing life. Staying safe, refusing to take any chances."

"Living like that is deadening," Edwina said in a husky voice that made Josie peer at her more carefully. "I think now—well, I've come to think that we ought to do our best to resist whatever keeps us from bearing the risk of really living."

"I have a feeling we're not just talking about Mama."

"No," Edwina said and wiped at the corner of her eye. "I was thinking of Jack Whitby. There was something so special between us, and I was afraid of it. I never allowed myself to dream it could be possible to be with him."

"He is not a gentleman," Josie said gently. "To choose someone like him would be to break with everything you'd ever known or wanted."

"I loved him," Edwina said with a catch in her voice. "Love knocked on my door and I wouldn't open it because I didn't like the way its knock sounded. I was afraid of what was different."

"Don't be so hard on yourself. It would have been a very bold step to choose him."

"It would have. And I've never been bold, have I?"

"Don't tell yourself mean things like that! It's telling yourself a lie and believing it's true. How can you know what you might do? You were bold in London—didn't *you* kiss *him*?"

A rueful bent teased the edge of Edwina's quivering lips. "I did, didn't I? I hadn't thought of it that way before. Even if kissing Jack led to disaster, it was also bold, wasn't it?"

She gave a watery smile. "I did something bold," she said, sounding surprised.

Josie gave her a hug. "And you shall do again, I make no doubt."

But Edwina only sighed. "I'm afraid chances for boldness don't come along too often."

Josie was sadly inclined to agree. A woman's place was in the home, sheltered from harm—and opportunity.

The following morning very early, though, she heard the sound of a cart approaching, and when she looked out the window to see, she felt a spike of hope that a chance was about to present itself.

❧

Edwina heard the cart coming too. The morning was cold, but she always kept her bedchamber window cracked for freshness into December, and it looked out over the front drive. It was very early for a delivery of any kind, and she had to finish pulling on her stockings before she could satisfy her mild curiosity as to the identity of their visitor.

Having plaited one side of her hair, she was just pinning it up when she wandered over to the window and saw a familiar brown-haired man setting a piece of furniture on the drive. Her heart lurched.

A second later she was rushing down the stairs and out the front door, where Sally was just directing Rickett to pick up the piece of furniture. It was a desk like the one she'd admired at Maria Westin's. And there, climbing back into the cart just as though he had no interest in seeing her, was Jack Whitby.

"Wait!" she called, and he turned. She rushed toward the cart, just catching sight of the exquisite petite desk as Rickett was carefully lifting it. She reached the cart as Jack took his seat, so that he was somewhat above her because of the height of the cart. He seemed uninterested in her arrival.

Behind her, Sally was lingering in the doorway as Rickett carried the sweet little desk inside. Mama was just appearing as well, and in the window above, Matthew was looking out. She supposed it would be only moments before Josie and Will and Lawrence were watching too, along with the kitchen maids. But Edwina didn't care who was watching. She'd had enough of hidden doings.

"You weren't going to leave without seeing me," she said. He didn't turn to look at her.

Her eyes drank in his dear profile, with that hint of a smirk that seemed to linger permanently at the edge of his mouth and those light blue eyes like none other. She'd missed him every single day.

"I didn't see the need," he said coolly. "I merely came to deliver the desk. Mrs. Westin knew you'd admired it, and she wanted you to have one just like it."

"You made it for me," she breathed in wonder, coming to stand in front of him so he'd have to really look at her. His expression was stony, but still the sight of him filled her with joy and hope. "I admired it in her sitting room, and she told you, and you made it for me."

"She placed an order, and I filled it. I'm only here to deliver it."

"But you made it with the care and artistry that you bring to everything you do. I know I shall always treasure it because you made it for me."

His eyes betrayed no reaction to the eager warmth of her words. He looked so distant, the sharp set of his chin forbidding, his blue eyes icy and closed off to her. He was a proud man, and she'd insulted him terribly, and overlooked so many of the fine values he held dear. She couldn't expect him to be glad to see her.

She grabbed at the pinned-up side of her coiffure and pulled it free to hang loose with the rest of her hair as she hurried to make him understand. "I know I behaved terribly to you. I was wrong."

He regarded her impassively, the mouth that had teased her and playfully kissed her set in a hard line.

"No, you weren't."

He dropped his gaze to the horses and lifted his hand to crack the whip as if that were all that could be said between them.

Before her disaster, this rejection would have been more than enough to make her feel spurned, to make her decide she didn't want what she couldn't get. But she was bold now, and she quickly put a foot on the cart and swung herself up to stand precariously next to him.

Now he was very close, and she towered above him as he sat. She might be bold, but she was also quivering in fear that he wouldn't bend—he was such a proud man.

"What on earth are you doing?" he said, but she'd cracked his cool a little, even if now he sounded angry.

"You can't just leave, Jack. Please don't throw away what's between us."

"There's nothing between us, and there can't be. We've already established that."

"All we've established is that I can be stubborn and you can be arrogant. They're qualities that can be positive or negative—it depends on what you do with them."

"Edwina," he said through clenched teeth, refusing to look up at her, "you've been raised all your life to marry a gentleman. I'm not a gentleman, which means that the way we are right now, with you hovering above me, is the way it would always be."

"I disagree. We always have choices. Move over."

And before he could even shift, she was dropping onto the small space between him and the end of the bench. She was slim, but still, only half of her backside fit on the small available section of the cart bench. She turned and smiled at him, her heart in her throat.

"Won't you please move over a bit?"

He drew in a breath that gave her a little hope, because it sounded tormented. He made room, although they were still touching all along their sides.

She welcomed the warmth of his body and sent up a little prayer that her own body was having an effect on him as well. She'd take whatever worked, if it would soften the resolve in the stiff spine beside her. It amazed her when she thought of how she'd once considered him capable of rough behavior, when in truth he was the most upright man she'd ever met.

"Edwina, this is a terrible idea," he said, still not looking at her. "We had a chance in London to try things out, and it worked out badly. I'm sure neither of us wants a repeat of that."

"There wouldn't be a repeat. If we were together, it would be the two of us as one. No one would find it very interesting at all."

"It wouldn't work, Edwina. You want a gentleman, a prince to make you feel royal."

She touched his arm, feeling the hardness of tendons and muscles held in tension.

"I only thought I did," she said softly, "until I met you. Darling Jack, you *are* a prince, in the only ways that truly matter. But I couldn't see that at first. I didn't know what I really wanted because I'd been so focused on what I thought I needed. When I found myself so drawn to you, I fought it. I was afraid. You showed me how much more life might offer, and it scared me because it was different from everything I'd ever thought I needed."

He finally turned to her then, and she saw that

his eyes had softened a little, and the sight lifted her heart. "You weren't wrong to want what you knew, Edwina. I shouldn't have pushed you."

She shook her head. "I was foolish and weak. I wanted a safe harbor." She never would have thought she'd be inspired by her mother, but Mama had left her own safe harbor and was beginning to create a new vision for herself, and Edwina wanted that too.

"I wanted a man whose adoration would make me feel proud, instead of a man I would feel proud to deserve. And I see now that is the only kind of man who could ever make me a good husband."

"Edwina"—his voice was husky—"I don't know that I deserve such generosity. I could hardly *not* pursue you. You were like a fascinating puzzle set before me, a woman wrapped up tightly inside a shell. And you've borne everything so bravely." His brows drew together as he looked at what must have been an enormous grin spreading over her face. "What?"

"I love that you didn't say I'm beautiful."

He laughed softly and reached up to cup her cheek. "Of course you are. You're beautiful when you're tormenting me, you're lovely when you're scheming, you're a sight when you're being kind to penniless strangers. It's *you* that's beautiful, *you* that makes your face the most exquisite one I've ever seen."

He dropped his hand between them, palm side up.

"There will be complications," he said in a grimly serious voice. "People will gossip. They'll say you've come down to my level."

She laid her hand in his, in full view of anyone who

cared to see. "There's no *down* about it. Just you and me together."

His eyes looked into hers, their ice melted to the soft blue of a summer sky.

"Edwina Cardworthy, will you do me the very great honor of becoming my wife?"

She threw her arms around him and squeezed tight. "Yes, Jack, yes! A thousand times yes!" He laughed, and she loved the sound of it.

She hadn't noticed that her family had gathered in the doorway at a respectful distance, but now she saw them and motioned them over. She and Jack got down from the cart and shared their good news.

Josie was smiling as though she couldn't have been happier, and when she drew close she whispered to Edwina, "Well done."

"It is the most wonderful thing in the world," Mama said, leaning a little against the cart but able still to take Edwina and Jack by the hands and press them together. "A love match."

# Twenty-three

THE DAY TURNED INTO ONE OF THOSE AUTUMN GLORIES that are like a final visit from summer, and the sun was at its warmest when Josie went into the garden late that afternoon. She sat on the bench behind the enormous oak tree at the back of the garden, a place that always felt like a secluded nook because it couldn't be seen from the house. She let her wrap fall to the bench as she basked in the soft sunshine.

Whitby had stayed for a boisterous lunch, and he was already a favorite with Josie's brothers. She supposed that, however much Papa had steered them wrong, the way he'd kept them apart from society had made them all less likely to care about society's strictures. And Mama had taken one look at the desk and declared that Whitby was an artist, and said how lucky they were to have him in the family. Josie could already imagine that her parsimonious parent would be finagling more than one piece of furniture out of her future son-in-law.

She leaned back against the tree trunk and wished for inner peace, but today—and every day of these last months—peace had been elusive. How could she be at peace when she was allowing herself to be courted by one man while she was in love with another?

There was an answer to this, one she'd been shying away from, but Colin was right. She now had nothing more than a sisterly affection for Nicholas, and it was partly out of guilt and concern for what everyone would think that she'd agreed to let him court her. But it would be wrong to marry him, and she would tell him of her change of heart.

The decision brought her a small measure of relief. She was left with the much larger problem of Colin. He'd asked her to marry him twice, and he'd been so importunate in recent days that she suspected he would soon ask again. But she didn't want a functional marriage of two people who got along fairly well—she wanted one built on love, and on a desire for each other that was physical *and* emotional.

And he wasn't offering that.

Lost in thought, she didn't realize she was no longer alone until she heard a soft rustle and turned to see Colin stepping out from behind an overgrown juniper bush like someone emerging from a game of hide-and-seek.

Her heart leaped giddily at the sight of him, then shrank back as though it had come up against a hot coal. She felt so vulnerable right now—the last thing she wanted was to see him. "Were you *hiding* in there?"

"I needed to see you, and you haven't been very available."

"That's because I don't want to see you."

He came closer. "Yes you do," he said in an annoyingly reasonable voice.

She looked away from him, summoning a bored tone. "Being an earl has gone to your head."

He stopped at the bench. She was glad her skirts were spread out over it so that there was no room for him to sit, but he simply pushed the fabric aside and sat down anyway. "I was always arrogant—you just never noticed."

That was true, she now knew, and she wanted to laugh, but she didn't want him to have the satisfaction of amusing her. The warmth of his body was already having an effect on her, and she slid over a few inches and examined her nails idly as though her heart weren't racing.

"I've missed you," he said. Out of the corner of her eye, she saw his grin. "Admit it, you've missed me too."

She abandoned her cuticles and crossed her arms. "What I miss is the way we used to be when we were friends. It was easy and carefree and now it's spoiled."

"I don't look at it that way at all. I think what's developed between us is marvelous."

"You just liked the kissing and the touching."

His grin turned wicked, making her feel weak. "I did," he said. He lifted his hand and ran a single fingertip along the skin of her forearm that was left bare by her three-quarter sleeve, making the little hairs stand up excitedly. "Your beautiful body is driving me to distraction."

She pulled her arm away and struggled against emotions he surely wasn't feeling.

"You're just interested because of the thrill of the chase. If I agreed that it was marvelous, you'd soon find the marvelousness faded."

"If you agreed with me," he said, leaning until his mouth was right next to her ear, "I'd be thrilled."

He kissed her earlobe.

"Stop that," she said weakly.

"Agree with me. It's marvelous."

"Oh, Colin," she murmured, her heart in her throat, "when did you turn into the devil?"

"When I met you."

And though she needed to keep herself apart and safeguard her heart, his nearness undid her good intentions, and, her heart twisting with bittersweet longing, she turned and met his lips with hers. She told herself this would be the very last time she'd ever kiss him.

She was simply going to have to leave Jasmine House—go to India after all, or less excitingly and more probably, ask to visit her mother's distant and unpleasant sister in Scotland. Anything so she wasn't in proximity to Colin.

Their kiss was a passionate mating. His hands were everywhere, sweeping up her back worshipfully and shaping the rise of her bosom. She let her hands run over the strong, flexed muscles of his back, and wanted to cry out with happiness when he pulled her firmly against him so that their bodies touched all along their thighs and hips.

He groaned and pushed her dress off one shoulder and began kissing the top of her bosom lavishly. The pleasure was like a drug, but sadness pierced her as she gazed at the dark head below her chin, knowing it was filled with thoughts he'd never share with her.

Colin, who hadn't looked up, moved upward to kiss her neck.

He gave a playful sigh. "I *suppose* we oughtn't to be doing this out here in the middle of the day, but"—he pressed his lips softly under her ear and chuckled—"I find no inducement to stop. I'm sure I never shall."

The lightness in his voice did her in, pouring more salt in the wound of her love for him. Touching her was about pleasure and bodily need for him. Colin wasn't a man to surrender to the kind of emotions that were swirling inside her: yearning, remorse, hope, despair. All of them, all at once.

Her love for him would keep pushing her to behave like a fool, and he might have affection for her, but he'd never love her back, not the way she needed him to. A tear welled up and began to slip down her cheek, and she wiped it angrily. She nudged Colin away from her and jerked her bodice into place.

She stood up, needing to break the spell of his nearness. "You have to leave. Go. Clearly I can't be around you. I can't be your—your plaything."

"Don't be absurd," he said. He stood up too. His eyes seemed so unreadable. They were remote. *He* was remote. "I love you, and I want to marry you."

She just stood there, blinking at his brazenness. How could he lie like this to get what he wanted?

"Marry me? Love me?" She made a scoffing sound. "You do not."

"*What?*"

"I don't believe you."

A dark flush spread over his cheeks. "What do you mean, you don't believe me?"

She crossed her arms tightly, willing herself to hold firm to what she knew was true. "I believe you like my company and my friendship. I believe you like to do sensual things with me. But I don't believe you love me."

His lips tightened. "And why not?"

"You're too cool for me! You hate messy, uncontrollable emotion, and I have loads of that. If you married me, you'd just want to go off by yourself all the time."

"I would not! So I like to spend time alone—that doesn't mean I don't also love spending time with you."

She shrugged. What was the point in arguing about the way people were? "It doesn't matter."

"Nothing could matter more than who you love to spend time with," he said. "That person for me is you. And I'm fairly certain it's also me for you. You have to make the honest choice. You can't choose Nicholas if you love me."

"I don't want to marry Nicholas."

He blinked. "You don't?" He seemed to have trouble absorbing this, but then he began to smile. "But that's wonderful. Now you can choose me."

"Don't talk to me about choices. We've already established that I'm impulsive. I make the worst possible choices, and I doubtless will continue to do so."

"Josie, Josie," he said warmly, clearly still delighted by the news that she didn't want to marry Nicholas, "you're exaggerating. So you've done a few ill-advised things—your spontaneity is actually one of the things I love best about you. Being with you pulls me into the whirl of life in a way I might never find on my own."

That sounded so genuine. It made her lips tremble as she thought about how she loved the way he, conversely, seemed to anchor her so that she wouldn't, like a kite tossed in a storm, be carried off by her flights of fancy.

But she mustn't be weak. Words were easy. Life was hard and real. Even with the best intentions, people behaved in predictable patterns, and Colin's patterns indicated a person who would always keep to himself.

"What if all the things you've done," he pressed, "all the impulsive things you regret, were really the right thing to do because they brought you to see what you would have overlooked?"

She rolled her eyes. "And I'm supposed to have been overlooking you."

"Of course you overlooked me—you saw me as a friend, not a man who could be your lover. I wanted you—needed you—all along. That first night you met Nick at my ball was the night I had planned to begin courting you properly and openly. But Nick showed up, and you turned to him. I had to spend a whole year wanting you and knowing you belonged to him."

Hearing this wasn't helping at all. She looked away from him, toward the tangle of forsythia fronds that leaned against the garden wall.

"You have to let this go, Colin. Let *me* go. You don't love me, not really. Not the way I'd need you to. I'm sorry to speak so bluntly," she said in a voice that was turning husky just when she so desperately wanted to banish emotion, "but it will save unhappiness later if I speak plainly. We'd never have the kind of deep, open connection that I dream about."

His jaw tightened. "And for that you think you'd

need an outgoing man like Nicholas," he ground out, "who's happy to talk all the time about love."

She made herself nod, even though she'd never felt for Nick anything like the rich, overwhelming, bittersweet love she had for Colin.

"I need openness," she said. "I could never be happy always wondering what you were thinking behind that reserved facade. And you wouldn't really want me. I'm needy! I'd poke at you and want to know what you were thinking all the time, and it would make you incredibly irritated. We'd end up with a marriage in which you'd go on ever more jaunts by yourself just to find the peace and quiet you crave, while I'd be left at home with the children and servants, feeling abandoned. And I'd hate that."

"Because you care about me."

"Of course I do!" she said angrily. "But I shall master it."

He looked very stiff, yet the vulnerable light in his eyes surprised her.

"So you don't think I'm capable of impulsive behavior," he said. "That scene in the London coach wasn't improper enough."

"That was just lust. Any man would have taken what I was offering."

"And it's not enough that I tell you I think you're the most fascinating woman I've ever met and I love spending time with you."

"I'd want a devoted husband, not a satisfied companion."

She sighed, so very worn out. She just wanted this all to be over: the conversation with Colin, and the

one she was going to have to have with Nicholas.
"But none of this matters because I'm not going to
marry you."

"Right," he said. Then he grabbed her by the
arm and began pulling her toward the gate in the
garden wall.

"What on earth do you think you're doing?"

"Helping you make up your mind," he said as they
passed through the gate.

"I know my own mind," she said through grit-
ted teeth, "and I don't need any help from you.
Let me go!"

But he didn't, and though she spluttered and protested as they hurtled along the path to Greenbrier,
this was Colin, and he was very good at not responding when he didn't want to. Silence was his friend,
and he'd never been bothered by awkward or charged
pauses, never mind the angry lashings of an outraged
woman. She tried to dig her heels into the grass, but
her efforts had no effect on his unrelenting stride.

And then he was pulling her up the steps of the
back entrance to Greenbrier. Josie had by now ceased
protesting, since it was having no effect, but she was
preparing a ferocious tirade to deliver the minute
they stopped. They passed through the tall doorway
and along the seemingly endless marble-tiled cor-
ridors of his manor, and into the two-story front
hall with its beautiful double staircase. His butler
appeared almost instantly.

"Ames, have Captain Hargrave called, please. Tell
him his presence is required in the front hall."

Josie gasped and tried again to reclaim her arm.

Colin kept talking pleasantly, as though he weren't holding her there against her will. Only the desire not to have Ames think something was going on between her and Colin kept the polite smile fixed on her face.

"Then send a footman over to Jasmine House," Colin continued, "to let them know Miss Cardworthy decided to stop here for a visit."

Ames left to do his master's bidding and they were alone for a moment in the hall.

"Have you lost your wits?" Josie snarled.

He made no reply except to let go of her arm, but it was too late for escape or even her tirade, because Nicholas, apparently alerted by the commotion, was coming down the stairs.

He grinned when he saw them. "What's all this about?" he said as he neared the bottom. "Not that I'm not happy you've come for a visit, Josie."

His eyebrows drew together as he noticed that neither Colin nor Josie was smiling.

"Is something amiss?"

"You'll doubtless find it so," Colin said.

*What was he doing?* Surely he couldn't possibly be planning some kind of public confession. He was a private man. He hated emotional spectacles. Ames was coming back, and two footmen had appeared near the stairs.

"Colin," she said warningly in a low voice. He didn't listen.

"I'm in love with Josie, Nick. And I mean to court her."

*Oh no! He'd done it!*

Nicholas blinked several times, then his face darkened with growing fury. She knew just how he felt because she was furious with Colin, too. Nicholas moved closer, his jaw hard with tension.

"What the devil do you mean by this, Colin? Is it some sort of jest?"

Nicholas looked at her then, and she wanted to cringe. "Josie?" he asked quietly.

"I…" What could she say? Now, when Nick was so recently returned, he was hearing about her betrayal. Their betrayal. And here, of all public places. Why had Colin done this?

"It's no jest," Colin said. "I had started to care for her before you were engaged, and I fell in love with her while you were away. You of all people can understand that a man would find her irresistible. I would never have declared myself now, but your engagement was broken."

"Only so I could court her again," Nicholas ground out, any trace of the congeniality she was used to in him replaced by the unyielding hardness of a man accustomed to battle. "You bastard."

He sent his fist crashing into Colin's jaw.

Josie gasped as Colin staggered backward, knocking a vase of flowers off the long, narrow table behind him. It shattered on the floor as he hit the wall.

Ames, who'd been watching the proceedings with a look of shock that was turning to outrage, stepped toward Nicholas, but Colin put up a staying hand.

"I deserved that." He looked Nicholas in the eye. "And I'm sorry. I know this all looks very bad, but I love her, and I believe she just might care as much for me. I won't let her go without a fight."

Nicholas took a step closer. "If it's a fight you want," he growled, balling up his fist again.

Colin jerked his head toward the corridor. "In the library."

*Now* he wanted privacy? She was ready to punch him herself.

Both men stalked toward the library with Josie at their heels. She pushed the door closed behind her and faced them. They were looking at each other, shoulders stiff, jaws hard, fists clenched.

The two most formidable men she'd ever known.

They were furious, and she was the reason why. She swallowed hard and forced herself to speak.

"Nicholas," she began, but neither man paid her any attention.

"And you called yourself my friend," Nicholas said in a voice laced with derision.

"If I believed that you both loved only each other, I wouldn't be here," Colin said coldly.

What did he mean by that? Did his remark have something to do with Nicholas's French lady-spy?

Colin's words sent Nicholas's fist crashing into his jaw again and knocked him backward over his desk.

He was on his feet in a trice. "This is for courting Josie while you were in love with another woman."

*Nicholas was in love with another woman?*

Then Colin, *reserved* Colin, punched his best friend and sent him crashing into a delicate round occasional table, which shattered under Nicholas's weight.

In a flash, he was upright and they were brawling.

"Stop!" Josie shouted, but they ignored her.

It was as though they'd entered some private competition and they were oblivious to everything but the punches they were raining on each other. Books and papers slid off Colin's desk as he shoved Nick along the top of it. Nick got up and slammed Colin into the wall, Colin's momentum knocking loose a pretty landscape miniature Josie had always loved.

She rescued it just in time but was unable to save the bust of Horace that toppled off its stand. They were going to destroy the entire room, never mind what they were doing to each other. Already Colin had a bleeding cut on his cheek and Nick's bottom lip was split.

She rushed out of the room, seeking help, and found the servants standing in the hallway, horrified. She asked for a bucket of water, which was quickly procured, then she rushed back into the room and threw it over them, aiming for their heads.

Startled, the men stopped for a moment, shaking the water from their faces. They looked ready to resume.

"Please!" she cried. "No more hitting."

They looked at her as though finally aware of her presence. Nicholas pushed a hank of dripping hair off his forehead and turned his gaze to her.

"Do you love him?" he demanded.

"I…" Her throat was suddenly a desert. How could she talk about this? And with both of them? She wanted to crawl away and curl up in a ball somewhere dark and hidden.

"Josie?" Colin pinned her with his eyes. "Will you tell the truth?"

"I don't want to talk about this!" she said as she watched the blood trickle down his cheek. "I don't even understand why you created such a spectacle."

"Don't you?" he said quietly. He took a step

toward her. "You think I keep my emotions so closed up that I have none to share with you."

He came closer still, to stand right in front of her as he spoke these astonishing, frank words. "You think I won't allow the mess of feelings, that I'm too bottled up to be the man who would love you as wholeheartedly and freely as you deserve."

A thought broke through, but she could hardly credit it. Had he truly just deliberately made an emotional, public spectacle of himself as a sort of bouquet for her, a way of showing her how much he cared?

"Oh," she said, her heart in her throat.

Something shone in Colin's eyes. "Yes, Josie," he said. "I did this for you. You have to understand that not only does my heart beat for you and no one else, it will always be open to you. Open to whatever happens. I would never close myself off to you, because you're the woman who makes me happy. Yes, I need solitude at times, but I would never retreat from *you*. I love you."

They stared into each other's eyes. This was it, the moment she'd hardly dared to hope for. This was true love, and it was real and untidy and emotional, an everyday love that also made her heart soar.

"I'm still here," Nick said from across the room.

They turned toward him where he stood by the desk. His lips pressed together grimly.

"Right," he said in a clipped voice. "It doesn't take a genius to see that there's quite a bit going on between you two."

Josie went to him. She wished he hadn't had to be caught up in her indecision. But in truth they *didn't* really know each other well. What was six weeks of giddy courting to a year and more of a soul-deep friendship turned to love?

"I'm so sorry about all this, Nicholas," she said softly, searching for understanding amid the anger and unhappiness in his eyes. "It's all been shifting so rapidly that I didn't know what to do. We were devastated when we thought you'd been killed, and Colin and I had been the best of friends. We were a solace to each other. By the time you came back, something had grown between us. But I cared for you and was honored that you cared for me, and it seemed right to try to make things work."

"I see."

She felt awful having to say such blunt things, but not being clear about what she wanted had been such a mistake.

"You deserved a much better fiancée," she said. "And I think you'll agree that I never was the paragon you thought me."

He looked away from her, his eyes settling on the floor. "Perhaps it was a mistake to want anyone to be a paragon." His voice sounded dull, but beyond the tightness of his jaw, there was nothing that spoke of a heart truly crushed by what she'd just said.

Josie thought about what Colin had said: *If I believed you both loved only each other, I wouldn't be here.*

Nicholas took in a deep breath and looked up. "In truth, Josie, I probably got exactly what I deserved: no fiancée."

She wanted to reach out to him in friendship, but things were too tangled for such a gesture. "You can't believe that. You're a wonderful man, and you deserve a wonderful woman with whom to share your life. I'm just not that woman."

"No," he said slowly. "You're not. While we're telling the truth…there is someone else, a woman I love. I wanted to tell you about her, but it's complicated. But"—he shot Colin a grim, rueful glance—"Colin was right. You deserved better than what I was offering."

He and Colin exchanged looks, and though they'd been battling each other only minutes before, it was as though a summer storm had come through, exploding the pressure of a sweltering day and leaving calm in its wake.

"I understand," Nick said to Colin. "And—perhaps I'll even say thank you."

Colin inclined his head in reply. The skin along his jaw, where Nick's fist had connected, was very red.

Nick walked out of the library, closing the library door behind him.

Colin came up and put his hands on Josie's shoulders.

"He told me about a lady-spy he'd met in Spain and admired," she said, "but he never said more. It's to do with her, isn't it?"

"Perhaps. None of that matters now, though," he said, stroking her cheek, "because I got the right girl. I'm still waiting, you know, to hear that I really did get the girl."

She felt a huge smile breaking over her face. "You did." She was hardly able to speak over the giddy joy bubbling up in her. "It took me a long time to realize that I loved you, Colin. But then when I knew, I was afraid to trust you."

"Yes," he said in a slightly pained voice. "I know. But I understand why."

"Maybe some part of me knew you were right for me all along, and that was why I felt so unsettled about marrying Nicholas."

"You almost undid me when you kissed me at the ball in London." He leaned his forehead against hers, and his breath fell softly against her skin.

"That kiss made me a little crazy too," she said. "I didn't understand why I couldn't stop thinking about you even though I was engaged to such a wonderful man."

"You will make me much happier if you stop talking about other men right now, especially ones you deem wonderful. Let's talk about how much you love me. Because I love you more than anything. I always will. And this time you're going to accept when I propose."

"Bossy again," she said in a mock scold. "But yes, yes I will marry you, Colin Pearce. I love you, and you're the only man for me, forever."

She reached up to cup his cheek. "Though I was ready to brain you when you announced to Nicholas in the foyer that you wanted to court me. I never realized you were capable of doing something so—"

"Stupid?"

"Yes, and impulsive."

He laughed and pulled her into his arms. "Actually, I'm getting an impulsive idea right now. But perhaps it's too wicked for you…"

"Now you'll have to tell me what it is."

"I'd rather show you. That is, if you feel you can slip down to your back garden tonight at midnight."

"Child's play."

They left Greenbrier and set out on the path back to Jasmine House. She pestered him the whole way back to tell her what they were going to do that night, but he wouldn't say.

❧

Josie stepped silently out into the Jasmine House garden as the case clock in the sitting room struck midnight. The night was chilly and very dark, and she saw that the moon was a crisp, silvery crescent. Though it offered scant illumination, the little curl of celestial light seemed cheery.

*Like a heavenly smile shining down on lovers who meet by night*, she thought, and grinned at her own ridiculousness.

And then Colin was by her side.

"So where are we going?" she whispered. "To the lake? A picnic under the stars?"

"Nothing so tame, and it's a surprise. Now, turn around."

He tied a blindfold around her eyes.

"Is this even necessary?" she said. "I could hardly see my hand in front of my face as it was. And as I haven't seen you since this afternoon, I was rather looking forward to seeing you now."

"It's definitely necessary. Now, if the nearly Countess of Ivorwood will march?"

Taking her hand, he led her carefully along. It was chilly, but she'd put on a thick wrap, and Colin's hand warmed her. A nightingale began to sing quite beautifully, or perhaps she heard it with new ears because of Colin's blindfold.

"I wouldn't have trusted you to lead me like this last week," she said. "Or the week before that."

"I know." She could hear the smile in his voice. "Though I wouldn't have said 'no' if *you'd* offered to blindfold *me*."

"There's something wicked in your words."

He just chuckled and directed her to take a large step to avoid something in her path, to watch her head, to be careful descending some small hill. It was possible that his directions were a ruse to give her wrong ideas about where they were going, but if they were, she didn't care because she was having too much fun.

"Did you know that Edwina had been making me a wedding dress all these months? It's amazingly beautiful, and it was to be a surprise. I think it was everything she ever wanted for herself in a wedding dress, and since she didn't think she'd have a chance to wear it, she made it for me."

"A grand gesture."

"It was the kindest, most sisterly thing. But I told her *she* must wear it, now that she and Jack are to wed. And Mama is very eager to take me shopping for a dress of my own. Imagine. She hasn't taken me to a shop in years. And we have you to thank for the idea of putting the divan out."

He laughed a little. "I think you must take credit for that. I never meant for you to put your mother out as well. And leave her in the rain."

"It *was* outrageous," Josie said. "But I'm so glad it worked."

She sighed. "I do worry, though, about poor Nicholas and his French spy. He's had such a hard road, and he deserves to be happy. I can't believe you split his lip today."

"Poor old Nicholas will be fine, and he left me with my own souvenir. He's promised to stay for the wedding, and then he's going back to France to see if he can find his lady-spy."

"Oh—that's wonderful! If he finds her and brings her home, we'll throw an enormous party to welcome them, and a ball in Town as well, and no one will care that she's French."

"Certainly," Colin said, and she could hear the smile in his voice. "If the future Countess of Ivorwood sets her mind to it, it shall be so."

Their footsteps began to make a quiet echo that told her they were inside a building and moving over a floor, and she smelled a scent of damp stone. Finally they stopped.

He untied the blindfold and she opened her eyes to a wonder. Candles were everywhere, so that their rich yellow radiance all around her was the first thing she took in. Then she realized where they were, and she laughed.

"It's your wine cellar, isn't it?"

"It is."

The candlelight picked out the dull gleam of dusty glass and thick cobwebs on row after row of shelves. "It's wonderfully old. I imagine some of these bottles haven't been touched in decades."

"Centuries," he said.

"I love it."

"Good, as it will soon be yours as well." He took her hand. "Come this way."

He guided her toward a little alcove along one wall where was nestled a table piled with pillows and luxurious blankets and surrounded by candles.

"Up you go," he said, lifting her to sit on the table-bed. He climbed up next to her.

"Now," he said, taking up a bottle that had been left open next to two glasses, "I had actually thought, given your love of potions, that I should track down a gypsy and see what could be procured. The potion you foisted on me did, after all, give me the most vivid erotic dream of you. It seems like turnabout would be fair play."

Happy warmth spread through her. "You had a dream about me? Can I know the details?"

"Perhaps some day."

She smiled. "Did the potion do anything else to you?"

"You seem inordinately interested in this topic."

"It was such a mischief-causing potion. When my brothers gave it to their tutor, he picked a bouquet of weeds for Edwina, and it made Mama sing inappropriate songs."

"You gave it to your mother?"

"She took it. Now, tell me everything it did to you," she said. "I've been so terribly curious."

He crossed his arms and gave her a very haughty look, and she sighed happily: he was her own darling earl. "I'll have you know it caused me to make a spectacle of myself. I shouted your name from the roof of Greenbrier."

"You did? Oh, Colin, how wonderfully romantic! I wish I'd heard you. Do you know, I think the gypsy who pressed that potion on me may have been right after all."

"How's that?"

"She warned me that if I didn't use it, I might miss out on the love of my life. And here you are."

He smiled a little through the haughtiness. "I suppose then I shall have to say I'm glad I suffered. But it was excruciatingly embarrassing, being discovered on my roof shouting things by Ames. I don't even want to consider what he thought about my sleeping up there."

"It's probably been chased out of his mind by the spectacle you made of yourself earlier today."

He groaned a little and laughed. "You're probably right. Ah well, it's been rather too quiet around here for years. I have a feeling Greenbrier's mischievous new mistress is going to make things quite a bit more interesting."

He was so adorable. She reached out and brushed her fingers through a hank of dark hair that lay across his brow. He captured her hand and kissed her palm.

"So, am I to have a potion?" she said.

"Of sorts. It occurred to me that if you were going to be having erotic dreams of me, I would hope to inspire them all on my own. So instead"—he reached behind him for the open bottle of wine—"I shall give you a historical potion. This was among the last bottles produced by the Château Lafite before the revolution and the guillotine relieved the family of the vineyard in 1794."

"It's rather old then," she said as he began pouring.

"Yes," he said. They each took a glass. "Like drinking history."

They sipped, saying nothing for a moment.

"It's amazing," she breathed. The cellar was wonderfully silent, like an ancient church.

"It is quite good, isn't it? I've been saving it for a special moment. And that moment came today, when you told me you loved me."

She moved closer to press against him. "I like to hear you talk like that. I'm imagining it's making you squirm, but you're doing it anyway."

He kissed her. And there was that magic that happened when he did, like a firework show starting in her.

They put their glasses down.

"Now," he said as he kissed his way down her neck, "if we didn't have the recent history that we do, I'd insist on everything being proper before we marry in two weeks. But the thing is, I'm afraid waiting to do a certain thing again will put too much pressure on us for the wedding night."

"Pressure?" Josie murmured. She found that her mouth was near his earlobe, so she licked it, which drew a little groan from him. She smiled and did it again.

"Yes. Creating worries that it might be like a certain carriage ride."

She laughed. "I'm not worried."

"You may not realize it, but likely you are," he said. His head dropped lower and he kissed the upper swell of her breast. "In addition, Miss Cardworthy, you've got this notion I'm very reserved and deliberate. It's important for you to thoroughly understand my capacity to do the impulsive, ill-advised thing."

He wasn't wearing a cravat, and she pushed the neck of his shirt wider and kissed his collarbone. "Like bringing your fiancée down to your wine cellar at midnight?"

"Yes." He leaned forward a bit and caught the hem of her skirts and began dragging them up her legs. "But quite a bit worse than that, actually. I mean to *do* things to you in my wine cellar at midnight. Inappropriate things."

"Oh good."

He took his time, teasing her, lingering when she would have hurried him. She tried to undo the ties of his breeches, but he captured her hands and held them gently but firmly behind her back.

He began a slow torment with his mouth, paying enthusiastic attention to her breasts and making her sigh shamelessly. With the dedicated, ardent focus of a scholar studying a fascinating work, he roamed lower, his warm lips and hands exploring her. And then he kissed her in the most astonishing place.

She moaned. "I take back everything I ever said about you being nice."

He gave a husky chuckle. "I give you fair warning that I have volumes of plans where you are concerned, Josie." And then he did something incredible with his tongue.

"You're…diabolical," she breathed. "How did you get to be so inventive?"

"Reading stimulates the imagination," he said.

And then he turned serious, his every touch

worshipping her. Their joining was a joyous celebration of love and life, and they held each other through the bliss, and for hours afterward as they lay among the pillows, sipping their wine and talking about everything.

It was very late—or rather, very early the next morning—by the time Colin walked her back to Jasmine House. They paused behind the cover of the enormous oak.

He kissed her, then sighed. "Two weeks is a long time to wait to have you sleeping under my roof."

"It is," she whispered. "We'll have to find some way to pass the time."

They were very resourceful in the ensuing days... roofs, cellars, even a much-neglected folly deep in the woods at Greenbrier—everywhere seemed to embrace the lovers.

And two weeks later, when Josie and Colin stood before their friends and family in the beautiful old chapel at Greenbrier, neither of them had any doubt that the future was going to be absolutely wonderful.

The minister pronounced them wed, and Colin bent down and kissed Josie. "You're the queen of my heart," he said, looking into her eyes.

"And you're the king of mine."

Awe stole over her. She knew now that they would always be able to speak the most important things to each other. But that also, in the deepest way, words might no longer even be needed.

Beautiful music carried them down the center aisle and out into sunlight.

# Acknowledgments

I want to thank to my patient, smart, and always enthusiastic editor, Deb Werksman, as well as Susie Benton, Skye Agnew, Danielle Dresser, Beth Sochacki, Eliza Smith, and all the dedicated and super-talented staff at Sourcebooks. Thanks also to my awesome agent, Jenny Bent, whom I am so grateful to have in my corner, and her staff.

And thank you to my wonderful, ever-supportive family and friends—you're the best!

If you enjoyed Emily Greenwood's *Mischief by Moonlight*, then read on for excerpts from more sparkling Regency romance:

*Noble Intentions*
by Katie MacAlister

*To Charm a Naughty Countess*
by Theresa Romain

*Once Upon a Kiss*
by Jayne Fresina

From *Noble Intentions*

GILLIAN LEIGH'S FIRST SOCIAL EVENT OF THE SEASON began with what many in the *ton* later labeled as an uncanny warning of Things To Come.

"Well, bloody hell. This isn't going to endear me to the duchess."

Gillian watched with dismay as flames licked up the gold velvet curtains despite her attempts to beat them out with a tasseled silk cushion. Shrieks of horror and shrill voices behind her indicated that others had spotted her activities, which she had hoped would escape their notice until she had the fire under control.

Two footmen raced past her with buckets of water and soon had the fire extinguished, but it was too late, the damage was done. The duchess's acclaimed Gold Drawing Room would never be the same again.

"Sealing my fate as a social pariah, no doubt," she muttered to herself.

"Who is? And what on earth happened in here? Lady Dell said something about you burning down the house, but you know how she exag...oh, my!"

Gillian heaved a deep sigh and turned to smile

ruefully as her cousin, and dearest friend, caught sight of the damp, smoke-stained wall.

"I'm afraid it's true, Charlotte, although I wasn't trying to burn down the house. It was just another of my Unfortunate Accidents."

Charlotte gave the formerly gilt-paneled wall a considering look, pursed her lips, then turned her gaze on her cousin. "Mmm. Well, you have made sure everyone will be talking about your debut. Just look at you! You've soot all over—your gloves are a complete loss, but I think you can brush the worst off your bodice."

Gillian snorted while Charlotte effected repairs to her gown. "My debut—as if I wanted one. The only reason I'm here is because your mother insisted it would look odd if I remained at home while you had your Season. I'm five and twenty, Charlotte, not a young girl like you. And as for setting the *ton* talking—I'm sure they are, but it will no doubt be to label me a clumsy Colonial who can't even be a wallflower without wreaking havoc."

Charlotte rolled her eyes as she dragged her cousin past the excited groups of people and out the door. "You're only half American and not clumsy. You're…well, you're just enthusiastic. And slightly prone to Unfortunate Accidents. But all's well that ends happily, as Mama says. The curtains can be replaced, and I'm sure the duchess will realize the fire was simply one of those unavoidable events. Come, you must return to the ballroom. The most exciting thing has happened—the Black Earl is here."

"The black who?"

"The Black Earl. Lord Weston. It's rumored he's going to take a bride again."

"No, truly? And this is an event we must not fail

to witness? Is he going to take her right there in the ballroom?"

"Gillian!" Charlotte stopped dead in the hallway. Her china-blue eyes were round and sparkling with faux horror. "You really cannot say such things in polite company! It's shocking, simply shocking, and I cannot allow you to sully my delicate, maidenly ears in such a manner!"

Gillian grinned at her cousin. "Honestly, Charlotte, I don't see how you can tell such awful whoppers without being struck down with shame."

"Practice, Gilly, it's because I pay the proper attention to perfecting a shy, demure look for an hour each morning. If you would do the same, it would do wonders for your personality. You might even catch a husband, which you certainly won't do if you continue to be so...so..."

Gillian chewed on her lip for a moment. "Unassuming? Unpretentious? Veracious?"

"No, no, no. Green, that's what you are. Utterly green and without any sense of *ton* whatsoever. You simply cannot continue to say what you think. It's just not done in polite circles."

"Some people like honesty."

"Not in society, they don't. Now stop dawdling and fix a pleasant expression on your face."

Gillian sighed and tried to adopt the demure look that spinsters of her age were expected to wear.

"Now you're looking mulish," Charlotte pointed out with a frown. "Never mind, your face doesn't matter in the least. Come, we don't want to miss Lord Weston. Mama says he is a terrible rake and isn't welcomed into polite circles anymore. I can't wait to see how depraved he looks."

"What has he done to make him unacceptable to the jades, rakes, and rogues who populate the *ton*?"

Charlotte's eyes sparkled with excitement. "Lady Dell says he murdered his first wife after he found her in the arms of her true love. He is said to have shot her in the head, but missed when he tried to murder her lover."

"Truly? How fascinating! He must be a terribly emotional and uncontrolled man if he didn't tolerate his wife having an *inamorato*. I thought that sort of behavior was *de rigueur* in the *ton*."

Gillian and Charlotte slipped past small groups of elegantly clad people and paused before the double doors leading to the ballroom. The heat generated by so many people inhabiting the confined space left the room stifling and airless.

Charlotte fanned herself vigorously as she continued to tell Gillian what she knew of the infamous earl. "He doesn't wear anything but black—'tis said to be a sign of his guilt that he's never been out of mourning even though he killed his wife more than five years ago. She cursed him, you know, and that's another reason he wears black. And then there are rumors of a child…"

Charlotte's voice dropped to an intimate whisper that Gillian had a hard time hearing. "…and was born on the wrong side of the blanket."

"Someone is a bastard?" Gillian asked, confused.

"Gillian!" Charlotte shrieked and, with an appalled look, pulled her cousin closer to the ballroom doors. "God's teeth, you're as uncivilized as a Red Indian. It must be living among them as you did that makes you so unconventional. Do try to curb your tongue!"

Gillian muttered an insincere apology and prodded her cousin. "Who is illegitimate? The earl?"

"Gilly, really! Don't be such an idiot. How can he be illegitimate and an earl? I was just telling you how Lord Weston murdered his first wife because she refused to bear him a son and turned to her lover for comfort. Isn't that thrilling? It's said she pleaded with him to give her a divorce so she could marry her lover, but he told her that if he could not have her, no man would. Then he shot her while her lover looked on." She sighed. "It's so romantic."

Gillian looked around at the dandies, macaronis, fops, elderly gentlemen in silk breeches, and other assorted members of that small, elite group who possessed the combination of fortune, rank, and reputation to admit them as members of the *ton*. "And this man is here tonight? Does he look evil? Does he have a hump on his back and a squint and walk with a limp?"

Charlotte frowned. "Don't be ridiculous, Gilly. The earl is not a monster; at least, not to look at. He is quite handsome if you like large, brooding men, which I most definitely do. When they're earls, of course. Come stand with me and we will watch to see if the rumor is true."

"Which rumor—that the earl killed his wife or that he is looking for a new one?"

"The latter. I will know soon enough if he is—men cannot keep a thing like that secret for very long."

"Mmm, no, I imagine not. If their intentions are not clear in the speculative gazes they impart on every marriageable female who can still draw breath, it's in the way they check the bride-to-be's teeth and make sure her movement is sound."

Charlotte tried to stifle a giggle. "Mama says I am not to listen to a thing you say, that you are incorrigible and a bad influence."

Gillian laughed with her cousin as they entered the ballroom arm-in-arm. "It's a good thing she doesn't know I've learned it all from you, my dear Char. Now, after we view this rogue of the first water, tell me who has caught your fancy. I'm determined you will end your Season with a stunning match, but I cannot help you become deliriously happy if you do not tell me who your intended victim is."

"Oh, that's simple," Charlotte replied with a wicked smile. "Everyone knows rakes make the best husbands. I shall simply pick out the worst of the bunch—one riddled with vices, bad habits, and a reputation that will make Mama swoon and Papa rail—then I shall reform him."

"That seems like a terrible amount of work to go to just to find a suitable husband."

"Not really." Charlotte whipped open her fan and adopted a coy look. "After all, you know what they say."

"No, what do they say?"

"Necessity is the mother of intention."

Gillian stopped. "Invention, Charlotte."

"What?"

"Necessity is the mother of *invention*."

Charlotte stared at her for a moment, then rapped her cousin on the wrist with her fan. "Don't be ridiculous, where would I come up with an invention? Intentions I have aplenty, and that's quite enough for me, thank you. Now let's go find this delicious rake of an earl. If he's as bad as Mama says, he might just suit."

From *To Charm a Naughty Countess*

*June 14, 1816*
*Lancashire seat of the Duke of Wyverne*

"THE MONEY IS GONE, YOUR GRACE."

*Finally.* After eleven years in Michael's service, his steward had abandoned the vague diplomacy favored by the previous Duke of Wyverne. Michael's father had been offended by bitter truths, preferring them sweetened into a palatable pap.

Michael was never offended by the truth, especially not a truth so obvious.

He wiped his pen and placed it next to the inkwell, almost hidden between ledgers and stacks of correspondence. "Of course the money's gone, Sanders. I have more titles to my name than guineas this year. I must simply borrow more."

He sanded his just-completed letter to the engineer Richard Trevithick. Only a few years before, the man had overcome financial ruin to introduce steam-powered threshing in Cornwall. A brilliant innovator. Michael requested his

opinion on whether steam power could be made useful
in irrigation.

This year, of all years, his dukedom needed as many
brilliant opinions as Michael could lay hands on.

Sanders cleared his throat, then hesitated. The
familiar headache began to prod at Michael's temples.

"Yes?" His voice came out more sharply than he
intended.

Another cough from Sanders. "The usual sources of
credit have dried up, Your Grace."

Michael's head jerked up. "Impossible. Has every
bank in England run out of money?"

As pallid as sand itself, Sanders's only color came
from gold bridgework he wore in place of three
teeth lost during a youthful altercation. Now his face
drained paler than usual, and he looked as pained as if
he'd had another tooth knocked out.

"England remains solvent, Your Grace, but... I
regret that your financial overextension is now common
knowledge. I have been unable to secure further credit on
your behalf. In fact, it is likely that demands may be made
for a repayment of your existing loans—ah, rather soon."

The headache clamped tight on his temples. Michael sat
up straighter. "Dun me for payment, as if I'm a common
cit? With whom do they think they are dealing?"

Sanders drew a deep breath. "I believe they have lost
trust in your judgment, if you'll forgive the frank speech."

Michael stared. "Yes, do continue."

"As long as the prosperity of the dukedom appeared
inevitable, securing credit for your estate improvements was not a problem. But with the unusual
climatic circumstances...ah..." Sanders trailed off in

a defensive flurry of careful language, his old habit of roundaboutation returning.

"My improvement plans remain unchanged, despite the persistence of winter," Michael said.

The damned winter. Until this year, Michael trusted two things in the world: his own judgment and his land. But this year, spring had never come, and it seemed summer would also fail to make an appearance. For months, the world had lain under a chilly frost. And now Michael couldn't trust the land, and no one else trusted his judgment.

"Exactly, Your Grace. This is what they find worrisome. During an unusual year, there is less tolerance for…" Sanders shifted his feet on the threadbare carpet of Michael's study. "Unusual behavior."

"This is an utterly unreasonable response," Michael muttered. "When infinite credit is extended to fribbles with silk waistcoats and clocked stockings."

"Waistcoats and stockings require a smaller outlay on the part of a creditor than do speculative mechanical constructions, Your Grace."

Michael's mouth twitched. "My speculative mechanical constructions, as you call them, will be the making of Lancashire." Or *would* have been.

He had planned so carefully: plowing moorland into canals; researching steam power. And finally, finally, he had a chance of reclaiming land no one had ever thought would be useful.

If his creditors were reasonable. Or if the world hadn't frozen solid. Now there was nothing to irrigate; all the crops were dead. There was nothing with which to water them; the canals were troughs of icy mud.

His signet ring weighed heavy on his finger; he rubbed at the worn gold band. "Well. Even if I am short of funds, Sanders, I will find a way to fix the situation."

"I can think of one possible way, Your Grace." The steward hesitated.

"Judging from your overlong pause, I'm not going to like it. Do tell me at once."

"You could marry an heiress." Sanders shaped the words as delicately as if he held glass beads between his precious gold teeth. "An alliance with a wealthy family would restore your creditors' confidence, and provide an infusion of cash to restart work on the canals." He paused. "Or even build those steam-powered pumps you are interested in, Your Grace."

"Bribery, Sanders?"

The steward's mouth turned up at the corners. "Good sense, Your Grace."

Michael leaned back in his chair and allowed his eyes to fall closed. Mentally, he pressed the headache into a ball and threw it to the side of his awareness. What was left?

The facts. The money was gone, and if Sanders were right, no more would be coming. Crops were scarce this year. There was barely anything to feed the tenants, much less their livestock or his own sprawling herds of sheep. The duchy was dying.

Sanders made a fair point; credit depended on appearances. If a man could maintain the appearance of wealth and power, it didn't matter if he had two sous to rub together.

Michael had little use for false appearances, but the polite world had little use for this eccentricity—so they had avoided one another for the past eleven years.

But if Michael's goal was to save the dukedom, he must get more money. And one day, he must get an heir. The steward's suggestion was perfectly logical: a wife would be simply the latest of Wyverne's improvements.

"Very well. I shall marry." Michael opened his eyes, and the headache roared back into his consciousness. Over its pounding, he said, "Shall we convene a house party, then?"

Now Sanders looked as if the glass beads had been shoved up his posterior. "I regret that that is impossible, Your Grace. I have, as you know, kept in contact with your London household over the years, and I hesitate to inform you that they have come into the possession of certain articles of interest regarding—"

Michael held up a hand. "Speak plainly, if you please."

The steward's gaze darted away. "The *ton* thinks you're mad, Your Grace. It's a frequent source of amusement in the scandal rags."

"Is it? After all the time I've been away, they still talk about me. How fascinating I am."

His words sounded carefree, belying the headache that now clanged with brutal force, or the queasy pitch of his stomach. Michael could ignore these distractions, but that word, *mad*—he had heard it so often that he had come to hate it.

He had never known he was *mad* as a boy—never, until he was sent off to school. If there had been nothing to do but study, he would have excelled, but the close quarters, the games, the initiations others handled so easily had turned Michael ill and shaking. He was eventually sent home. A sin for which his father had never forgiven him. But hard-won solitude had been

Michael's, save for a brief interlude in London more than a decade before.

A wholly unsuccessful interlude that revived whispers about the old duke's mad son. Michael had hoped these whispers were silenced after so many years. But no: if the polite world was again questioning his sanity, that was undoubtedly why no more credit was forthcoming. Anyone would loan to a genius, but no one would risk a farthing on the schemes of a madman.

Unfortunate that the line between the two was slim and easily crossed.

"If I might make a suggestion," Sanders ventured.

"Go on."

"If you travel to London at once, Your Grace, you may take part in the final weeks of the season. You will find many potential brides." Sanders's thin, sun-browned face softened under its thatch of grayish hair. "Once they meet you in person, Your Grace, they will surely be charmed, and all scurrilous gossip will be refuted."

"Charmed, Sanders? I haven't charmed anyone since I learned to walk and talk." Except for that brief, bright flash of time in London.

Years ago. Unnecessary even to recall it. At this stage of life, he was as likely to charm a wife as he was to plop a turban on his head and charm a cobra.

"I would be delighted to travel to London in your stead, Your Grace," Sanders said, "but I doubt I should answer the purpose to the young ladies of town."

"Shall I, though?" Michael rubbed a hand over his eyes. "A madman. The mad duke. 'The mad duke's bride hunt.' Why, the scandal-rag headlines almost write themselves."

From *Once Upon a Kiss*

*August 29th, 1815 A.D.*

*Today I splashed Mrs. Dockley from head to toe, broke a china plate, and failed to heed Mama. Thrice. All these things, but for the last, were quite accidental. I was quarrelsome on four occasions and fibbed regarding the china plate, pieces of which will one day be found buried in the herb garden and not in the possession of a wild-eyed, knife-wielding gypsy with a wart and a wooden foot. Although I think my version of events is better.*

*Sometimes real life is very dull, or simply inconvenient, and things never turn out quite the way one expects or hopes. I have heard it said that challenges are sent to try us. I would like to know who is sending so many to me, for I believe they have been misaddressed. I am quite tried enough, and I suspect that someone, somewhere, is completely light since I have all their calamities as well as my own.*

*Speaking of which, today I thought of the Wrong Man again.*

*I know not why he continues to plague me, unless it is a developing, chronic case of Maiden's Palsy. It has been over a year.*

*All I can say is, the blasted town of Bath has a great deal to answer for and I would not go there again for ten thousand pounds and a life supply of hot chocolate.*

Anyone coming upon Justina Penny's diary would be shocked, not only by the fullness of its pages, but by the fastidious attention to detail.

Her sister, Catherine, kept awake every evening in the bed beside her while she recorded these "trivial happenings and idle thoughts," proclaimed it to be a wicked form of self-indulgence.

"Your time would be better spent in somber internal reflection and prayer, Jussy," she said primly. "Why you bother committing all your terrible shortcomings to paper, I'll never know."

To which Justina replied, "Really, Cathy! How can I be sure of making proper recompense to those I wronged if I do not keep track of my daily malefactions?"

*I cursed inventively when I caught my skirt in the kitchen door and again when I found a splinter in my finger.*

*At approximately ten o'clock, when I saw Lucy in her new scarlet cloak, I was wracked with envy. But it lasted only until a quarter past, at which time she shared a jam tart with me and lamented the fact that her hair will never hold a curl so well as mine. Ah, vanity—one is hounded by it relentlessly when one has so little to be vain about.*

*Yesterday we sat in the hayloft and watched Major Sherringham's hired harvest hands at work.*

*Briefly I lusted.*

*That is when I thought of the Wrong Man again. But even I do not suffer the Maiden's Palsy as often as Lucy, who will*

*confess—when pressed—that she is seized by wicked desires
at least twice daily, even with no militia encamped nearby. I
suspect this may be due to the fact that she was once a sickly
child. I shall advise her to eat nettle soup. And a quantity of it.*

Catherine peered over the edge of the coverlet.
"If you feel the need to write your sins down, would
it not be less time-consuming to behave properly in
the first place?"

Ah, it was easy for *her* to say, thought Justina. Her
sister was never tempted by the perfect target of a
backside bent over, or a man needing his opinion
adjusted. Catherine was angelic goodness itself, never
lured into trouble by an unbound curiosity. Even laid
flat in bed she managed to be upright.

"No other young lady in this village feels the need
to leap over puddles, Jussy."

"That's their fault. It is a tremendous thrill to be
flying through the air."

"Sadly one must always come down again, and in
your case the landing has a propensity to be sudden,
heavy, and lacking in ladylike elegance."

While Justina allowed this to be true, she still
maintained it was not her fault that anyone else's pet-
ticoats were splashed in the descent. "How was I to
know that Mrs. Dockley would come out of her gate
at the exact moment I landed in the flooded lane?"

"Perhaps by considering the possible consequences
before you indulge yourself in another of your *thrills*?
No, I suppose that would be too much to ask. I
wouldn't want to spoil the joyous spontaneity for you."
Cathy burrowed again, mole-like, under the covers.

"Sarcasm is unbecoming, sister dear. It will give you wrinkles and dyspepsia. Possibly also gum boils."

The next words were muffled. "For which I shall blame you."

*The sky remains calm, although according to the rusted weathercock on Dockley's barn, North is now South. Some say it is a bad omen. I, for one, am glad. It's time things around here were turned on their head. Perhaps something interesting will happen.*

"Honestly," Justina muttered, pen scratching furiously across the page, "it's no surprise to me that Nellie Pickles ran away with some lusty sailors. There is no fun to be had in this village."

The sheets churned beside her again and Cathy reemerged. "Nellie didn't run away with any sailors. Who told you such a terrible thing?"

"No one tells me anything," Justina replied gloomily. "I have to imagine it for myself most of the time."

"Well, I wish you would not. You spend too much time dwelling on these...unsavory ponderings."

"With entertainment so thin upon the ground, is it any wonder?"

"But—"

"If people answered my questions, I wouldn't have to make things up, would I? No one tells me what I want to know."

"Because the things you want to know about usually aren't suitable subjects for young, unmarried ladies. Lusty sailors, indeed!"

Justina sighed in disgust as a large ink blot dripped from her pen. "Do you not want to know either, Cathy? Have you no curiosity about your wedding night, for instance?" She didn't have to look at her sister to know she blushed. "I'm sure you have questions about that, just as I do."

"I do not think of it," Cathy replied. "It is not for me to know anything about."

"Why? Is the man supposed to do it all? What if he doesn't know either?"

"Of course he'll know. He's a man."

Justina laughed at that. "Saints preserve us! If everything were always left up to men, where would we be? If men can do it all without us, why are we here? I shall tell you, sister. Women exist to put right all the wrongs men do and to keep them from making a complete pig's ear of the world."

Cathy groaned. "Oh, do finish and put out the candle, Jussy. You've wasted an inch of wax tonight at least."

"Very well, but first you must admit Nellie Pickles left Hawcombe Prior to become the plaything of a shipload of sailors. 'Tis all there is to it."

"That is the fate *you* decided for her, is it?"

"I am resolved upon it."

Nellie Pickles was a scullery maid up at Midwitch Manor, the grandest house in the village, until she disappeared, never to be seen again and with no explanation left behind. Three years later, folk still talked about the incident in hushed tones, everyone pretending they knew more about it, and more about Nellie, than they possibly could, considering she was a mute, unable even to write her own name.

"If she did not run off with the navy, there is one other option I will allow." Justina waited for her sister to ask, but upon hearing only a weary sigh, she continued, "Old Phineas Hawke did away with her. There, is that not better? Murder, I suppose, would be preferable to scandalous ruin at the hands of a half dozen sailors."

"Jussy!"

She snorted. "Phineas Hawke was a mean and miserly master to all his servants. I shouldn't be at all surprised if she's buried somewhere in the overgrown garden at Midwitch Manor. *If* he didn't eat her minced in a pie with his supper one evening."

"Did away with her, how?" her sister demanded. And then, she added a hasty, "For pity's sake." Cathy, of course, would never want to be caught encouraging her younger sister's wicked imagination.

"Strangled her, perhaps with her own stockings," Justina replied, perusing the ceiling and stroking her chin with the end of her quill. "Drowned her in the cider barrel, plucked out her eyeballs with a shoehorn, or threw her down the stairs in a fit of rage."

"That frail, grumpy tyrant? I don't believe he'd have the strength. He was wheeled about in a Bath chair for the past five years at least. May I remind you that Nellie Pickles was a stout, solid girl who could have pulled a plow?"

Justina shrugged. "Well, it is too late to make old Hawke confess his wretched crime." Phineas had been found dead in his bed a week before. Whatever became of the missing scullery maid, it seemed unlikely the truth would be uncovered. Suddenly an idea came to her. "Perhaps the ghost of Nellie Pickles returned to settle the score with her rotten master."

"What nonsense you speak, Jussy. There are no such entities as ghosts. Now, do put out the candle."

# A Little Night Mischief
## by Emily Greenwood

───────────── ❧ ─────────────

### Every prize come with complications

A game of chance saves James Collington from the prospect
of debtors' prison, and grants him ownership to Tethering
estate. Little does he know that his winnings come with
serious complications—not least of which is the beautiful
but impoverished young lady who insists his new manor
belongs to her.

### If he can't stop her, he might as well join her

Felicity Wilcox is determined to run Mr. Collington off her
land, though James's charm and devilish good looks are a
serious distraction. What she doesn't know is that she may
be haunting him right back.

───────────── ❧ ─────────────

"There's a certain whimsical nature to the plot,
the hero is quite devastatingly gorgeous, and the
writing is well-crafted."—*All About Romance*

"A lovely, lighthearted, historical romance.
Lovers of romance, you should definitely give
this book a read."—*Imagine a World*

### For more Emily Greenwood, visit:

www.sourcebooks.com

# *Gentlemen Prefer Mischief*
## by Emily Greenwood

—— ✧ ——

**When adversaries clash, mischief ignites passion…**

If it hadn't been for the crazy rumors, Lily Teagarden would never have approached her neighbor, Hal, Viscount Roxham—the careless rogue who broke her fledgling heart. But strange noises and lights on his property are causing serious problems for her, and she needs his help.

Trouble is oh-so-diverting for Viscount Roxham, and what could be more amusing than investigating what's plaguing his prim, beautiful neighbor—haunted sheep, of all things. Every time he seems to make progress, though, she throws mischief in his path, and his attraction to her is becoming extremely distracting…too bad Lily's the only woman in England who doesn't think he's Lord Perfect.

—— ✧ ——

"Emily Greenwood's delightful characters that are so well developed and the humor that threads through the plot make *Gentlemen Prefer Mischief* captivating."—*Long and Short Reviews*

"A mix of delicious sensuality in a nicely written and, at times, emotional read."—*RT Book Reviews*

**For more Emily Greenwood, visit:**

www.sourcebooks.com

# About the Author

Emily Greenwood has a degree in French and worked for a number of years as a writer, crafting newsletters and fundraising brochures, but she far prefers writing playful love stories set in Regency England, and she thinks romance novels are the chocolate of literature. A Golden Heart finalist, she lives in Maryland with her husband and two daughters.